Alison Roberts has been lucky enough to live in the South of France for several years recently, but is now back in her home country of New Zealand. She is also lucky enough to write for the Mills & Boon Medical line. A primary school teacher in a former life, she later became a qualified paramedic. She loves to travel and dance, drink champagne and spend time with her daughter and her friends. Alison Roberts is the author of over 100 books!

Withdrawn From Stock
Dublin City Public Libraries

Also by Alison Roberts

Miracle Baby, Miracle Family
A Paramedic to Change Her Life
One Weekend in Prague
The Doctor's Christmas Homecoming

Discover more at millsandboon.co.uk.

SECRET SON TO CHANGE HIS LIFE

ALISON ROBERTS

HOW TO RESCUE THE HEART DOCTOR

ALISON ROBERTS

MILLS & BOON

All rights reserved including the right of reproduction
in whole or in part in any form. This edition is
published by arrangement with Harlequin Enterprises ULC.

This is a work of fiction. Names, characters, places, locations
and incidents are purely fictional and bear no relationship to
any real life individuals, living or dead, or to any actual places,
business establishments, locations, events or incidents.
Any resemblance is entirely coincidental.

This book is sold subject to the condition that it shall not, by way of trade
or otherwise, be lent, resold, hired out or otherwise circulated without the
prior consent of the publisher in any form of binding or cover other than
that in which it is published and without a similar condition including
this condition being imposed on the subsequent purchaser.

® and TM are trademarks owned and used by the trademark owner
and/or its licensee. Trademarks marked with ® are registered with the
United Kingdom Patent Office and/or the Office for Harmonisation
in the Internal Market and in other countries.

First published in Great Britain 2023
by Mills & Boon, an imprint of HarperCollins*Publishers* Ltd,
1 London Bridge Street, London, SE1 9GF

www.harpercollins.co.uk

HarperCollins*Publishers*
Macken House, 39/40 Mayor Street Upper,
Dublin 1, D01 C9W8, Ireland

Secret Son to Change His Life © 2023 Alison Roberts

How to Rescue the Heart Doctor © 2023 Alison Roberts

ISBN: 978-0-263-30596-8

02/23

This book is produced from independently certified FSC™ paper
to ensure responsible forest management.
For more information visit: www.harpercollins.co.uk/green.

Printed and Bound in Spain using 100% Renewable Electricity
at CPI Black Print, Barcelona

SECRET SON TO CHANGE HIS LIFE

ALISON ROBERTS

PEARSE STREET BRANCH
BRAINSE SRÁID PIARSACH

MILLS & BOON

CHAPTER ONE

THE ADDRESS WAS in an ordinary street, in an ordinary suburb towards the northern side of Bristol, a three-bedroom, end-of-terrace house not dissimilar to the one Brianna Henderson lived in herself.

As she pushed open the gate to the straight, narrow concrete path that led towards the front door with its honour guard of tidy rose bushes on either side, there was nothing to suggest something very *un*ordinary was happening inside this house.

Nothing to warn her that a split second could change *everything*...

This felt more like a dream come true, in fact. This was Brie's first callout, on her first official shift as a newly qualified paramedic—the achievement of a dream that could so easily have been seen as completely dead in the water not that long ago.

Okay, so maybe it was only an activation of a personal medical alarm—the kind that so many elderly, frail or disabled people could use to summon assistance. Her senior crew partner, Simon, had actually rolled his eyes when the call came through.

'Don't get too excited,' he'd warned. 'Bet you they've pressed the button on their pendant by accident. Either that or they've fallen out of their chair and need some help to get up off the floor.'

'But don't they usually contact family members or neighbours first unless there's something really wrong? This is a priority call.' Brie was already several steps ahead of Simon now. The vehicle they were heading for was parked in the garage at the back of one of Bristol's largest ambulance stations.

'They will have forgotten to put their hearing aids in so they won't have heard anyone calling through the loudspeaker to find out what's going on.'

'What about the banging noises they could hear? And the scream?'

'I bet the telly's on in another room. Really loud because of the no hearing aids.' But it must have been very clear to Simon that Brie was not about to dismiss this call as a waste of time and resources. 'You can drive,' he'd told her with a smile. 'It's a good chance for you to play with all the bells and whistles.'

Apparently it was also a good chance for Brie to take the lead in assessing the situation and she took a big breath as she climbed the couple of steps at the end of the path and knocked on the door that was slightly ajar.

'Ambulance,' she called as she pushed the door open. 'Hello…? Where are you?'

Simon was right behind her, the handle of the defibrillator in one hand and an oxygen cylinder in the other. This might turn out to be a false alarm but protocol made it necessary to carry whatever they might need if they found themselves faced with something as serious as a cardiac arrest.

The silence that met Brie's call was the first sign that something wasn't quite right. Someone who was alone and waiting for help would always answer that call if they were able to. If they weren't alone, there would probably have been someone waiting at the door, or the gate, to direct them to where they were needed. Or was the explanation simply that someone couldn't hear the call because they had forgotten to put their hearing aids in?

They were in a small hallway that had a staircase leading upstairs to where bedrooms and a bathroom would most likely be. Brie assumed that the door ahead of them on the right would lead to a living room and kitchen dining area, like her own house and, given the time of day, it was more likely that the elderly or disabled occupant of the house would be downstairs. With a glance over her shoulder to confirm that Simon agreed with her choice, she walked forward, knocking on the interior door again before pushing it open.

'Ambulance,' she called again. She didn't want to give an elderly person a horrible fright by barging in without any warning. 'Is anybody here?'

It only took that split second, after stepping into the room, to capture what she could see but it took another beat of time to process something so unexpected.

An elderly woman was sitting, bolt upright, on a couch in front of the bay window that faced the street. Brie could see the ambulance she'd been driving less than a minute ago, parked on the road outside. She had turned the siren off well before turning into this suburban street but the blue lights were still flashing on the roof.

The woman looked terrified and she was clutching her chest as if she was in the kind of pain a heart attack could cause but she wasn't looking back at Brie. She was staring straight in front of her to where a much younger woman was being strangled. Her face was bright red and her eyes were bulging as she clawed desperately at the two hands around her neck. The man who was doing the strangling was the only person looking at Brie and she'd never seen such a look of sheer rage.

Training told her she needed to get out of there as fast as possible. Her own and her crew's safety was paramount because if they got hurt they wouldn't be able to do their job and help anyone. But Simon was right behind her, blocking the door, and he was still taking in what he was seeing in what seemed like a frozen scene in front of them.

Suddenly, it wasn't frozen. The younger woman crumpled and fell to the floor as the man let go of her neck and shoved her away with a vehement curse. The elderly woman on the couch cried out in fear as he began moving but he was heading straight for Brie, who instinctively stepped out of his path. Her training in self-defence was kicking in and she slipped the backpack off her shoulders and held it in front of her as she moved, ready to use it by throwing it at the man or as a barrier in case of a knife attack.

But it seemed that the angry man was more intent on escaping the room and he rushed to the door, pushing Simon out of the way with such force that the senior paramedic's feet almost left the floor as he hurtled backwards. Brie could actually hear Simon's head strike the wooden edge of the staircase with a sickening crunch.

It was Brie's turn to freeze for another moment. The crumpled woman on the floor was moving, pushing herself up to a sitting position. The woman on the couch was crying and still clutching her chest. It was the groan from Simon outside the door that had to take priority, however. She found him sitting, holding his head, his eyes shut.

'Call for backup,' he told Brie. 'And get out of here.'

'I'm not leaving you,' she said, dismayed to hear her voice shake.

'He might…come back…'

Brie swallowed hard, her mind racing. Having her own life in potentially immediate danger on her very first shift was the last thing she'd expected. How would her mother cope if the worst happened? How on earth had she thought that following the dream of this career had been a good idea? Back in the days when she'd been working as a triple nine call taker and dispatcher for the ambulance service, she'd always been so frustrated by trying to assist with critical situations from the other end of a telephone line. Coaching people to provide CPR or, ironically, advising them to try and find a safe space if they were in a situation where their own lives could be in danger. She'd never forgive herself if chasing that dream of doing what she'd wanted to do so much—being the person who took over when the telephone contact was no longer needed—ended up ruining the lives of the people she loved the most. Her mum. And her son…

But she'd never forgive herself if she ran away from people who needed help either. Brie knew she had no choice, but she did have to think fast and the first thing she needed to do was to try and prevent the situation getting any worse. She slammed the front door shut and locked it. She'd check the back door next but, first, she had to get backup on the way. She reached for the radio clipped to her shoulder and pressed the button to transmit her voice, which wasn't shaking nearly so much now.

'Unit Four-Zero-Three to Control,' she said clearly. 'Code Black. I repeat… Code Black.'

A code she'd never dreamed of having to use. One that would alert any emergency vehicles nearby that assistance was urgently needed for a situation that was dangerous enough to be a threat to life.

'Roger that, Four-Zero-Three.'

'It's a violent assault,' Brie added as she crouched beside Simon. 'At least two victims. Paramedic down. Attacker still in the area.'

'Roger that, Four-Zero-Three. Standby… We've got assistance on the way.'

Simon was trying to get up but fell back with another groan. 'Too…dizzy…' he said.

'Don't move,' Brie ordered. 'I'll be right back. I've got to check on the others and make sure the back door's locked.'

Fear for her own safety had evaporated as an adrenaline rush galvanised Brie. She raced back into the living room. The older woman hadn't moved from the couch and still looked terrified.

'Is he gone?' The words wobbled. 'Really…gone?'

'I've locked the front door,' Brie assured her. 'Help's on its way. I'm going to check the back door now. Who was he—do you know?'

'My husband…'

It was the younger woman on the floor who spoke, as Brie moved past her into the kitchen. Her voice was croaky and Brie could hear a whistling sound as she grabbed a breath after speaking. How much damage had that near strangulation caused? Was she in danger of losing an airway that was only just patent?

Brie could see that the back door of the house was ajar and then, to her horror, she caught the ominous shape, in her peripheral vision, of someone moving fast down the side path through the kitchen window. With shaking hands, she pushed the door shut and heard the snib lock catch just as the handle got rattled. A volley of swear words followed.

'I'll get you!' the man shouted, banging on the door. 'Just you wait…'

The pane of glass in the top of the door shattered and Brie pressed her hand to her mouth, waiting for the hand to reach in to undo the lock. Instead there was more profanity from outside.

'I've *cut* myself… This is all your fault…'

Brie held her breath. In a sudden silence outside she could hear the sound of a siren, which could well be the first available unit responding to her Code Black. She hoped it would be the police responding first. With a violent offender still present, the scene would have to be secured before any other medics could be allowed in and she needed help as fast as possible. Simon was out of action, the elderly woman on the couch might have chest pain that could indicate something serious like a heart attack, but the younger woman who'd been attacked was in respiratory distress so she needed the most urgent care. It was the top of the list in the ABC of assessment. Airway, Breathing and Circulation.

The high-pitched whistling sounds of obstructed breathing were even louder as Brie dropped to her knees beside the woman, who was now sitting and leaning forward—another sign of respiratory distress.

'My name's Brie,' she said. She unzipped the pack she'd carried in and then opened a pouch inside it. 'I'm going to put a mask on you and get some oxygen on, okay?'

As she picked up the oxygen cylinder that was lying by the door where Simon had dropped it, Brie could see that her crew partner was still holding his head in his hands.

'I'm okay,' he told her. 'But if I try and move I'm going to throw up.'

'I heard a siren,' Brie said. 'Backup's not far away.'

The woman on the couch was watching what she was doing. 'Her name's Carla,' she said. 'She's my daughter. She came here to try and get away from her husband. I didn't know what to do… That's why I pushed my button…when he wasn't looking…'

'You did exactly the right thing,' Brie said. She pulled a plastic mask from its packaging and unfurled the tubing to attach to the oxygen cylinder. She had the mask in one hand and the elastic to pull over Carla's head in the other but, even before she could get the mask near her patient's face, Carla's head slumped as she lost consciousness and she toppled sideways.

In the same moment, she heard glass being broken again in the kitchen and then the unmistakable sound of a door opening. Brie could feel her heart actually stop for a split second as she looked up, but the first impression of the uniform this man was wearing was enough to reassure her that this wasn't Carla's violent husband back for another go. It was, unexpectedly, a critical care paramedic—part of an elite squad that worked alone, as part of an air ambulance service or a general station like the one Brie had been fortunate enough to get a position at. The critical care paramedics had well-equipped vehicles with gear and skills that enabled them to respond to major, life-threatening events to provide the highest level of pre-hospital care.

It was the best backup that Brie could have hoped for but that didn't stop her heart skipping another beat as she saw the man's face clearly for the first time.

It *couldn't* be…could it?

Jonno?

The man who'd changed her entire life in the space of a single night?

The last man she'd thought she would ever see again?

'What's happened?'

The query was crisp but he wasn't looking at Brie. He'd dropped to his knees beside Carla and he gripped and shook her shoulder. She didn't have time to answer him before he spoke again, but she still wasn't the focus of his attention.

'Can you hear me?' he asked Carla loudly. 'Can you open your eyes for me?'

Getting no response, he tipped Carla's head back to open her airway and then touched the red marks on her neck to assess any injuries and find her pulse, focusing on what he could see and hear of her breathing at the same time. He slid a rapid sideways glance in Brie's direction.

'So what's happened? I was just round the corner when the Code Black alert came through.'

'Attempted strangulation,' Brie responded.

Did he recognise her voice? Was that why he fired that sharp glance at her face? Brie was desperately trying to bury her own recognition of this man and not only the visceral response her body was generating but what the potential repercussions in her own life could be. She couldn't let herself go there. Not yet.

'She was conscious and talking but the stridor got worse,' she added quickly. 'And…she just lost consciousness a few seconds ago.'

'Grab a bag mask for me, would you?' His gaze was back on their patient and his voice was calm. 'I need both an oral and nasal airway as well, and how 'bout cranking that oxygen up to full tilt. Fifteen litres.'

He looked over his shoulder to where Carla's mother was staring at him. Brie saw him frown as she handed him the curved plastic oral airway, the soft rubber tube that was the nasopharyngeal airway and the mask with the ventilation bag and a soft reservoir bag attached. He slipped the devices intended to keep airways open into place and then snapped open the compressed ventilation bag, taking another concerned glance at Carla's mother.

'Have you got chest pain?' he asked.

She nodded.

'Have you had it before? Do you get angina?'

She nodded again.

'Is this pain the same as normal?'

'Yes… Should I use my spray, do you think? It's in my pocket.'

'Yes, please do.'

Jonno smiled at the elderly woman and if Brie had been in any doubt that this was the man she remembered all too well it vanished in that moment. She'd spoken to Jonathon Morgan via radio transmission for years when she'd worked in the control room. More than long enough to hear about the charismatic paramedic's exploits and develop rather a serious crush on him, but it wasn't until she'd met him at that party and he'd smiled at her—just like that—that she'd really fallen for him. Hook, line and sinker. Head over heels. A brief fantasy that had been fulfilled beyond her wildest dreams. For one night. Because that had been the first and last time Brie had seen Jonno. Nearly seven years ago now.

'We'll look after you just as soon as we can,' Jonno told Carla's mother.

Then he looked back at Brie and she saw the flash in his eyes that was the moment he had definitely recognised *her*. Not that he was going to acknowledge it in any way. He knew better than she did that this was most definitely not the place or the time and, to his credit, Jonno was ultimately professional. He didn't miss a beat in his focus on what was going on around them.

'Are you working alone?' he asked.

'No—my partner, Simon, got attacked. He's in the hallway. Conscious, but he's had a hard knock to his head and he's too dizzy to move.'

As if to back up her explanation and add to the feeling of chaos, they could hear a groan from Simon and then the sound of him being sick.

'The guy that attacked him might still be around,' Brie warned. 'That's why I called a Code Black. He tried to break in through the back door just before you arrived.'

Jonno's eyebrows rose a fraction and Brie could almost see him processing all the implications and assigning priorities. There was a frisson of something like respect in there as well. Because she hadn't run away from a terrifying situation herself? Or did he realise how huge a fright he must have given her by breaking in through the back door the way he had?

'The police won't be far away,' he said. 'Don't worry

about what might or might not be going on outside. It could mean that we'll have to work by ourselves in here for a while, though, until they get the scene secured. You okay with that?'

Brie nodded but she bit her lip. 'I'm just glad you're here,' she murmured.

'Same.' Jonno raised his voice. 'Simon? Can you hear me?'

'Yeah…'

'Hang in there, mate. We'll come and have a look at you in a sec.' He lowered his voice to speak to Brie again. 'He's conscious and talking so he has a patent airway. Our first priority has to be here.' He squeezed the bag he was holding to pump more oxygen into Carla's lungs. 'Those marks on her neck suggest some soft tissue injury that could start causing enough swelling to close her airway.' He shifted his glance to where the life-pack Simon had been carrying had been abandoned by the door. 'Can you get a pulse oximeter on and some ECG dots? A blood pressure would be good too. I'm going to get IV access and I think we'll be looking at intubation sooner rather than later.'

Taking basic vital signs was something Brie was more than confident to do. She stuck the sticky dots for monitoring Carla's heart into place and clipped the oxygen saturation probe onto her finger while the trace on the screen settled. Then she wrapped the blood pressure cuff around one arm and pushed the button for an automatic reading to be done. Jonno was unrolling pouches from his own kit between delivering puffs of oxygen to Carla and Brie felt a beat of nervousness as she saw the instruments and drugs that it would be years before she could become qualified to use. Was she even capable of being a useful assistant with something as invasive as intubating a patient?

Maybe Jonno could see those nerves as he glanced up because his gaze was reassuring and his tone still perfectly calm.

'Can I get you to come and take over the bagging while I get IV access, please, Brie?'

The subtext to his request was just as clear.

We've got this. I know you're scared but it's okay... I'll talk you through anything you need to do...

And...he'd remembered her name. Brie scrambled to kneel above Carla's head, holding the mask firmly over her mouth and nose with one hand to make sure the air couldn't leak out and squeezing the thick plastic of the bag with her other hand to force the oxygen in.

But...wow... There was a tingling sensation in Brie's body that was impossible to ignore. After so many years and having only really met her on that one occasion, Jonno remembered her name. Did he remember anything else about that night? With something like desperation, Brie shoved the memories that were so keen to surface aside. She knew that they had the potential to be overwhelming.

Not now, she told herself. *Please...not now...*

Jonno was working swiftly and smoothly, sliding a cannula into a vein in Carla's arm and attaching it to a bag of saline. He was keeping a close eye on the numbers the screen of the defibrillator was displaying and Brie could see that it wasn't looking good. The heart rate was increasing steadily and the level of circulating oxygen was dropping. What they were already doing to try and keep Carla's airway open and her breathing adequate was clearly not working well enough.

If Jonno could hear the more than one approaching siren outside that Brie was aware of, he didn't acknowledge them. Instead, he looked completely focused on what was directly in front of him as he caught Brie's glance.

'I'm going to draw up the drugs I need and set up for a crash intubation,' he told her. 'I'll need your help, so try and ignore whatever else might happen, okay?'

Like the shouting that was happening outside only seconds later?

'Come out with your hands in the air,' she heard a male voice command. 'We've got the shed surrounded.'

'Oh, my…' Carla's mother had got to her feet to stare out of the window. 'They've got guns, those policemen.'

'Sit down, love.' Jonno's instruction sounded like a casual invitation but Brie could hear a thread of steel beneath it. 'You don't want to distract anybody from doing their job out there and it's probably best to stay out of sight. Have you had your spray now?'

'Yes.'

'How's that chest pain?'

'Better.' She sank back onto the couch. 'Why isn't Carla waking up? What are you doing?'

'She's having a little trouble with her breathing so we're going to help her by putting a tube into her throat.' Jonno caught Brie's gaze again. 'Ready?'

Brie nodded. She was. What was happening outside to secure the scene so that more emergency personnel could come into the house became a background hum. Even any concern for Carla's mother or for Simon was temporarily shelved. They had one job to do here that could very well save this woman's life and that one

glance from Jonno had been enough for Brie to summon the confidence *she* needed.

She *could* do this.

Technically, she knew that a crash intubation was a
way to rapidly sedate and paralyse a patient who needed
airway protection because they couldn't maintain or
protect their airway themselves.

'Right…' Jonno picked up a loaded syringe. 'Can
you put some cricoid pressure on, please?'

Brie had done this many times, but only in training.
Only on a mannequin. It felt very different to be doing
it on a real person but she knew she was feeling for the
hard, ring-like structure beneath the cricothyroid cartilage. She also knew that the manoeuvre was used to
avoid aspiration of stomach contents that was the complication of airway management that carried the highest risk of fatality. She held the ring between her thumb
and forefinger and applied pressure.

'That's the rocuroniumin,' Jonno murmured moments later. He picked up another one of the syringes
he'd prepared. 'We wait fifteen seconds and then it's
time to push the ketamine.'

We. They were a unit. A team. Brie liked that.

She knew to increase the pressure once the drugs had
taken effect. Then Jonno tipped Carla's head back and,
with the same smoothness and confidence with which
he'd gained IV access, he inserted the laryngoscope into
her mouth to get a view of her airway. Then he reached
down, without taking his eyes off what he could see, and
put his fingers over Brie's. She knew what he was doing
even though nothing was said and she was aware of a
fleeting memory of the jokes in training about doing
BURP. Jonno needed backwards, upwards and to the

right pressure on the cartilage, to help him see what he was doing more accurately. He was going to find the best position and then it would be her job to maintain it until the endotracheal tube was placed and the cuff inflated to keep it secure.

It seemed to be only seconds after Jonno had put her fingers in the right place that he pulled out the bougie wire from inside the tube, emptied the syringe full of air to inflate the cuff and then attached the bag mask to the end of the tube. He held the mask out for Brie to take and then picked up the earpieces for the stethoscope hanging around his neck.

'Give her a few breaths while I check we're in the right place and then we'll get it all secured. Sounds like we're about to get company.'

The background hum suddenly came back into focus. The banging on the front door and someone calling and Simon's voice telling them he could unlock the door for them and yes…he thought it was safe to come in. There was someone coming in through the back door at the same time, calling to reassure them that they were the police and not a returning offender.

There was another paramedic crew coming in as well but, while Jonno acknowledged them, it was Brie he was talking to as he looked at the screen of the defibrillator.

'Still tachycardic at one twenty-two and her BP's still lower than I'd like, but her oxygen saturation is going up and her end tidal CO_2 is sitting at forty-two, which is just where we like it.' He smiled at Brie. 'Good job.'

It was then he turned to the new crew and began to bring them up to speed. Another ambulance crew arrived and then more police officers and the house became so crowded it was overwhelming. Carla's mother was being attended to, having a twelve lead ECG taken to rule out an evolving heart attack. Simon was being carefully assessed as well, but Brie was relieved to see that he was looking better than he had earlier. She stayed where she was, supporting Carla's breathing, until the chaos settled a bit and the new crew took over.

'Looks like your partner's got a good concussion,' a paramedic told her as she got to her feet and stepped out of the way so they could lift Carla onto a stretcher. 'He's going to need a scan and observation for a while. Are you going to be okay on your own to get your truck back to your station?'

Brie nodded. 'Of course. What about Carla's mother?'

'She's stable. No sign of an infarct and her chest pain's resolved. We've got another crew coming to transport her for a more thorough checkup, though. Jonno, are you okay to follow us in? We'll be heading for the Central Infirmary.'

'Sure thing. Right behind you.' He was packing up his kit but glanced up at Brie. 'Where's your station?'

'Not too far. I'm with Westwood Ambulance EMS.'

'No way. That's where I'm based at the moment. How come I haven't seen you around?'

Brie blew out a breath. 'Maybe because this is my first shift?'

A huff of breath that sounded very close to laughter escaped Jonno. 'Well, you've certainly jumped in at the deep end, haven't you?' He zipped up his kit and got to his feet. 'But you used to work in Control, didn't you? Ages ago? Before I headed offshore?'

'Mmm…' How hard would he need to rake through his memories to find what was demanding attention again inside Brie's head right now? That totally unforgettable night that still haunted her dreams—in a very good way?

Apparently not that long.

'I remember you,' Jonno said softly.

A flash of something in his eyes was gone as fast as it had appeared, but it had still been long enough for Brie to register that that attraction that had led to the most memorable night of her entire life might very well still be there on his part. There was no doubt it was still there on her side of the equation. The tingle that had been sparked by him remembering her name was nothing compared to the spear of sensation she was experiencing now. And she knew it had to be her imagination but her knees really *did* feel weak for a heartbeat.

Jonno seemed to be trying to hide a smile as he refocused and turned to follow the crew taking Carla from the house. 'How 'bout I come and find you back on station so we can catch up properly?'

He was gone before Brie could respond, but what on earth would she have said, anyway?

Good idea—it's been far too long? Or perhaps, *No, I don't think that would be a good idea at all. I didn't think you were ever coming back and now I'm not at all sure I want you finding out that you're the father of my son...*

CHAPTER TWO

'MUMMA'S HOME...'

The joy in the excited cry, as Brie opened the back door of her house and stepped into her kitchen, brought a smile to her face despite the fatigue and worry weighing her down.

The fiercely tight hug of a six-year-old's arms around her neck as she crouched down to where Felix was sitting in his wheelchair beside the kitchen table was so good it brought a lump to her throat. Or maybe that had something to do with this new knot of anxiety that had lodged in her belly since she'd found out that Jonno Morgan was back in town?

'Mumma, I did it all by myself today. I rode Bonnie all by myself.'

'Really?' Brie exaggerated her most impressed expression. 'Felix Henderson rode a horse all by himself?'

Felix was beaming as he nodded vigorously but his grandmother's smile was reassuring. 'Don't worry, I was walking on one side and Kylie was on the other.'

'But I did it myself,' Felix insisted. 'I held the reins and made Bonnie walk.' He sighed happily. 'I love Bonnie.' Then he held his arms up for another hug. 'I love you too, Mumma.'

Brie kissed her son's soft curls and straightened the red plastic frames of his glasses before she stood up. 'Love you too.' She ruffled the ears of the curly-haired dog gazing adoringly up at Felix—or was it the plate on the tray across the armrests of his wheelchair that their beloved pet was more interested in? 'You haven't been feeding Dennis any of Nana's lasagne, have you?'

Felix shook his head but he was still grinning. And Dennis was licking his lips.

'I had to make your favourite dinner.' It was Brie's mother, Elsie's, turn for a hug. 'We needed something to celebrate your first day on the road. How was it?'

'Unforgettable.' Brie summoned a smile. 'I'll fill you in when our famous Paralympian equestrian in the making goes to bed.'

'What's a 'questrian?' Felix asked.

'Someone who rides horses,' Elsie responded.

'That's *me*.' Felix was beaming again. 'And I know what the Paralympics is. That's for people like me too.'

'It totally is,' Brie agreed. 'But future famous equestrians have to eat their broccoli to make sure they're getting all their vitamins.'

'But I don't like broccoli.' Felix made it sound like a perfectly legitimate excuse not to eat the green vegetable still on his plate. Dennis was lying down now. He didn't like broccoli either.

'You know what to do, darling.' Elsie picked up a floret of broccoli and held it out by the stem. 'You're the dinosaur and this is the tree. Scare the world and eat it in one giant bite.'

'I think I could eat the rest of your lasagne in one giant bite,' Brie said. 'I'm *so* hungry.'

'Sit yourself down.' Elsie smiled. 'There's plenty of broccoli left for us too.'

'I'll take my uniform off first. And I'll run a bath for Felix. Why don't you put your feet up and have a glass of wine? You've had a busy day today too, with the RDA after school.'

Riding for the Disabled was only one of many therapeutic activities built into Felix's life and it was his absolute favourite. Mind you, he'd look this happy if he'd been to a physiotherapy session or speech therapy or his dance class. He'd been a happy little boy from the moment he'd arrived in the world, loving life despite—or was it because of—the extra challenges that came with having spina bifida?

Felix didn't need his wheelchair most of the time but it was useful for covering longer distances or when he needed a rest, such as when he'd had a big day including pony riding. He'd taken off his foot and ankle braces already and his crutches were propped up in the hallway so, a short while later, Brie carried her little boy up the stairs and supervised his undressing and climbing into the bath, which he'd become determined to do on his own lately.

It was hair-washing night tonight and Felix screwed his eyes tightly shut and tipped his head back so his mum could use the plastic beaker to sluice the shampoo foam away.

'On my face too.'

He opened his mouth to catch some of the waterfall and then sprayed the water out.

'Did you see my whale spout, Mumma?'

'I did, sweetheart.' Brie was laughing with him as she tipped a last beakerful of water over his head.

'Okay, I think you're squeaky clean. Let's get you out and into your jimjams.'

Felix was yawning by the time she turned him round to dry his back. As always, something snagged at her heart as she saw the scars from his multiple surgeries, including one that had happened well before he'd been born—the one that had probably helped the most and had made Felix one of the lucky few spina bifida children who didn't have to live with major bowel or bladder issues.

He was almost falling asleep before Brie had read more than a couple of pages of his favourite story about a spotted Appaloosa pony called Nobby who ran away to join a circus. She turned on the night light—the one that made stars shine on the ceiling—pulled up his duvet and leaned down to plant a very soft kiss on the dark curls that smelt so deliciously of baby shampoo.

'Time for a wish?'

Felix nodded and they whispered their modified version of the rhyme together. *Star light, star bright, first stars I see tonight. I wish I may, I wish I might, have the wish I wish tonight...*

Brie felt her heart squeeze with her love for him as she watched his little face scrunch up in concentration.

'What did you wish for, Bubba?'

'That I get to ride Bonnie again next time...'

His words trailed off and his face softened into sleep but Brie took another moment, just to look down on this small person she loved so much that the squeeze on her heart tightened enough to hurt—in a good way.

Felix had been a blessing from the time he'd taken his first breath. He loved the world and the world, especially his mother and grandmother, loved him back wholeheartedly. If she could help it, Brie was not about to let anything, or any*one*, change that in any way.

It was then that the new challenge she was so unexpectedly facing suddenly got a whole lot bigger. A whole lot scarier. So Brie did what she'd always done when she had something big and scary to face.

She went to find her mum.

Elsie Henderson had dipped in and out of her nursing career over the years. She'd stopped working when Brie was born and had then changed from hospital shift work to more child-friendly hours in the local medical centre when Brie started school. She'd gone back to a position at Bristol's Central Infirmary when Brie was in her teens but had stopped again when Felix was born, to support Brie as a single mother to a special needs child.

It was only recently that she'd gone back to work again, this time in Bristol's St Nicholas Children's Hospital, in her favourite role as a paediatric nurse. She was only planning to work part-time and she and Brie were working out how to juggle their shifts so that they could both work in the careers they loved because, as Elsie said, if they wanted to be the best parent and grandparent they could be, they had to look after their own needs as well and do things that they were passionate about. The immediate future promised to deliver the best of both worlds and they would not only be able to give Felix all the supportive parenting he could possibly need and give their own lives an extra, fulfilling direction, but it would also make them financially secure enough to meet any other needs he would be facing as he grew up.

But Elsie hadn't bargained on her daughter having such a dramatic start to her new career.

'I'm horrified,' she confessed. 'Are you sure you wouldn't rather go back to working in the control room? With your new training and experience on the road you'd be able to handle anything over the phone.'

Brie shook her head as she ate another bite of her lasagne. 'It would be even more impossible to be happy being sat behind a desk and trying to coach people— who've never been trained—to do CPR or stop a major haemorrhage. Can you imagine if it had been that woman's elderly mother, with her own chest pain, and I was trying to tell her how to keep her daughter alive until help arrived?'

'Thank goodness it *did* arrive as soon as it did. You must have been so relieved to see that critical care paramedic coming in.'

'Yeah…' Brie put her fork down, her appetite suddenly fading.

It took only a split second of silence for Elsie to realise there was something she wasn't being told. 'What's wrong, Brie?' she asked quietly.

There was no point in beating around the bush.

'Jonno's back in town. He was the critical care paramedic I was working with today.'

This time, the silence was much longer and a lot deeper. In fact, Elsie didn't say a word until she'd got up and opened the fridge.

'I'm going to break my own rule and have another glass of wine. Can I pour you one?'

Brie closed her eyes. She had a difficult conversation coming up. 'Yes, please. Just a small one.'

Elsie sat down at the table again. 'So… Jonno Morgan, huh?'

'Mmm…'

'He's not related to someone who works at St Nick's, is he? Anthony Morgan? The best paediatric cardiac surgeon in the city, they say. I haven't met him yet but I've been caring for a few of his patients and know how highly people think of him. He must be around the right age to have a son who would be in his thirties.'

Brie shook her head. 'That night I met Jonno, he told me he was leaving because there was nothing to keep him in Bristol. I can remember that he specifically said he had no family here.'

Elsie took a sip of her wine. 'I guess Morgan's hardly an unusual name.' She let her breath out in a sigh. 'So… what are you going to do, darling? When are you going to tell him?'

'I don't know,' Brie said. 'I don't know if I *should* tell him.'

Elsie looked shocked. 'You can't *not* tell him. He has a child. Felix has a father.'

Brie tried to swallow that beat of fear along with her wine. 'It's not as if I didn't try and tell him when I found out I was pregnant. I did everything I could. Someone gave me his phone number but it had already been disconnected. Emails bounced back as undeliverable. When I finally found him on social media and asked him more than once to contact me, he never bothered responding. The messages never even got marked as having been read. And nobody here knew where he was by then. Everybody knew he'd gone to the Mount Everest base camp in Nepal but, by the time my snail mail letter got there, he must have moved on and the letter came back with a stamp saying to return it to the sender. Do you know, I think I've still got that letter somewhere? It arrived back after Felix was born.'

Brie shook her head slowly. 'Anyway…it was about the time I posted that letter that we found out about what was wrong with Felix and contacting Jonno didn't seem that important any longer. I had to make choices about whether I wanted to have in utero surgery or wait until after he was born or whether I was going to continue with the pregnancy, even. It was hard enough just for the two of us to have to face that.'

'I know…' Elsie reached out to touch her daughter's arm with a sympathetic rub. 'It was a horrible time.'

'I stopped even trying to contact Jonno then because the last thing we needed was for anyone else to try and make a choice like that for me. And part of me didn't want to hear what Jonno would have said because I think I'd already made up my mind that I had to do whatever I could to save my baby.'

'How could you be so sure that you knew what he would have said?'

'Because of who he is?' Brie shrugged. 'I'd always heard about the way he pushed himself physically to the nth degree. Both in his training and his hobbies. It seemed a no-brainer that he might have thought that a life where you were too disabled to do the kind of things he's so passionate about would be a life that wasn't really worth living. What if he'd persuaded me that was true and Felix had never been born?'

Elsie smiled. 'That would never have happened. You've been as fiercely protective as a mother lion ever since you learned that your baby was going to need special help.'

'And maybe I still need to protect him now, Mum. What if I told Jonno and he wanted to see him? Or worse, wanted to be involved in his life?'

'He does have that right,' Elsie said quietly. 'And Felix has the right to know that he does have a father. He's old enough now to know that it's something missing from his life. One of these days he's going to start asking questions that we can't ignore or brush off by telling him that not everybody has a daddy they live with.'

'Never did me any harm not having a father,' Brie muttered.

'That's completely different and you know it. Your dad died before you were even born. I never had a day of not wishing he was here to meet you and see what a wonderful baby and little girl you were. And the young woman you grew into being. I could be completely honest and tell you that he would have loved you to bits.'

'Yeah...well...what if Jonno didn't think Felix was wonderful? Or love him to bits? If he couldn't see past the crutches or glasses? If Felix was made to feel...' Brie had to search for a word that could encompass everything she never wanted her son to have to feel. '... to feel *less* than who he really is...'

'At some point in life, that's something he's going to have to deal with.'

'I know. And he does already to some extent with those kids at school that have given him a hard time. But how much worse would it be if his dad turned out to be a kind of superhero who goes around saving lives and, in his spare time, jumps out of planes with a parachute or leaps off mountains to go hang-gliding or does a bit of deep-sea diving or an iron man challenge in

Hawaii?' Brie caught her breath, to stop the small avalanche of all the things she'd heard about Jonno Morgan before she'd even met him. 'What if…' she added
quietly, 'Felix discovered he has a dad like other kids
he knows and then that dad decides that he's going to
go off on another adventure and leave town for the next
seven years? How damaging would *that* be?'

Elsie looked as disturbed as Brie was feeling. They
both knew what the right thing to do was but the need
to protect Felix—and themselves—was paramount.

'Will you be seeing Jonno again?'

'He's working out of the same station. He said that
he'd come and find me so we could catch up properly.'

Elsie bit her lip. 'How do you feel about that?'

Brie smiled wryly. Oh, there was a question…

She couldn't deny that part of her had felt thrilled
that he remembered her name. Maybe she'd dreamed
about Jonno—and that night—often enough over the
years that it had made it easy for her body to remind
her what his touch was like and wrap it up with the kind
of yearning she would have when she woke from those
dreams. But right now?

'Terrified,' Brie said aloud. 'What if someone tells
him I've got a six-year-old kid?'

'He won't know anything unless you tell him.'

Brie swallowed hard. 'I have to, don't I? At some
point, I'm going to have to tell him.'

Elsie didn't say anything but she reached out and
covered Brie's hand with her own, a silent signal that
the support was there for when she was ready to do the
right thing.

She wasn't ready yet. Far from it.

'I'll have to find the right time,' she said quietly.

'I need to know how long he's planning to be around. How he might feel about finding out he's a father. For all I know, he could be married with kids that he *does* know about. There could be more people than just us that this might affect.'

'I hadn't thought of that,' Elsie conceded. 'But the longer you leave it, the harder it might get to tell him. At some point in the future, he might want to find out more about his father. What if he finds out that Jonno was living here and had never been told about his existence?'

Brie took a deep breath. 'I *will* tell him,' she promised. 'Just not yet.'

CHAPTER THREE

It was Jonno's idea and he ran it past the duty manager, Dave, first thing the next morning.

'Brie…ah…' It was only then that Jonno realised he'd never known her last name, which felt a bit weird given he knew so much else about her, physically, at least. Even seven years ago, he'd felt as if he knew her before he ever met her because her voice was so familiar. He'd heard it on the radio so many times as he got dispatched to jobs and often kept her talking to get as much information as he could. It had been the first thing he'd recognised when he'd found himself in her company in a totally unexpected situation yesterday.

Brie had been one of the best dispatchers in the control room but he'd never expected her to turn out to be the most beautiful woman he'd ever seen when she'd turned up at his farewell party. That soft cascade of curls framing an elfin face that made her eyes look so huge. Eyes that he could see were reflecting the attraction simmering in the air between them.

'Henderson?' Dave raised his eyebrows. 'The newbie who got caught up in the violent offender incident yesterday?'

'That's the one.'

Dave let his breath out in a huff that was almost a chuckle. 'Her first shift as a graduate and not a trainee observer. That'll go down in station history. What about her?'

'How's her partner? Simon?'

'Nasty concussion. He could be off work for weeks. Fingers crossed he doesn't end up with post-concussion syndrome, which could keep him grounded for months.'

'Where are you going to put Brie? It'll be her second day shift today, yes?'

'Yeah. She'll be here any minute. I haven't decided, to be honest. We haven't got space on a crew with the kind of mentor I'd like her to have, but I don't want to take her off the front line and put her on a patient transfer ambulance. I can use her for cover but no one's called in sick today.'

'What about putting her with me?'

'What? You're in a rapid response vehicle.'

'It's not unusual to be a mentor at the same time.'

'Yeah, but that's for people about to complete their critical care training, not a complete newbie. And you go to jobs that could break someone without enough experience.'

'She didn't break yesterday. She did a good job. Why not let her get some real experience—when you haven't got any gaps to fill or until you find a suitable crew partner for her on a general truck?' Jonno smiled at the senior officer. 'I promise I won't break her.'

So that was why Jonno was waiting for Brie when she arrived on station that morning.

Or one of the reasons, anyway. The other was that he hadn't stopped thinking about her after work yesterday. He'd gone back to the apartment he was living in while he renovated it to get it ready for sale and it seemed that stripping wallpaper created a mindset that was like a time warp.

Hardly surprising given that particular room he was redecorating, but the sense of being sucked back in time was deeper than that. Seven years ago, he couldn't wait to escape. From this city. From this apartment that was like a symbol of the sham marriage and lifestyle his mother had maintained, but mostly he had to get away from the man who was making another attempt to be part of his life as a father figure, which was the absolute last thing Jonno needed. Or wanted.

He'd found his way in life by then and he was doing it on his own terms. With no family and especially no dependants, it didn't matter if he killed himself doing something stupid like a base dive or having a go in a jet-pack wingsuit, if he was ever lucky enough to have the chance to do that. He could spend all the money he still had left from his inheritance from his mother on his expensive adventure sports if that was what he wanted to do, but he could also get the satisfaction of working in an often action-packed job where he got to save lives.

Like yesterday.

By the time he was winding down, steaming, scraping and tearing shreds of paper from his bedroom walls, he was thinking about another benefit of being a lone wolf in his mid-thirties. He wasn't—and never had been—hemmed in by a committed relationship. Not that he put it about with reckless abandon or anything. No… Jonno was very particular about the women he chose to take to his bed, and if it was something special there was no harm in letting it carry on for a while. Not long enough to turn into something serious, of course, but long enough to enjoy every minute.

Brie had been something special.

Not that his memories of the unexpected night they'd spent together, in this very apartment, was even in the back of his mind when he'd made the suggestion that she rode with him in the rapid response vehicle for the next shift or two. He'd been impressed with how she'd handled herself yesterday and he had the feeling that Brie Henderson might be special in more ways than he knew about. Plus, he was curious about the woman who'd chosen to leave the safety of handling emergency calls from the other end of a telephone line to being on the front line.

He was even more curious when he saw Brie's shocked expression when she found out who she was going to be working with today. There was nervousness there, as well. Of the job?

Or of him?

He gave Brie his best smile. 'Don't worry,' he told her. 'I'll look after you.'

Being this close to Jonathon Morgan was…well, it was disturbing, that was what it was. On several levels.

One was that Brie was being driven faster than she would have believed possible through the heavy traffic of a big city on a busy weekday. Jonno's driving wasn't just fast, it was very clever. He seemed to have the ability to sense a complication like a panicked driver swerving the wrong way having just noticed a vehicle with lights and sirens right behind him, someone deciding to plough on through a junction to get out of the way, a delivery truck driver who threw open his door without looking and even a dog that had apparently appeared from nowhere. It was kind of like riding a roller coaster, Brie decided. Scary but undeniably rather thrilling.

On top of that, it felt as if fate was throwing them together. How weird was it that her crew partner had been injured on her first shift, there weren't any other gaps that needed filling on other crews and Jonno was on the rapid response vehicle that the station manager had decided to put her on for some extra experience.

Or had Jonno had something to do with that decision? Brie suspected it was not a common way to provide a rookie paramedic with some additional training.

Most of all, though, it was disturbing because it wasn't just the experienced, confident driving that was exciting.

It was being this close to Jonno. Thinking that perhaps it had been his idea that she rode along with him because *he* wanted to be this close to her? To pick up where he'd left off seven years ago, perhaps? Not that that was going to happen but it was, admittedly, flattering to think it might be even a part of the motivation behind this unexpected change in her duties.

The way Brie was feeling was like an emotional coin that kept flipping. Excited but then scared. Delighted but then super wary. Wishing she could be somewhere else—as far away as possible—but then feeling privileged to be this close and to have an opportunity to learn from the best.

There was nothing to suggest that Jonno had chosen to have her work with him either, and no hint of anything other than professional communication, but there hadn't exactly been any time for that to happen yet. This call had come in within minutes of the news that she would be second crew on this rapid response vehicle and this particularly fast ride was going to put them first on scene to a three-year-old child who had potentially swallowed a dangerous amount of his grand-father's heart medication.

'Just one or two tablets of a calcium channel blocker like this one can be lethal to a ten-kilogram toddler,' Jonno said, giving a bus driver a wave as he overtook the vehicle that had been pulled out of their way. 'Cardiovascular medications are among the top twenty-five drugs for potentially toxic ingestion, but they're the third most common substance resulting in the death of a child under five years old.' He gave Brie a sideways glance as they turned off the motorway and headed into a residential suburb. 'What sort of symptoms should we be concerned about?'

'Cardiac effects to the heart rate and/or rhythm?'

'Yep. What else?' Jonno killed the siren as they found the street they were looking for.

Brie tried to remember her training module on poisoning. 'Blood pressure changes,' she said. 'Hypotension?'

'Yep. That's the most common symptom. Worst case scenario is a cardiovascular collapse so we'd better be prepared for anything.' Jonno switched off the beacons on their vehicle, turning his head to peer at house numbers.

To her relief, there was no sign of an imminent cardiovascular collapse as they entered the house. The toddler was sitting happily in front of the television, in fact, watching a children's programme.

His mother was a lot less happy. 'I'm so glad you're here,' she said. 'I'm worried sick about George...'

'So what's happened?'

'I was getting my dad's pills ready for today. He's got dementia and he lives with us. So I had all the pills out to put into the little boxes and I heard him calling out in the bathroom.' George's mother looked distressed. 'He'd got confused over how to flush the loo and he was getting upset because the taxi was coming to take him to the day care group he goes to. Anyway… I was in there for a minute and then the taxi arrived, so he needed help to get to the gate, but I could hear that George was happy singing along with his programme. And then I came in here and there were pills everywhere from the bottle of Dad's heart medicine. I don't know how many are missing.'

The quirk of Jonno's eyebrow let Brie know he wasn't too worried himself yet. He went to crouch down by the little boy.

'Hey, George. Is this a good show?'

George nodded. He pointed at the screen, where people dressed in colourful animal costumes were singing a song.

'I hear that you're a good singer.' Jonno sounded impressed.

George nodded again. 'I can touch my tummy!' he sang, along with someone in a penguin costume. His singing was enthusiastic but not at all tuneful. 'Pat, pat, pat…'

Jonno was grinning. It was easy to tell what the next line of the song was going to be, thanks to the actions of the person dressed as a tiger. 'I can touch my head,' he sang. 'Pat, pat, pat…'

'Have you noticed anything unusual about his behaviour?' Brie asked.

'No. But I know he's eaten some of the pills. I had

to wipe some white stuff off his chin and I found a half chewed-up pill on the floor. See?'

'Can I see the label on the bottle? And the pill organiser? I should be able to see how many might be missing.' Brie had to smile as she saw that both Jonno and George were now doing the actions to the song, along with singing the lyrics.

'I can touch my toes, pat, pat, pat…'

Her smile wobbled then. Because she had a sudden image in her head of Jonno on the floor, playing with a child like this, only it wasn't with a patient. It was with his own son…

How much would Felix love to have a daddy who would engage with him like the way Jonno was with George? How much was missing from his life because he only had his mum and his nana?

Brie shoved the thought aside, focusing on the job at hand. She was confident Jonno would be quite satisfied with the information he was getting from his somewhat unique method of interacting with a young patient. If Brie had been using the paediatric assessment triangle of appearance, work of breathing and circulation, she would be confident that George's vital signs were all within normal parameters. He clearly had no issues with his breathing if he could sing like that, his skin colour was good and he seemed to be behaving like any other happy child would. On the other hand, she was unsure of what they would do next.

'I'm pretty sure there are two pills missing, not counting the half chewed one,' she reported to Jonno.

'Are they slow release?'

Brie checked the bottle. 'Yes.'

Jonno stood up, leaving George to pat his ears by

himself. 'Let's give his face and hands another wash,' he suggested to the mother. 'Just in case there's something still on his skin. I'm going to call for someone to come and take you into hospital as well, so that George can be monitored for a few hours.'

'Oh, no… Do you think he's really sick?'

'He seems absolutely fine,' Jonno assured her. 'But, because the pills are slow release, if he has swallowed any, it could take longer for any symptoms to show up. I'm sure you'll be happier to be somewhere that people can keep a close eye on George. While we're waiting, Brie and I will see if we can get an ECG, just to make sure his heart's doing exactly what it's supposed to.'

Brie opened the pouch on the side of the defibrillator to find the packet of electrodes as Jonno made a call requesting an ambulance to transport mother and child to hospital.

'I've got a new game,' Jonno told George as his mother was wiping his face and hands with a damp cloth. 'Can you touch your chest? Pat, pat, pat? Good boy… Do you want some special stickers to go on your chest?'

George nodded eagerly.

'Okay… Mum's going to take your tee shirt off and then Brie's going to help me put the special stickers on. Oh…look at that…' A small white pill rolled out of the elastic waistband of George's pants as the tee shirt was pulled out. Jonno picked it up and handed it to Brie. 'Only one missing now,' he said.

George could see what he was holding. 'Yucky,' he said.

'Sure is,' Jonno agreed. 'Did you try and eat them, George?'

George avoided his gaze and shook his head firmly. 'Too yucky.'

Jonno's lips twitched. 'Time for the sticker game,' he said. 'Can you lie as flat as a pancake on the floor? Show me where the stickers are going to go? And Mum? Maybe you could pack a bag with some toys and snacks and things that you might need with a few hours in the observation ward?'

By the time they had the ECG recorded, an ambulance had arrived to transport George and his mum to hospital.

'He could still develop symptoms, couldn't he?' Brie asked as they headed back to station, having transferred the care of their patient and seen them both into the ambulance. 'Especially for slow-release medications?'

'They'll keep a close eye on him for about six hours. If nothing's happened by then, he should be fine. If something shows up soon, they may give him some activated charcoal but that should be within the first hour or so of ingestion.'

Brie could see the ambulance turning onto the motorway ahead of them. 'You're really good with kids,' she said. 'I can imagine getting an ECG on most toddlers could be a bit tricky.'

'Maybe I've never grown up properly myself.' Jonno threw her a grin. 'And I love kids.'

Oh… Brie's heart skipped a beat. She couldn't help the flash of fantasy that was an extension of imagining Jonno playing with Felix. This time, it was an image of them all together. As a family…

Maybe she should have tried harder to contact him.

Maybe it wasn't too late?

Her mother was right. The longer she left it, the harder it was going to become.

She took a deep breath and hoped she would be able

to sound as if her question was simply a response to what he'd just told her.

'So…you've got some of your own now?'

'What…*kids*?' Jonno sounded horrified. 'Not that I know of. Thank goodness.'

The fantasy crashed and burned.

'I love them when they're someone else's,' he added. 'That way, they don't mess with the stuff I love to do.'

Brie managed to find a smile. 'You mean travelling? Having adventures?'

'Absolutely. And doing the kind of things that you'd never do if you had anyone dependent on you like a wife or kids. You know…like flying with one of those jet-pack wingsuits? Have you seen the video that came out recently of that guy flying beside a passenger jet in Dubai?' The gleam in Jonno's eyes advertised both admiration and envy. 'Crazy…'

Brie shook her head. 'No, I haven't seen it.'

'I'll show you later. I've got it downloaded on my phone.' Jonno's attention seemed to be caught by a hardware shop they were passing. 'That reminds me. I've got to get some paint after work today. I've nearly finished stripping the wallpaper in my bedroom. Maybe I should get your advice about a good colour?'

Brie looked out of her window to avoid meeting any glance that might be coming her way. At some point, it was inevitable that something was going to be said about the time that Brie had been in that room. About the unprecedented—on her part, anyway—passionate encounter they'd shared.

The fact that they had a past history, albeit very fleeting, was there, simmering away between them beneath the professional veneer, as if they might both be waiting for a signal that it didn't need to be a secret.

'I didn't have you pegged as a DIY type,' she said lightly.

'I'm not. I'd rather be racing planes like a superhero, to tell the truth. But I need to sell the apartment. It's my last tie to Bristol and when it's gone, I'll be gone too. For good, this time.'

Brie took a moment longer before she let him see her face. Any inclination to tell Jonno about his son right now was evaporating as convincingly as that snapshot of a happy family including a daddy for Felix. Telling him at all was becoming even more of an issue, in fact. Jonno had no intention of hanging around for very long at all so it would only break a little boy's heart if he found out he had an amazing father, who actually *was* a superhero in real life, only to have him vanish again.

'I'm only filling in as a locum here,' Jonno added. 'It's a race to see whether I'll get the apartment sold or be out of a job first. Not that it matters when the prize is the same—a fresh start. A new adventure. I'm thinking maybe Australia. Or New Zealand. Did you know that Queenstown, in New Zealand, is the adventure capital of the world?'

'No, I didn't know that.'

'I haven't tried bungee jumping yet.'

'I'm happy to say that I never want to.' It was easier for Brie to find a smile this time because it felt as if the decision of whether or not to tell Jonno he was a father was being made for her and it was proving to be a huge relief. Maybe she had the perfect excuse not to tell him, seeing as he was going to be on the other side of the globe very soon and would never be coming back. If Felix ever tracked him down in decades to come she could honestly say that keeping silent had been to protect him. To protect everybody involved, in fact, because the last thing Jonno wanted was to have a continued connection to Bristol.

It's my last tie to Bristol and when it's gone, I'll be gone too. For good, this time...

'So...' After the outbound journey from station on the way to the potential paediatric poisoning, it felt as if Jonno was driving super slowly now. His smile was just as relaxed. 'What do you reckon? About the colour I should paint my bedroom? I'm thinking a nice strong colour like aubergine or a dark blue. Mind you, even a lurid pink or something would be better than the wallpaper that was there. Don't suppose you remember those things that looked like upside-down pineapples?'

And there it was...

The window into one single night that had happened a very long time ago, but Brie could remember every single detail. Including the hideous wallpaper in Jonno's bedroom and the first words he ever said to her that weren't over the radio.

'You're Brie, right? Like the cheese?'

'Yeah...like the cheese.'

'I feel like I know you... But I've never seen you before. How crazy is this?'

'Same. I've heard your voice on almost every shift I've done.'

'You've always looked after me. Dispatching me to the best jobs and trying to make sure we got enough of a break to get something to eat.'

The noise of the rowdy private party happening in

a local pub was all around them but, for Brie, it was nothing more than static. A fuzziness in the background of the real picture. She was meeting Jonno Morgan, a medic who was universally admired and respected throughout Bristol's emergency services and...he fancied her.

'I wish I'd known...'

'Known what?'

'How gorgeous you are...' He touched her face with a single fingertip, tracing a line from her eyebrow to skirt her cheekbone and then slide to her mouth, where it paused for a heartbeat at the corner before skimming her bottom lip.

'Same...'

Brie knew she was blushing but she'd always been so shy when it came to talking to men. She would never have dreamed of flirting like this with anyone, let alone Jonno. Perhaps being dragged to this party by a friend from the control room without being given time to find an excuse had something to do with a new confidence. More likely, it was due to the second glass of wine she'd just finished—or had that been the third? The fact that Jonno was so attracted to her was probably due to the amount he'd had to drink as well, but Brie didn't care. Because she'd never felt like this before. As if she was actually desirable—to someone like Jonno Morgan?

'Let me get you another one of those.'

Jonno's hand was over Brie's, about to take possession of the empty glass, but then it stopped and she knew why.

She could feel it too. The jolt like an electric shock as their hands touched. The heat that was being generated by the prolonged contact.

Brie couldn't look away.

'I want to kiss you,' Jonno said, and he was proba-bly shouting, given the noise of the party around them, but it felt as if he were whispering in her ear. 'But not here...'

He took the glass from her hand and put it down on the nearest table, and then his hand was holding hers again.

'I live just round the corner,' he said. 'How 'bout we find somewhere quieter so we can get to know each other a bit better?'

'But this is your party.'

'Nobody will miss me. They're all having far too good a time. And, hey...if it's my party, don't I get to choose to be with the person I most want to be with?'

There was no one Brie wanted to be with more than Jonno. Who wouldn't want to find themselves in a real-life fantasy with someone they'd had a crush on from the moment they'd heard their voice over the radio? They were both adults. Both single. She didn't even have to worry about something as mundane as birth control because she'd been on the pill for months now, to try and regulate an annoyingly unpredictable cycle.

Jonno bought a bottle of champagne on the way out. They held hands as they walked to his apartment. They drank the champagne and talked as if they'd known each other for years. They laughed about the upside-down pineapples on the wallpaper in his bedroom.

And then they didn't talk again.

Dawn was breaking outside when Jonno finally fell asleep. Brie was still awake, still stunned by the wild-est and yet the most attentive lovemaking she'd ever experienced. Every cell in her body was still humming and her head was spinning, but maybe that was the last of that champagne catching up with her and pushing her over the edge.

When her stomach started tying itself in knots, she slipped quietly from Jonno's bed and carried her clothes in her arms to get dressed downstairs. To escape before she could spoil the most perfect night in her life, and a fantasy that had exceeded all expectations, by throwing up everywhere...

Perhaps it was because Brie had relived that fantasy so many times over the years since that night that it could flash through her mind in a tumble of images and emotions that took no longer than the blink of an eye.

'Definitely not aubergine...' Brie made it sound as if she'd given the query about paint colour some careful thought and she caught Jonno's gaze briefly so that she could make her denial more convincing. 'And no... I don't remember the pineapples but they do sound truly awful.'

He knew she was lying.

It was unfortunate that they were queued behind the traffic at a red light because it meant that Jonno didn't have to look away in a hurry. Brie could feel her cheeks getting pink. She'd never been any good at lying.

Jonno knew she remembered.

And the way his eyes seemed to become an even darker shade of brown sent a spear of sensation right through her body. She'd seen Jonno's eyes darken like that before. Before he'd kissed her for the first time...

He wanted to kiss her again.

And, heaven help her, but Brie wanted him to.

Perhaps heaven did help her because the radio crackled into life at that exact moment.

'Echo One…how do you read?'

Jonno was still holding Brie's gaze as he responded. 'Loud and clear, Control.'

'We're dropping a job on you. Cardiac arrest. Dog walker at the south end of Castle Park. Bystander CPR underway. Details coming through…'

'Roger that…'

Jonno switched on the beacons and eased the vehicle out of the stalled traffic. By the time he did a U-turn and activated the siren, that conversation with Brie was clearly forgotten.

And thank goodness for that.

It was still there.

That extraordinary attraction that had pulled them together for a night that Jonno had never forgotten.

He'd never forgotten that stab of disappointment when he'd woken up to find he was alone in his bed. Why hadn't she stayed? Not being able to say goodbye, let alone tell her that it had been the best night of his life, had left him with the feeling that he was leaving town with something unfinished.

Something important.

But there was nothing he could have done about it. He had to get his bag packed, hand over the keys to his apartment to the agency who would be managing the rental and get to the airport. He would be winging his way to Nepal in a matter of hours, with a group of climbers who had employed him to stay at base camp as their medic while they made possibly more than a single attempt to climb Mount Everest.

One adventure had led to another as Jonno became known for being the best in the business and prepared to take on even the wildest terrain. He'd meant to come back ages ago to sort out the loose end in his life that his apartment represented. The last thing he'd expected was to find that he still had that other loose end—the woman who'd rocked his world and then vanished into the night like a puff of smoke from a fantasy that had just imploded.

Maybe he would have simply let it go when Brie told him she didn't remember—or didn't want to remember—her visit to his apartment, but then he'd seen the colour creep into her cheeks.

The way it had at that party, when he'd finally shaken off so many well-wishers and managed to capture the attention of the most beautiful woman he'd ever seen. He'd known then that she was lying about not remembering. Perhaps there was unfinished business there for her too?

Jonno was here to make sure he could leave this city for good with no regrets. If there was a chance that he could revisit that fantasy and give it the kind of ending it should have had the first time, perhaps for both of them, well…why not? Life was short and his time in Bristol was even shorter.

But something was telling Jonno that there could be a good reason for Brie to not want to go jogging down memory lane with him, and he knew that was most likely because she was no longer single. Or had she fled that night because she hadn't been single then? No… Jonno threw that idea out. He was a good judge of character and he would never have picked the Brie he'd met that night as someone who would cheat on a partner.

That didn't mean she was still single now, of course. She wasn't wearing a wedding ring but that didn't mean much, did it? You could be in a committed relationship with someone without ever getting married. Jonno fully intended finding out but he didn't get a chance to try and satisfy his curiosity until a rather busy shift was ending.

'Come and look at this, Brie.' He tapped the triangle on his screen. 'It's the wingsuit video I was telling you about.'

'Wow…' Brie's eyes widened as she saw the improbable clip of a human flying alongside an enormous passenger jet.

'That's an Airbus A380,' Jonno told her. 'Biggest plane in the world.'

'Unbelievable…' Brie shook her head. 'And you're planning to do that?'

He grinned. 'It's on my bucket list, that's for sure. There's a few logistics to work out, like how much it would cost.' He put his phone away. 'You heading straight home?' If she wasn't, Jonno intended to suggest they went somewhere for a drink. Or coffee. Or anything that would give them some time together away from work.

But Brie nodded. 'Yeah… I need to run. That last job has made me a bit later than usual.'

'Dependants, huh?' Jonno tried to make it sound like a good thing. 'I never did ask whether *you* had kids by now. Or a husband.'

'No husband.' Brie was heading towards the locker room. 'But I do live with someone.' She threw a smile over her shoulder. 'And Dennis the menace, of course.'

'How old is Dennis?'

'Almost four.'

Wow…

The stab of disappointment was real.

Oddly, it was even sharper than the one he remembered from waking up to find she'd vanished from his bed.

But that was that. Jonno had a firm rule not to get involved with anyone who was in a relationship.

Even if he knew damn well that she was still attracted to him…

CHAPTER FOUR

IT HADN'T REALLY been a lie.

She'd just fudged the truth a little.

So why did she feel as if she'd made a huge mistake? Done something unforgivable, even?

Brie *did* live with an almost four-year-old called Dennis. And she was living with someone in a relationship that had not only given her the support to be the kind of single mother to a special needs child that she could be proud of, but had even accommodated her training in the career she'd dreamed of for years. The new adjustment to her shift work was working well so far too.

Brie got to have a day with Felix the next day, after her mother had left early to work a day shift on the paediatric surgical ward. Having done two day shifts herself, Brie had the first of two nights to work, which meant she had her day clear to take Felix to school in the morning and to a physiotherapy session in the afternoon. There were no out-of-school activities scheduled for tomorrow, which was a good thing, as Elsie was working another day shift and Brie would have to sleep during school hours to be ready for her second night shift.

Any day, like today, that included a session in the

specialised physiotherapy hot pool was always a treat. With the heat of a comfortable bath and the reduction of gravity the water provided, the range of movement and stamina exercises were so much easier and more fun that it had been a favourite since Felix had been a toddler. Brie loved seeing the grin that never faded and hearing the way his shrieks of laughter echoed in the tiled pool area.

The pleasure was more than a little dampened today, however, by the guilt that Brie was struggling with. The conversation she'd had with her mother last night had an echo far less agreeable than Felix's laughter.

'*You still have to tell him,*' Elsie had said. '*Even if he's not planning to be around for long. You never know—he might change his mind when he knows. You have to do the right thing.*'

'*But it has to be at the right time. We might have been working together today, but it's hardly the appropriate time to drop a bombshell like that on someone.*'

'*So, find a way to spend some time with him away from work. Go out to dinner or something. I'll babysit.*'

'*Mum! I'm not going to ask Jonno out to dinner!*'

At least Brie didn't have to let her mind wander in the direction of the 'or something' her mother had suggested. The way the atmosphere had changed the moment she'd told Jonno that she was living with someone—and, okay, had deliberately given the impression that she had a child called Dennis—had been palpable. Any hint that he might be thinking they could pick up where they'd left off seven years ago had disappeared like the flame of a snuffed-out candle.

She'd known she was completely safe at that point. She would have been disappointed, in fact, if Jonno

Morgan hadn't made it obvious that someone being in a relationship was a no-go area for him. She'd always thought of him as one of the 'good' guys. The kind you'd dream of having as a partner.

Or a father for your child?

Yes, but not if it presented a danger to a world that she had poured her heart and soul into creating for her son. And Jonno did present a danger. He could break her son's heart by walking out on him—or getting killed. For heaven's sake, she just had to remember the video he'd shown her of the person flying beside that huge plane to have her blood run cold at the thought of Felix watching his father doing something that dangerous.

And, while it was less important, there was a personal danger there as well, because Brie knew that the attraction that had led to Felix being part of her life in the first place was still very much alive and kicking. Not just undiminished but quite possibly enhanced beyond reality because her memories of that night were the closest thing Brie had had to a sex life since she'd become a mother. That pull—which could magnify the new complication in her life—could not be allowed to develop any further.

But did that justify the barrier she had deliberately put up to protect both herself and Felix?

The fudging of the truth that, okay, most people would consider a lie, wasn't sitting at all well with Brie.

Having Jonno smile at her as she arrived on station that evening made it quite clear to Brie that she had made a mistake. Instinct told her that Jonno had never been anything other than honest with her and he didn't deserve to be treated with any less respect himself.

But how could she put things right?

She certainly wasn't going to get an opportunity on this shift because someone had called in sick and she was put on an ambulance with another paramedic, Liz, an experienced medic in her late forties. It was a busy night but none of their callouts involved trauma or medical events serious enough to request advanced backup so Brie didn't even see Jonno again until nearly seven a.m. when her shift was finishing and the station locker room was busy with people both arriving and preparing to leave.

'I need coffee,' Liz declared, closing her locker. 'A real coffee. Anyone fancy coming out to breakfast?'

'Sure. Count me in.' Jonno looked as though he'd managed to catch some sleep overnight. He looked, in fact, as if he'd just got out of bed, with his hair all rumpled and some designer stubble shading his jaw. And he was smiling at Liz but Brie could feel something deep inside her own body trying its best to melt.

He looked…impossibly gorgeous…

'Brie?'

'Sorry, Liz, I've got to get home.' Brie pulled her bag from her locker and checked that her car keys were inside.

'To Dennis,' Jonno supplied helpfully.

'Mmm…' Brie bit her lip. 'He'll be wanting his breakfast.'

Jonno blinked at her but Liz actually laughed. 'You called your kid *Dennis*?'

'Not exactly,' Brie admitted. 'Dennis is a fur baby. Bit of everything, including some poodle. Very cute, but he was a very naughty puppy. Dennis the menace seemed to suit him.'

'Dennis is a *dog*?' Jonno stepped out of the way of someone reaching past him to open a locker and that put him right beside Brie as she turned to walk out. 'And the person you're living with? Is he just a flatmate?'

'Um…not exactly.' Brie didn't dare catch Jonno's gaze. 'I ended up moving back home a few years ago so I'm living with my mum again.'

Tell him, said the small voice at the back of her head. *Here's your chance…*

Except it wasn't a chance. She couldn't just tell him she had a six-year-old child without the possibility that he'd do the maths instantly and be blindsided in front of the people he was currently working with. That was hardly treating him with the respect he deserved, was it?

The scramble of Brie's thoughts was making her walk faster towards the main doors of the station but Jonno's long legs were keeping up with her effortlessly. Then he dropped back slightly as he slowed his steps.

'Wait a minute…' he called softly.

Brie found herself instantly slowing her own pace.

'Are you telling me you don't have a partner?' Jonno's voice was quiet behind her but she could hear him clearly. 'That you're…single? Why on earth did you want me to think that you weren't?'

'Um…' Brie stopped in her tracks, mortified. She had never blushed quite this hard, judging by the level of heat she could feel in her face, and she didn't dare look back. Until she heard the huff of sound from Jonno that was almost laughter.

'I get it,' he murmured. 'And I know…it's weird, right? I wasn't expecting it either…'

Brie tried to pull in a breath as she met his gaze but it felt as if most of the oxygen in this building had been used up. That might also explain why her response came out sounding slightly hoarse.

'What is?'

'That it's still there,' Jonno said.

Brie wasn't going to ask what he meant. She didn't need to because she knew exactly what was still there. That once-in-a-lifetime, totally irresistible attraction that was equal enough on both sides to pull them together with all the force of a human nuclear reaction if they got close enough.

She could see the gleam in Jonno's eyes that suggested he would be up for getting that close—if she was. A gleam that told her she wasn't anywhere near as safe as she'd thought she was this morning. A gleam that scrambled her brain enough to want things that she couldn't—or *shouldn't*—have. Especially not with this particular man.

Liz overtook them. 'You coming, Jonno? I can smell the coffee from here. Some bacon and eggs too…'

Jonno's smile was lazy. 'Lead the way.' He walked past Brie. He didn't have to say anything more. That subtle almost wink he gave her as he passed was enough to let her know that their conversation was nowhere near finished.

It was that lazy smile that stayed with Brie as she tried to top up on her sleep once Felix was safely delivered to school.

Or maybe it was the confidence that was behind it. Did Jonno think that it was inevitable that she would end up in his bed again? That this was just some kind of game and that, if he played it without breaking too many rules, he was bound to win. Because things had probably always worked out like that for him?

Well…not this time.

Even when just the thought of being with Jonno—being kissed, or…dear Lord, being touched by him—was creating havoc in various parts of her body and making it impossible to get her mind anywhere near the quiet space it needed in order to slide into sleep. Part of that havoc was a small voice that seemed to be gaining enough of an audience to make it refuse to go away.

How long? it was asking. *How long is it since you felt like this?*

The answer was built into the reason the question was being asked. Brie knew perfectly well that there had only ever been one man who'd made her feel like this. As if every cell in her body had woken up and was quietly fizzing. Waiting for that kiss. That touch.

No. It couldn't happen. Brie wasn't a single young woman now, with the freedom to do whatever she wanted and to follow her heart's desire. She was a mother. And a paramedic. Her life was all about being responsible and supporting other people, especially those she cared most about. Even allowing herself to sink into these feelings at all felt somehow wrong. Selfish. So she couldn't afford to play games with Jonno, even if she was reasonably confident she could stop him winning in the end.

Even when she found she was crewed with Jonno again on her next shift, which meant they were going to be spending an entire night together. Because this was work. The professional arena where any kind of personal games were not only inappropriate, it would be unforgivable if they interfered with patient care in any way.

What Brie hadn't bargained on was that Jonno seemed to be prepared to play a long game. When they found themselves alone in the staffroom, waiting for their first call, there was no hint of flirting in the glance that grazed Brie's. He looked…curious.

'So… Dave tells me you left your job in Control not long after I went off to the Himalayas. How come?'

'I needed a break.' Brie's heart rate kicked up, both at the idea that Jonno had been asking about her and because this could be exactly the opportunity she needed. Was this the way it would happen? That the truth would emerge in a casual conversation? She cleared her throat. 'I had a few…um…health issues.'

She could actually feel Jonno's focus narrowing. That brilliant mind of his was probably throwing up all sorts of possible 'issues', including those involving mental health. He would be offering her the respect of not asking questions she might not want to answer but there was no doubt that he was interested. Concerned, even.

Because he *cared* about her? As more than simply a long-ago one-night stand?

Oh, help…the feeling of being cared about was almost as seductive as being desired.

But she couldn't tell him about Felix right now. They were on the start of a shift and messing with his head with something that huge would be a distraction for the rest of the night. She had no idea how to start telling him, anyway. The words were dancing in her head like fireflies that would be too hard to catch.

Jonno's calm voice was easy to focus on. 'But you're okay now?'

'Never better,' Brie assured him.

'Good to hear.' That focus in his eyes softened with a warmth Brie could feel right down to her toes.

'And you decided to train as a paramedic instead of going back to the control room? That was a big change to make.'

Brie nodded. This was safe ground. 'It had never occurred to me that I could be brave enough to be out there on the road, dealing with the kind of scenarios I was hearing about in those frantic triple nine calls for help but, you know, it got more and more frustrating when the calls got disconnected as soon as an ambulance, or someone like you, arrived. Or worse, when speaker phone was left on and I was listening to what was going on and then another call would come in so I was the one who had to disconnect and start all over again, trying to calm a panicked person enough to get the information needed to dispatch another crew.'

At some point, as Brie was talking to Jonno and he was nodding his understanding of why her old job had become so frustrating, something clicked in the back of Brie's mind. There were two separate things going on here, which was making everything so much more complicated.

There was her attraction to Jonno that she knew was still there, on both sides.

And there was the fact that Jonno had a son he didn't know he had.

Telling him something that was going to change his life—possibly in a way that would make him unhappy or angry, even—was a far more difficult prospect than dealing with any sexual tension that was, in fact, rather surprisingly delicious…

It wasn't that she was never going to tell him. It was, as she'd explained to her mother, a matter of choosing the right time. Maybe she *did* need to find a way to spend some time with Jonno away from work. Perhaps, if this *was* some kind of personal game, the card with Felix on it needed to be slipped up her sleeve for now, leaving Brie to play with the cards she was already holding, which were purely about each other.

One of them was also about this new space in her life. An adult, child-free space that was completely separate to her life as a mother and a daughter. This was an independent space that was about who she was in her own right—the core of the person she'd always been, before she'd willingly given up so much for her baby. And, somewhere in that core, was a yearning that Brie hadn't actually acknowledged. A need for something that was missing from her life? Something that it had taken Jonno's sudden appearance to bring to the surface?

Something her mother had said in the wake of Jonno's return popped into the back of Brie's mind. About how, if she wanted to be the best parent she could be, she had to look after her own needs as well. Could one of those needs be as simple as a physical connection with someone? A sex life?

Maybe she was being offered an opportunity to find out the answer to that question and, if it was something really important she was missing, maybe it was time to think about dating again. Starting a search for a life partner—something she knew Jonno Morgan could never have been because any dependants were the last thing he wanted in his own life.

That didn't necessarily mean Jonno couldn't help her discover the answer to this new question of how much a gap not having a relationship was creating in her life. Hypothetically, of course. Having the father of her child around was quite complicated enough without allowing this attraction to get out of control.

Something wasn't quite adding up and it was making Jonno cautious.

Why was Brie so wary of being close to him?

It was almost as if she had been—was *still*, even—upset about what had happened all those years ago, but that didn't make sense. She'd known it was his last night in town so it was never going to be the start of anything. It had been a memorable night, but that was all it could have ever been. Surely Brie hadn't expected him to stay in touch afterwards? He'd given up on using social media because the patch of the globe he was heading towards didn't allow for easy communication with anybody. He'd had enough trouble getting a phone and email connection to work. He'd discovered he didn't miss social media at all and, while he'd still thought of Brie surprisingly often, he had no real desire to contact her again. Because he didn't do relationships. Besides, Brie had been the one to disappear without saying goodbye—or even leaving him her phone number.

But now he was curious, dammit. Even more so now that he knew she was single. What kind of health issues had she had? And why on earth was she living with her mother? Jonno couldn't imagine being in the same room with his father, let alone sharing the house he'd grown up in, a huge old dwelling with an even bigger garden in one of the leafy, more affluent suburbs in Bristol, where you might expect a renowned paediatric cardiac surgeon to reside.

He didn't want to push too hard, however. He already knew how disappointing it was to have Brie vanish without a trace and while that couldn't physically happen while they were working together, it could happen on a personal connection level and Jonno wanted to avoid that. Because he was curious. And because he was still attracted to her in a way he hadn't been to any woman, before or since that one night with Brie Henderson. Had it really been as amazing as he remembered it being or had he dreamt even a part of what had exploded between them?

One thing he could be sure of was that Brie was passionate about her new career and that was obviously going to be an easy way to reconnect with her safely. Being in a position to give her the chance to consolidate and expand her skills exponentially by being involved in critical cases was a gift he was only too happy to offer. And Brie was clearly equally happy to accept.

He saw the way her eyes lit up with the priority call they got just after midnight that night.

'Sixty-eight-year-old female with severe, ten out of ten, left-sided abdominal pain. Conscious and breathing.' Jonno glanced at the GPS route highlighted on the dashboard screen as the automatic gates slid open from the station entrance. 'First thoughts?'

'Too many,' Brie confessed. 'Renal colic? Bowel obstruction? Ruptured appendix? Any other information?'

'Her GP increased her blood pressure medication a couple of days ago after she went to him with a bad headache.'

'Ah…' Brie was chewing her lip. 'Do we know if the onset of the pain was sudden?'

'Good question.' Jonno nodded approvingly and then responded to the person in the control room, telling him an ambulance was being sent as backup for transport but could be ten minutes behind them. 'Roger that,' he said. 'Our ETA is currently six minutes.'

Brie was waiting for him to finish the exchange. 'Triple A?' she suggested. 'Acute coronary syndrome? Thoracic aortic dissection?'

Jonno nodded again. 'My guess is a triple A.'

'An abdominal aortic aneurysm,' Brie said slowly. 'If it's ruptured, we might well be too late.'

'Let's hope it's just a dissection. What's the difference?'

'An aneurysm is a bulge in an artery wall where it's weaker. A dissection is where the wall tears and blood leaks between the layers of the artery wall. A rupture is when all the layers tear and it can lead to massive internal bleeding that's very likely to be fatal.'

'What would be a major diagnostic factor to look for?'

'A pulsatile mass in the abdomen?'

'Which may or may not be obvious. Depending on how distressed our patient is, I'll get you involved in the assessment.'

'Okay.'

He could actually hear the way Brie sucked in her breath, preparing herself for anything, and it almost made him smile. He'd been that new once. Scared of what he might find when he arrived on scene but so determined to do whatever he could to save a life.

An extremely anxious husband was waiting for them at the address and took them straight to their patient, Maria. She was lying on her bed, constantly shifting with the pain, sweating, very pale and clearly terrified.

'I'm Jonno,' he introduced himself. 'And I've got Brie with me. We're going to have a quick look at you and do something for that pain you're in and then we're going to get you to hospital as quickly as we can.' He hoped his smile was reassuring. 'Can I have a look at your tummy while Brie puts some sticky patches on so we can see what your heart's up to?'

Maria nodded. So did her husband. 'Please,' he begged. 'Do whatever you can. I've never seen her like this before.'

Brie was opening the pouches on the defibrillator cover, preparing to get a set of vital signs and a rhythm strip. Maria was in too much distress for it to be appropriate to let Brie take part in an urgent assessment and treatment but he knew she would be soaking it all in and they could spend all the time they needed later to go over every detail.

Jonno uncovered Maria's abdomen and gently laid his hand on the first quadrant he was going to palpate on the other side to where the pain was located.

'Tell me about this pain,' he said. 'Can you describe it?'

'Like something was tearing.'

'Are you having any chest pain as well?'

'No… I don't think so.'

It wasn't easy to assess her abdomen because Maria was unable to stay still due to the pain, but Jonno had moved his hand to her left side and he could feel the unmistakable pulsing beneath his palm.

'Have you ever been assessed for an abdominal aneurysm?' he asked.

It was her husband that answered as Maria groaned and rolled her head to one side.

'Yes,' he said. 'But they said it was only small and shouldn't be a problem, especially if she stopped smoking. They said they'd keep an eye on it.'

Smoking, along with high blood pressure were two of the biggest risk factors for a complication like this.

'Is that what's causing this?' Maria's husband sounded alarmed.

'I think so.' Jonno caught his gaze and could see that the man was well aware of how serious this situation was. He reached for his wife's hand.

'Heart rate's sixty-four,' Brie told him. 'Sinus rhythm with a few ectopic beats. Blood pressure's one ninety over one hundred and four, and the oxygen saturation's down to ninety-two percent.'

'Let's get an oxygen mask on,' Jonno said. 'And I'll get you to help hold her arm still for me so that we can get an IV line in.' He leaned down. 'Maria? I'm going to put a needle in your arm so that we can give you something for the pain, okay?'

Maria's response was another agonised groan but she nodded. Her husband had tears on his face but his voice was calm.

'I'm here, my love,' he told his wife. 'I'm right here…'

Brie drove the rapid response vehicle so that Jonno could travel in the ambulance with their patient with the triple A dissection. Maria was still alive when they got her to hospital and they bypassed the emergency department to get straight to Theatre, where a surgical team was waiting for her.

Jonno went over the dramatic case with her in the kind of detail that reminded Brie of swotting for her exams, but it felt even more satisfying to know that she was achieving a great score. And it wasn't the only benefit of being crewed with someone who was so knowledgeable.

There was more drama to come that night, with a night worker at a processing plant amputating several fingers and an employee getting knocked off his bicycle as he went to start work at a bakery just before dawn. Brie followed the ambulance again to collect Jonno from the emergency department and found him chatting to one of the doctors, having transferred their patient to the team in Resus.

'Maria's come through surgery,' he relayed. 'She's in ICU but it looks as if we got her here in time.'

'She's one of the lucky ones,' the doctor said. 'Good job, guys.'

Back on station, Jonno started quizzing her on whether she thought they could have done anything differently in their treatment of Maria, like doing something to try and lower her blood pressure? And why had he given her an anti-nausea drug?

'I'm guessing vomiting could have put additional pressure on a dissection and turned it into a full-on rupture? I don't know about the blood pressure management.' Brie held her hands up in surrender. 'I think my brain's fried. It's been quite a night.'

'Sorry.' Jonno's smile was apologetic. 'I've been act-ing like you're getting ready for sitting your critical care paramedic assessment. Not very fair, is it?'

'I loved it,' Brie assured him. 'I can't believe I'm lucky enough to be doing a few shifts with someone like you so I can learn so much. If I ever do get to be a critical care paramedic, I'll have you to thank for giving me a head start.'

'It's my pleasure,' Jonno said. 'It's the sort of thing that I love doing for a friend.' One side of his mouth curled up in what looked like a hopeful smile this time. 'We can be friends, yes?'

Brie felt her heart sinking. She wanted to be but it was impossible while she was keeping the truth from Jonno. She tried to smile back and hoped it would be enough of an answer.

It seemed to be. Jonno's smile widened. 'That's great. I'm heading off for a bit of rock climbing in Scotland with my mate, Max, tomorrow but I'll be back before you start your next shift. Dave tells me that Simon might be back on deck by then so I might not see so much of you. How 'bout I get your phone number and then I can ask you a favour. As, you know…' there was a sparkle in his eyes now that matched that smile '…a friend.'

'Sure.' Brie pulled out her phone and tapped the screen. 'Give me your number and I'll send you a text.'

She put the numbers in for a new contact and put a smiley face in the message line and hit the send arrow. As she put Jonno's name in the contact details it felt oddly significant. As if Jonno was officially part of her life now.

'I need a friend to help me with some painting if you have a bit of spare time when I'm back,' Jonno was saying as she slipped her phone back into her pocket. 'I'm not so bad with a roller but I'm really hopeless with a brush for doing the outlines.'

Brie didn't believe that for a minute but she knew what the real request was here. Jonno wanted to spend some time with her away from work. Maybe he had more in mind than getting some help with his renovation, but that wasn't what was foremost in Brie's thoughts right then.

This was exactly the opportunity she'd been waiting for.

A private space, away from work, to tell Jonno what he needed to know.

No excuses, this time. She would go to Jonno's apartment and tell him about his son. Because it was the right thing to do.

And because there was just the faintest hope that he might not react the way Brie feared. That she wasn't going to make his life implode in what could be his worst nightmare.

That, once Jonno got his head around it, there was even a chance that they *could* be friends? That he could, somehow, be a part of his son's life without breaking his little heart?

CHAPTER FIVE

TEN O'CLOCK IN the morning seemed like the safest time possible to be alone with Jonno Morgan.

It was during daytime hours, which removed any romantic associations that could have come from candle-light or the moon. It wasn't lunchtime, which removed any incentive for alcohol to be offered at this time of day, and Brie was hardly dressed to impress. She was wearing her oldest tee shirt and a pair of dungarees that had splatters of paint all over them from being used for her own DIY decorating projects in the past.

Not that Brie was anticipating wielding a paintbrush once she had dropped that paternity bombshell onto Jonno. Unless he wanted to talk about it in detail, in which case, doing something at the same time could possibly defuse some of the inevitable tension?

What Brie hadn't bargained on, as she arrived to knock on the door of Jonno's apartment, were memories waiting to ambush her. The way she'd come down this path last time, with her hand lost in the grip of Jonno's. The way she'd held the cold bottle of champagne so he could find his keys and unlock the door. And the way he'd given up the search so that he could use both his hands to cradle Brie's face and kiss her for the very first time.

She also hadn't factored in that Jonno might also be wearing old, ragged, paint-spattered clothing. That his tee shirt had a ripped hem that revealed a triangle-shaped patch of his skin. That oh, so soft skin on his side, just above his hipbone and below his ribs. That his jeans looked a size too big and were hanging so low on his hips the waistband of his underwear could be seen. Or, heaven help her, he didn't look as if he'd shaved in several days and his hair certainly hadn't seen a brush in a while. There were even flecks of paint adorning those wild, black waves.

And the smile…

Jonno looked so happy. A smile that would be obliterated very soon, when he heard what Brie was about to say. The sooner the better, in fact, because she could feel her resolve ebbing away under the effect of a smile that advertised how delighted he was to see her. Had he thought that she might change her mind and not turn up, given that her text response to his invitation had only said she'd do her best to come to help this morning if nothing got in the way?

She'd been giving herself an insurance policy, hadn't she, in case her nerves got the better of her?

'Hey…' she said by way of a greeting as Jonno opened the door.

'I'm so glad you're here,' he said. 'Please, come in…' He held the door open, but the gap for Brie to move past him was narrow enough for her to feel the heat of his body.

Oh, help…she hadn't expected that either. Or that she could be aware of the scent of him despite the paint

fumes in the apartment and it was triggering an avalanche of memories she didn't dare acknowledge.

'I had to come,' she said, pulling in a determined
new breath. 'There's something I really need to tell
you, Jonno.'

'Me too,' Jonno said, pushing the front door closed.
'You were right.'

'What about?'

'Come and see…' He took hold of her hand as he
caught up with her in the narrow hallway and pulled
her to the door opposite the open-plan living area she
was heading for. Before she had time to even say another word, he was leading her through the door to the
bedroom. 'The aubergine would have been a disaster.'
He waved his free hand at a test pot sample he'd painted
on the wall. 'But…what do you think of this? It's a half-
shade of olive-green.'

'It's lovely. Good choice.' But Brie's gaze strayed
from the pretty pale green as she tried to collect her
thoughts and find a way to open the conversation she
should have already had with Jonno. Years ago.

But she found herself staring at the wall beneath the
window where there were still patches of wallpaper that
needed stripping.

She could see one of those damned upside-down
pineapples. That avalanche of memories was coming for
her. She could see it moving so fast, there was a layer
of mist above it—one that already seemed to be making her brain feel foggy. Just what had that opening line
been to tell Jonno that he had a son? In desperation, Brie
jerked her gaze away from the pineapples. She turned
away from them completely, only to find that she was
not only standing too close to Jonno to allow for that

turn to offer an escape route, she was also under a very intense gaze from a pair of dark, dark eyes.

Jonno wasn't smiling now. In fact, his face was more than serious. He almost looked…sad? Poignant, anyway. As if he was thinking of something bittersweet.

'Why did you run away while I was asleep that night, Brie?' he asked softly. 'You didn't even leave a note. Did I do something that upset you?'

'*No*…' Brie's eyes widened. How on earth could he be thinking that when every single thing he'd done that night had been beyond wonderful? 'It was nothing like that.'

'What was it, then? I've always wondered.'

'I…um… I was feeling a bit sick. I would have been so embarrassed if I'd thrown up in your apartment. I'd had way more to drink than I usually do.'

Jonno's face stilled. 'Is that what it is? Why you're keeping your distance? Did I take advantage of you?' His words were quiet. 'I could have stopped, you know. You only needed to say the word. But I thought you wanted it as much as I did.'

'I *did*…' Brie whispered. Dear Lord, she could remember the level of that desire so clearly. Probably because she could feel the tendrils of that need tying themselves in a knot again right now, deep in her belly.

You *do*…you mean. That little voice in the back of her head was correcting her, even as she spoke. You still want it, you know you do. This is how you find out what's missing in your life and the fact that you want it *this* much is telling you how important it is.

She couldn't look away from Jonno's gaze but his silence was unnerving her. She had to break it.

'You've got some paint on your face.' Her voice sounded oddly raw. 'Right by the corner of your eye.'

'Oh?' Jonno lifted his hand and used his middle finger to brush at his skin.

'Not there. The other eye.'

He tried again but still missed the splash of paint and, without thinking, Brie lifted her hand and touched the paint that was crinkled by his smile lines. Jonno caught her wrist loosely with one hand as she touched his skin and he used his other hand to touch *her* face even though they both knew perfectly well that she didn't have any paint that needed wiping off.

His touch was feather-light but startling enough for Brie to have caught his gaze directly again. She could see the clear message that he would back off if she moved even a fraction away from that touch. He would drop his hand and that would be that. The music would be killed and the first steps of this dance would be the last.

But Brie didn't move away. As she closed her eyes she could feel herself leaning her cheek into the palm of Jonno's hand. And then she heard the way his breath came out with an undertone of sound that was exactly what she was feeling.

Raw need.

Pure desire.

Exactly the way this had started the first time.

Brie didn't open her eyes because she wanted to feel the heat of Jonno's lips taking her by surprise as they touched hers. She knew that heat would spark a reaction that she had no desire to dampen. She had to feel this again.

Just once…

* * *

He hadn't misremembered.

Or hyped up anything about that night with Brie into some kind of dream that had no basis in reality.

In actual fact, this new reality was better than anything Jonno had remembered. The sheer magnitude of the attraction that only built on itself from the first touch and *taste* of Brie's skin. The exquisite pain of slowing things down that pushed desire to limits he'd only ever discovered existed because of that night with this woman.

One kiss that led into another, deeper conversation between their lips and tongues. Questions that were instantly answered. Pleasure that was both given and taken in equal amounts. Buttons being undone, tee shirts being lifted for hands to find bare skin. It was a physical dance with a sense of urgency dampened only by the knowledge that if they went too fast this would all be over far too soon.

The bed that had been in this room the last time this had happened was long gone. Right now, the only furniture was a mattress on the floor that was covered with a drop sheet. The room smelled of fresh paint and, if they weren't careful, they might knock over a tin of pale, olive green liquid, but Jonno couldn't have cared less.

What he did care about was whether there was some reason why this shouldn't be happening at all.

'Do you want this?' he whispered against the side of Brie's neck as his fingers paused against her back, poised to unfasten the clasp of her bra. 'Is it okay?'

Her head tipped back to expose that vulnerable dip in her neck where Jonno could see how fast her heart

was beating. 'I want it,' she murmured. 'Don't stop…
Please don't stop…'

Desire kicked up several more notches. Who knew
that had even been a possibility?

'Are you still on the pill?'

'*No*…' There was a note of something like anguish
in Brie's tone. She must want this as much as he did if
she felt like this at the prospect of having to stop.

'That's okay… I've got something…'

Of course he did. Tucked into a hidden pocket in
his wallet. Jonno would never take risks with anything
like birth control. And you never knew when you might
meet an amazing woman who was happy to live in the
moment and take pleasure in a one-off encounter of
such an intimate nature.

This wasn't a one-off, of course, because they'd done
it before. But that had been so long ago that it felt like
it could be a first time with each delicious surprise of
an unexpected touch…or lick. Then again, there was a
feeling of safety. Of familiarity. Of knowing that this
was even better than the first time because of that emotional umbrella that felt like trust.

He heard Brie cry out with the first stroke of his
fingers and then again as he entered a space that had
haunted his dreams for so many years. It was the sound
of a woman in ecstasy. A woman who'd just been given
exactly what she'd needed the most. And then he felt
Brie's legs wrapping around his, the pressure urging
him on. It was *his* turn now. She wanted to give him
the same gift.

It was a long time before Jonno had any vaguely
coherent thoughts he could collect but, gradually, despite the continued floating sensation that was the af-

termath of a release like no other, he became aware of the warmth and shape of the woman he was holding gently in his arms and the rise and fall of her breasts as her breathing slowed.

'You okay?' he queried softly. Jonno didn't open his eyes because he didn't want to break this spell.

'Yeah…' He could hear the smile in Brie's voice. 'Never better.'

Jonno pulled her a little closer. He pressed a slow kiss against the top of her head.

'You want to get up? Are you hungry? Did you know I'm probably the world's best cheese toastie maker?'

He loved the sound of Brie's laughter. 'No, I did not know that.'

'Do you like cheese toasties?'

'Who doesn't?' But Brie snuggled closer. 'I don't want to get up just yet, though. Talk to me?'

'What about?'

'Anything… Everything…'

The warning bell sounding faintly in the background of Jonno's thoughts was enough to make him open his eyes and stare at the ceiling. He would never stay in one place long enough to talk about 'everything'. This was all about the sex. And friendship, if Brie could be one of those rare women who didn't expect it to automatically grow into something more. Or she didn't find a proper relationship where a close friendship with another man wasn't acceptable.

'You do know I'm not going to be around that long, don't you?' His words were quiet.

'I know.'

'And I don't believe in marriage. Or long-term relationships. I've never wanted my own family.'

Brie didn't say anything this time but Jonno could feel the shape of her body become more defined in his arms. Muscles had tensed and he knew he'd broken that blissful spell, but this was important. He couldn't let her think for a moment that this could be anything more than what it was, because that was the way people got badly hurt. He didn't usually go into details but Brie was different.

Because this wasn't the first time.

And Jonno was kind of hoping it might not be the last time.

'I grew up in what looked like the perfect family,' he told Brie slowly. 'From the outside. A successful father, a beautiful mother who devoted her life to charity work and helping less fortunate people. I got into a prestigious boarding school. I was the luckiest kid ever. Until I was about fifteen and it all fell apart in such spectacular fashion that there was no way I was ever going to believe in happy families again.'

'What happened?'

Jonno closed his eyes again. He let out his breath in a long sigh. He never talked about this but… Brie was different. And he wanted her to understand. So that she wouldn't get hurt. Or maybe it was so she would understand in case he'd hurt her somehow the first time they'd been together, without intending to.

'There was an accident,' he said. 'A nasty car crash. One of Bristol's leading philanthropists was driving. My mother was in the passenger seat. They were both killed instantly, and that was when the scandal broke.'

Brie was silent. Waiting…

'It turned out the guy was just the latest in a string of affairs my mother had been having throughout her entire marriage. She'd used this apartment to keep her liaisons private. Everyone who was anyone in Bristol seemed to be involved and everyone was shocked. My parents had presented the façade of a perfect marriage. My father would be there in his tuxedo at every glittering charity event and my mother, in one of her gorgeous ballgowns, would be hanging onto his arm, playing the adoring wife. There were photoshoots at home occasionally and I'd be in the background somewhere—the perfect child of the perfect mother. It was all a total sham. Totally fake.'

Brie made a sound as if something hurt. He felt her fingers move against his arm as if she wanted him to know she was right there. On his side?

'It would have been awful enough to lose a parent,' she said softly. 'Without finding out any of that. Especially at that age, when it's enough of a challenge to figure out the world and where you fit into it.'

'I didn't fit,' Jonno said. 'Not for a very long time. I'd lost the mother I adored, but she wasn't who I thought she was. I felt cheated. And angry. I used to go to friends' houses for school holidays, so I barely spoke to my father for years. He tried to tell me that he'd married my mother because she was pregnant and then he stayed with her because he didn't want to lose his son, but I was never going to forgive either of them. When I was eighteen I got access to what my mother had left me, which was this apartment and rather a lot of money, and it gave me an escape route. I told my father that I'd done a DNA test and he wasn't even related to me biologically. It didn't surprise him at all.'

He could feel the brush of Brie's hair against his

skin as she shook her head in sympathy. Or disbelief, perhaps.

'So there you go. I was expected to follow in my father's footsteps and go to medical school but I took off. The money I inherited meant I could do whatever I wanted. I got a job as a ski instructor in the Swiss Alps and met people who introduced me to all sorts of adventure sports. And then I got involved in an accident up in the mountains and that was when I decided to train as a paramedic. The rest, as they say, is history. What goes around comes around. My mate Max and I got involved in a mountain rescue a couple of days ago up in the Cairngorms.'

Was Brie aware that he was deliberately changing the subject? If so, she didn't seem to mind.

'Really? What happened?'

'It was another group of rock climbers. They got caught in a rockfall and one guy got a nasty compound fracture of his femur. Luckily, I carry a good first aid kit so we could give some decent pain relief before we splinted his leg and carried him to a spot the helicopter could land.'

'Sounds like a mission.'

'It was. We had to give up our plan to tackle Squareface.'

'Squareface?'

'It's a nice, gnarly climb that we've had on the bucket list for a while now. Never mind… We've booked another couple of days up there next month and we'll have to do it then or the weather will get worse and too much rain makes it hard to get through the river, and who knows when we'd get another chance? Anyway… Max messaged me this morning to tell me there's a picture of us on the front page of half a dozen newspapers.'

Brie gave a huff of laughter. 'I always knew you were destined to be famous. Way back, when I kept hearing people talking about you even before I was the one who got to dispatch you the jobs where all hell was breaking loose.'

'Just the way I like things to be.' Jonno grinned. 'Living on the edge. Apart from the times I like things to be just…like this…' Jonno smiled, shifting her in his arms so that his lips could find hers. '*Exactly* like this…'

Oh, man…the way she could respond to what felt more like a thought than a physical touch was mind-blowing. It was no wonder he'd never been able to forget Brie Henderson. He'd never met someone who was so in tune with how he rolled. Who he was. A random thought that, if things had been different, Brie would be his perfect life partner drifted through Jonno's mind some time later, when he truly felt too exhausted to move. And then another thought pushed it out of the way.

'What was it?' he asked, his voice sleepy.

'What was what?'

'The thing that you said you had to tell me? The reason you came today?'

Brie's intake of breath a beat later was almost a gasp. 'Oh, my God…what time is it?'

Jonno reached for the watch he'd dropped beside the mattress. 'Just after half past two. Must be time for that toastie, huh?'

But Brie was already on her feet, pulling on her underwear. 'I can't stay.' She reached for the paint-splattered tee shirt and pulled it over her head. 'I'm sorry but I've… I've got to be somewhere.'

'That was what you had to tell me?'

'No…not exactly…' Brie was halfway into her dungarees now and looking around for her shoes.

'But you can't stay,' Jonno finished for her. 'Are you running away from me, Brie? Again…?'

Brie froze, her shoes in her hands. She shook her head but she was looking wary again.

Guilty, even?

Yeah…he'd been right to feel that something didn't add up here. And maybe what he needed to do was back off. He didn't need, or want, to get involved in someone else's life to the extent that it interfered with his own life.

'It's no big deal,' he assured Brie. 'You go and do what you need to do.' He reached for his own scattered clothing. 'I got a bit distracted from the things I need to be doing myself.' He walked towards her, to drop a slow kiss onto her lips. Just to let her know there were no hard feelings, even if she *was* running away from him again.

She kissed him back. As if she simply couldn't help sinking into one final kiss.

And then she was gone.

CHAPTER SIX

SHE'D NEVER FELT like this.

Ever.

Brie arrived in the nick of time to collect Felix when his school day ended at three o'clock.

She'd never felt this guilty before. She'd thrown away the perfect opportunity to do what she knew she had to do, which was to tell Jonno that he had a son. But how could she when he'd opened up about some really traumatic things that had shaped him into the person he was today? Brie had a whole new understanding of made Jonno Morgan tick and her heart had gone out to that troubled teenager he'd once been. He'd felt betrayed by a mother he said he'd adored. He'd hated the man he'd thought was his father, who had contributed to the sham marriage they'd had. And what about his biological father that he hadn't mentioned? Did he feel as if he'd been betrayed by him as well? His family had clearly been a disaster he never wanted to repeat, so how could she have told him he was a father himself in that moment?

Okay…she could have told him as soon as she'd arrived at the apartment, which had been her absolute intention. But she'd been sucked back into the past, thanks to that damned wallpaper.

Taken back to a time in her life when everything was all about herself and there were still endless opportunities in her search for her place in the world and true happiness. To a time when dreams could actually come true and the man she'd hero-worshipped from afar had not only noticed that she existed but he'd *wanted* her.

Brie had been pulled back to that very brief window in time—the space of one night—when it had felt as if every bit of romantic nonsense she'd ever heard was actually true. That you could find 'the one' you were meant to be with. The person who could touch your soul at the same time as your body and that combination was so intense that you knew you could never, ever find it with anybody else.

Even another glimpse of that dream was something Brie had never thought she'd find and the temptation to actually *feel* it again had been totally irresistible. Just once.

And the result was that, yes, she felt more guilty than ever before. But she'd never felt this *happy* before either.

It felt a whole lot like being in love…

Which put Jonathon Morgan firmly amongst the people that Brie cared about.

The people that needed to be protected.

Feeling like she was protecting everyone involved made it easier not to let the feelings of guilt become overwhelming. This needed to be dealt with one step at a time and surely the fact a new, stronger connection was being forged between herself and Jonno was a step in the right direction? Laying the foundation for a future that all the people she cared about the most would be sharing to some extent?

Guilt versus happiness. Selfishness versus caring for others. Add them all together and the result was confusion.

It was doing Brie's head in, but she wasn't about to let Felix see the dark side of her thoughts. She took him and Dennis to the park after school because the sun was shining, and they were both in fits of laughter as they watched Dennis plough into drifts of autumn leaves and then pop out of the centre of the pile. She bought ice creams on the way home and had dinner ready for Elsie when she got home from a yoga class to get ready for a night shift on the paediatric ward.

It wasn't until Felix was tucked up in bed and Brie went to help her mother with the dishes that she found herself under her mother's watchful gaze.

'So it went well? Better than you expected?'

'Um...' Oh, wow... Brie dried a plate rather more thoroughly than it needed and turned away to put it in the cupboard. As close as she was to her mother, there were some things that weren't up for discussion and sex with Jonno was currently at the top of that list.

'You did tell him, didn't you?'

'Not exactly.'

'Oh... *Brie*...' Elsie sighed. 'Why not?'

'Because he told me that he doesn't believe in marriage or long-term relationships and he's never wanted a family of his own. He stopped believing in families at all after the horrible way his own family disintegrated when he was about fifteen. No more than a kid, really. He doesn't want anything to do with families, so it was hardly a good time to tell him he's got one of his own, was it?'

Elsie just shook her head.

'I feel like I know him a whole lot better than I did, Mum. It was the first time we've really talked, you know? He was trusting me with some pretty personal information. If I told him now, he might just take off and we'd never see him again.'

'You make it sound like he's going to do that anyway. What happened that was so terrible in his own family?'

It was Brie's turn to shake her head. It wasn't her story to share. 'He trusted me,' she repeated. 'And if I can prove that he *can* trust me, it could change everything. Oh...guess what?'

'What?'

'There's a photo of him in the paper today. I bought a copy when Felix and I had an ice cream on the way home from the park. Want to see what he looks like?'

'Of course.'

There was an undeniable feeling of pride as Brie showed her mother the picture of the hero paramedic who'd saved a man's leg, if not his life, in the mountains of Scotland.

Pride mixed with the memory of how it had felt lying in his arms today. Feeling his heart beating against her own. Feeling as if there was no other place in the universe that she could ever feel quite like this.

If Jonno was feeling anything like she was tonight, surely it *could* change everything?

Because it felt as if a few hours of being with Jonno was never going to be enough.

That even a lifetime might not be enough?

Yeah...this certainly felt an awful lot like being in love...

* * *

Elsie Henderson had a baby in her arms and she couldn't put him down.

If she did, his face would crumple and he'd start to whimper and she'd already spent too much of this night shift trying to get this miserable six-month-old baby boy called Tommy to settle enough to get some much-needed sleep.

She had been walking up and down the central corridor for some time now, talking to Tommy in the soft whisper that was apparently very soothing. Elsie had long since run out of things to say about the antics of all the animals crowding the brightly decorated walls of this paediatric ward and, a while ago, she'd started simply thinking out loud, finding something personally soothing about releasing thoughts that were starting to pile up enough to be concerning.

'So, you know what I think, Tommy? I think she's dating him. I *think*…she might have slept with him, though she's not telling me anything. She's got this… I don't know…*glow* about her. And she's so happy. If I didn't know better I'd say she was head over heels in love…'

Elsie smiled down at Tommy as she shifted what was becoming quite a heavy weight in her arms.

'I'm not saying it's not good to be in love. Or happy, for that matter. We all want to be happy, and it's all we want for our children. And that's why I haven't said anything. The only thing I do know is that she hasn't told him yet and I'm not happy about it at all. Surely she could have found the right moment today? I get that it might spoil what could be happening between her and Jonno, but that's just selfish, isn't it? This has to be about what's right for Felix. And his daddy. Even if Brie is happier than I've ever seen her…'

Elsie let her breath out in a long sigh. Her arms were starting to ache and she needed to put Tommy down, or at least sit down herself for a while. One of those comfortable armchairs in the corner of the staffroom would be perfect. She walked past the central desk in the ward and another one of the night nurses looked up.

'Is that Tommy?'

Elsie nodded. 'He's finally asleep,' she said, as quietly as she could. 'But I can't put him down without him waking up.'

'Don't put him down. I'll keep an eye on your other patients. It's only an hour or so before the day shift starts arriving and that wee guy should be due for some more painkillers by then.'

Elsie carried on towards the staffroom but Tommy was moving his head and making little grunting noises as if he was thinking of waking up.

'Shh…' Elsie bounced him very gently in her arms. 'It's okay… Here we go, let's find that comfy chair.'

There were two armchairs on either side of the coffee table by the window, but one of them was already occupied. By someone she would never have expected to be using it, especially at this time of night. Elsie bit her lip as she eyed the other chair.

'I'm not in your way, am I? I can go…' The man hurriedly put the mug he was holding down on the table. Too hurriedly, because it tipped over to soak a section of a messy, well-read newspaper. He groaned as he grabbed the mug and it sounded as if this might be the final straw.

'Don't worry about it,' Elsie told him. 'That paper

looks due to go into the recycle bin anyway.' She was watching his face and could see deep lines of fatigue around his eyes. 'And don't get up. Please. You look like you need a quiet space even more than Tommy and I do, Mr Morgan.'

'Please, call me Anthony...'

She smiled, liking his informality. 'I'm Elsie, I've just started recently on this ward. I've seen you around before, of course, but not usually at silly o'clock.'

The surgeon met her gaze for the first time. 'It has been rather a long night. I've been in PICU since midnight with a wee girl who looked like she might not make it. She had a fairly major surgery today and ran into problems with arrhythmias that put her into acute heart failure.'

'Oh... I'm sorry.' Elsie held his gaze for a heartbeat longer. She knew that Anthony Morgan had a reputation for being one of the best paediatric cardiac surgeons in the business but this was palpable evidence of how much he actually cared about his young patients and Elsie couldn't help but be seriously impressed. But then her eyes widened.

'It wasn't Victoria, was it? I knew she was having her surgery.'

Shutters came down that told Elsie he wasn't about to break rules concerning privacy and she had another very strong impression about this man. He could keep a secret for ever if he needed to.

'Sorry,' she said again. 'I shouldn't have asked. It's just that I spent some time talking to Vicky's mother the last time I was on duty. I'm helping to raise a grandson with spina bifida so we had a connection. And Vicky's just an adorable little girl. She gives the best cuddles in the world—just like my Felix.'

Those shutters in his eyes had been lifted in a slow blink. Anthony was even smiling. 'She's okay. She's a wee fighter. Her cardiologist has got her electrolyte balance sorted now, so she may well come onto the ward in the next day or two and you might be able to get another one of those cuddles. Is your grandson the same age?'

'No, he's six—a couple of years older. We've been through a few surgeries ourselves, but nothing as serious as an open-heart procedure.'

'I'm glad he hasn't needed it.' Anthony nodded but then stifled a yawn. 'I don't actually need to be here for Vicky any longer but if I went home I would no sooner get there than I'd have to turn around and fight my way through rush hour traffic to come back. I've got a full Theatre list this morning so I thought I'd put my feet up here instead. And have a strong coffee.' He glanced down at the empty mug in his hand. 'So much for that plan.'

Tommy seemed to be enjoying the sound of their voices. Elsie could feel him sink into deeper slumber as she took his weight on one arm. 'Here…give that to me.' She held her hand out for the mug. 'I'm well practised in making a coffee one-handed. Why don't you put the newspaper in the recycle bin by the fridge?'

'Sure.' Anthony started to gather up the sections of the paper.

'How do you take your coffee?'

'Black, thanks. No sugar.'

It was easy to pour coffee from the glass carafe that was part of the drip coffee percolator. Elsie took the mug back to Anthony, to find that he hadn't got very far with moving the coffee-splattered newspaper. He had it in his hand instead and was staring at the picture on the front page.

Elsie had seen that picture herself. A few days ago now. Because Brie had brought the paper home with her. After throwing away what must have been the best opportunity she could have had to tell him about his son.

'*Look, Mum,*' she'd said. '*That's Jonno. He and his friend were rock climbing in Scotland and they ended up rescuing this guy who'd broken his leg. I thought you might like to see what he looks like.*'

Elsie had done more than simply admire the action shot of the paramedic with his grateful patient as he got loaded into a rescue helicopter. She'd cut the picture out and had it in safe keeping because one day—hopefully very soon—she would be able to give it to Felix. To put the first picture of his daddy on the wall, even?

Anthony didn't seem to notice Elsie putting the mug of coffee down beside him. Or that she was watching him as she sank into the other armchair, careful not to disturb Tommy. There was something about how still Anthony was that made the back of her neck prickle. Something that made those lines of weariness in his face look a lot more like…grief?

'Do you know him?' she asked softly. 'Is he a relative of yours?'

Anthony didn't seem to notice that it might be odd she could remember the surname of someone she'd seen in the caption of a newspaper image. He seemed lost in the photograph.

'Yeah…' The tone of just that one word was raw. It had an echo of fatigue that almost sounded like despair. 'Jonathon Morgan is my son.'

Elsie froze. Brie had been quite sure that Jonno was not related to this surgeon with the same surname.

He specifically said he had no family here...

But had that been the truth? What about what she'd said after she'd spent time with him the other day?

He stopped believing in families at all after the horrible way his own family disintegrated when he was about fifteen...

Anthony put the paper down. Then he closed his eyes and rubbed his forehead with his fingers. 'Sorry,' he murmured. 'Maybe the night's been longer than I realised. I'm quite sure you don't want to hear about my personal life.' He had a smile on his face as he opened his eyes but he didn't meet Elsie's gaze. 'Families, huh?' He reached for his coffee. 'They can be complicated, can't they?'

Elsie's sound of agreement was a little strangled. She was staring at him. He had no idea just how much more complicated his family might actually be.

Anthony Morgan was clearly well aware of the difficulties in his relationship with his son.

What he couldn't possibly know was that his son had a child he still didn't know he had.

That Anthony had a grandson he didn't know he had.

The weight of Elsie's concern about the way Brie was handling this whole situation had just become a whole heap bigger. As if he could sense the tension, Tommy woke up with a start and decided to let the world know that he was a long way from being happy.

Elsie got to her feet and excused herself as the baby's cries rapidly became ear-splitting. She needed to get Tommy back to his room so she could check on his nappy and see whether he was due for a feed or that his medication dose could be brought forward if necessary. She could feel the misery of this howling infant settling around her own heart as she carried him and it was morphing with that concern about Brie.

How was she going to tell her daughter that Jonno had lied to her? That Felix's father might not be trustworthy? That there was now another grandparent in the picture, and didn't Anthony Morgan have the right to know about Felix as well?

Families were complicated, all right.

Elsie had no idea where she could even start to try and sort the unexpected issues that were landing on her own family but one thing was clear.

As much as Elsie adored her daughter, Felix was the person who mattered the most right now. Whatever she decided to do, or not do, could affect her grandson's whole future.

CHAPTER SEVEN

BRIE HENDERSON MIGHT be thirty-two years old and a highly competent single mother but she knew she might have made a mistake in not paying enough attention to the words of wisdom from her own mother.

Elsie had warned her that the longer she left it, the harder it was going to be to tell Jonno.

And Brie's intimate reunion at Jonno's apartment had just made it a whole lot harder.

When he smiled at her like *that* it was impossible to think of anything other than the way it felt to have Jonno touching her. There were moments when she could feel a glance from him burning through her clothes from the other side of the station staffroom. Even the sound of his voice, or his laughter, could send a delicious shiver down her spine and she had to be careful not to let eye contact linger long enough for it to be blatantly obvious that they were more than colleagues.

It was just as well they weren't working together.

Brie's original crew partner, Simon, was back at work but, in the wake of his recent head injury, he was being sheltered as much as possible from any stressful situations that might be too much of a challenge so the calls they were being dispatched to were low acuity. Not that Brie was about to complain because this was the kind of experience she needed and Simon was happy to take the role of a mentor and let her take the lead.

She assessed a twelve-year-old boy who'd fallen off his bike on the way to school and had a Colles fracture of his wrist and Simon was pleased with the way she splinted the injury, remembering to put something soft for the boy's fingers to curl around and keep the fracture stable. She dealt with a known epileptic who'd had a seizure in a video arcade but refused transport to hospital by the time Simon and Brie arrived on scene. He confessed he hadn't been taking his medication recently and he also knew that the flashing lights of the arcade games were a trigger for him. He apologised for wasting their time and Brie assured him that this was what they were here for. She made him promise to take more responsibility for his own health from now on.

'It could have been worse, you know? What if you'd been riding your bicycle and you'd fallen off in the middle of traffic?'

There was a pregnant woman who thought she might be in labour and wanted a ride to the hospital and a very elderly gentleman whom they found sitting in an armchair with a bag beside him. Brie could see the neatly folded pyjamas and a plastic bag with a toothbrush and toothpaste on top of it. It sounded as if Clive had also googled and then memorised all the classic symptoms of a heart attack.

'I've got terrible central chest pain, love,' he said to Brie. 'And it's radiating to my left arm and my jaw. I feel lightheaded. Faint, even…and I'm really short of breath.' He took a couple of quick gasps.

'Have you been sick at all?'

'Not yet. But I feel like I could be. Any minute.'

'How bad is the pain? On a scale of zero to ten, with zero being no pain and ten being the worst you can imagine?'

'Oh…' Clive screwed his eyes shut and pressed a fist to his chest. 'Ten…' He opened his eyes and smiled bravely at Brie. 'Maybe just a nine. I'm pretty tough, you know?'

Brie smiled back. 'I know. But it's a bit scary if you're feeling sick and there's no one around. Do you live alone here?'

Faded blue eyes had a sparkle that looked like imminent tears as Clive nodded. This was a lonely old man and, if they weren't needed urgently elsewhere, what was the harm in spending some time to give him some attention and reassurance? They had to take any report of symptoms like this seriously anyway, even if Clive didn't look as if he was at all unwell or suffering from severe pain.

'I'm going to give you the full work up,' Brie told him. 'I'll take your pulse and your blood pressure and look at the oxygen saturation in your blood. We'll do a twelve lead ECG as well. Have you had one of those before?'

'I have indeed.' Clive lay back in his armchair. 'You do whatever you need to do, darling. I have complete faith in you.'

So did Simon as their shift drew to a close. He had let her take the lead in every callout, including the last one, which had been a lights and siren response to a medical alarm.

'You're already way more confident in your assessments,' he told her as they headed back to station. 'And you just got that IV line in on your first attempt.'

'My hands were a bit shaky,' Brie admitted. 'I've never had to deal with a case of hypoglycaemia that severe. I thought she was dead when we first walked in. And her veins were so hard to find.'

'Giving the IV ten percent dextrose is a bit of magic, isn't it?' Simon was smiling. 'I know it's not as exciting as being out as crew on one of the Echo trucks but it's always been a favourite job for me. Especially like Glenys today, when they wake up like a light switch going on.'

Brie laughed. 'She was so with it. The way her eyes popped open and she said, "Oh, no… I've had a hypo, haven't I?" She was so annoyed with herself.'

'At least she had the good sense to activate her alarm when she felt the first symptoms. She could have been in real trouble if she hadn't.' Simon was rubbing his forehead.

'You've got a headache again, haven't you?'

'Yeah… I'm glad it's nearly home time.' His eyes narrowed as they slowed down. 'What's with this traffic?'

'I don't know. Oh, wait… I can see some beacons behind us.' Brie pulled the ambulance closer to the side of the road as a police car pushed its way through the traffic. Moments later, the flashing lights of another emergency vehicle appeared in the rear-view mirror and, at the same time, the radio in the ambulance crackled into life.

'Unit Four-Zero-Three, how do you read?'

Brie pushed the talk button. 'Loud and clear, Control.'

'Your location is Queen's Road, correct?'

'Roger that.'

'Please proceed to the intersection of Queen's Road and Charlotte Street. There's a car that's gone through the window of a coffee shop. Details coming through. You're backing up Echo One.'

The vehicle with its flashing blue lights and the siren sounding was passing them as Brie activated the lights on the ambulance and pulled out to follow it. She knew who was driving the rapid response vehicle. Her heart rate would have picked up even if this didn't appear to be the most exciting call she and Simon had had all day.

The fact that she was about to be in the same place at the same time as Jonno was just as exciting as any major trauma case could be. Brie hit the air horn as another car tried to pull out in front of them. She wasn't about to let anything get in her way or slow her down.

The scene was a mess.

A car was half in the café and half on the footpath with broken pieces of the outdoor tables and chairs scattered around. Police officers were trying to direct traffic and clear space and spectators, which was not an easy task because of the busy junction nearby.

Jonno was first on scene for medical assistance and left the beacons on his vehicle flashing as he got out, looking for whoever had already taken charge of the scene. He could see a fire engine approaching from one side and an ambulance was arriving from the same direction he'd come from. A police officer standing at the rear of the crashed car waved him over.

'Was anybody sitting outside?' Jonno asked.

'Fortunately not,' the police officer responded. 'And there's only a couple of people with minor injuries inside. They had time to jump out of the way, apparently. The driver of the car is elderly. Seems like they were intending to park but hit the accelerator instead of the brake. Unless there's something medical going on. He's refusing to get out of his car. There's a doctor in there talking to him.'

'Okay… I'll take a quick look but it sounds as if I'm not really needed here.'

A glance over his shoulder showed Jonno that the ambulance had found a space to park and it sounded as if their crew would be easily able to handle whatever was happening inside the café. When he saw it was Brie getting out of the driver's seat in the ambulance, however, Jonno found himself dismissing his plan of making himself instantly available for another call. When his gaze caught hers, even across a gap as big as this, in the middle of a chaotic accident scene, he was aware of what could be seen as a rather unprofessional desire to stay here.

But, on the other hand, he was nearing the end of his shift so there would be another rapid response vehicle available very soon and maybe he needed to take a bit more time to assess this situation. Driving through a shop window had the potential to be quite a serious mechanism of injury, didn't it?

And…what if Brie needed his help? Her crew partner was looking a bit pale himself. Had he come back to work too soon after getting that nasty concussion? Jonno wasn't about to have Brie left to deal with everything on her own, like she had when he'd found her looking after that woman who'd nearly been murdered by her husband.

So he walked into the café with Brie. Side by side.

He could see the back of the man, presumably the doctor the police officer had told him about. Had he happened to be in here for a coffee, perhaps? They weren't far away from St Nick's children's hospital here. Whoever he was, the man was crouched beside the open driver's door, his hand on the wrist of the elderly driver, who was still gripping his steering wheel and staring straight ahead. A table lay on its side nearby, along with a splintered chair and broken crockery on a carpet of shattered glass.

There were several other people in the café's interior, possibly because the crashed car and all the emergency personnel were blocking the café doors. A man in a chef's apron had a bloodstained tea towel wrapped around someone's arm. Two middle-aged women were still sitting at a table with plates of cake in front of them, staring wide-eyed at what was going on, and there was another woman in the corner closest to the door they had just come through. Beside the only intact part of the front windows of the café. She had streaks of grey in her hair and an alarmed expression, but what Jonno was most aware of was that she was holding onto the handles of a wheelchair that had a small boy sitting in it. A small boy who was also wide-eyed. Even more so when he saw Jonno and Brie walk inside. The astonished expression on his face now was almost comical.

'Mumma!' he shouted. 'Look, Nana…it's *Mumma*.'

Confused, Jonno turned to see that Brie now looked far paler than Simon had.

She looked beyond shocked, in fact, as she moved towards them.

'Mum…what on earth are you doing here? Are you

hurt?' Brie dropped to crouch in front of the wheelchair. 'Felix? Are you okay, darling?'

The small boy was climbing out of his wheelchair and Jonno could see the braces he was wearing on his lower legs. From the corner of his eye he could see the man who'd been talking to the driver of the car getting to his feet but he wasn't ready to talk to him yet. Because he was watching the little boy wrap his arms around Brie's neck and the way she got to her feet with him clinging to her like a little monkey.

Holding him the way a mother would hold her child so that she could reassure him. Or reassure herself that he wasn't hurt?

So Brie did have a child, not just a dog.

Had she lied to him about being single, as well?

Distracted far more than he should ever have been in a professional situation, Jonno tried to centre himself. He turned away from watching Brie cuddling her son to talk to the doctor who had already assessed the driver who'd come through the wall of this café.

But the distraction of seeing Brie with her child was nothing compared to the shock that Jonno was now faced with. He was standing within touching distance of a man he hadn't seen for a very long time, but it wasn't long enough.

Because this was a man he'd believed he never wanted to see again.

But he'd never realised he would feel this…*pull*… towards this man if he did see him again.

His father…

His only family…

For a heartbeat the two men stared at each other. And then Anthony Morgan's gaze went past him, towards

Brie and her mother and the kid, and Jonno knew instantly that this couldn't be simply a coincidence. There was a link here and it had to do with Brie.

And his connection to Brie.

He could feel the axis of his entire world shifting beneath his feet. Kind of like the way it had when he'd been hardly more than a kid himself and he'd been told his mother was dead. When he'd found out that the world as he'd known it hadn't actually existed.

But it made absolutely no sense that it could be happening again.

He turned back to his father. 'What the *hell* is going on here? No…' He held up his hand as he saw the older man about to respond. 'It can wait. I've got patients who need attention. Simon?' He turned his back on his father. 'Could you give me a hand here, please?'

'What *is* going on, Mum?' Brie echoed Jonno's angry question as she put Felix back into his wheelchair. 'Who is that man? Someone said he's a doctor, so what's so wrong about him helping the driver of that car?'

'Nothing.' Elsie shook her head. 'He *is* a doctor. He's Anthony Morgan.'

Part of Brie's brain was trying to join dots so that she could make sense of this, as another part reminded her at the same time that it was her job to find any people other than the elderly car driver who might need medical attention. Like that man with the tea towel wrapped around his arm. Yet another part was noticing the way her mother was swallowing hard, as if she had something difficult to say. Felix didn't seem to be aware of any sudden tension. He was watching the actions of police officers and firemen again with total fascination.

'He's also Jonno's father.' Elsie was avoiding Brie's gaze now, her voice deliberately casual and low enough not to attract Felix's attention. 'He…um…wanted to meet his grandson.'

Those dots didn't just connect. They smashed into each other.

'How *could* you?' There was only one way that this stranger could have learned of any connection to Jonathon Morgan's son and Brie felt utterly betrayed, but this wasn't the time or place to confront her mother. 'Take Felix home, please.'

'But…'

'*Now…*' Brie turned away, managing to find a smile for Felix. 'I'll see you soon,' she promised. 'But I've got work I have to do right now.' She stepped towards the man with the tea towel. 'Can I see your arm?' she asked. 'How did your injury happen?'

'Bit of flying glass,' he said. 'I pulled it out but it wouldn't stop bleeding.'

As Brie began unwrapping the bloodstained cloth she glanced up to see the doctor—Jonno's *father*—moving past her, leaving Jonno and Simon to reassess the man in the car. He wasn't looking at her. Anthony Morgan's gaze was on her mother.

'I'm so sorry,' she heard Elsie say to him. 'We shouldn't have come here.'

'I'm glad we did.' Anthony Morgan sounded remarkably calm, Brie thought. There was a warmth to his tone as well that made her question the impression Jonno had given her that he wasn't a nice man. 'But I do think it's time we left. Let me help you get Felix back to your car.'

The laceration beneath the tea towel was a clean cut that was only oozing a small amount of blood now. Brie found a sterile dressing in her kit and a bandage to hold it in place.

'You're going to need a couple of stitches,' she advised. 'Have you got someone who can take you to your GP or the emergency department?'

He nodded. 'My girlfriend's over there.' He shook his head. 'We only came in for a coffee to takeout. Who knew something like this could happen?'

Brie wound the bandage around his arm swiftly. 'You were lucky you weren't standing any closer to the window.'

There were fire service personnel working with police officers as they assessed what needed to be done to remove the car and make the scene safe. One officer was talking to Jonno and others were helping to get the dazed-looking elderly man out of the driver's seat. Simon had hold of his arm.

'Just watch your feet, Mr Baxter,' he said. 'There's all sorts of broken stuff and I don't want you tripping up. We've just got to get out of the door and into the ambulance so we can take you to hospital for a proper checkup.' He turned his head, looking for Brie. 'You good to go?' he asked. 'Is there anyone else that needs us?'

'All good,' she responded. 'I'll just pack up my kit.' She gathered up the packaging from the dressing and bandage and stuffed it into her pocket before standing up again, with her backpack in her hands.

Only to find that Jonno was standing right in front of her. His face was pale, which made his eyes look even darker.

Even angrier...

'Did you know about this?' His voice was low. Dangerously quiet. 'Why *my* father and *your* mother were meeting?'

'*No*... I had no idea.'

'But you know *why*, don't you?'

Brie had to nod. She'd never felt this miserable in her life. She knew she had only seconds before she had to walk out of this café and finish the job she was responsible for. Time had run out. These few seconds were her last opportunity to tell the truth.

'My mother obviously thought your father had the right to meet my son...' However impossible it felt, Brie had to hold Jonno's gaze. She could see that Jonno knew what she was about to say but he wasn't going to make it any easier for her.

And why should he?

Her voice was no more than a ragged whisper as she finished her sentence. '...because you're Felix's father.'

Yep... Jonno had already guessed the truth and yet he'd managed to do his job without letting the bombshell interfere in any discernible fashion. Brie needed to channel that focus. She had an elderly patient who might not be seriously injured or unwell but he was probably already in the back of her ambulance and it was time to transport him to hospital.

But she couldn't break that eye contact quite yet. She knew Jonno had something he wanted to say and, however painful it might be, she owed it to him to let him say it.

It turned out to be more painful than she'd expected.

'I didn't think you were like *them*,' he said, his words dripping ice. 'But you're just the same, aren't you? You've been lying to me ever since I met you.'

CHAPTER EIGHT

'ECHO ONE, HOW do you read?'

'Echo One, reading you loud and clear.'

'Priority One call. Unwitnessed cardiac arrest of unknown duration. Private house. No bystander CPR underway. Police have been informed. Address should be on your screen now.'

Jonno flicked on his beacons and activated the siren, although, given the details he'd just received, it was unlikely that rushing to this scene would be of any benefit to the victim. His role was more likely to be that of being able to pronounce someone dead so that the police and coroner could take over but he was grateful for the automatic priority of the call.

He needed the buzz of the adrenaline rush that, even after so many years, still came from the sound and lights of a life-threatening emergency. From having to drive fast and think even faster so that he could anticipate and avoid hazards. This feeling was a drug and the effect that Jonno was most grateful for right now was that it made it impossible to think about anything else.

He reached the address within three minutes, well before any police were expected, but he knew that the scene of a sudden death was unlikely to be high on their priority list unless there were indications that it hadn't been natural. Jonno had to get there as quickly as possible, however. Just in case there was a chance it wasn't too late.

Jonno could sense that it was too late the moment he stepped through the front door to the house that had been left wide open. It wasn't simply the sound of a man sobbing, it was the oddly empty feeling in this house that he instinctively knew only came from being near someone who had no flicker of life left in their body.

The man was sitting at the table in his kitchen, a phone lying beside him, his face in his hands. His body was shaking with the effort to control his sobs when he looked up to see Jonno enter the room and he pointed to another door.

'She's in there… She said she felt tired and went to lie down…hours ago…' He pulled in a ragged breath. 'I thought she was just asleep…'

'Stay here for a minute. I'll be back…'

Jonno put his kit and the defibrillator down as he entered the bedroom because it was obvious as he approached the bed that the woman was deceased and there was no point in beginning a resuscitation. Her eyes were open and staring, her jaw drooping and he could see a bloodless pallor to her face and lips. He knew he would find her skin cool to the touch and her pupils fixed and dilated when he shone his penlight torch into her eyes. He still needed to observe her for long enough to be absolutely sure and Jonno put his stethoscope to her unmoving chest to listen for any sounds of life.

His protocol called for an ECG to be performed to demonstrate no cardiac activity but there was something more important to take care of first. Jonno went back to the kitchen and crouched so that he was at eye level with the grieving man.

'I'm so sorry for your loss,' he said quietly. 'Is there someone I can call to be with you?'

'My son's on his way.' The man rubbed at his dripping nose and sniffed loudly.

'My name's Jonno. I'll be with you until your son arrives but there are a few things I need to do for…?' He raised his eyebrows. 'I'm really sorry, I wasn't told the name of your…wife, is it?'

He nodded. 'Margaret. But everyone calls her Peggy. We've been married for more than fifty years…'

'That's a long time.' Jonno smiled. 'And you are?'

'Trevor.'

'And Peggy wasn't feeling well today?'

'I thought she was fine. Just a bit tired…'

'Does she have any medical problems she was being treated for?'

'Oh, yes…she's had trouble with her heart for a long time now. And her blood pressure. Her breathing wasn't so great either, but she was doing well. We just celebrated her birthday last week. She's only seventy-three…' Trevor dissolved into tears again.

Jonno straightened, putting his hand on Trevor's shoulder. 'I'm going to put the kettle on,' he told him. 'And I'll be back to make you a cuppa. I've got a couple of things I need to do to tick the boxes on some paperwork, but after that would you like to come and sit with Peggy?'

The sound of Trevor's grief followed Jonno back into the bedroom. Any buzz of the adrenaline rush of getting to this scene had completely worn off now and, if anything, Jonno was feeling worse than he had before this call.

And that had been quite bad enough.

It was two days since he'd walked out of that café with an anger building to rival the worst of those teenage years when he'd felt betrayed by the people who should have cared about him the most. An anger that burned so brightly it was easy to channel it into action, focusing intently on his work and attacking all the remaining renovation work he could do himself out of work hours. Lack of sleep as he kept himself busy enough not to have to think about things had, no doubt, contributed to the weariness that was weighing him down now. Along with a disappointment that was so deep it actually hurt to breathe if he let himself think about it.

Jonno gently closed Peggy's eyes before opening the pockets on the defibrillator to find the electrodes he needed to stick to her skin to take his ECG recording. He found himself murmuring an apology as he pulled back the duvet and then lifted Peggy's clothing, treating her as respectfully as he would have if she had still been alive.

With all the electrodes in place, he turned on the defibrillator and watched as any artifact on the screen settled into the expected flat line. He pushed a button and the paper trace began to emerge, capturing the lack of any cardiac activity. He let it run for a few seconds and then stopped the trace, ripping off the recording so that he could attach it to the paperwork he needed to do.

He stared at that flat line for a long moment. Because it felt like a reflection of how he was feeling himself?

As if something had died?

But it had died a very long time ago, hadn't it? Why was it that the moment he'd recognised his father he'd become aware of this dark space in his heart? A family-shaped hole that he'd been living with for more than half his life, so it should have been filled by now with the satisfaction of his chosen career and the adrenaline-fuelled hobbies that were the focus of his free time.

He couldn't still love his father enough for this to be hurtful all over again, could he? Or had his anger diminished over the years enough to leave something exposed, but because he'd turned his back on it so long ago he hadn't seen it?

Jonno took a minute to get the room ready for Trevor to come back in to be with his wife. He tucked the duvet around Peggy's body. He closed the curtains and turned on a soft bedside lamp. He put a chair beside the bed and then took one of Peggy's hands to lay on top of the duvet, so it could be held by grieving relatives.

It was then he noticed how beautifully manicured her nails were. Perfect ovals with a glossy red polish on them. She had a large diamond ring on her finger and there was something about that sparkle and those nails that took Jonno back in time with a jarring sensation. If Peggy's hand had a few more diamond rings on it, and a few less wrinkles, it would look exactly like his mother's hand had looked the last time he'd seen it.

Oh, man…that emotional hole was getting darker. Deeper. Jonno needed to get out of this room and do something that would distract him. The interruption of the middle-aged police officer who put his head around the door in that moment was more than welcome.

'Need any help?' he asked.

'I'm all done,' Jonno responded with a shake of his head.

'Nothing untoward?'

'No.' He hadn't noticed any red flags, like any sign of a struggle or evidence of drugs or alcohol being consumed. 'And there's a history of various medical issues. 'I'll be able to get out of the way as soon I've finished the paperwork.'

He'd be able to find something new to focus on, as well. Hopefully a complicated medical crisis that would allow nothing from his personal life to even enter his head. Because there was something even worse than having been reminded of a long-ago betrayal.

It was having history repeating itself.

But why had he expected anything to be different?

Jonno scribbled notes on the forms that needed filling and signed his name. He stapled the ECG trace to the back of the certificate and left a copy with the police officers present. Trevor's son and daughter-in-law had arrived and it was time Jonno left the family to have some time with their loved one before the next steps in the process had to occur.

He strapped the defibrillator back into its slot and shut the side hatch of his vehicle. Getting into the driver's seat, he was about to advise the control room of his availability but, instead, found himself closing his eyes and pulling in one of those unexpectedly painful breaths.

He had expected something different because he had *trusted* Brie.

He'd let her touch a part of his heart that he hadn't realised wasn't protected enough any more.

So now he felt betrayed all over again.

Because he'd felt closer to her than he'd allowed himself to be with any woman. With any person, come to that, after learning that his parents' marriage and, by association, their love for him, had been nothing more than a pretence.

He'd never felt like that about any woman.

He'd been in love with her, dammit.

She had been lying all along, but this time he couldn't run from the truth. He couldn't turn his back on people and places in order to shield himself.

He had a child.

A son. A small boy called Felix. And, if that wasn't enough to turn his entire world upside down, he had a child with special needs that made him even more vulnerable.

A child who had existed for years, but he'd never been told about him.

It was unforgivable. But Jonno wasn't about to walk away.

That would be more than unforgivable. It would be utterly unacceptable.

Letting his breath out in a sigh, Jonno reached for his phone and opened a contact he had resisted deleting in those first hours when he'd been so angry with Brie. He tapped in a text message.

We need to talk. And then I want to meet my son properly.

They met at Sugar Loaf Beach on the Severn Estuary.

Brie had suggested it because it gave her an excuse to take Dennis with her and she had a feeling she might need the comfort of her dog's company. Going to the beach was his favourite thing in the world, which also meant that at least one of them would be happy.

Jonno certainly wasn't. The look in his eyes as Brie walked towards him felt like a physical blow.

He hated her, didn't he?

And she couldn't blame him.

He barely made eye contact before leaning down to pat the dog's curly hair. 'So…this is Dennis?' His tone was polite. Cold.

Brie nodded and then realised Jonno wasn't about to look at her again so she cleared her throat. 'Yes… I hope you don't mind that I brought him. It's not often he gets to go to the beach.'

'I haven't been here since I was about Dennis's age.' Jonno tilted his head.

'Really? But you grew up in Bristol, like me, didn't you? These are our closest beaches.'

'I lived in Leigh Woods, which was the perfect place to grow up in with the forests and mountain bike trails to play in. For me, going to the beach meant a trip to Spain or the Maldives with my mother. My father could never get away from work, apparently, but, oddly enough, my mother would usually find a friend of hers who happened to be on holiday at the same time. In the same place. Always a male friend, of course—on holiday alone.'

Brie said nothing. Was he deliberately reminding her of that happy family image that had been contrived for public consumption? The lies he'd grown up with? That he considered her to be 'one of them'?

She wasn't. Deep down, she'd only ever wanted to be completely honest with Jonno. She'd been too shy in the beginning, given up too easily along the way and, most recently, too afraid to risk damaging the lives of the people she loved the most. Or too selfish, because she'd wanted that small piece of the fantasy back?

Jonno wasn't looking at her. He seemed to be staring at the coast of Wales across the calm waters of the Severn estuary.

'Let's walk, shall we?' His tone was clipped. He didn't really want to be here, did he? He didn't want to have had his life tipped upside down.

Brie let Dennis off the lead and he raced ahead of them to get to the pebble beach that they appeared to have to themselves, which made the silence between them even more noticeable. Brie found a stick to throw and Dennis barked joyously as he chased it into the water. Then he found a seagull to chase instead and ran in circles as it flew overhead. The silence was feeling awkward now so Brie gathered her courage.

'I'm sorry,' she said.

'What for?' Jonno's words were still terse. 'That you got pregnant or that you got found out for lying for so long?'

'I'm not sorry I got pregnant.' Brie's response was swift. 'Felix is the best thing that's ever happened in my life.'

Apart from you, she added silently. *And the way you made me feel...*

'So...you lied to me about being on the pill? You *wanted* to get pregnant?'

'*No!*' The accusation was an insult. 'I'd never do something like that. I told you I'd left because I felt sick. I threw up, off and on, all day. I didn't miss any pills— it just didn't occur to me that it might have messed with my contraception.' Brie could feel her anger ebbing. She couldn't blame Jonno for thinking along those lines. 'I'm sorry that you found out the way you did,' she added. 'I didn't lie, exactly, but I should have told you sooner...'

Jonno gave a huff of unamused laughter. 'You think? Oh, right...maybe seven or so years ago?'

'I tried every way I could to contact you,' Brie said quietly. 'But it was weeks after you'd left. Your phone was disconnected. You never responded when I tried to message you on social media. Nobody knew where you were.'

'So you just gave up?'

'It was during those weeks I found out that the baby I was carrying had spina bifida.' Brie's tone changed. She might deserve Jonno's anger but she wasn't the person he thought she was. She hadn't set out to lie to him. 'My priorities kind of changed at that point.'

That silenced him. Brie walked ahead and found another stick to throw for Dennis. Then she turned.

'I never expected to see you again,' she said. 'But when I'd had a bit of time to get used to you turning up out of blue like that, I did try to tell you—the day I came to your apartment.'

She could hear the echo of what she'd said to him then, in spite of the background shriek of the seagulls. She knew Jonno could hear it as well.

'I had to come... There's something I really need to tell you, Jonno...'

They both knew why she hadn't ended up telling him that day.

'You could have told me well before then. Like when I asked you if you had any kids.'

'Oh...yeah... Right after you'd been telling me how

thankful you were that you didn't have any dependants? How much you'd hate to have a wife or kids that might stop you doing all the crazy, dangerous things you love so much? How do you think that made me feel?' Brie's voice hitched. 'I was still trying to get my head around it myself. How was I going to tell my son that his daddy was back in town but might not want to have anything to do with him because he had better things to do with his time? That he wasn't even planning to be around long, anyway. He was going to get rid of the last tie he had here and then he'd be gone again. For ever. Probably on the other side of the world in Australia or New Zealand.'

'I said those things because I didn't *know*,' Jonno countered. 'Do you really think I'm someone who'd walk away from a responsibility like having a child? That I wouldn't *care*?'

Brie swallowed hard. Of course she didn't. She found herself blinking back tears. 'I couldn't put your name on the birth certificate officially,' she said softly. 'But I wrote it on the back. Maybe I was hoping that one day Felix would be able to find you.'

Oh…*dammit*…

Maybe Jonno had wanted to hang onto his anger because it was easier than feeling *this*…

That, perhaps, he was the one in the wrong. That he'd gone off on his great adventures and deliberately cut all contact with the people he'd left behind. That Brie had had something so massive to face—not only single parenthood but knowing that her baby was facing physical challenges that could make life so much harder. That he had been careful to make it clear that he would never be interested in long-term relationships or having a family of his own. How thankful he was, in fact, that he didn't have any kids.

That he'd lied to *her* about not having any other ties in Bristol other than that apartment.

He knew Brie was covering up the fact that she was crying by throwing sticks for the dog. He saw her brush tears away as she stooped to pick up the stick and this had to be the worst feeling of all. Wanting to be able to comfort Brie and knowing that it simply wasn't possible. That he could do nothing to change everything she'd gone through so far and that they now had to sort out changes that were going to be life-changing for everybody concerned.

There was a large driftwood log on the beach just ahead of them.

'Come and sit down for a bit,' he called to Brie.

She turned her head and Jonno's heart broke a little at the pain he could see in her eyes. He remembered how he'd seen the wariness in her face when he'd landed back in her life. Fear, even? And he remembered the look of joy on that little boy's face as he'd reached up his arms to his beloved mumma. His son was very much loved—*genuinely* loved, unlike he had been himself—and there was a big part of Jonno that was very grateful for that.

'Please…' he added. 'I want to hear about it all. Right from the start…'

CHAPTER NINE

How WAS IT possible to feel this close to someone yet, at the same time, to feel further apart than ever before?

Seven years was a lot of time to catch up on but it was such a relief for Brie to be able to be completely honest with Jonno that the words just tumbled out. She did start right at the beginning, apart from skipping over how that single night with Jonno had been a dream come true because this wasn't about *them* any longer.

Whatever might or might not have been simmering between Jonno and herself had become irrelevant because Brie knew it was dead in the water as far as Jonno was concerned. He had dismissed her as being 'just like *them*' which, presumably, meant his parents? Because they hadn't been honest. Because he'd seen his whole family as a sham.

So Brie was being completely honest. She did start right at the beginning as far as Felix was concerned, by telling him how shocked she'd been to find herself pregnant. And that she'd been even more upset to learn that there was something wrong with her growing baby.

'I was about twenty weeks along when I got the results of the second trimester alpha-fetoprotein test that were elevated. Then the roller coaster began with seeing all the specialists and having an MRI and the advanced ultrasound tests. And, after I'd seen him on the scans so clearly, they still gave me the option of ending the pregnancy...' Brie couldn't stop fresh tears from rolling down her face. 'But it only made me want to protect him even more... That was when they told me about the possibility of having surgery before he was even born. That they could open me up and then put the spinal cord back into the spinal canal and close the tissue and skin around it to protect it from exposure to the amniotic fluid. It wasn't happening in the UK then so I would have to travel to the States or Switzerland or Belgium but it would be very expensive and there were so many risks. He could have been born prematurely. Or died. I can only ever have a baby by Caesarean because of uterine scarring.' Brie let out her breath in a huff that was almost laughter. 'Not that I'm ever planning to have another baby. But when they told me that foetal surgery can prevent the most severe brain malformations and mean that a child might be able to walk independently, I had to give him that chance, even though the risks were terrifying.'

She told him how it had turned their lives upside down to travel to Switzerland and have meetings with a huge team of prenatal specialists and social workers and psychologists. That she'd had to stay in the hospital for a week after the surgery and then have weeks more bed rest nearby before they'd let her go home, as long as she could travel to London every week for monitoring, and the focus on the baby she was carrying had only become more intense after he was born by elective Caesarean at thirty-seven weeks and needed more surgery in his first few days in the world.

Her voice wobbled as she told him it had become even harder when he was old enough to understand what was going to happen when he'd needed a shunt put in and corrective surgery on his feet, but she could smile with genuine happiness as she shared moments of joy at the milestones her brave little boy was determined to meet. There was laughter, even, as she answered Jonno's query of what he was like.

'I barely saw him at the café but I could see how close he is to you. How much he loves you—and your mum.'

'Felix loves everybody in his life and everybody adores him. He's such a...*happy* kid, I guess. Even when things are difficult or something hurts he can still find something to smile about. It's like he can find joy in thin air and then make it grow enough to share it without even trying. The world's a better place because Felix is in it.' Brie's smile seemed misty but then laughter bubbled. 'He learned to blow raspberries when he was a tiny baby and it made him laugh every single time. Then he discovered he could do a whale spout with a mouth full of water—in the physiotherapy pool—and that was the funniest thing ever. He still does it in the bath sometimes and it still makes us laugh.' She finished with a shrug. 'What can I say? He loves life. He's just the best kid in the world. It's partly how I chose his name because Felix means happy. And lucky. But I'm even luckier—that he's mine...'

Brie wrapped her arms around herself, feeling suddenly chilled from sitting here for so long. Or maybe it was something else that gave her that sudden shiver.

'I'd protect him with my life,' she said quietly. 'And I'm not going to let him be hurt, if there's any way I can help it. I don't want him to know that you're his father and get attached if you're just going to disappear on your next adventure and make him feel like he's not... I don't know, good enough to hang around for or something...'

'I'm not going to disappear.'

'You're going to stay in Bristol? For ever?'

'I don't know.' Jonno met her gaze directly and there was a new connection there that had absolutely nothing to do with any physical attraction. This was about honesty. About a very different kind of trust. 'I do know I won't make any promises I'm not going to keep. And I will promise that I won't do anything that could hurt Felix.'

Brie closed her eyes as she nodded slowly. She badly needed to believe that.

'Thank you for talking to me,' Jonno said.

'Thank you for listening.'

Jonno had listened to her story with what felt like compassion. He had seen her tears and her smiles. He'd reached down once or twice to pat Dennis, who'd curled up, finally tired out, by their feet but he hadn't touched Brie. He hadn't held her gaze long enough for it to be anything more than you might do in polite conversation.

They were close enough to be talking about their son.

But distant enough to make physical contact unthinkable.

Brie looked down at the gap between them on the log. Only a matter of inches but it felt like miles. Whatever had happened between them since Jonno had been back in town was over but she wasn't even going to think about how much that hurt.

'I need you to do something else for me too, Brie.'

The sound of her name on his lips was bittersweet. It made her look up instantly to catch his gaze.

'I want to meet him. I get that it's too soon to tell him the truth, but I want to spend some time with him. Somewhere that you think will be safe.'

Brie nodded again. She'd already thought about this. About how she could still protect Felix when it happened.

'Why don't you come to his next riding class? There are lots of volunteers that help out at the RDA so it won't seem like anything out of the ordinary.'

For Felix, anyway. It would be huge for Brie but she knew it was going to be even bigger for Jonno. If he, as a parent, was going to feel even a fraction of how she felt about Felix, he had every reason to feel nervous about it, so she offered him a smile that felt almost shy.

'You'll love it,' she said. 'It's great fun and, like I said, he's the best kid in the whole world.'

'Have you had much to do with ponies?'

Jonno smiled at Kate, the woman in charge of this session at the RDA facilities. 'I worked in Mongolia for quite a while, for an adventure tourism company that took people on horseback through the desert or out onto the Steppes.'

'Wow...' Kate's eyes widened.

Jonno thought he heard Brie mutter something like *Of course you did...* which sounded rather like some kind of reprimand. An unjustified one because he hadn't done anything wrong. Not intentionally, anyway.

'I took part in the endurance charity challenge ride once,' Jonno added. 'The Gobi Gallop? We covered seven hundred kilometres in ten days.'

Kate was shaking her head. 'Well, all you need to do here is walk on one side of Bonnie—the pony Felix is riding. His mum can walk on the other side and I'll take the lead rein. You're just an insurance policy in case Felix loses his balance.' One of the helpers getting Felix onto the pony waved in their direction. 'Looks like he's ready to go.'

'This is Jonno.' Brie's voice sounded a little tight as they took their positions on either side of Bonnie. 'He's going to help us today, okay?'

On top of the small pony, Felix was at the same level as Jonno. He eyed him up and then beamed at this new person in his life. 'I'm a 'questrian,' he told Jonno. 'I'm going to go in the Paralympics when I'm big.'

'That's very cool.' Jonno had to clear his throat and find a suitably impressed smile but there was something making his chest feel oddly tight.

That smile. That instant willingness to accept someone new in his life along with the sparkle in this little boy's eyes was sucking him in.

They were brown eyes. Dark brown eyes.

Just like his own.

Oh, man... This felt so weird. He'd been around hundreds of kids in his lifetime. He'd taken care of them as patients and had always felt the need to do everything he could to care for such vulnerable little humans. He knew the joy of winning a battle to save a small life and he also knew the trauma and grief of losing one.

But he'd never felt quite like this. As if this bright, happy little boy was gripping his heart as tightly as the reins he was clutching in his hands.

Felix squeaked with excitement as Kate clicked her tongue and encouraged Bonnie to start walking and the sound made Jonno's smile stretch into a grin. But then he caught Brie's glance across the pony's back and suddenly he had to blink away an unexpected moisture in his eyes.

'Can you make Bonnie turn right?' Kate asked as they reached one end of the sawdust-covered arena. 'Do you remember which rein you use, Felix?'

'*This* one.' Felix lifted his right arm, with the rein hanging in a very loose loop, but Bonnie obligingly turned towards the right. Felix tilted his head, trying to stay upright in the saddle but look down at his mother at the same time. 'Did you see me, Mumma? I did it. All by myself.'

'You did, darling. I'm very proud of you.'

That tightness was there again. Good grief…was this pride that Jonno was feeling as well? Like a parent might feel?

'I can ride all by myself,' Felix announced a few minutes later as they came to the other end of the covered arena and completed a turn to the left. 'Can I go faster now, Kate?'

Kate caught Brie's glance. 'Maybe we could try trotting just a couple of steps for the first time? What do you think, Mum? Are we ready?'

Brie looked across at Jonno, a question in her eyes.

'I've got this side covered,' he said. He did. If Felix got bounced out of the saddle he'd catch him in a heartbeat. He had the feeling it wouldn't be necessary, mind you.

'Hang onto the handle on the front of your saddle,' Kate told Felix. 'Don't worry about your reins this time.' She took hold of Bonnie's bridle and patted the pony's shaggy black neck. 'And…away we go…trot on, Bonnie…'

Bonnie appeared to understand the verbal instruction and broke into a gentle trot. Felix bounced up and down in the saddle and then lost his grip on the handle, but perhaps Bonnie felt him lose his balance because she slowed back to a walk at precisely the same moment. After teetering wildly enough for Brie to reach towards him but not quite grab him, Felix anchored himself again by catching the handle attached to the pommel. Jonno could hear him pull in some air and it was only then that Jonno realised he'd been holding his own breath since Felix had started this first attempt at a faster pace.

His son's face was glowing with a mixture of astonishment, pride and sheer excitement. '*Again...*' he commanded. 'I want to do it again.'

Jonno could feel Brie's gaze on him again but he couldn't turn to meet it. Not until he'd blinked a few times, anyway.

Yeah...this was pride, all right. And something a whole lot bigger. Possibly the biggest feeling he'd ever had?

Jonno was looking a bit shellshocked, Brie thought as she fastened the buckle on Felix's car seat and closed the door.

'He'll probably fall asleep before we even get home,' she said. 'That was a lot of excitement for one day.' She swallowed hard. 'And he didn't even know the half of it, did he?'

'Trotting for the first time was quite enough excitement for one day. He did so well, didn't he?'

'He did.' Brie knew her smile was one of deep pride. 'But you know...he is a 'questrian.'

Jonno didn't laugh. His smile was decidedly crooked, in fact. 'I felt so proud of him. Is that weird?'

Brie shook her head. It wasn't weird at all, although she hadn't expected he might feel such an instant bond with Felix. She wasn't exactly sure how she felt about it either. Her smile was rapidly vanishing.

'I'd better get him home,' she said. She turned away with a sigh.

'You okay?' Jonno's voice was quiet behind her. 'I know that this can't be easy for you either, but this was a brilliant idea and… I really appreciate the way you've made it easy for me to meet Felix.'

Brie turned back. 'It's not you,' she told him. 'Things are a bit…um…strained at home, I guess. I still can't believe that my mother thought it was acceptable to tell your father he has a grandchild before you even knew about it yourself.' She shook her head. 'We're not exactly happy with each other right now. I'm even thinking it might be time for me and Felix to find a place of our own.'

'I'm sorry to hear that…'

'She thinks I should have told you sooner. And she still thinks Anthony had the right to know, even though he isn't actually related to you, biologically.'

'Who told you that?'

'Seems like my mother and your father had a big heart-to-heart. She's a paediatric nurse and they met at St Nick's. It was that photo of you in the newspaper from that rescue in the Cairngorms that started it. He told her that you were his son. It was only after she told him about Felix a few days later that he said he wasn't actually your real father, but my mother said that of course he was.' Brie's shrug was apologetic. She was embarrassed by her mother's interference but she also didn't want to lose the new honesty that she had with Jonno and he deserved to know what was being said behind his back. 'She said he was the man who'd brought you up. And when she asked if Anthony would still like to meet Felix, he just nodded. She said she thought he had tears in his eyes.'

Jonno's lips were a thin line. 'At least you and your mum are still talking. I'm sure you'll sort it out. It's so many years since I spoke to my father, I wouldn't know where to start. Or even if I want to.'

He turned away from her and Brie could see that Felix was watching him through the window as he waited patiently for his mum to get into the car. She saw him smile at Jonno and, when Jonno smiled back without hesitation, her heart melted a little. With relief? Or something a whole lot deeper?

'Maybe you should talk to him,' she said quietly. 'Mum said that when he saw your picture in the paper he looked really sad. And when he talked about you later he was obviously very proud of you.'

This time, when Jonno turned away, he started walking away from her. Increasing this new distance which made it feel as if she was being shut out of a big part of Jonno's life.

Of being allowed to connect to the person he really was?

'Thanks again,' he said. 'I'll see you at work tomorrow, yeah? Maybe we can find time to talk about what we're going to do next.'

'Sure. I'll make a copy of his timetable for you so you can see what you might be able to come along to.

There's a movement and music class coming up if you're free that day?'

'Sounds fun. Let me know where and when.' Jonno turned his head to catch her gaze. 'And one other thing, Brie…'

'Yes?' A splash of hope blossomed somewhere deep inside Brie's chest and grew astonishingly quickly. Was Jonno going to say something that might suggest he didn't hate her? That there was hope they could not only navigate this new space they found themselves in but that it could connect them even more significantly on a personal level?

But there was no warmth in Jonno's eyes. 'If you've got any copies of the medical records for Felix, I'd really like to see them.'

Hope was being pulled out by the roots to die a quick death, which was remarkably painful.

'I've kept everything,' Brie told him. 'I'll bring the folder into work tomorrow.'

Brie hadn't been exaggerating about keeping everything.

And it was astonishing how images and words on paper could tell a story that let you get to know someone on a completely new level.

Not just his son, although he could read between the lines of the medical reports he was browsing in his late evenings and actually feel the courage of a small boy recovering from surgeries or that determination to learn to walk unaided. He could also feel the love of a mother who'd kept the first ultrasound images of her baby, the first recording of his heart, X-ray images from before and after surgeries, even the first prescription for glasses that would help him see clearly. There was a note scribbled on the form to say that Felix had his heart set on the brightest red frames if possible.

He must have had several changes of prescription and frame size since then but his colour preference hadn't changed. He'd been wearing his bright red glasses at his riding lesson and he was wearing them again when Jonno arrived in time for the music and movement class he'd been invited to attend and went to sit with Brie and the other parents to watch.

But Felix was waving at him. 'I want Jonno to do it with me,' he called. 'Please…?'

Jonno could sense that Brie was a little taken aback by the plea and was about to say he was happier to simply watch but then Brie caught his glance.

'There are quite a few kids who like their parents to do the class with them,' she said.

How could Jonno say no to that? Felix might not know he was a parent—*his* parent—but he wanted Jonno to do this class with him and that was even more impossible to say no to. And it *was* fun. There were songs to be sung and instruments to be played. Felix chose a tambourine. Jonno decided to shake some maracas and earned a grin from a man who was helping his son bang a drum.

Felix led the way with Jonno close behind when the teacher sent them all over the hall with suggestions of how they could move to a frequently changing variety of music.

'Be an aeroplane,' she called. 'Or a butterfly. And now you're all robots…'

Finally, before they were all too tired, there was an enormous rainbow-coloured parachute and everybody—parents and children—got to hold onto the edges and lift it up and down to make it float. It was hard to try and do it in time to the music but it didn't matter and if someone lost their grip there were shouts of laughter as they tried to catch it again.

Jonno helped the teacher fold the parachute while Brie got Felix into his coat and settled into his wheelchair for a rest.

'I haven't seen you before,' the teacher said. 'Are you Felix's dad?'

'I am,' Jonno told her. 'And you'll be seeing me again soon, I hope. I haven't had so much fun in ages.'

'Felix obviously loved having you here,' she said with a smile. 'He always looks like such a happy kid but today he was just glowing.'

Yeah… Jonno could feel that glow himself. Maybe that was why he suggested they went to a nearby fast-food restaurant for an early dinner instead of saying goodbye outside the hall. They ate hamburgers and he made Felix laugh by showing him how to put French fries under his top lip so they stuck out like walrus tusks. He expected Brie to tell them to stop playing with the food when she shook her head but she was smiling.

'Can I go in the playground, Mumma?' Felix asked.

'It's time we went home,' she said. 'Dennis will be wanting *his* dinner.'

'But I want to show Jonno how I can climb in the tunnel,' Felix protested. 'And go down the slide by myself.'

'Maybe just for a few minutes. Jonno might need to go soon too.' Brie caught Jonno's gaze and there was a question there. Maybe it was simply a small question about whether he wanted to spend a little extra time with Felix today. But it felt like a much bigger question, about how much of the rest of his life did he want to devote to his son and that was…disturbing?

Because it was…huge, that was what it was.

If he wanted to be the kind of father he hadn't had himself—one that was available and interested and truly present in his life, it represented a very different future to anything Jonno had planned. Or wanted…?

Felix was climbing out of his wheelchair.

'Wait for me, buddy.' It was a relief to have an excuse to turn away from Brie and the prospect of confirming a commitment he was still coming to terms with. 'Am I allowed to go on the slide as well?'

CHAPTER TEN

THE SMELL OF lasagne was enough to bring tears to Brie's eyes when she stepped through the back door into the kitchen. She couldn't remember when her mother had last cooked her favourite meal.

Oh, yeah...that's right. It had been the day that Jonno had crashed back into her life. Her first day on shift as a qualified paramedic and that dramatic job that she would never forget.

Brie was never going to forget today's last job either. And it seemed that the horror of it was still written on her face because Elsie went pale herself.

'What's happened?'

Elsie was on her feet as she spoke, pulling Brie into her arms in the same way she had always done as a completely automatic response to her daughter needing comfort, but it had been a long time since Brie had felt an embrace like this. Too long.

'Are you okay, love?'

Brie let herself sink into that familiar warmth for a heartbeat longer. With the background of the aroma of the hot food in this small room, it felt as if she were being transported back to her childhood. To a time when the world was a safe place because she and her mum had each other.

'Not really,' Brie admitted as she pulled away. 'I'll tell you about it in a minute. I... I just need to give Felix a kiss. I'm guessing he's asleep by now?'

'I hope so.' Elsie bit her lip. 'He was a bit quiet this evening. He didn't eat much of his dinner either, and he loves lasagne as much as you do.'

'Was he upset that I was going to be so late?'

'I think it's more likely he's just coming down with a cold or something.'

Brie was already on her way upstairs. Her little boy was sound asleep. His breathing was regular and his skin felt a normal temperature when she touched her lips to his forehead gently enough not to wake him but he stirred and opened his eyes. Then he smiled at her. His words were slurred by being sleep-drunk.

'Love you, Mumma...'

'Love you more, Bubba.' Brie brushed a lock of hair off his forehead and kissed him again. 'Sweet dreams...' She glanced up at the star-spangled ceiling of his bedroom. 'Did you make a wish?'

Felix nodded. 'Special wish...' he mumbled.

'What did you wish for?'

But he was asleep again and this time Brie wasn't going to disturb him.

Elsie had poured a glass of wine for her when she got back to the kitchen. 'I know it's a day shift for you tomorrow but...'

But she was a mother and she'd needed to do something to comfort her child? Brie understood completely. 'Thanks, Mum.'

'You hungry?'

'Not really.' But she knew that the food was another peace offering. 'Maybe later? It smells amazing.'

Brie took a sip of her wine. 'I'm sorry I'm so late. My station manager, Dave, wanted me to have a chat to a counsellor before I went home.'

Elsie had worked in the medical world long enough to know why that might have been important. 'Oh, no... Was it a child?'

'Just a baby.' Brie nodded. 'Three months old. Got put down for an afternoon nap and never woke up.' She picked up her glass and took a long sip. 'She was still warm,' she said softly. 'But we were way too late. We did everything we could. We had critical care backup and continued CPR all the way to the hospital. *They* did everything they could but...' Brie closed her eyes. 'She was so tiny, Mum, on that hospital bed. And her mother was so utterly broken...'

'Oh, love...' Elsie put her hand over Brie's and squeezed it. 'There's nothing worse. I'm so sorry...'

'It's part of the job, as you know all too well. You had to cope with that little girl dying on *your* watch not that long ago. And, as the counsellor told me, knowing how that mother was feeling was part of what's going to make me very good at my job, but I've got to protect myself as well or I'll burn out fast. He told me to go home and cuddle my son and take comfort in being with my family.' Brie blinked back new tears. 'I'm sorry, Mum.'

'Whatever for?'

'I've been horrible to you lately. We've hardly been talking.'

'That was my fault, not yours. I shouldn't have put

my oar in and told Anthony about Felix. I forced you into a conversation you weren't ready for.'

'And I should have had that conversation earlier. I didn't because…' Brie stopped abruptly. She could say she'd been trying to protect Felix, and that was absolutely true, but there was a selfish aspect about it that she wasn't proud of. She'd wanted to step back into that fantasy, hadn't she? *So* much…

Elsie's tone was tentative. 'Because there's something happening between you two?'

Brie shrugged. 'Not now. I'm not sure there ever was…on Jonno's side, anyway.' She slid a sideways glance at her mother. 'How did you guess? I never said anything.'

'I could feel it. And I knew there had to have been something there in the first place or you would never have gone to bed with him. Are you still in love with him?'

Brie avoided a direct response. 'I feel the same way I've always felt about him. It's never been anything… real.'

The silence that fell between them threatened to push them apart again.

'Was it Jonno that backed you up today for that horrible job?' Elsie asked.

'No. He'd taken the afternoon off. There's a rumour that he went to a job interview at the air rescue base.'

'For a permanent job? Here, in Bristol?'

'Maybe.' Brie's glass was half empty now. 'He hasn't said anything to me about it.'

'But he might be planning to stay.' Elsie sounded hopeful. 'He gets on well with Felix, doesn't he?'

'He's brilliant with kids. And Felix thinks the sun shines out of him.'

'He certainly talks about him a lot. On the way home from school today, I got to hear all about the ponies that Jonno galloped across the desert. Are you... I mean, have you talked about when you'll...' Elsie bit her lip.

'No... I'm not going to ask. I'm keeping my oars firmly in my own boat from now on.'

'When we'll tell him?' Brie finished her wine as well as her mother's query. 'Soon. As soon as I can be sure Jonno's not going to do a disappearing act. He's still planning to sell his apartment. It's on the market already, in fact. He said he can't wait to get rid of it.'

And Brie hadn't been able to stop herself wondering if that had anything to do with the reminders of what had happened between them in that bedroom? Because he still hadn't forgiven her for what he saw as dishonesty? They were still navigating this new space, connected by parenthood but with spiky boundaries around everything they had shared in the past.

'But he might be applying for a job here,' Elsie said. 'And he seems to want to spend more time with Felix. How did the dance class go yesterday?'

Brie finally found herself smiling again as the trauma of her day began to fade. While this new space she was in with Jonno felt fragile and restricted, there were still moments of unexpected joy to be found.

'Jonno joined in the dancing like it was his favourite thing ever,' she told Elsie. 'Then we went out for hamburgers and Jonno showed Felix how to make walrus tusks with his fries. They were both laughing so hard they couldn't eat them.'

Elsie was smiling too. 'Speaking of eating…are you at all hungry yet?'

'Do you know, I think I am… Have you had *your* dinner?'

'I was waiting for you…'

Brie let her breath out in a sigh, relieved that the recent tension between them seemed to have evaporated. Home was definitely the place she'd needed to be this evening. It was even better to remember the pleasure of seeing Jonno interact with his son yesterday and… maybe hope was contagious because Brie found herself wondering if that rumour had been true and Jonno was thinking of taking a permanent job in Bristol.

That could change everything.

It would mean Jonno would become a real part of their lives.

Of *her* life.

Could she cope with that? Knowing that the man she was in love with was only there because of her child? *Their* child?

Yeah…if he was going to bring more joy and love into the life of that precious child, Brie would welcome his presence. Because that was what mothers did—they put their children first.

'You must be starving.' Brie smiled at Elsie. 'Let's eat…'

The offer that came through on the apartment within just a few days of it going on the market was a bit of a shock, to be honest.

It wasn't that Jonno couldn't deal with another life change. He was, after all, an expert in tipping his life upside down and then shaking it to see what fell out and whether he was tempted to give something completely different a good try—preferably something that had a bit of danger or unpredictability about it.

Oddly, however, in these last few weeks, it was predictability that he was placing the most value on. Like knowing the times he was going to spend with Felix in his activities outside school hours, which meant he was getting to know his son and getting used to the shock of discovering that he was a father.

The email from the estate agent that pinged into his phone as he arrived at work a day or two later, with a better-than-expected offer from a client already on her books that she had taken to view the property before its first open home, should have been a pleasant surprise but Jonno wasn't sure how he felt about it yet. Because it meant that decisions needed to be made a lot sooner than he'd thought he would have to make them, even if he could push the settlement date out by a month or two.

Big decisions might need even longer than that to be sure about, though. Like where he was going to live. Should he buy a kid-friendly sort of house for when the stage might be reached that his son would want to have a sleepover at his dad's house? The kind of house he'd grown up in himself, with room to play hide and seek inside and a garden that was big enough to kick a football around in? Near that wonderful park with the forests and bike trails or close to the sea in a suburb near Portishead or Sugar Loaf Beach?

It was something he'd been putting off even thinking about for precisely this reason. Because it made him think about what had been good about his own childhood, and that made him think about his father and he wasn't ready to think about that when he was still get-

ting used to being a father himself. Despite Brie's advice to talk to him which kept replaying itself in the
back of his mind, Jonno didn't feel remotely ready to
talk to his father.

It was all too soon. Jonno was still processing the information in his son's extensive medical records, learning about every surgery he'd ever had and those still
to come. He still hadn't come to the end of the folder,
in fact, because Brie had included copies of school reports and dental examinations in the meticulous range
of documents she had collected. He was still reading
and absorbing every summary of outpatient clinic visits to his neurosurgeon and orthopaedic surgeon and
urologist over the years.

Jonno hadn't even had any time alone with Felix
yet. How could he, when the boy hadn't yet been told
that Jonno was his father? Brie was, understandably,
very protective and that made Jonno suddenly wonder
whether she would let Felix stay in this hypothetical
house by himself with his father or would she want to
have a sleepover as well?

Oh, man… No. He had to stamp on that line of
thought hard. Getting that close to Brie wasn't going to
happen again. This was more than complicated enough
as it was. Having been so determined not to allow history to repeat itself that he had avoided any long-term
relationships himself, here he was on the cusp of com-
mitting to the longest term one imaginable—that of a
parent and child. Not only that, it would also be a commitment to the mother of that child—the only woman
Jonno had ever trusted enough for her to get past the
protection that had been in place around his heart.

He had trusted her enough to feel betrayed by her not telling him sooner about Felix.

Enough to feel as if something important had died. The potential future with the only woman he'd ever fallen in love with, perhaps?

How was he going to be able to make this work so that he didn't end up as distant as his own father had been when it was this complicated and there were the kind of huge emotions he'd been so careful to steer clear of?

Like trust.

And love.

Jonno felt a familiar urge to escape. To go and do something a bit dangerous that didn't allow for anything but complete focus if you wanted to stay alive. Like hang-gliding. Or rock climbing. He made a mental note to call his mate, Max, later today and check that their trip to Scotland was still on.

The day shift crews were checking over their vehicles as he walked through the garage and seeing Simon carrying a defibrillator towards an ambulance sent his thoughts straight back to Brie. She was probably in the back of that ambulance right now, making sure they weren't missing any supplies that might be vital today. That firm tug, somewhere deep in his gut, that made it irresistible to go and put his head around the open back doors of the vehicle to say hello was a warning he shouldn't ignore.

It should, in fact, be pushing him towards another big decision that was now looming as well—whether he wanted to accept the offer of a permanent job with the air rescue base that he'd received after Max had persuaded him to go and do that interview yesterday afternoon. If he was going to stay in Bristol, would it be better if he and Brie were working out of different bases to keep their professional and personal lives as separate as possible?

'You looking for Brie?' Simon caught up with Jonno before he reached the ambulance. 'She's not here. I'm going solo for the day.'

'What? Where is she?'

'She called in sick.'

Okay, that was another warning, that kick in his gut at the idea of Brie being unwell.

'It's not her,' Simon added. 'Sounds like her kid is a bit off-colour so she's keeping him out of school today.'

The idea of Felix being unwell was turning that sensation in his gut into an unpleasant knot. 'What's wrong with him?'

'No idea. Not much, I don't think, but Dave said he thought it was probably a good idea if Brie had a day off. After yesterday…'

'Yesterday?' Jonno could feel his frown deepening. 'Have I missed something?'

'Last job of the shift was a three-month-old baby that was DOA. SIDS. Don't know about you but I sure remember my first one. Brie coped amazingly well on scene, but afterwards she looked like she'd been hit by a truck.'

Jonno *felt* like he'd been hit by a truck. He was pulling out his phone as he walked away from Simon. He had fifteen minutes before his shift was due to start so he could ring Brie and check that she was okay. That Felix was okay.

Except he didn't get the chance. He could see the station manager, Dave, striding into the garage.

'Jonno—good, I was hoping you were in early. Are you able to take a priority call right now?'

'Ah…sure…' Jonno turned to walk to where the rapid response vehicle was parked but he fired a sharp glance at Dave. This was a really odd way to be responded to a call.

Dave knew why he was getting the look. 'Control gave me a heads-up,' he said quietly. 'It's Brie's house.'

Jonno felt a chill run down his spine. He pulled open the driver's door. 'Do you know any details?'

'Yes. It's her kid. Six-year-old boy who has spina bifida. Apparently he's having, or has just had, a seizure. I'll send Simon as backup in case you need to transport.'

'You might need to get someone in to cover the rest of my shift too,' Jonno said. 'It's not just Brie's kid. It's mine.'

Dave's jaw dropped. 'I can't send you for first response. You're too involved.'

'Don't try and stop me,' Jonno warned. 'I need to be there. Now…'

'Then I'm coming with you.' Dave pulled open the passenger's door of the rapid response vehicle.

Jonno was already in the driver's seat. He could see the suggested route on the GPS on his dashboard screen as soon as he turned the ignition key. He put his safety belt on as he waited impatiently for the huge garage doors to rumble up far enough to get out without catching the beacons he already had flashing on the roof of his vehicle. He flicked on the siren as the barrier arm in the car park swung up to let him into the traffic.

And then he put his foot down. It didn't matter how quickly he was going to be able to get there.

It was still going to take too long.

CHAPTER ELEVEN

DESPITE MOVING SO quickly as he led the way into Brie's house, Jonno found himself hyperaware of tiny details.

Like this neat little suburban house where his son lived with his mother and grandmother. An ordinary little three-bedroom, end-of-terrace house that reminded him of… Oh, yeah…the surprising location of the violent situation he'd discovered the day he'd answered the emergency Code Black alert to find Brie on her first shift as a paramedic, working alone as she tried to manage a woman about to go into a respiratory arrest.

Was she alone again right now? Trying to keep her son alive?

Their son…

He found her in the kitchen. On the floor. Holding Felix in her arms. He could see the little boy was not conscious. He could see the terrible fear in Brie's eyes.

He knew what he should be doing. He had to find out whether Felix was at all responsive. Was he simply asleep and easily rousable, in a postictal state after a seizure and sleepy and confused, or was he unconscious for a more sinister reason? He needed to check his heart and respiratory rate, listen for any sounds of an impaired airway and check the colour and temperature of his skin at the same time.

But, for one horrible, frozen moment, as he saw how limp Felix was and how pale his face was, it occurred to him that his son could be dead.

It was a good thing Dave had come with him on that wild ride to get here as fast as possible and Simon would not be far behind with his well-equipped ambulance, but the quick glance from Dave with his silent query about whether he needed to step back was enough for Jonno to take control of his emotional reaction. He owed it to Brie to do whatever he could for their child. He owed it to Felix to do his best to protect him.

Brie let him take Felix out of her arms and put him down gently on the floor.

'Hey, buddy…what's happening?'

There was no response to Jonno's voice. Or to the pinch on his earlobe that should have elicited a response to pain. And he wasn't moving at all.

He broke his initial visual assessment of Felix to catch Brie's gaze for a heartbeat. 'What happened exactly?'

'I'd taken Dennis outside. I heard a thump and I came in to find Felix on the floor in a full tonic-clonic seizure. I'm not sure if he fell off the chair or just knocked it over.'

Jonno lifted an eyelid and shone his penlight torch, relieved to see that Felix's pupil sizes were equal and that they reacted to the light with normal speed.

'Have you noticed any sign of a head injury?'

'No.'

Jonno was feeling the small skull beneath his fingers, anyway. He couldn't feel any lumps or bumps and there was no sign of any bleeding. 'And he was unwell enough this morning for you to decide to keep him home from school? Was his behaviour unusual in any way?'

'He was slow to wake up, which isn't like him, but I guess it started last night. Mum said he didn't want his dinner. She thought he might be coming down with a cold and he had a bit of a temperature this morning. He was rubbing his eyes, which usually means he's got a headache, so I gave him some paracetamol. It was Dennis who was really behaving oddly. He refused to leave Felix and go outside to pee. That's why I took him out…'

From the corner of his eye, Jonno could see Dennis huddled in the corner, under the table. The little dog looked as frightened as Brie.

'Has Felix vomited at all? Complained of anything hurting?'

'No…' Brie's breath hitched. 'But he never complains. Not unless things get really bad.'

Jonno was watching the way Felix was breathing, looking for signs that he was in difficulty. The rate of breathing was higher than normal but he couldn't hear any sounds of airway obstruction. He lifted the little boy's clothing to look for retraction of the muscles between his ribs but he needed to check his skin for any evidence of a rash that might indicate a medical emergency like meningitis and he also wanted to stick some ECG electrodes in place. An oxygen saturation probe completely covered one of Felix's tiny fingers but Jonno was happy to see that his cardiac rhythm and oxygen levels were okay.

'How long did the seizure last for?'

'I'm not sure. It felt like ages but it was probably

only about two minutes. I was already ringing triple nine as it stopped.'

'Has he woken up at all since?'

Brie shook her head.

'Has he had seizures before?' Dave had a paediatric oxygen mask in his hand as he connected the tubing to the cylinder he'd brought in.

'No, never.'

'He's had borderline increased cranial pressure in the past, though, hasn't he?' Part of Jonno's brain was lifting any relevant information from Felix's medical records. 'That was why he had the shunt put in to redirect cerebral spinal fluid?'

'That's nearly four years ago now. And the only symptoms he had were to do with his eyes. The squint and the blurred vision.'

'It's possible that an obstruction could be causing problems.' Jonno watched Dave fit a cover to a tympanic thermometer. 'What's his temperature?'

'Thirty-seven point eight.'

High enough to suggest an infection but not high enough to cause a febrile convulsion. Jonno was mentally listing other potential causes of a seizure in a paediatric patient, like high or low blood sugar, an electrolyte disturbance like low sodium levels, concussion from a head injury, the ingestion of drugs or the presence of a brain lesion when two things happened.

Simon arrived.

And Felix began having another seizure.

It was Dave who made the call of status epilepticus. 'That's two seizures in a matter of minutes without regaining consciousness in between.' He was opening equipment packs. 'Let's get IV access, but I'd like to get some intranasal midazolam on board stat.'

It was Simon who administered the medication and drew up another dose in case it was needed. Dave set up what he needed to put an IV cannula in when the jerking of Felix's limbs had subsided. Jonno was watching the little boy like a hawk, finding himself having to resist the urge to cradle his head to protect him from any injury from the wooden floorboards. It felt as if Brie was reading his mind when she pulled the jumper she was wearing over her head and folded it to provide a thin pillow. One minute stretched into another but still the seizure continued. Another dose of medication was administered.

Jonno watched the oxygen saturation levels dropping to less than ninety percent before the medication could take effect on the seizure and, when it slowed enough for Dave to find a vein in Felix's hand to slip the needle into and the interference on the monitor screen to settle, Jonno could see that Felix's heart rhythm was abnormal. His lips were becoming an alarmingly dusky shade of blue, as well.

Simon reached for a bag mask unit to try and improve the oxygen levels.

'Oxygen saturation isn't coming back up.' It was Simon that Dave was speaking to. 'Keep bagging him. I'm going to get ready for a rapid sequence intubation in case those levels don't improve in the next couple of minutes.'

'I can do that.' Jonno reached for the airway kit but Dave shook his head.

'Sorry, Jonno. I can't let you do that. You know the

rules about invasive procedures on members of your own family.'

His own family...

Shocked, Jonno moved out of the way as Dave and Simon took over managing what was becoming a critical situation for Felix. He found himself closer to Brie. The mother of his child. Did that automatically make *her* a part of his own family too?

In this moment, it certainly felt like it. And he knew how scared she was because he was feeling a good dose of that fear himself, especially when they both had to shuffle back and give Dave and Simon the room they needed to take over control of Felix's airway and breathing. He could cope with watching Dave draw up the medications that would paralyse and sedate a small body, choose a paediatric size of laryngoscope blade and endotracheal tube and even Simon pre-oxygenating Felix before removing the bag mask to allow Dave to position the small head and open his mouth to insert the blade of the laryngoscope.

But then it suddenly became too real. This was a fight to keep Felix breathing. To keep him alive. The start of a journey to find out what had gone wrong in the first place and to provide treatment that would hopefully make sure it wasn't going to happen again. They had no idea right now what was going to happen in the next minutes, hours or days and...

And it was unexpectedly terrifying...

Jonno wasn't sure whether it was him or Brie that stretched out a hand first but it didn't matter. They both needed one to hold and who better to hold it than the other person who was so deeply invested in keeping this child safe.

His fingers felt numb by the time Felix was successfully intubated and his oxygen levels were steadily rising.

'Let's get him on the stretcher.' Dave nodded. 'I'll come in the ambulance with you and we'll call ahead to let them know we're on our way. Brie, you'll want to come to with us, yes?'

'Please…' Brie let go of Jonno's hand and went to help settle Felix onto the stretcher. 'I'll grab my phone. Mum's at work. She'll want to be with us when we get there.'

Jonno was packing up some of the gear but he could feel the touch of Brie's gaze and he knew what she was thinking but was not about to say aloud.

That his father was Felix's other grandparent.

That he should know what was happening too.

Jonno got into the rapid response vehicle to follow the ambulance. He tapped a contact number in his phone and it came through on Bluetooth as he pulled away from Brie's house.

'St Nicholas Children's Hospital. How may I help you?'

'Could you page Dr Anthony Morgan for me please?' Jonno knew he sounded brusque but this was no time to be hesitant. 'It's urgent.'

'Who's calling, please?'

Jonno took a deep breath. 'Jonathon Morgan. I'm his son.'

That Brie's life had fundamentally changed had never been more obvious than when she found herself watching Dr Peter Jarvis, the head of paediatric neurosurgery at Bristol's St Nicholas Children's Hospital, walk away from the discussion they'd just had, with Jonno Morgan standing beside her and not her mother. For the first time ever, Felix had both his parents involved in any decision-making on his behalf. Two people who could sign the necessary consent forms.

Elsie was in the intensive care unit, through the double doors in the corridor behind them, sitting beside the bed where Felix lay, sedated and on a ventilator, holding her grandson's hand. An operating theatre was on standby for the next step in managing what felt like the worst crisis Brie had faced so far in her son's life and her head was spinning with all the information she was trying, desperately, to retain.

Jonno was watching her. 'Are you okay?'

Brie was fighting tears. 'Not really…' she admitted. 'I might need a minute before I go back in. I don't want to scare my mum. Or Felix. What if he's aware of what's happening around him at some level?'

'I'm quite sure that he's deeply asleep. The atmosphere around him is different when he has people that love him there, but he's got that right now. His nana obviously adores him. He's probably dreaming about riding that pony he loves so much. What's its name?'

'Bonnie.' Brie's response was more like a strangled sob.

'Come in here for a minute…' Jonno touched her shoulder, guiding her into an empty relatives' space that had comfortable seating, tea and coffee-making facilities and a large-sized box of tissues on a coffee table. 'You can talk to me about anything that's scaring you. Sometimes just talking about it can help to keep you strong. And Felix needs you to be strong.'

The calm encouragement in Jonno's tone, along with

the touch on her shoulder, was already helping and Brie knew it could be some time before Felix would be taken to Theatre. She sank onto the edge of a couch cushion and buried her head in her hands to try and gather her strength. 'I forgot to bring a notebook,' she said. 'I'm never going to remember everything Dr Jarvis told us.'

Jonno crouched in front of her. 'You don't have to,' he said gently. 'All those results from the blood tests—the white cell count and the metabolic panel and the blood gas—have ruled out a lot of things. It's clear that Felix is fighting a nasty infection and the most likely cause for that is a shunt infection. That pocket of fluid they found near the end of the shunt on the abdominal ultrasound was the reason Dr Jarvis went ahead with collecting the sample of cerebral spinal fluid from the shunt valve reservoir and, as soon as they get the initial results on that and make sure they've got him started on the best antibiotics, he wants to take him straight to Theatre to remove the shunt.'

Brie nodded. Watching them put a needle under the skin behind Felix's tiny ear to find that cerebral spinal fluid reservoir had been yet another procedure that Brie hadn't expected and could never be really prepared for. Nowhere near as awful as seeing him being intubated at home and then rushed into Emergency but it had been another graphic reminder of how vulnerable her little boy was right now and… Brie was feeling almost that vulnerable herself.

Vulnerable and so very frightened. Maybe Jonno could sense that because she felt his hand rubbing her knee in a gesture of empathy.

'I get why they need to remove the shunt.' Brie's indrawn breath was shaky. 'But I'm not sure I understood what he was saying about administering the antibiotics.'

'If they take out the shunt, they need to put in an external ventricular drain. It's a system that works on gravity to help drain excess cerebral spinal fluid. They can use the same system to deliver intrathecal antibiotics straight into the CSF and monitor the intracranial pressure at the same time. Felix will need to stay in the ICU while that's in place and will have nursing staff with him at all times.'

Brie felt a tear trickle down the side of her nose. 'He's never been this sick before,' she said quietly. 'And he's had so many surgeries already.'

'Even before he was born,' Jonno agreed. 'The reports about that surgery in his folder were just clinical but I remember you talking about it on the beach that day and I can only imagine how hard that must have been for you.' He reached behind him and pulled tissues from the box on the table to press into Brie's hands. 'And you got through that. Even when you had to travel to another country to have it done. And stay there for weeks and weeks. You're strong, Brie. You're right about him being the best kid in the world but, you know what?' He didn't wait for her response. 'You're the best mum.'

Brie shook her head. 'I've never felt like that. I've just tried to make the best decisions I could.' She swallowed hard, remembering another time she had to struggle to take in everything a medical team were telling her. 'And I didn't do it alone. I couldn't have. Mum was the amazing one. She got a mortgage on her house so we could afford to go to Switzerland and have the surgery. She resigned from her job. She's been with me every step of the way.'

She heard the way Jonno cleared his throat as if it was painful.

'I wish I'd been there,' he said softly. 'I'm sorry you had to go through that as a single parent. I *would* have been here if I'd known…'

'I know…' Brie blew her nose. She did believe that. In a way, it might have been a good thing that she hadn't been able to contact him and tell him about his impending parenthood. He might have come back to Bristol. He might even have thought he needed to 'do the right thing' and offer to marry her so they could raise their child together, but that could well have been a disaster. It hadn't exactly worked out well for his parents, had it?

'I need to go back to Felix and bring Mum up to speed with what's been decided.' But Brie took a moment to take a deep breath to gauge whether she could control her tears. 'What was that other thing that Dr Jarvis mentioned? That he said we could wait and talk about later? After they get on top of this infection?'

'There's a surgery he could have that would mean he doesn't need another shunt put back in, maybe for the rest of his life, so the danger of another infection would be gone. It's called an EVT—an endoscopic third ventriculostomy.'

Brie's brain was refusing to make sense of the words. It was more than she could cope with to think about further brain surgery for Felix.

Jonno must have seen that in her face. 'You don't need to even think about that yet,' he told her. 'One step at a time, okay? You've done it before and you can do it now. We're going to get through this. *All* of us. I know I'm very new at being a father but…you know how much I love Felix, don't you? That I'll do anything I can to protect him?'

It was that wobble in his voice that told Brie he was just as scared as she was. And maybe he'd only known his son for a very short time but she could clearly remember the first time she'd laid eyes on her baby—with that first ultrasound—and she knew how instantly it was possible to fall in love with your child. She knew how much Jonno loved Felix. He was here now and she knew he would be here for his son whenever he was needed from now on.

And then, kneeling on the floor, Jonno wrapped his arms around her in a physical connection unlike anything Brie had ever felt before. The only times before this that she'd been this close to Jonno was when they had been making love. This had absolutely nothing to do with any physical attraction but it was a form of love.

Of caring.

Of sharing. Because Brie knew how much Jonno already loved his son and this had to be just as traumatising for him as it was for her.

So she held him back. Tightly.

So tightly she didn't see someone coming into this space.

'Oh…excuse me…' It was a male voice. 'I didn't mean to interrupt.'

Oh…no…

Jonno let go of Brie and hurriedly got to his feet. He hadn't been anywhere near ready to let go of Brie so his first reaction as he faced his father felt like resentment. She'd needed the comfort of that hug.

He'd needed it.

But, for some unidentifiable reason, he was embarrassed that his father had seen them. Was it because he didn't want Anthony to think there was anything going on between himself and Brie? That he might be considering a relationship with the mother of his son—marriage, even—simply because they shared a child?

As if…

You only had to look at his own family to know what a terrible idea that was.

His resentment was hard to hang onto, however, as he saw how strained his father's face was. How embarrassed he was that he might have interrupted an emotional moment.

'I'm so sorry I couldn't be here any earlier. I was in the middle of a Fontan procedure for a three-year-old with hypoplastic left heart syndrome. It's a complex surgery that I couldn't hand over to anyone else.'

'It's not a problem,' Jonno said. 'It's not as if you could have done anything. I just thought you should know.'

Anthony's nod was slow. 'Thank you.'

Brie was on her feet now. 'I need to get back to Felix. I want to stay with him until he has to go to Theatre.'

'Theatre?' Anthony's eyebrows rose. 'The message I got was that he'd had a seizure.'

'I'll get him up to speed,' Jonno told Brie. 'You go and be with Felix.'

'Thank you.' Brie smiled at Anthony. 'And thank you for coming.'

'If there *is* something I can do, please don't hesitate to ask.' The older man's face was serious but there were crinkles at the corners of his eyes that suggested a smile. 'You know, it's quite extraordinary, but looking at you is like seeing your mother a few decades ago.'

'And you look like an older version of Jonno.' Brie bit her lip. 'Oh…sorry… I shouldn't have said that, should I? When you're not…'

'Jonathon's biological father? It's okay…you're not the first person to say that but DNA doesn't lie.'

Jonno was cringing inside. He'd accused Brie of lying to him and being just the same as his parents but he was no better, was he?

'I never actually did a DNA test,' he said. 'I just said I did.'

There was a long moment of stunned silence in that small room.

Anthony closed his eyes. 'It was always a possibility,' he said. 'That's why it was so believable.'

'I could do one now. So we'd all know the truth.'

Anthony shook his head. 'It wouldn't make any difference.' He opened his eyes and looked straight at Jonno. His words were quiet and straight from the heart. 'You'll always be my son.'

The emotion in that room was overwhelming. It was Brie who made it bearable.

'And you'll always be Felix's grandpa,' she told Anthony. 'And you know what?'

'What?'

'I've always seen Jonno in Felix. Now I can see where they've both got their Morgan genes from. You've all got the same eyes. Like peas in a pod.'

Brie's own eyes were filling with tears again and Jonno wanted nothing more than to stay close to her and offer her whatever support and reassurance he could. Perhaps he wanted to try and explain why he'd lied to his father all those years ago, but she was already through the door and heading back to the ICU.

He wanted to follow her. So that he too could be near his son before he got wheeled up to Theatre. Instead, he was going to have to sit and talk to his father for the first time in so many years. For the first time since he'd learned he was a father himself. It was getting too close to painful, shut-off places to even think about Anthony saying he would always be his son but the least he could do was to apologise for that lie.

Jonno took a very deep breath.

'I'm sorry, Dad,' he said.

Anthony shrugged. 'It's ancient history,' he said quietly. 'How 'bout you tell me what's going on with *your* son?'

Talking about clinical matters was so much easier. They sat side by side on the couch and Jonno told him everything they had found out so far and what the plan was to treat the infection Felix had somehow picked up.

What he didn't say was how heartbreaking this was. That he'd only just discovered he was a father but he felt as if he was failing in the only responsibility that really mattered, which was to protect his child.

But maybe he didn't need to say anything. It was Anthony who broke the heavy silence when Jonno stopped talking.

'It's never easy,' he said softly. 'Being a parent.'

The silence became even heavier. To his horror, Jonno could feel tears gathering at the back of his eyes. 'How would you know?' he heard himself asking, his voice raw. 'You were never there...'

'I wanted to be. I tried to be. You were the reason I married your mother but that meant she made all the rules in the marriage. I couldn't break them because she had all the power.'

'You didn't break them because you were weak,' Jonno muttered.

'I didn't break them because, if I had, I would have lost my son. Julia would have taken you away and I might never have seen you again and…and I couldn't let that happen.' Anthony's outward breath was a sigh. 'But I ended up losing you anyway. And I couldn't blame you for being so angry.'

'I hated you then,' Jonno admitted. 'But I hated the whole world at that point and, after I'd found a way to escape, I never wanted to go back.'

'I know.' Anthony got to his feet. 'And I couldn't force you to do anything. Especially when I knew it was quite possible that I wasn't your biological father. Your *real* father…'

Jonno stood up. He was about to open his mouth and apologise again. Maybe to tell him that being a 'real' father was about a lot more than simply biology. But Anthony put his hand up and stopped him speaking.

'You need to be with *your* son right now,' he said. 'We can talk another time.' His smile was tentative. 'I hope…?'

Jonno gave a single nod.

'I might see if Elsie would like a bit of a break.' Anthony turned towards the door. 'I could take her down to the café for a coffee, maybe. And that way, you and Brie can stay with Felix together.'

Jonno led the way back into the ICU but he was very aware of the man following him.

His father.

He was a father himself now. Had Anthony ever felt

about him the way he felt about Felix? How would he feel if Brie wanted to control how close he could be to his son? Maybe his father hadn't thought that his work as a famous paediatric surgeon was so much more important than his own family. Maybe giving more and more of himself to that work had been his way of coping with heartbreak. The way that Jonno's passionate involvement in adrenaline sports had been the way he'd learned to cope when emotions got too big?

It was only a short time after Elsie had accepted Anthony's suggestion of going for a coffee that Felix was taken up to Theatre to have his shunt removed. Jonno and Brie followed his bed. They went past the relatives' room and then waited at the lift to go up a floor. They walked the long corridor to the Theatre suite, where they were allowed into the anaesthetic room adjacent to the operating theatre for a minute or two before they had to say goodbye.

Jonno had been holding Brie's hand ever since the journey to Theatre had started. He was still holding it as she bent to smooth a dark tress of hair from Felix's forehead to place a soft kiss on his pale skin.

And he still hadn't let go when they both went back to the relatives' room to wait, because he had the strong feeling that Brie didn't want him to let go.

There wasn't much that he could do, but at least it was something.

CHAPTER TWELVE

THE WAITING WAS the hardest part.

Waiting for Felix to come out of the operating theatre after having his shunt removed. Waiting to see how quickly the pressure inside his skull could return to normal so that he would no longer be at risk of any seizures. Watching the fluid collect in the CFS drainage system that relied on gravity and had valves that had to be carefully closed and then opened again whenever Felix changed his position. Waiting for the antibiotics to get on top of the infection that had made him so sick.

The first twenty-four hours were the worst and there was no way Jonno was about to let Brie and her mother keep vigil alone. He barely left the room himself that first day. Anthony came and went throughout the day and into the evening, between commitments to his patients. Elsie ferried coffee from the café and tried to persuade both Jonno and Brie to take a break and find something to eat much later that evening after the café had closed but Brie wasn't going anywhere.

'I can't,' she said quietly. 'I have to be here when he wakes up.'

'I'll go, then,' Elsie offered. 'I could bring you both back a hamburger or something?'

'I can do that,' Jonno said. 'I might duck back to my apartment and have a quick shower and change out of this uniform. I'll bring food back.' He closed his eyes briefly, as he remembered that it was only a couple of days ago that he and Brie and Felix had been eating hamburgers together after that dance class. That he'd made his son laugh and laugh and laugh by using the longest French fries as walrus tusks. He had to swallow hard to get rid of that lump in his throat. 'Cheeseburger for you, right?' He smiled at Brie. 'With extra bacon?' He turned to Elsie. 'Can I get you something as well?'

Elsie shook her head. 'I'll go home when you get back,' she said. 'I'm going to need a shower myself.'

'You should go home and get some sleep soon, Mum,' Brie said. 'I'm going to be here all night. I'll call you if anything changes.'

Elsie shrugged. 'Maybe…but I'm not going to leave you here by yourself.'

'She won't be by herself,' Jonno said. 'I'll be back very soon and then I won't be going anywhere.'

He met the steady gaze of Brie's mother and held it until he saw some of the deep lines around her eyes and mouth soften a little. Until he knew she'd got the message that he could be trusted.

She was still there when he got back and this time she smiled at him with a warmth that made him remember what his father had said to Brie about how like her mother she looked and he could see it himself now. Elsie Henderson was still a very beautiful woman.

'Go and have your dinner,' she told them. 'I'll hold the fort until you get back and I'll come and get you if Felix wakes up, but I have the feeling he's going to sleep for the rest of the night.'

'His temperature's come down,' Brie told him as they walked to the relatives' room where he'd left the paper bags of hot food outside the ICU. 'So has the intracranial pressure. Dr Jarvis popped in while you were gone and he's happy with how he's doing. Your dad came in too. He's got a post-surgery patient in the unit that he's with at the moment.'

Hamburgers really hadn't been the best choice of food, he decided a few minutes later, when he saw Brie unwrap hers and simply stare at it. And then she picked a French fry from the small cardboard container and her gaze flew up to meet his and he knew she was thinking about the walrus tusks. Jonno could see the moment her eyes filled with tears and how determined she was to blink them away and stay strong.

'What's in the other bag you brought in?'

'My laptop. I thought I could find something to entertain Felix with when he wakes up. And I brought that folder of his medical notes too. I haven't quite finished reading all those school reports.' Jonno put his hamburger down, still wrapped. He wasn't feeling very hungry either. He reached into the carrier bag and pulled out the folder and as he did so an envelope fell out.

'Oops...' He reached down and picked it up. Puzzled, he turned it over in his hand. The envelope was sealed and stamped. It had several date stamps from seven years ago as well as the postage stamp. And it was covered with other stamps of words, only a couple of which were in English. Words like 'Return to Sender' and 'Unknown at this Address'.

The address of the Mount Everest Base Camp, Khumbu, Nepal. With his name above it.

'Oh, my God...' He raised a startled gaze to find Brie. 'You wrote to me? Snail mail?'

Brie was watching him back intently but she didn't say anything. She simply nodded.

Jonno shook his head slowly. 'There are two base camps,' he told her. 'The south camp is in Nepal. The north one is in Tibet, on the opposite side of the mountain.'

Brie's eyes widened. 'I didn't know that. And you were in the north camp?'

It was Jonno's turn to nod. 'Can I...open it?'

She shrugged. 'Not much point now.' She offered him a wry smile. 'It's kind of old news.'

But Jonno opened the envelope anyway. It only took seconds to read but then he took another breath and read it again more slowly.

Dear Jonno,

I know this will come as a shock, but I have to tell you that I'm pregnant with your baby. I wasn't lying to you when I said I was on the pill, but I was sick the next day and something went wrong. I'm sorry.

I'm past my first trimester now. I don't expect anything from you at all and it's fine if you don't want any part of this—I just thought you should know that you are going to have a child in the world in about five months' time. A baby that I'm going to keep and am going to take care of and love in the very best way I can.

I will love him—or her—enough for both of us and I'll tell them about their father and how very special he is.

All the best, Brie.

There was a smudge on the paper below that line. It could be words that had been rubbed out. Or tears that had fallen?

PS, she had added. *I will never forget you. Or that night.*

Brie was watching closely enough to see the moment that Jonno remembered accusing her of having lied to him from the moment they'd met. Not that this letter was proof that she had been taking an oral contraceptive that night, but it was certainly proof that she'd done everything she could to contact him when she knew she was pregnant.

She could see the apology in his eyes.

And she thought she could see him offering her the gift of trust and that was huge, coming from Jonno, when he'd had his ability to trust broken so badly at a time when he had so needed something solid to hang onto in his life.

It *was* huge. But it also felt fragile so Brie didn't want to risk saying anything that might make Jonno take a step back. Instead, she put her uneaten food back in the bag.

'I might go back and see how Felix is doing,' she said quietly. 'Thanks so much for bringing the food, though. I can always heat it up later.'

'I'll come with you.' Jonno's voice sounded rough, which might be why he needed to clear his throat. 'I'm not that hungry myself now.'

They found Anthony in the room with Elsie. 'I'm trying to persuade your mum to go home and get some sleep,' he told Brie. 'But she said the couch in the relatives' room would be good enough.'

'Go home, Mum.' Brie gave her mother a hug. 'I'll call you if anything changes, I promise.'

'Are you okay to drive?' Jonno asked. 'I could call you a taxi.'

'There's no need for that,' Anthony said firmly. 'I'm heading home myself and I can drop you off, Elsie.'

'Oh…' Elsie blinked. 'In that case…' She turned back to Brie. 'Are you sure you don't want me to stay?'

Brie shook her head. 'We'll be fine,' she said.

And she didn't mean herself and Felix in that 'we'. She meant herself and Jonno—in what felt like a partnership that had just moved into a different space. One that had the beginnings of things that were much more solid than an irresistible physical attraction.

Things like forgiveness. And trust.

Only the following day Felix was sitting up in bed, feeling so much better he was wondering what all the fuss was about. Amazingly, he was far less bemused by the fact that someone he'd only known as a helper at his riding class and as a friend of Mummy's was visiting him so often, but maybe a lifetime of medical support and therapies had brought so many adults into his life on a regular basis it was no big deal. And maybe it was just wishful thinking, but it felt as if there was a real connection there. That Felix already loved his daddy even though he still had no idea who Jonno really was?

There seemed to be an unspoken agreement between Jonno, Brie, Elsie and Anthony that it was time to tell Felix why his family had suddenly doubled in size but, equally, there was a silent pact to wait until he was well enough. Nobody wanted to upset him in any way. They were, in fact, all going out of their way to make him feel as good as possible.

A few days later, when all four adults happened to be visiting at the same time and they decided to go to the café for some coffee because Felix was sound asleep, the consensus was that if there had been a competition going on for who could make Felix feel happiest then Jonno would have won it hands down.

'How did you know,' Elsie asked, 'that his favourite book was the one about that spotty pony Nobby running away to join a circus?'

'He told me. When I had been telling him about riding ponies in the desert. He thought Nobby would like to do that.'

'Why did I never think to try and find out if there was a sequel?' Brie was shaking her head but smiling at the same time. 'Who knew that Nobby would think circus tricks were so silly he didn't want to do them and he'd get sold to a cowboy?'

'And who knew that somebody would be smart enough to make a Nobby soft toy to sell along with the book?' Elsie's smile was misty. 'Did you see the way he was hanging onto him and using him for a pillow while he's asleep?'

Jonno was embarrassed by the appreciation of his gift. 'I just did a search online,' he said. 'It was no big deal.'

Except it really was, wasn't it? The way Felix's face had lit up. The squeeze of those small arms around Jonno's neck as he'd thanked him had felt as if they were actually tightening around his heart hard enough to take his breath away.

'It's a big deal for Felix,' Brie assured him. Her eyes

were thanking him all over again. 'He thinks you're more amazing than Father Christmas.'

'We'll have to make sure Dennis doesn't get hold of Nobby when we get home,' Elsie warned. 'He's got such a talent for eating the ears off any soft toy animals.'

'That might be a wee while yet,' Anthony warned. 'They want to keep a close eye on him and watch for any sign of increasing ICP until he's been clear of the infection long enough to replace the shunt. Or do the EVT?' He looked from Jonno to Brie. 'Has Peter Jarvis talked to you both about that again?'

Brie nodded. 'I was trying to explain it to Mum this afternoon.' Jonno could see the careful way she was taking a deep breath and it made him notice how tired she looked. He'd never seen shadows that deep beneath her eyes. 'I know it would be great if it meant he would never need another shunt but it sounds really scary.'

'It's a well-established, minimally invasive endoscopic procedure now,' Anthony said. 'With promising results. I had a good chat to Peter about it today.'

'I don't really understand it all,' Elsie confessed. 'But deliberately making holes in someone's brain does sound a bit horrific.'

Anthony gave her a quick reassuring smile. 'It's a tiny hole,' he told her. 'And the procedure only takes about thirty minutes. It's called minimally invasive because it's not a major surgery.'

'That's a risk in itself, isn't it?' Brie asked. 'With the hole being so small, it can close up.'

'But the long-term complication rate is lower than it is for shunts,' Jonno put in. 'And I certainly don't want to see him go through another infection in the years to come.'

His own words seemed to catch in the air. Jonno could see that Anthony and Elsie weren't listening because his father was drawing on a paper serviette to explain the procedure of an endoscopic third ventriculostomy more clearly to Elsie but he could also see—or, rather, sense—that Brie had gone very still.

In the years to come...

It would be a rather casual way to be making a public commitment to being involved in his son's life, if that was what he was doing.

Was it?'

Was he making a promise to be here as Felix's father, alongside his mother? Like a real family?

Good grief...they even had an extended family with the grandparents already involved.

It was Jonno's turn to take a deep breath. It wasn't that he didn't trust Brie enough to know that they could make it work. How could he not trust her after finding that letter that proved the lengths she had taken to try and tell him he was going to become a father?

But his own father was back in his life again and that was stirring some big emotions. Memories of how it felt to believe that he'd never been loved as much as he'd desperately wanted to be. Of needing to escape because there was nothing in the world that could really be trusted.

Jonno could feel that need to escape hovering at the back of his mind, fanned by the knowledge that he'd already made a big decision today. Did Brie see that in his face when she caught his gaze? Or had she actually tuned into his thoughts?

'When's the settlement date on your apartment?' she asked.

'Not for another month.' But the clock was already ticking, wasn't it? 'My mate Max is happy for me to crash on his couch for a while but I do need to start looking for another property. Especially since I told the Air Rescue management that I'm happy to sign up for that job.'

He'd been speaking quietly but that didn't stop his words catching their parents' attention. Talking about being involved in the years to come was one thing. Taking on a new career and investing in property was something else. Something that could mean Jonno's involvement in Felix's life—and, by default, in Brie's life, along with her mother and *his* father—was going to be life-changing for them all.

'You're taking the job on the helicopters?' Elsie asked. 'Oh…that's such exciting news.'

'You're looking for property?' Anthony asked.

'I'm selling the apartment,' Jonno told him quietly. 'It's something I should have done a very long time ago. It's time to move on.'

He let his gaze rest on Brie for a heartbeat, hoping that she would understand that there were some memories associated with that apartment that he didn't necessarily want to move on from? Memories that were theirs and theirs alone? It took only another beat of time to know that the message had been received. Even better, that Brie wasn't about to forget them either. She'd already told him that, hadn't she? In that postscript in her letter.

I will never forget you. Or that night…

Thank goodness nobody else was picking up on any intimate silent communication.

'It's time I downsized,' Anthony said. 'I'd like something about the size of your place, Elsie. That garden of mine is taking up far too much time to maintain and I barely use most of the rooms in the house. I've only kept it because I grew up there myself.' He reached for his coffee cup to finish his drink, but then replaced it carefully on its saucer as he caught his son's gaze.

'It's where *you* grew up,' he said softly. 'It's as much your home as mine, Jonno. You should have a say in whether it gets sold or not. Maybe you'd like to live there again yourself? Felix would love the garden, wouldn't he?'

Jonno had told Brie that the house had been a perfect place to grow up in, with the nearby forest park and bike trails, but in reality his life had been a long way from perfect. Would it be a huge mistake to revisit the past to that extent, in the hope that history could be rewritten?

'Thanks,' he said to his father. 'It's certainly something to think about.'

But his tone was dismissive and an awkward silence fell that seemed to be overflowing with things that maybe both father and son wanted—or needed—to talk about but neither of them had any idea how to start, or if they even *should* start. Jonno was aware of a sensation as if there were walls closing in around him. Of being trapped…?

Elsie was the first to respond to the tension. She got to her feet. 'I'll head back upstairs,' she announced. 'I'm sure Felix is still sound asleep but I'd like to tidy up his toys before I go home tonight.'

'I'd better get moving too.' Anthony was clearly relieved by the escape route Elsie had engineered. 'I've got some patients I need to see before *I* head home.'

* * *

A new silence between Jonno and Brie when they were alone, but before Brie could think of a way to break it there was a buzzing sound from his phone lying on the table beside his coffee cup. He silenced the vibration.

'It's just Max,' he said to Brie. 'I'll call him back later.'

But his phone buzzed again against the tabletop and Jonno grimaced as he must have guessed why his friend needed to talk to him so urgently. 'Oh, *no*...'

'What is it?' Brie asked.

'That trip we planned to the Cairngorms to do that rock climbing we missed out on last time, thanks to getting involved with that rescue?'

'I remember. The climb with that odd name. Squareface?'

'That's the one. Fancy you remembering that.'

Jonno sounded impressed, but how could she ever forget when it had been such a part of all of this? Jonno's trip away had given Brie the time and courage to decide she had to tell him about Felix, only to be so thoroughly distracted when she'd arrived at his apartment. That photo of him and Max in the newspaper, which had been how Elsie had found out Anthony was Felix's grandfather. Jonno finding out he was Felix's father, thanks to that meeting Elsie had arranged.

Jonno's tone was almost a groan. 'It's this week. The day after tomorrow, in fact. I'd been planning to get in touch with him to talk about that trip, but that was the day Felix got sick and it totally fell out of my head.' He picked up his phone. 'I'll call him back. I'll have to cancel it now.'

Brie watched him pick up his phone again, a cascade of thoughts flashing through her head, following on from the series of events that had happened since his last trip to the Cairngorm mountains in Scotland.

She thought of that gleam in his eyes when he'd been talking about how much he would love to try one of those wingsuits that could make you feel as if you were flying. How disappointed he'd been not to get the chance of facing the challenge of that 'gnarly' rock face he and Max had wanted to climb.

She wondered if he was planning to cancel every adventure he might have dreamed of doing in the years to come. The years to come that he was planning to spend helping to keep his son safe and loved as he grew up. Did that go some way towards explaining the tension she'd felt when his father had suggested he went back to living in the house he'd grown up in? A tension that had suggested old wounds were being exposed. That Jonno felt a need to escape? Did he need some time to clear his head—the way she had needed it that first time he'd gone away for a few days with his best mate, to do something they were both passionate about?

Without thinking, Brie put her hand on Jonno's arm to stop him picking up his phone.

'Wait…' she said.

Jonno looked up. 'What is it?'

'It's something Mum said to me a long time ago, when it felt like it might be impossible for us both to be able to combine looking after Felix with other things in life we both wanted to do. Like me becoming a paramedic and Mum going back to her nursing.'

Jonno looked puzzled. He obviously couldn't see how this related to him calling Max.

'She said that if we wanted to be the best parent and grandparent we could be, we have to look after ourselves too. We have to be able to do things that we're passionate about.'

'Your mum is a wise woman.'

'So you'll go? Have some fun doing the kind of stuff you love so much?'

But Jonno looked torn. 'I can't. Not while Felix is in hospital.' His gaze on Brie was intense. 'This has made me realise how much you've had to go through by yourself. It's not going to be like that from now on, Brie. I'm going to be here too.'

In the years to come...

Hearing Jonno say aloud that he was planning to be involved in his son's care in the future was one thing. Taking on a new career and investing in property was even more significant. Jonno's presence in Felix's life—and, by default, in Brie's life—was going to be life-changing for them all.

But...how perfect would it be to be hearing those words because he wanted to be here for *her* and not only to support her in caring for their child? Brie wasn't about to let a flash of heartbreak cloud the significance of the promise Jonno was making, however. And she didn't want to push him away by making it obvious how much more she was longing for, so she kept her tone light.

'He's happy. Thanks to you, he's got Nobby. And a new story we'll probably have to read until we all know it by heart and everyone other than Felix will be sick to death of it.' Brie smiled. 'You'll be back by the time he has to go to Theatre again. And didn't you say that if you didn't go now the weather would get too bad and it might be ages before you got another chance?'

'That's true.' Jonno was holding her gaze. 'Are you sure you don't mind?'

Brie's heart was being squeezed so hard it hurt. Jonno had been prepared to give up something he loved that much for Felix. This was a gift that only she could give him, wasn't it?

'I'm sure,' she said softly. 'Go... Enjoy...'

It wasn't just Brie who missed Jonno being around.

'Where's Jonno?' Felix asked yet again, as Brie tried to settle him for the night.

'He's away, just for a few days,' Brie told him. 'And when he's back he'll be able to tell you all about his exciting adventures climbing mountains. Do you want to look at some pictures of people climbing mountains on your tablet?'

But Felix shook his head. Very uncharacteristically, he even stuck out his bottom lip. 'I want him to read me the story about Nobby and the cowboys.'

'We might be able to find a picture of exactly where Jonno's gone, in the Cairngorms in Scotland. Did he tell you he was going to climb part of a mountain that's got a funny name? A big rock called Squareface?'

Felix still looked mutinous.

Brie sighed. 'Okay... I'll read you the story about Nobby and the cowboys.'

Felix pulled the spotted soft toy horse into his arms as he snuggled down on his pillows. His sigh was even louder than Brie's. 'We're ready, Mumma...'

She had to read the story three times but, while Felix was looking a lot sleepier, he still wasn't looking happy.

'I want to go home,' he said sadly.

'I know.' Brie ruffled his hair and bent down to kiss

him. 'It won't be long. Dr Jarvis said we're going to do some more tests and then you might be ready for the operation that will fix things so we can all go home. You and me *and* Nobby.'

But Felix didn't smile back.

'I want to go home now. I want to see my stars and make a wish.'

Brie could see his eyes filling with tears and it was so unlike Felix that her heart broke a little. She picked up his tablet. 'How 'bout I find a picture of some stars?'

'Okay…'

'*Star light, star bright, first stars I see tonight…*' Felix showed little enthusiasm for the rhyme but he closed his eyes tightly as they finished.

'What did you wish for?' Brie asked.

'Same as last time.'

'The special wish?'

'Yeah…' Felix was drifting into sleep, his cheek buried in Nobby's soft neck.

'What was it?'

'Can't tell you or it might not come true…' his voice was getting the familiar slur that told Brie he was barely conscious now '…and then Jonno will never be my daddy…'

Oh…

Brie needed some air. She walked out of Felix's room and down the main corridor of the ward. As she went through the main doors to where a group of comfortable chairs had been placed in front of the windows opposite the lifts, a set of steel doors slid open.

Elsie walked out of the lift.

'Mum…' Brie could feel the blood draining from

her face. 'What's wrong? Has something happened to Dennis?'

'No...he's fine. He had a lovely walk. It's something else...' Elsie was right in front of Brie now. 'You'd better sit down, love...'

But Brie couldn't move. 'Tell me...'

'I just heard it on the radio in the car. There's... there's been an accident...'

She knew. Even before Elsie said anything else, Brie knew what had happened. That her worst fear had come to pass.

'They're not giving out any details yet. They just said that a climber's been killed in the Cairngorms. On a peak the locals call Squareface... Oh, love... I'm so sorry...' Elsie's arms were around Brie. 'It might not be Jonno. We can't assume the worst.'

Except that it was impossible not to.

Somehow Brie made it to one of the chairs near the window. She sank onto the edge of it but couldn't find any words. She just stared straight ahead, too stunned to even process what was happening.

'I tried to call Anthony,' Elsie said. 'If it is Jonno, they would have told him first, I'm sure. But I think his phone's switched off, which isn't a good sign, is it?'

'Anthony was here a while back.' Brie's voice was toneless. 'He had to take a patient back to Theatre for some reason, but he didn't think it was going to take too long. If he's finished, you might be able to find him in the ICU.'

Elsie shook her head. 'I can't leave you.'

'I'm okay. I think I need a few minutes by myself, to be honest, Mum. I can't seem to get my head around this.'

'I know…' Elsie had tears running down her cheeks. 'I can't believe it. And the first thing I thought was that you'd been right all along…'

Her words made no sense. 'About what?'

'About not telling Felix. About how awful it would be for him to find out he has a daddy, only to have him disappear.'

Brie found herself fighting to take a breath as her chest tightened painfully. 'You go, Mum. See if you can find Anthony and then we can be sure about what's really happened.'

Except that, deep down, Brie *was* sure.

The worst *had* happened. Brie had lost Jonno and she'd never even told him how much she loved him.

Felix had lost his father before he'd even known he had him.

What seemed even more heartbreaking was that her precious son had a wish—a special wish—that was never going to come true.

CHAPTER THIRTEEN

SHE LOOKED AS though she'd been sitting there for ever.

Frozen.

Head down and eyes closed as if she was dealing with a very private, very painful battle.

Dear Lord… Had she heard the news already? The police had informed him that no names would be released until members of the family had been told, but that might have only made it worse. He'd tried to call his father but had only been able to leave a voice message. Did Brie think that *he* was the one who had died? Surely he didn't matter so much to her that she would look as though the world had ended?

Or did he…?

The mix of overwhelming strong emotions like grief and fear and…hope…only made it harder to know what to do in this moment so as not to give Brie a horrible fright.

So he called her name. So softly, it was a whisper he could barely hear himself.

'Brie…?'

She heard him. She looked up and shock was written all over her face as she stumbled to her feet, which was hardly a surprise. He knew he looked terrible. He was still in his climbing gear and there were bloodstains on his clothes. He had what felt like dried dirt or blood on his face and he hadn't even thought to try combing his hair because he'd been too desperate to get here.

To do *this*…

To hold Brie in his arms and let his cheek rest against her hair. To feel her heart beating against his chest and her warmth that he'd known was the only thing that could thaw the ice in his chest. And it did…

Jonno could feel it starting to melt, with trickles of pain that cut like knives as tears rolled down his face.

Brie was crying too. But she'd never even met Max.

'I thought it was you,' she whispered. 'Oh, God, Jonno. I thought I'd lost you for ever.'

He could feel her shaking in his arms, which made him hold her even more tightly. He'd felt this shattered when he'd been holding his best friend's body in his arms after that fall. When he'd travelled with him on the long journey to bring him back to Bristol, to where his family would be waiting for him.

A journey during which Jonno had realised there was only one person who could help him get through his world falling apart for the second time in his life.

One person he could trust enough to let her hold his heart—if he was brave enough to give it into her care.

If she wanted it…

There had only been one way to find out. One that had brought him here with such urgency he hadn't even bothered to comb his hair or wash his face. And he'd known that, even if Brie didn't feel the same way, he had to tell her.

Because life was so horribly fragile and you never

knew what might be around the next corner. Brie deserved to know how special she was.

How much he loved her...

And Felix had to know that he had a daddy who loved him with all his heart. A heart that might be hurting unbearably right now, but that wasn't simply because it had lost something precious. It was because it was getting bigger. Cracking open. And yeah, that meant that it was open to pain, but it also meant it was open to the opposite of pain.

To the warmth and light and pure joy that love could bring in the good times.

And the comfort and support and hope it could bestow in the not so good times.

So Jonno held Brie even more closely in his arms, just for a heartbeat, because he knew he would have to let her go so that she could take a breath very soon.

'I love you,' he whispered, right against her ear. 'I love you, Brie...'

She felt his arms loosen, which was a good thing because she really needed to take a breath. But the last thing she wanted was for Jonno to let her go.

Ever...

Free enough to tip her head back, Brie looked up at the man she loved so much and her heart hurt for him because he looked so shattered.

There was happiness there as well, though. Sheer relief that he had not only survived some terrible accident that had claimed his best friend, but that he had chosen to come and find her to hold and be held.

Pure joy that he'd said those three, totally life-changing words and she'd known he'd meant every one of them with his whole heart.

It was her turn now. She reached up to touch his face and smooth away some of those tears.

'I love you, Jonno,' she whispered back. 'I always have.' She had to sniff and brush away tears on her own face. 'I could see you in our boy and I've missed you being in our lives, even though you never had been, and…and while I've been sitting here, thinking the worst, I realised that I always *will* love you and I hated that I hadn't told you that. I hated that we'd waited to tell Felix the truth.'

'We don't have to wait any longer, do we?' Jonno pulled her back into his arms. 'From now on, we need to make the most of every minute we can be together as a family.'

Brie tightened her arms around him. 'We might need to wait just a little bit longer,' she said. Not that she was going to tell him he might give Felix a fright if he went in looking like he'd fallen off a mountain himself.

Jonno was nodding agreement but he seemed to be giving her words a very different meaning because he bent his head to touch her lips with his own. Softly. Slowly…

She should take him home, Brie thought. He needed a shower and a change of clothes. It would be good if she could persuade him to eat something, but what he needed most of all was comfort.

Love…

There would be time for everything else after that. They had the rest of their lives to work out how to become the best family they could possibly be. Brie heard the lift doors sliding open behind her and turned her head to see Anthony and Elsie walking out towards them. She could see an oddly similar expression on their faces and she understood exactly why. They were parents and they were both looking at their children with the kind of love that clearly didn't diminish over so many years.

'Oh, thank goodness…' Elsie was smiling through her tears. 'Anthony had already got your message, Jonno. We were coming down to tell Brie but…'

'I think we might be interrupting, Elsie,' Anthony said. 'Shall we go and check on Felix instead?'

'We were just going to do that,' Brie heard herself saying.

Elsie knew what she was saying. Her eyes widened. 'We'll go and get some fresh air,' she said. 'Maybe a coffee. We can come back later.' She gave Anthony a look that made him blink and start following her instantly.

Jonno's eyebrows were raised and he put his hand to his hair as if he'd just remembered how messy it was. 'He won't want to see me like this.'

But Brie smiled. That didn't really matter, did it? Jonno could give his face a quick wash and put a gown over his clothes but Felix would probably only see his daddy's smile, anyway. And the look in his eyes when he found out that both his parents loved not only him but each other… That they were going to become a family.

'He wants to see you more than anything.' Brie took Jonno's hand in hers. 'You have just been given a magic power to make a little boy's wish come true.'

'I hope that's true.'

'I promise you it is.'

Jonno pulled her closer. They were alone in the foyer

again and Brie knew he wanted to hold her again for a moment before they went in to see their son. Maybe he wanted to give her another one of those oh, so tender kisses.

And that was fine by her.

Because it wasn't just Felix's wish that was coming true…

* * * * *

HOW TO RESCUE
THE HEART DOCTOR

ALISON ROBERTS

MILLS & BOON

PROLOGUE

Just a day or two before...

IT WAS FIVE O'CLOCK in the morning, the staffroom was empty and the full pot of coffee on the automatic percolator was too tempting to resist after the long night that paediatric cardiac surgeon, Anthony Morgan, had just had. A quiet moment to sit down and enjoy a mug of hot, strong coffee was exactly what he needed.

Only seconds later, however, a nurse came in carrying a baby in her arms and he couldn't blame her for looking so taken aback to see him there.

'I'm not in your way, am I? I can go...' He put his mug of coffee down on the low table beside the chair he was sitting in, but somehow he managed to tip its contents onto the pile of folded newspaper on the tabletop. He couldn't quite stifle his weary groan.

'Don't worry about it.' The tone of the nurse's voice was kind. 'That paper's due to go into the recycle bin anyway. And don't get up. Please. You look like you need a quiet space even more than Tommy and I do, Mr Morgan.'

'Please, call me Anthony...'

'I'm Elsie, I've just started recently on this ward. I've seen you around before, of course, but not usually at silly o'clock.'

She had a rather lovely smile. She also had silvery grey streaks in her hair that told him she was older than most of the nurses here at St Nick's.

'It has been rather a long night,' Anthony admitted. 'I've been in PICU since midnight with a wee girl who looked like she might not make it. She had a fairly major surgery today and ran into problems with arrhythmias that put her into acute heart failure.'

'Oh... I'm sorry.' She was frowning but then looked shocked. 'It wasn't Victoria, was it? I knew she was having her surgery yesterday.' He could see her almost wince as she realised she was stepping over privacy boundaries. 'Sorry,' she said again. 'I shouldn't have asked. It's just that I spent some time talking to Vicky's mother the last time I was on duty. I'm helping to raise a grandson with spina bifida so we had a connection. And Vicky's just an adorable little girl. She gives the best cuddles in the world—just like my Felix.'

He was catching undercurrents to her words. She was a grandmother? What was it that made her want to be doing shift work? But he'd been right about the kindness he could hear in her voice. She'd taken the time to connect with not only a young patient but with her family and, with experience of a child with special needs, she would have been able to do that better than most. She also clearly adored her grandson. Anthony found himself smiling. He didn't have to keep any barriers up. Vicky would hopefully be back on the ward within a very short space of time. This nurse was part of his own team, wasn't she?

'She's okay. She's a wee fighter. Her cardiologist has got her electrolyte balance sorted now so she may well come onto the ward in the next day or two and you might be able to get another one of those cuddles. Is your grandson the same age?'

'No, he's six—a couple of years older. We've been through a few surgeries ourselves but nothing as serious as an open-heart procedure.'

'I'm glad he hasn't needed it.' Anthony managed to stifle a yawn. 'I don't actually need to be here for Vicky any longer, but if I went home I would no sooner get there than I'd have to turn around and fight my way through rush-hour traffic to come back. I've got a full Theatre list this morning so I thought I'd put my feet up here instead. And have a strong coffee.' He glanced down at the empty mug in his hand. 'So much for that plan.'

He saw Elsie shift the weight of the baby in her arms, who looked to be soundly asleep. 'Here…give that to me.' She held her hand out for the mug. 'I'm well practised in making a coffee one-handed. Why don't you put the newspaper in the recycle bin by the fridge?'

'Sure.' Anthony started to gather up the sections of the paper.

'How do you take your coffee?'

'Black, thanks. No sugar.'

He put the last section of the newspaper on top of the pieces he was already holding. It was the front page, with the banner at the top, a date of a few days ago and a photograph of a rescue helicopter with a backdrop of mountains. There was a man standing beside the stretcher about to be loaded into the aircraft. A hero who'd helped save the life of an injured climber.

Anthony couldn't look away. He couldn't even take a breath because it felt as if his chest was being squeezed in a vice. How long had it been since he'd seen this man's face in real life? Nearly ten years? How long had it been since he'd felt welcome in his life? Probably not since his mother's funeral even longer ago.

Until he heard her speak, he'd barely registered that Elsie had put a fresh mug of coffee down on the table beside him. Or that she was sitting down herself. Watching him.

'Do you know him?' Her voice was soft this time. A little tentative, perhaps. 'Is he a relative of yours?'

Anthony still didn't look up from the photograph. He shouldn't say anything but the words seemed to get torn out of a deep place in his chest.

'Yeah… Jonathon Morgan is my son.'

Why on earth had he told a complete stranger something that personal? It might be nearly twenty years but he'd never forgotten what it had been like to be the hot topic of gossip on the hospital grapevine.

Anthony dropped the paper and rubbed at his forehead. 'Sorry,' he murmured. 'Maybe the night's been longer than I realised. I'm quite sure you don't want to hear about my personal life.' He pasted a smile on his face. 'Families, huh?' He reached for his coffee. 'They can be complicated, can't they?'

The sound Elsie made suggested that she had no desire to hear any more about his personal life. Or maybe this had suddenly become awkward because she already knew about that old scandal? Anthony focused on the smell and taste of his coffee to avoid any eye contact.

It was a relief when the baby she was holding woke up and started crying miserably. It was even more of a relief when Elsie got up and excused herself.

Left alone, Anthony drank his coffee, his gaze drifting back to that front page photograph. That tightness in his chest was still there, along with a twinge that felt like a very familiar pain.

So Jonno was back in the country…

The son who wanted nothing to do with him…

Anthony drained his mug and got to his feet. He was ready to deal with this the way he'd dealt with unpleasant emotional issues for far longer than he cared to remember. By focusing on the problems of others that he could potentially fix. Medical problems to do with little hearts that were broken in some physical way.

He could feel a wry smile teasing the corners of his mouth as he quietly left this ward staffroom. How ironic was it that his own heart had been broken by something that couldn't be fixed?

CHAPTER ONE

UH-OH...

Luckily, Elsie Henderson saw him before he saw her so probably had time to avoid getting any closer. Anthony Morgan had his back to her, in fact, as he spoke to someone behind the main desk of this cardiac surgical ward.

Did she have time to take Vicky, the small girl who was balanced on her hip with her arms around her nurse's neck, back to her bed? It was quite possible that Mr Morgan was coming to see Vicky, who was one of his patients, but Elsie didn't want him to see *her*.

She'd only met the man for the first time a couple of days ago but she knew something about him that he *didn't* know.

Something very personal.

Something he had the right to know.

But Elsie wasn't sure she had the right to tell him and she'd been wrestling with the dilemma ever since.

The split second of indecision about how to avoid a face-to-face encounter in the ward corridor was almost too long. As Elsie was turning to go back in the direction she'd come from, she could see in her peripheral vision that Anthony was turning as well. Towards her. She stared at the open door to the playroom she had just come out of.

'Let's go back in here for a second, darling. I don't think I showed you what was inside the Wendy house, did I? Do you know there's a little stove with an oven door that actually opens?'

Vicky shook her head but her eyes were drifting shut. 'I want to go back to bed,' she told Elsie. 'I feel funny…'

'Do you?' Elsie was now safely screened by a tall bookshelf in the play area but an alarm bell was ringing at the back of her head for a different reason this time. 'What sort of funny, darling?'

Vicky was a few days past open heart surgery to repair congenital defects. She'd only come back from the intensive care unit yesterday but, in the astonishing way children were capable of bouncing back from even major surgery, she had desperately wanted to get out of bed to play. It was only the side rails that were raised on her bed that had thwarted her attempt to climb out.

'How 'bout I go and get you an ice cream?' her mother, Julie, had suggested. 'I'm pretty sure I saw your favourite kind in a freezer in the cafeteria. The one with the strawberry jelly in the middle?'

'And I could take you for a little walk while Mummy's gone,' Elsie had suggested. 'Just for a couple of minutes. Maybe we could have a look at the playroom for when you get better. No walking yet, though, and we'll have to be very careful. I can find a wheelchair for you or I can carry you. Which would you like better?'

Vicky had held her arms up in the air by way of response, a wide smile on her face, and Julie had given

Elsie a grateful smile. Maybe the young mother needed a few minutes to herself after days of intense anxiety about her daughter. Elsie had bonded with both Vicky and Julie when the little girl had been first admitted to have all her pre-surgical tests and checks done. Heart issues were only one of the challenges Vicky was facing in life. She'd also been born with spina bifida—a birth defect that Elsie had become an expert in over the years since her own grandson had also been born with the condition so her connection with both Vicky and Julie had been instant.

As a nurse, she was also an expert in sensing when something wasn't right and she could hear an odd note in Vicky's voice. She could also see how pale that little face was becoming.

'My head's going...roundy roundy.' Vicky had to stop to take a breath after only a few words and then she coughed. '*Ow*...' She sounded close to tears now. 'It *hurts*...'

Okay... Any personal preferences became totally irrelevant as Elsie moved swiftly back towards the doors into the main corridor. She wasn't worried about seeing Anthony Morgan now. She would welcome seeing him. Or anyone else who might be in a position to assist her.

Because something was going wrong. Fast enough to be frightening.

She could feel Vicky slumping in her arms. Was her level of consciousness dropping? Her respiration rate had certainly increased. Her small patient was almost gasping.

'What's happening?' Anthony Morgan was only a

few steps away as Elsie stepped into the corridor and he must have seen the fear in her eyes. 'Is that Vicky?'

'Something's wrong,' Elsie said. 'Her LOC's dropping. She's short of breath...'

'This way...' Anthony put a hand on her shoulder, guiding her across the corridor and into the ward's treatment room that had a bed in the middle and was lined with cupboards and shelves stacked with all the medical equipment and supplies that could be needed for even major procedures and emergencies. 'Put her on the bed.'

Anthony unhooked the stethoscope from around his neck as Elsie laid Vicky on the bed. He slid the disc under a pink pyjama top that had a sparkly picture of a unicorn on the front.

'Her heart sounds are a bit muffled,' he said moments later. 'And she's tachycardic at one forty. See if you can find a radial pulse?' He put his hand on Vicky's head, smoothing her hair back. 'Hey, Vicky...can you open your eyes?'

Vicky's eyelashes fluttered, which suggested she could hear him, but she didn't open her eyes. She was opening and closing her mouth, however, in an increasing struggle to get enough oxygen. She looked like a fish out of water, Elsie thought as she tried to find a radial pulse in the tiny wrist she was holding between her fingers and thumb.

'I can't feel a pulse.' Elsie was surprised at how calm her voice sounded when she could feel the claws of panic digging in, deep in her gut. Vicky's blood pressure could be dangerously low.

'Bring the defibrillator trolley over. We need to get an ECG and a blood pressure if we can. I might need an airway adjunct as well.' Anthony was frowning heavily. 'Her jugular veins aren't distended but with muffled heart sounds and being hypotensive, it could be Beck's triad forming.' He glanced up at Elsie as she pushed the trolley closer, to see if she understood the reference.

She did. And it was enough to make her swallow hard. 'Cardiac tamponade?'

Bleeding into the pericardial space around the heart was a well-recognised complication following cardiac surgery. It could also be dangerous because, if it happened rapidly, it could be enough to stop the heart functioning well before they'd have time to get her back to Theatre.

Anthony nodded when Elsie reached for the defibrillator pads first, rather than any electrodes to record a more detailed ECG or a cuff to measure blood pressure. She helped him remove the unicorn pyjama top and stick them on but they could both feel the change as Vicky crashed and stopped breathing. Anthony barely waited for the static on the screen of the defibrillator to settle and confirm a rhythm of ventricular fibrillation—incompatible with life—before he hit the red 'cardiac arrest' button on the wall to summon urgent help.

Elsie grabbed the bag mask unit from the trolley but Anthony took it from her hands to hold over Vicky's mouth and nose himself. He tipped her head back and squeezed the bag, watching the chest rise and fall.

'Shall I start chest compressions?' Elsie was poised, flashes of a recent training session to keep nursing staff up-to-date with CPR protocols foremost in her brain.

Place the heel of one hand in the centre of the chest. Keep your arm straight and elbow locked.

Push hard and fast with a ratio of thirty compressions to two breaths.

Except…this little girl was only just beginning to heal after major heart surgery. How much damage could be done by pushing hard on that fragile-looking chest with its sutures still in place under the clear adhesive dressing?

Anthony Morgan must have seen the question in her eyes. 'Hold off on compressions. We'll shock first. What's her current weight, do you know?'

'It was almost twenty kilograms this morning.' More than a healthy weight for a four-year-old girl but it was a common problem with children who had major mobility issues.

'Charge to forty joules, then,' Anthony instructed. 'We'll go to eighty if we need to repeat.'

Elsie held her breath as the defibrillator's whine changed to a strident beeping to announce that the charge was set.

'Stand clear,' she warned, watching to make sure Anthony lifted his hands and that his body was not touching the bed, before she pushed the discharge button. She felt herself wince as Vicky's tiny body jerked with even the small jolt of electricity going through her heart.

'Still in VF.' Anthony's voice was calm as he watched the screen. 'Charge again. Eighty joules this time, please.'

Elsie adjusted the setting, thankful that the training session had included practice with the latest models of defibrillators like this one. She was even more thankful that more staff were arriving in response to the urgent summons of a cardiac arrest alarm. She recognised an anaesthetist, who immediately took over airway control and oxygenation, a paediatric cardiologist and Laura, one of this ward's most senior nurses. The mobile arrest team arrived shortly afterwards, pushing two more trolleys laden with equipment.

These people were all far more experienced than Elsie in dealing with an emergency like this but, as she stepped back with the intention of leaving, Laura shook her head.

'Stay,' she said. 'Watch and learn…and we might need a runner…'

So Elsie stayed, watching the team sort themselves into positions under Anthony's leadership. Because he was the cardiothoracic surgeon and the decision had already been made to perform a resternotomy and reopen that small chest. If it was a tamponade that had caused the cardiac arrest, the pressure had to be released as quickly as possible to have any chance of saving Vicky's life. There was no time to take her to Theatre.

Anthony and one other doctor had ripped open sterile packs and were donning gowns, gloves, hats and masks. Someone else took a folded drape, pressed the centre of it onto Vicky's chest and then unfolded each side. The little girl that Elsie had been talking to and holding in her arms only minutes ago vanished beneath the sterile green cloth, her entire body covered. Only her chest was visible through the clear plastic adhesive window as a kit of instruments was emptied onto the sterile field. The strings of Anthony's gown were still being tied by Laura as he reached for a scalpel. His assistant picked up something that looked like a pair of pliers.

It should have made this easier to watch by creating

a distance that made it possible to focus simply on a potentially life-saving procedure and not something ultimately invasive that was happening to a small human that Elsie had been able to bond with all too easily as she'd cared for her—and her mother.

Perhaps it was the thought of Vicky's mother, Julie, that brought the prickle of tears to the back of Elsie's eyes. She'd asked Elsie if she could stay with Vicky for a few minutes while she went to the cafeteria to buy a favourite brand of ice cream for her daughter. Elsie had promised she wouldn't leave her alone for a second and she wasn't about to now. She had to be able to tell Julie that she'd been here. That everything possible was being done to save her precious child.

It gave her the strength to be able to watch what was happening as Anthony cut through the external sutures and then another layer. He swapped the scalpel for a tool to cut the wires holding the sternum together and his assistant used the pliers to twist and remove the segments of wire.

Seeing the blades of the retractor being slipped into place and a spanner being used to wind it open was enough to make Elsie close her eyes for a moment. She could hear Anthony asking for suction and heard the unit attached to the wall beside the oxygen outlet whirring into action.

'Not much blood loss,' she heard someone close to her say. 'Maybe it's not a tamponade?'

'If it happens fast it takes a lot less blood to cause trouble,' someone else responded, 'Two hundred mils in an adult. But only two mils in a neonate.'

The other doctor who had gowned up was speaking to Anthony. 'Can you see any active bleeding?'

'No.'

'Have we got a rhythm yet?'

Elsie opened her eyes but she couldn't see the screen of the monitor. She could, however, hear the grim note in Anthony's voice.

'I'm going to try some cardiac massage. Are the internal paddles ready to use for defibrillation?'

'Yes...'

There seemed a moment of hope a short time later when Vicky's heart responded to the massage and began beating but the comments Elsie could hear were concerned with continued bleeding and the danger of hypovolemia. Instructions were being given to make a dash to Theatre, where they might be able to buy enough time to find the source of blood loss and control it.

'Have someone holding the lift doors open,' someone called. 'We'll be ready to move very soon.'

Laura caught Elsie's gaze and she nodded. 'I'll do that.'

It was a relief to get out of the treatment room. She ran to the lifts and pushed the button to summon it, then stood in the doorway to keep the doors open and stop anyone else using it. Seconds later the team emerged from the treatment room—a bed surrounded by people moving swiftly towards the lift. It was obvious that an emergency was in full progress. Anthony was still wearing a blood-stained gown as he strode alongside the bed.

People jumped out of the way, looking shocked. They were still staring after the doors of the lift closed and it began moving up towards the theatre suite. Laura was beside Elsie and they both realised that Vicky's mother was amongst the onlookers. It was obvious that Julie was fearing the worst. Laura spoke quietly to Elsie.

'Stay with her. You're the best person to be looking after her. I'll make sure your other patients are covered for the rest of your shift.'

The ice cream, in its packet, that Julie was holding, slipped from her hand to land on the linoleum floor as Elsie began walking towards her and Elsie knew she had to scrape up the same kind of courage that she'd needed to stay with Vicky during that dramatic resuscitation attempt.

This was going to be even harder. Elsie was a mother herself and she knew the unbearable level of fear that Julie was already experiencing. She had to let her know that everything possible was being done to save Vicky and she couldn't leave Julie alone for a moment while she waited to see if a miracle might be happening upstairs either. Which meant she'd have to be there if the news was as bad as she feared it might be.

At least Elsie knew she could do this as well as anybody else. Better than some, in fact. Because she was a mother herself. Because she understood the challenges and triumphs of raising a child with special needs and just how much of your life and heart they captured.

She also cared very deeply about her patients and their families. This was why she had been so determined to return to the career she'd loved so much—especially her favourite area of paediatrics. This was the downside of the fun and cuddles that came with letting yourself get so involved with these small, vulnerable patients. It was also, arguably, one of the most important aspects of her job.

Elsie walked to Julie, who was still staring at the closed doors of the lift and the lights above it, showing it had reached its destination. She knew that the operating theatres were on that floor. Her voice was no more than a whisper.

'Was that…?'

'It was a sudden collapse.' Elsie put her arm around the younger woman's shoulders to support her because she could feel the shockwave she was delivering herself. She needed to take her somewhere private and then answer all the questions she could while they waited for an update. 'They're taking Vicky up to Theatre now. They're doing everything they possibly can.'

'I don't understand…' Julie's voice was wooden. 'I was just bringing her an ice cream…'

CHAPTER TWO

THE POPULAR BRANDON HILL PARK was an easy walking distance from Bristol's St Nicholas Children's Hospital in the central city. It was a popular spot with hospital staff who needed a break or wanted to have a picnic lunch outside in nice weather and parents loved it as a place to take their children, thanks to the large sand-pit and play area. Paths led up to the landmark of the Cabot Tower at the top of the hill but there were plenty of bench seats to take a rest and admire the view.

Anthony Morgan wasn't planning to sit anywhere. He just needed a bit of exercise and some fresh air. Day-light was about to start fading so it wasn't the best time to be heading into a central city park, but when he'd got to where his car was parked he'd realised he wasn't ready to go home yet. He needed a distraction from the rawness of what had been a very bad day at work.

Something like the noise and activity of that group of teenagers using the sloping paths to practice their skateboarding skills. The children's playground was de-serted, which wasn't surprising given the time of day, so there was no distraction there, but he could watch the people who were taking their dogs out after they'd been confined all day. Halfway up the grassy hill, a man was throwing a frisbee for an exuberant collie whose joyous barking as he chased the flying toy towards the trees almost brought a smile to Anthony's face.

He paused for a moment to catch his breath when he reached the tower but was about to turn back and retrace his steps when his attention was caught, seeing someone sitting on one of the seats positioned to have the best view.

A woman.

A woman wearing jeans and long boots. As Anthony got a little closer he could see the silvery streaks in her hair and, even though she had her head bent, he recognised her. And he knew exactly why she was sitting here, alone in this park.

Looking rather like he was feeling himself.

As much as he might have preferred to keep himself to himself, the way he did as much as possible out of work hours, he couldn't simply turn away and leave her here. It wasn't a particularly safe place to be for a woman on her own, for one thing. And he knew too much about her for another.

He knew that her day at work had been as bad—if not possibly even worse—than his. For the same reason, which gave them a connection he couldn't ignore. Not only that, she'd been kind to him when he'd been clumsy enough to spill coffee everywhere the other night. Kind people deserved kindness in return.

He walked towards the bench. 'It's Elsie, isn't it?'

Anthony watched as she used the back of her hand to catch a drip from her nose before looking up at him and those tear-drenched, expressive eyes touched some part of his heart that was usually very well protected.

He took the neatly folded handkerchief from the top pocket of his suit jacket and offered it to her but she shook her head.

'It's okay... I've got a tissue somewhere.'

'Please...'

Anthony pressed the handkerchief into her hands and was rewarded with a shaky smile as she accepted it. The vigorous nose blow that followed made him smile as well.

'Mind if I sit down for a minute?' he asked, even though he was already starting to fold his long legs so that he could sit beside her. 'I think we might both need a bit of company, yes?'

She was still clutching his handkerchief. And then she burst into tears all over again.

Oh, dear Lord, how embarrassing was this?

Elsie Henderson wasn't an inexperienced, newly graduated nurse who had yet to learn how to cope with the more difficult aspects of their chosen career. She was fifty-eight years old, for heaven's sake. A mother. A grandmother. Four decades past being a junior nurse who could be excused for falling apart on the job.

Except she wasn't at work. She'd changed out of her scrubs at the end of one of the most difficult shifts she'd ever experienced but couldn't bring herself to go home straight away. Her grandson, Felix, would have sensed how upset she was and how could she tell him that a little girl, who could so easily have been one of his friends from the support group for spina bifida families, had died today. On top of that, her own daughter, Brie, was about the same age as Julie so it had all been far too close to home, and that had made it even more devastating to have been the last person to hold little Vicky while she was still alive. Elsie would be haunted for ever by that whispery voice telling her that her head was going *'roundy roundy...'*

And now here she was, bawling her eyes out in front of the surgeon she'd been trying to avoid for days. Blowing her nose on the pristine square of soft white cotton with a blue stripe around its neatly hemmed edges. Who used real handkerchiefs these days, anyway? And who ironed them for Anthony Morgan? A housekeeper? His wife?

Oh…no… Elsie screwed her eyes shut. There it was again—that thing she knew about him that he had no idea of. It was easy to push aside, however, because there was something she really needed to ask far more than anything she might think she needed to tell.

'Was it a huge mistake, taking her out of bed like that? I was so careful when I picked her up and it was only for a minute or two.' Elsie could feel tears gathering again. 'Could it have been enough to start something bleeding?'

'It's looking as if it could have been an arrhythmia rather than a tamponade that caused the arrest.' Anthony sounded weary. As if he'd been going over and over every detail himself in the hours since his small patient had collapsed? 'We came close to losing her that first night after her surgery because of rhythm issues.'

'I remember,' Elsie said. 'That was the night I found you in the staffroom getting a coffee at five a.m.'

Anthony's nod told her that he hadn't forgotten. 'We might end up not getting a definitive answer on what caused Vicky's death, but there are always risks with major surgery like that and one thing I *can* tell you is that it wasn't caused by anything you did. There was no obvious damage to any of the repairs that were done to her heart. And even if she'd still been in the intensive care unit and hooked up to monitors we would have done exactly what we did on the ward and then in Theatre and I doubt very much that it would have made any difference to the outcome.'

It was comforting to hear the reassurance. Elsie looked up with the intention of thanking Anthony, only to find herself under a steady gaze.

'I remember something else about meeting you the other night.'

To her astonishment, Elsie could feel a bit of warmth colouring her cheeks. She wasn't used to men remembering things about her. It was a little embarrassing to have a man even thinking about her, in fact.

'You told me you were helping raise a grandson with spina bifida.'

'Yes. Felix is six years old. My daughter Brie is a single mum so she's been living with me ever since we knew that there were problems with the pregnancy.'

Anthony's gaze softened. 'Today must have been very hard for you. I'm sorry…'

Elsie nodded. But she could see the lines of stress around his eyes and how weary it made him look. Feeling a bit shy, as if she might be overstepping a boundary, she caught his gaze again. 'For you too,' she said softly.

Anthony didn't say anything but, after a moment's hesitation, he nodded slowly, letting his breath out in a sigh and looking away from her to the view of the city in front of them. Lights were coming on here and there now and it was getting colder. She should be heading home but there was something about that sigh that kept her from moving. She already knew how much this man cared about his patients.

She had seen those lines of weariness in his face before and, okay, it had been after being up all night with Vicky straight after her surgery, but she'd thought at the time that there was something a lot deeper than being overly tired. That he'd looked incredibly sad as well. Lost, even, as he'd stared at a photograph in the newspaper he was holding.

A photograph of his son. A paramedic who'd caught the attention of a journalist by being involved in a mountain rescue. A young man that Elsie knew shared the same surname as this surgeon, but Brie had assured her they weren't related. He'd told her that.

He specifically said he had no family here...

But she'd known there was a connection. Nobody would look like that if it had been a stranger who simply had the same common surname.

'*Do you know him?*' she had asked softly. '*Is he a relative of yours?*'

'Yeah...' That single word had carried an astonishing undertone of pain. '*Jonathon Morgan is my son.*'

How hard would it be to have to tell parents that

they'd lost a child, as he'd had to do with Julie and her husband this afternoon, when he had a son himself, even if there was clearly a difficult relationship between father and son? What was it he'd also said that night?

Oh…yes… How could she have forgotten? He'd said he was sure she wouldn't want to hear about his personal life. And then he'd looked away with a wry smile on his face and dismissed the subject with a throwaway comment about how complicated families could be.

And that comment had been haunting her ever since. It was the reason she'd been trying to avoid Anthony Morgan today, when she had her first day shift after her days off. Even now, despite knowing that he was probably as upset as she was about Vicky, she knew she couldn't tell him what he didn't know. That her daughter would probably never forgive her if she did.

'I should get home,' she heard herself saying. 'Brie will be starting to wonder where I am, even though I warned her I was going to be late.'

'It is getting dark.' Anthony followed her example and got to his feet. 'So I can't let you walk back through the park on your own.' He offered her a smile as they began walking. 'Tell me about Felix,' he invited. 'He's a couple of years older than Vicky, you said?'

Elsie blinked. He remembered more than she would have expected of that first conversation, didn't he?

'He's six,' she confirmed. 'And the degree of his spina bifida is much less severe than Vicky's was. He had in utero surgery to close the defect in his spine when Brie was about twenty-five weeks pregnant.'

'Really? I didn't realise that was happening here then.'

'It wasn't. We had to go to Switzerland. It was about then that I decided to give up work to support Brie.'

'You were nursing at St Nick's then?' They were leaving the shadow of the tower behind them as they went downhill. 'I don't remember seeing you around.'

As if he would, Elsie thought. Women started to become a lot less visible in their forties. By the time they hit their fifties they were pretty much part of the background.

'I was working at Central then, but my first love has always been paediatrics. I had a stint as a general practice nurse too. The hours worked a lot better for me when Brie was at primary school and I was a single mum. It's been a recent thing to go back to nursing but I needed something else in my life and... I'm loving it...' Elsie's voice suddenly wobbled. 'Apart from today...'

'There are always bad days,' Anthony said. 'But, fortunately, they're outweighed by the good ones.' She could hear a smile in his voice. 'And we need nurses like you, Elsie. People that understand what the parents, as much as their children, are going through.'

They walked in silence for a minute or two and then they were out of the gates to the park and on the road leading back to St Nick's.

'How are you getting home?' Anthony asked as they waited for the lights to change and let them cross a busy junction with a group of shops on the other side of the main road. 'Can I offer you a lift?'

Elsie shook her head. 'I have my car at work.'

'And your daughter will be at home when you get there? And Felix?'

'It will be exactly what I need,' she confessed. 'I just needed to get a good cry out of the way before I got there.' She bit her lip, knowing that she was treading on personal ground. 'I hope you've got some company at home too?'

Anthony gave her an odd look. 'I lost my family a very long time ago,' he said quietly.

Elsie knew she shouldn't take an even bigger leap into that personal space but she couldn't fight the urge. Not when she was this emotionally exhausted and couldn't bear the thought that this man who'd been kind enough to offer her comfort—not to mention his hanky—despite being so upset himself, would be going home to an empty house.

'But…' she snatched a breath '…you have a son… Jonno…'

The lights changed and people nearby walked away but Anthony was staring at Elsie and she couldn't move.

'How on earth did you know that?' he asked.

'You told me. When you saw the photograph of him in the paper.'

'But I told you that his name was Jonathon. How did you know Jonno has always been my son's nickname?'

It was too late to stop now. Apparently that step into this personal space was actually the top of a slippery slope that was even steeper than the hill they'd

just come down together. And the emotional conse-
quences after such a traumatic day had done something
more than exhaust Elsie. They'd removed any barriers she'd had about telling Anthony what she knew.
It was suddenly blindingly clear that he had the right
to know, and at the end of a day like this perhaps he
needed to know.

'My daughter knew him,' she heard herself saying
calmly. 'She met him just before he went overseas a
while back. Before…she knew she was pregnant…'

Their chance to cross the road on this cycle had gone
but Anthony didn't seem to have noticed. His gaze was
locked on Elsie's. He might be as tired as she was but
that wasn't stopping his brain from working with im-
pressive speed.

'Are you saying…that my son is the father of your
grandson?'

Elsie took a deep breath. 'Yes,' she said.

Anthony gave his head a tiny shake. 'One of the last
things he said to me was that he was never going to get
married. Or have children. That the last thing he would
ever do would be to live the kind of lie I'd been living.
Unless…' He was frowning now. 'Unless it was history
repeating itself and it was an accident…?'

'It was.' Elsie nodded. 'Brie was on the pill but she
got sick…'

The expression on Anthony's face was unreadable
now. Stunned, even. 'But that means…'

'Yes.' Elsie kept holding his gaze. 'Felix is your
grandson too.'

There were people gathering beside them to wait

for the next window of time to cross the road but Elsie didn't move an inch. She could see the moment that the implications of what she was telling him registered with Anthony. She was getting a glimpse of a part of this man that she instinctively knew was usually kept very private.

Just for a heartbeat she could see the flare of something that looked like longing in his eyes, but then he blinked and it was gone.

'Jonno's not really my son,' he said. 'Not biologically. I just…thought he was until he did a DNA test when he was about eighteen.'

Oh…wow… No wonder she had sensed a whole world of pain beneath his words when he'd seen that picture of his son in the newspaper. It seemed very unfair that a man that Elsie already knew to be kind and caring might have been hurt badly enough to feel the need to deny something that was clearly so important to him.

'You raised him,' she said quietly. 'You loved him. You're his dad and that makes him your son as far as I'm concerned.' She was ignoring the curious glances of strangers moving past them to cross the road as the traffic waited. 'And that also makes Felix your grandson.'

Maybe it was a trick of the light, with darkness falling around them and the traffic light beside them changing colour, but Elsie was almost sure she could see tears in Anthony's eyes now and that pulled her heartstrings so hard she could feel tears of her own gathering again. Without thinking, she put her hand on Anthony's arm, as if she needed to confirm the connection they had. She also wasn't really thinking when she opened her mouth to speak again.

'Would you like to meet him?' she asked.

CHAPTER THREE

It turned out to be remarkably easy.

As if it had been meant to happen?

All it took was for Elsie to suggest a new park to go to on the way home from school. One that had a big sandpit and a climbing frame and a tall tower on top of a hill.

'It's near where Nana works,' she told Felix. 'At your hospital.'

'Do I have to go to hostible again?' Felix had always had trouble with the pronunciation of the institution he'd spent too much time in already in his six years.

'No.' Elsie gave him a cuddle. 'It's just that I went there the other day and it was so nice I thought you might like to see the tower. It might be nice for Dennis to have a new place to walk too, don't you think?'

And how natural did it seem when Nana came across a friend of hers from work who was taking a break that afternoon and just happened to be walking near the play area when they got there?

'I'm pleased to meet you, Felix.' Anthony crouched in front of the small wheelchair so he wasn't towering over the small boy. 'My name's Anthony. And who's this?' He reached out to scratch the ears of the small woolly dog sitting by the chair's footplate.

'Dennis,' Felix told him. 'We've come here to have a walk and go to the playground.' He beamed at Anthony. 'There's a tower here too. On top of the hill. It's really tall.'

'It's an awesome tower.' Anthony returned the smile, the way everybody automatically did when Felix smiled at them, but this time Elsie's heart melted a lot more than usual. Because this man was another grandparent for Felix and she could remember that astonishing joy when she'd held him in her arms for the first time, knowing that he was the child of her child, which made him a part of her own heart. Was Anthony feeling that unique kind of love already? His smile suggested that he was because Elsie had never seen him smile like that before.

And it was a lovely smile. Felix seemed to be basking in it.

'I want to climb it,' Felix confided to Anthony. 'But Nana said maybe not today because my legs might get too tired. That's why we brought my chair. I *can* walk, you know. Would you like to see me climb and go down the slide?'

'I would indeed.'

'You sit there,' Felix commanded, pointing to a bench seat. 'With Nana.' He was climbing out of his wheelchair. 'And Dennis,' he added as an afterthought. 'Because he might think he's at the beach and dig holes in the sand.'

So Elsie and Anthony sat on the bench. Dennis sat beside Elsie's feet and watched the squirrels, who darted closer in the hope of being offered something to eat, but the adults were watching Felix as he made a bee-line towards the climbing frame.

'Is he okay to do that on his own?' Anthony asked.

Elsie nodded. 'He'll be careful. And it's got handrails and those logs for steps on the ramp. He'd hate me to be hovering over him like a helicopter nana, especially when he's arranged a captive audience.'

'He's a happy wee chap.' Anthony seemed to be watching Felix carefully. 'And confident. It doesn't look that easy for him, walking through the sand, but he's not letting it slow him down.' He smiled. 'He reminds me so much of Jonno at that age, which is a bit odd.'

'Well... I had another look at that photograph of Jonno in the paper.' Elsie gave Anthony a quick, shy glance. 'I cut it out to keep for Felix—not that he knows about his father yet. Jonno doesn't know about Felix either, but that's a whole different story.' She shook her head. 'What I was going to say is that I thought you and Jonno look remarkably alike, so it's not surprising that Felix reminds you of your son.'

Anthony shrugged. 'Maybe it's the colouring. Dark hair, dark eyes... I'd always thought he looked far more like me than his mother, but there you go... DNA doesn't lie. And I'd always known it was a possibility.'

Elsie blinked. 'Really?' She turned to check on Felix as he negotiated the ramp of the climbing frame. 'How?'

Anthony was quiet for a moment and then she heard him take a deep breath. 'I guess people don't talk about it so much these days.' He let the breath out in a sigh. 'Maybe it's only me that feels as if the scandal is a permanent shadow over my life.'

'I don't listen to gossip,' Elsie told him. She offered him a smile. 'And you don't have to tell me about it. As far as I'm concerned you're Felix's grandpa and that's all that matters.'

'Except…it isn't, is it?' Anthony's words were quiet. 'It matters that Jonno doesn't know he's a father, doesn't it?'

Elsie nodded. And then she echoed Anthony's sigh. 'I've made my feelings very clear about that to Brie—my daughter—but she says she's got to find the right moment.' She waved at Felix, who'd reached the top of the ramp. 'I should tell you that she did do her best to contact him as soon as she knew she was pregnant but he was long gone. Off to the Himalayas and he never responded to her on social media. And then she found out that her baby had spina bifida and…well…life changed for both of us. Trying to track down someone Brie had only ever been with once didn't seem that important. Especially when nobody knew where he was exactly.'

'He's good at flying under the radar.' Anthony nodded. 'Even when he was still in the UK, I had trouble trying to stay in touch.'

'He's not planning to stay here for long either. Brie says he's going to sell the apartment he owns and then he'll be gone again. For good, this time.'

'Oh…' The syllable was drawn out. As if Anthony had expected little else? Elsie wasn't about to ask, but she had to admit she was curious about what could have caused such a breakdown in the relationship between a father and son. Surely it wasn't only because it was lacking a biological link?

'Brie's worried about how it might affect Felix if

he discovers he has a daddy who then walks out on him and disappears, but I've said that he has the right to know. And that maybe he'll change his mind about going somewhere else when he knows he has a son.' But Elsie was frowning now. 'Have you not heard anything from him since he left? In nearly seven *years*?'

'Longer than that. He pretty much turned his back on me after his mother's death. He blamed me for the accident. For the whole scandal, in fact.'

There was that word again and it just didn't fit with this man who seemed as dignified as the pinstriped suit he was wearing. As caring as the smile he'd given to Felix had suggested? Maybe Elsie's confusion was written all over her face because Anthony made a wry face.

'You should know about it,' he said. 'It's part of what makes this situation so very complicated.'

The shriek of glee from the small boy as he went down the slide was anything but complicated. Felix was living in the moment and having a great time.

'Did you see me, Nana? I went down the slide by myself.'

'I *did* see you, darling. It looked like great fun.'

'I'm going to do it again.' Felix climbed off the slide but found himself behind another child about to climb the ramp. 'When it's my turn…' He was grinning at a girl who was standing behind him now. 'It's the bestest slide, isn't it? What's your name…?'

It wasn't just the colour of his hair or eyes that was reminding Anthony of the son he'd raised.

It was that *charm*…

He was under its spell already himself—even more

than the little girl with pigtails who was watching with open admiration as Felix climbed the ramp again.

'Jonno's mother was a nurse at St Nick's,' he told Elsie, his voice without expression. 'It could be a case of history repeating itself with Jonno, but on my first date with Julia...' he cleared his throat delicately '...we got a little carried away. We went out a few more times over the next month or so and then she told me she was pregnant.' He was silent for a long moment. 'Long story short, we got married. Jonno was born and he was the best thing that had ever happened to me and I did think we could make it work, but I was wrong. I found out Julia was having an affair before he was even a year old, and it was only the first of many.'

'Oh, my goodness...' Elsie sounded horrified. 'But you stayed married to her?'

'We lived in the same house.' Anthony nodded. 'But it was never a real marriage. She didn't need the money—she was wealthy in her own right—but she wanted to be a surgeon's wife and the Morgan name has been well known in certain circles in Bristol for generations. It can open doors no amount of money could have done.' He paused to take a slow breath. 'She would have taken Jonno away from me if I hadn't agreed. I would never have seen him again. Not that I was allowed too much time with him, mind you. He got sent to boarding school at a young age and if she thought he was getting too attached to me when we did get time together, she'd whisk him away on holiday. Somewhere tropical usually, with her latest lover in tow.'

Elsie was silent but he could feel her shock that he would have put up with the situation and, looking back, he felt ashamed. She didn't say anything. She seemed to be focused on Felix, who'd given up on the slide. He was playing in the sand with his new friend with the pigtails. It looked as if they were making roads and using small sticks and stones as cars.

'I spent more and more time at work,' he admitted quietly. 'I didn't want to break up Jonno's family when he was young and have him turned against me but it happened anyway. When Julia was killed in the car accident, it became public knowledge that she was in the car with a man who wasn't her husband and it was big news because he ran one of the biggest national charities and people had all thought he was completely trustworthy. And then it all came out. The string of affairs, including other high-profile men. The discreet apartment she owned that she used as her 'love nest'. The public face she'd maintained in her involvement with all sorts of charities and the glamorous fundraising events she loved. The complete farce of her marriage…'

He took a breath but it was too swift to give Elsie the chance to make any comment. He hadn't got to the part that she probably needed to know.

'Jonno blamed me. He'd adored his mother and had no idea what was really going on. With all the wisdom of a fifteen-year-old, he decided that if I'd been a better husband she wouldn't have gone looking for anyone else. And if I'd been a better father I would have spent more time with him. He was grieving. And he was very angry. He went back to boarding school and when the holidays rolled around there were always friends that invited him to stay. Or go on adventures. He got into skiing in a big way. Rock climbing. Scuba diving. Any sport that created enough adrenaline to distract him, I guess. I encouraged it even because I thought he'd get past it as he grew up a little more, but he refused to ever discuss it. When he was eighteen he inherited the apartment and rather a lot of money from his mother's estate and he moved out. That was when he did the DNA test I told you about.' Anthony's words trailed into silence. He'd said more than enough.

Too much, perhaps? Did Elsie see him as most people had back then—including his son—as being weak? A total failure as a husband and a father? The reason his mother had been unfaithful and, by extension, the cause of her death?

Felix had given up on the game in the sand and he was coming towards them, limping a little.

'I'm hungry, Nana,' he announced.

'So are those squirrels,' Elsie said. 'We must remember to bring them something to eat next time we come.'

Next time? Anthony wanted to catch her gaze in case that was a subtle invitation for them to do this again. He rather hoped it was, but Elsie was making sure Felix was comfortable in his wheelchair.

'I'm a bit hungry myself, come to think about it,' she said. 'How 'bout we go to one of those cafés near where we parked the car and have a treat for afternoon tea? That way, we can put Dennis in the car to wait for us.'

'Can I have a sausage roll?'

'I'm sure they'll have sausage rolls.' Elsie turned to Anthony and her smile suggested that his interpretation of an unspoken invitation to meet again was not wrong. It also told him that she didn't think any less of him after hearing his story. If anything, her smile was even warmer than he'd seen before.

Warm enough to light up tiny golden speckles in those brown eyes that were an unusual colour that made him think of milk chocolate. Or had those flecks been there all along and he just hadn't taken any notice? Like he hadn't noticed that there were parts of Elsie's hair that weren't grey and it was that same shade of brown as her eyes? There were crinkles around her eyes as well that told him she smiled a lot.

Who wouldn't with the joy that her adorable grandson would bring into her life?

Their adorable grandson?

'Come with us,' she invited. 'Do you like sausage rolls too?'

Something was squeezing in Anthony's chest, hard enough to make it hard to take a breath.

'They're my absolute favourite,' he lied. And then he told the truth. 'I'd love to come with you.'

The sausage rolls were hot and savoury and they even had tomato sauce in squeezy plastic tomatoes, which Felix highly approved of.

'It's got a green stalk, just like a *real* tomato.' His tone was awed.

Elsie and Anthony shared a glance. 'I wonder how much of any *real* tomatoes are inside,' she said. The way Anthony quirked his eyebrow made her realise he wasn't about to let anything like nutritional guidelines undermine the sheer pleasure Felix was getting from this treat and she liked that. She could feel the connection growing between this man and his grandson. Between all three of them, in fact, and she liked that too.

She liked it a lot.

The café was not too busy. Two women were carrying plates with wedges of delicious-looking chocolate cake to a nearby table and a man and woman were waiting near the coffee machine having placed a takeaway order. The table closest to the window was ready to be cleared of its crockery but the young woman behind the counter was busy making the coffees. Nobody could have had the slightest idea of what was about to happen in this small café as Elsie tried to collect some of the flaky pastry crumbs that were landing all over Felix's jumper.

It took a moment for Elsie to even process what was happening when the huge glass window shattered with such a loud bang and the whole frontage of the café seemed to be caving in. Both she and Anthony instinctively moved to try and shelter Felix. Elsie was closest and she put her hands on the back of the wheelchair and hunched her body to create a human wall in front of her precious grandson. Then she felt Anthony's arm coming around *her* shoulders. He was trying to protect both of them. From what? A bomb going off?

The thought was so horrific Elsie twisted to try and see and her gaze caught on Anthony's.

'Are you okay?' he asked. 'And Felix?'

'I think so…' Elsie was still stunned. 'Felix? Are you okay, darling?'

Felix nodded. He was trying to peer past his grandmother. 'Look…' He pointed his finger. 'There's a *car… inside…*'

Sure enough, there was a car that had crashed through the plate glass window, demolishing the table that hadn't been cleared so there was now a lot of broken crockery amongst a deep layer of shattered glass on the floor. The man who'd been waiting for his coffee order was holding his arm and had blood dripping from his hand. The two women had completely forgotten about their cake and were staring in shock. A man in a chef's apron came rushing out from the back with a tea towel draped over his shoulder.

'I've called the police,' he shouted. 'And an ambulance. Don't move yet. There's glass everywhere.'

'I'm a doctor.' Anthony stood up. He was moving towards the car.

Elsie could see a dazed-looking elderly man in the driver's seat who appeared to be conscious. She saw the way Anthony scanned the whole scene. He needed to get to the car as fast as possible because the engine was still revving. If the driver put his foot on the accelerator could it come any further inside? Elsie moved to pull Felix's wheelchair further back, wondering if there was a back door in the kitchen that they might be able to escape through.

The flying glass hadn't reached the two women but it had clearly caught the man with the bleeding arm, who was the first person Anthony got to.

'I pulled the glass out,' the man said. 'But it's bleeding too much, isn't it?'

Anthony turned to the chef. 'Can you fold that tea towel to make a pad? That cut needs pressure on it to stop the bleeding. I need to check on the driver. And it might be a good idea if you can all move back a little in case the car gets past whatever's obstructing it.'

Suddenly, Elsie realised that Anthony might be putting himself in danger going anywhere near the car and her own level of alarm increased markedly. What if the car moved and hit him? Or it caught fire? What if the elderly driver had a head injury and became aggressive? Part of her wanted to go and help Anthony but an even bigger part was keeping her where she was, to protect Felix. At least it wasn't going to be long before the experts in dealing with emergencies like this arrived on scene. Amazingly, Elsie could already hear an approaching siren outside.

She backed Felix into what seemed to be a safe corner and decided it was definitely better to stay where they were for the moment. It didn't look as though her first aid skills were going to be needed either, because Anthony seemed to have things under control already. He'd managed to open the driver's door of the car, turn the engine off and he was now crouched beside the elderly man, asking him questions. She saw the man shaking his head as if he had no idea of what was going on and was finding it all very alarming.

There wasn't much left of the front door to the café but that was where Elsie saw the first emergency service personnel arriving only moments later and for a moment she felt as stunned as the elderly driver seemed to be. How on earth could this be happening? It was Felix who knew exactly what was going on.

'*Mumma!*' he shouted. 'Look, Nana…it's *Mumma.*'

Her daughter, Brie, who was a recently qualified paramedic was part of the team responding to this emergency and being found out in what had been supposed to be a secret rendezvous was the last thing Elsie would have wanted to happen. Not that Brie had any idea of what she'd done yet but she was going to find out any minute because, thanks to that picture in the newspaper that had been the catalyst for this meeting in the first place, Elsie had recognised the uniformed man who'd walked in with Brie as being Jonathon Morgan.

Felix's father.

Anthony's son.

It was a ticking emotional time bomb but the only thing Brie was worried about so far was that her son had been part of a traumatic incident. She veered away from Jonno and rushed towards the corner where Elsie and Felix were.

'Mum…what on earth are you doing here? Are you hurt?' Brie dropped to crouch in front of the wheelchair. 'Felix? Are you okay, darling?'

Felix had already climbed out of his wheelchair as he saw his mother coming towards them so he was ready to throw his arms around her neck and be gathered up into a comforting cuddle.

'The car came through the window, Mumma,' he told her excitedly.

'We came to Brandon Hill Park for a walk after school,' Elsie added hurriedly, although the plan of pretending they'd met Anthony Morgan by coincidence was seeming completely unfeasible now. 'It's got a nice playground. Felix got hungry so we thought we'd treat ourselves to afternoon tea.'

'I had a sausage roll, Mumma. And look…the tomato sauce is in a *real* tomato…'

But, having been reassured that both Felix and her mother were unhurt, Brie wasn't listening. She had turned to scan the area and see where she needed to be to be doing her job. Another paramedic was entering the café, carrying more equipment, but it was Jonno that caught both Elsie and Brie's immediate attention.

Elsie knew why Jonno looked so shocked when Anthony stood up from where he'd been crouched beside the driver, with only his back visible, and turned to face Jonno. This was the first time in so many years that father and son had even seen each other, let alone be standing with only a matter of inches between them.

In that moment, Anthony must have realised that there was going to be a price for Elsie to pay for having arranged their meeting because his gaze flew to meet hers and, even from this distance, she could see understanding, if not an apology, being offered. She could also hear the icy anger in Jonno's voice in the first, fierce words he said to his father.

'What the *hell* is going on here?'

Brie was hurriedly putting Felix back into his wheelchair. The other paramedic was moving in to help Jonno and Anthony was stepping back.

'What *is* going on, Mum?' Brie demanded. 'Who is that man? Someone said he's a doctor, so what's so wrong about him helping the driver of that car?'

'Nothing,' Elsie confirmed. 'He *is* a doctor. He's Anthony Morgan. He's also Jonno's father,' she added, quietly enough not to distract Felix from his fascinated attention on what was happening near the car. 'He... um...wanted to meet his grandson.'

She could see the shock of Brie realising what had been going on. The shock of feeling completely betrayed was only a heartbeat later and Elsie's heart sank like a stone. She'd known she was taking a risk but she'd thought it would all come right with a bit of time. After Brie had done what should have been done already and told Jonno that he was Felix's father?

The choice of when that happened had just been taken away from her, hadn't it?

'How *could* you?' Brie's tone was like a physical blow. 'Take Felix home, please.'

'But…'

'*Now*…' Brie ignored her mother and touched her son's head. 'I'll see you soon, but I've got work I have to do right now.' She walked away, towards the man with the bloodstained tea towel. 'Can I see your arm?' Elsie heard her ask. 'How did your injury happen?'

Anthony was beside them again.

'I'm so sorry,' Elsie said. 'We shouldn't have come here.'

'I'm glad we did,' Anthony said calmly. 'But I do think it's time we left. Let me help you get Felix back to your car.'

Firemen helped lift the wheelchair over the debris and onto the footpath outside. A police officer took their details and told them that they would be contacted soon to make a statement about what they'd witnessed. Someone lifted the bright yellow and black tape that was keeping spectators away from an emergency scene and, only a few minutes later, Anthony was helping Elsie lift Felix into his car seat and fold the wheelchair to go in the back of her hatchback.

'What about the man?' Felix asked when Anthony leaned down to say goodbye.

'What man?' It was Elsie who answered. Quickly,

in case it somehow slipped out that Felix had just seen the father he didn't know he had.

'The man in the car? Was he dead?'

'No, no...' It was Anthony who provided instant reassurance. 'He wasn't really hurt at all because he was wearing his seat belt and the airbag in the car protected him as well. He was a bit confused about what had happened and I think that was because he'd put his foot on the wrong pedal and gone faster instead of stopping.' He was smiling at Felix. 'But don't you worry. Nothing really bad happened and it's all going to be okay.'

His smile faded as he straightened to catch Elsie's gaze, however.

They both knew that something had happened. Something that had nothing to do with a confused elderly man who'd put his foot on the wrong pedal.

Something that was going to change the lives of everybody involved.

And...it might not turn out to be okay at all...

CHAPTER FOUR

'ARJUN, PUT THAT down right now! The nurse wants to take your temperature.'

The eight-year-old boy made a frustrated sound but obeyed his mother and put his tablet down reluctantly. 'But I'll miss my frog's heart dividing, Mummy. It's going to have three chambers now.'

'You know this game off by heart, Arjun.' His mother, Shayana, was shaking her head but her smile was proud.

'I've got four chambers in my heart, haven't I, Elsie?'

'You certainly have.' Elsie looked down at the screen as she put the tip of the tympanic thermometer in Arjun's ear and pressed the button. 'That looks like a great game. I bet my grandson Felix would absolutely love it.'

'I can dissect my frog. I'll show you.'

But Elsie caught his arm. 'In a minute, sweetheart. Your doctor's coming to see you any time now and if I haven't done your blood pressure and heart rate and everything else, he'll growl at me.'

'Will he?' Arjun's face lit up in a smile. 'Mummy growls at me a lot.'

'I do not,' Shayana protested. 'He's such a good boy,' she told Elsie. 'How could I growl at him a lot?'

Elsie smiled as she fitted her stethoscope to her ears. 'See how quiet you can be for just a bit, Arjun. I need to be able to listen so I can hear your blood pressure.' She could almost feel the little boy bursting with impatience as she inflated the cuff around his arm and then let it down slowly.

'Can you really hear my blood?' he demanded as soon as she lifted the disc of the stethoscope from his arm. 'What sort of noise does it make?'

'Dub-dub-dub...' Elsie told him. 'It's part of the same noise your heart makes, which is lub-dub, lub-dub, lub-dub...'

Arjun laughed and mimicked the sound, bouncing up and down on his bed at the same time, but Elsie could see his mother wiping tears from her eyes.

'You can play your game again now,' she told Arjun. Then she reached for the chart on the end of his bed to record her observations and spoke quietly to Shayana. 'Are you okay?'

She nodded. 'I'm just so happy,' she whispered. 'It was such a big operation and it was only last week and look at him now...'

'Come and see,' Arjun commanded. 'I'm going to start the dissection of my frog now.'

'A dissection? Goodness me, what's going on in here?'

They all turned to see Arjun's surgeon come into the room with one of his registrars and what looked to be some medical students who were observing his ward round this morning. Anthony Morgan's smile was

most likely the kind he gave all his small patients and
their mothers but, because Elsie was standing beside
Shayana, she got the full benefit as well and her day
instantly got a little brighter.

Hurriedly, she began filling in the empty spaces on
Arjun's chart with the latest recordings but Anthony
didn't need it yet. He was sitting on the side of the bed
looking at the screen of the tablet with great interest.

Arjun wasn't at all bothered by how many people
had just come into his room. He was focused on his surgeon. 'So I pin him like this.' Arjun tapped the screen
on several points. 'And then I can cut his skin and fold
it back and see all his organs. See?'

'Wow...' Anthony looked suitably impressed. 'I think
you'll be doing my job in no time flat. Has your frog
got a heart?'

'Of course. I'll find it for you. I can even take it out
and put it on the tray.'

'You do that while we talk about you for a minute,
okay? These visitors are learning to be doctors and
someone like you is very interesting for them to know
about.'

Arjun nodded absentmindedly. He was busy with
the game that was directing which organs he needed
to find first.

'Arjun is just over a week post-op now after coronary
artery bypass graft surgery to repair a giant coronary
artery aneurysm,' Anthony told the students. 'And, as
you can see, he's doing very well.' He caught Elsie's
gaze. 'Are you happy with him this morning?'

'I am,' she responded. 'All his vital sign recordings
are within normal parameters. There are no issues with

his cardiac rhythm or his fluid balance, there's no sign of infection in his wound and he hasn't needed any pain relief except for the paracetamol.'

'I'll let my registrar fill you in on Arjun's past medical history,' Anthony said to the students. 'I'm just going to have a quick read of the notes made since I saw him yesterday.' He stepped closer to Elsie.

'Okay…' His registrar, Ruth, stepped to the other side, nearer the students. 'So Arjun got Kawasaki disease when he was five months old and, despite aggressive therapy, he had an acute infarct three weeks later. He was in hospital for nearly three months.'

Arjun was completely engrossed in his game but his mother was listening to the recap. 'That was such a terrible time for the whole family,' she whispered.

'It must have been,' Elsie sympathised. Anthony flashed a glance at her, looking up from the notes. He knew she wasn't having the best time herself right now, with her own family. He'd been checking in when they found a quiet moment on his ward visits and, to be honest, it had been a relief to have somebody to talk to about what was going on in her private life so Elsie knew she'd probably told him more than he actually wanted to know.

Brie was still absolutely furious with her for having engineered that meeting between Anthony and his grandson. Mother and daughter were barely talking to each other right now and Brie had even made a comment about it being ridiculous to be her age and still living with her parent and maybe it was time she started looking for her own home.

'So Arjun was carefully monitored by Cardiology

and the cardiothoracic surgical teams throughout his childhood but CABG could be postponed until his arteries were larger because he was getting a good blood supply from collateral vessels.' Ruth didn't have to look at their patient's notes. She had done her homework well. 'The latest round of tests showed extensive ischaemia, however,' she continued. 'We found a complete occlusion of his left anterior descending artery and ST depression on a ECG treadmill test so we decided it was time for the surgery. Are you all familiar with the process of coronary artery grafting?'

The students all nodded. 'What vessel was used for the graft and how many vessels were grafted?' one asked.

'Two vessels grafted.' Anthony rejoined the conversation. 'And current practice is to use internal thoracic arteries as conduits for coronary bypass grafting in children with Kawasaki disease. They show significantly better results in long-term functionality.' He glanced up at the clock. 'How 'bout you talk about this more with these guys on your way upstairs, Ruth? I'll see you up there shortly, but it could take a while to get everybody sorted for their Theatre observation session. You could give them a bit of a tour of the Theatre suite if you have time.'

The rattle of the food trolley delivering lunch could be heard as the students followed Ruth into the corridor. Anthony hooked the chart back on the bed and smiled at Arjun.

'I can hear your lunch arriving. Can I have a quick look at your zipper before it gets here?'

Arjun grinned and unbuttoned his pyjama top to

show off the sutures in the middle of his chest beneath the clear plastic dressing. Again, just for a heartbeat, Anthony Morgan's gaze caught Elsie's and she knew they were both thinking of the same thing.

Vicky…

And maybe that was why, when Anthony had completed a swift check of Arjun's progress and moved aside to let his mother bring in the lunch tray, he smiled at Elsie.

'Got time for a coffee? There's another patient I'd like to talk to you about.'

'Go,' Shayana said to Elsie. 'I can give Arjun his lunch. You didn't even get morning tea, I don't think.'

'Are you sure you've got time?' Elsie asked as she followed Anthony into the corridor. 'There are some eager students waiting for you to demonstrate your skills upstairs.'

'It's their first time anywhere near a theatre. They'll be so excited, it'll take ages to get them kitted out. My patient isn't even due to leave the ward for at least half an hour. And I could really use a coffee.'

'Me too. Shayana's right, it's been so busy I haven't even sat down for five minutes yet.'

Moments later, they were both sitting in the same armchairs they had used the night they'd first met. The pile of folded newspaper on the table looked the same. The coffee tasted exactly the same. What was very different, however, was how comfortable they were with each other, even after the tension of what had happened in the café that day. Maybe it was actually because of it? There was no hesitation on Elsie's part to ask a personal question today when they found they had the staffroom to themselves.

'Has Jonno been in touch with you yet?'

Anthony shook his head. 'I don't really expect him to be,' he admitted. 'He's got a lot on his plate, hasn't he? How has he taken the news that he's a father, do you know?'

'Brie's still not really talking to me,' Elsie told him. 'But I do know that he's spent some time with Felix. He went to a session at Riding for the Disabled and I think he's going to a music and movement class with them this week. I can't ask Brie. I've already interfered too much.' She sipped her coffee and then sighed. 'It's all a bit miserable, to be honest. I get the feeling that she's got some pretty deep feelings for Jonno but I doubt very much that he feels the same way. He's a bit of a lone wolf, isn't he?'

Anthony made a sympathetic sound. 'I can't imagine he's finding any of this easy. Relationships can be so very complicated, can't they?'

Elsie's smile was wry. 'Sometimes I'm rather thankful I'm single.'

'Me too.'

'Really?' Elsie blinked. She'd certainly got the impression that Anthony lived alone, but that didn't necessarily mean he didn't have a partner.

'Really,' Anthony said firmly. 'Once was more than enough for me. Marriage was certainly nothing like I hoped it would be.' He lifted an eyebrow. 'Were you a single mother by choice?'

'Oh, no...my husband died just before Brie was born.'

'I'm sorry to hear that.'

'I was lucky that looking after my baby got me through the worst thing that had ever happened to me. It might have only been a short marriage but it was perfect.'

Anthony drained his coffee mug and got to his feet. 'You were lucky to have had that,' he murmured. He lifted an eyebrow before he turned. 'I'm surprised someone hasn't come along and swept you off your feet since, though.'

Elsie laughed. 'I'm way past any nonsense like that.'

Anthony was smiling as well. 'It's rather nice, isn't it?'

'What? Being single?'

'Being past all that angst.'

'Yes. I feel rather sorry for Jonno at the moment.'

The glance they shared was one of mutual agreement—that it was a relief not to have to deal with the emotional upsets that romantic relationships could bring—but it was a fleeting moment of connection as a nurse poked her head around the door.

'Ah…someone said you might be in here, Mr Morgan. You wouldn't have a minute to talk to Penelope's mum, would you? She's got herself in a bit of a state about her upcoming surgery.'

'No problem. I'll be right there.' Anthony picked up his empty mug. 'Have you met Penny? Three-year-old with hypoplastic left heart syndrome? She's in for a cardiac catheter before her Fontan procedure later this week. It's not as risky as the first operation she had as a newborn but it's still a pretty big deal. I'm not surprised her mum's finding it difficult.'

Elsie held out her hand to take Anthony's mug. 'I can

rinse that. You go. Families are our patients too, aren't they? Oh…was Penny the other patient you wanted to talk to me about?'

'No…' Anthony's smile was a little embarrassed. 'That was just an excuse to have a chat.' He turned to leave but then turned back. 'Don't feel too sorry for Jonno,' he said quietly. 'The timing might not have been the best but he needed to know and I'm sure Brie will understand that eventually. And please don't be sorry that you let me meet Felix. I'm really hoping that we can do that again when things settle down a little.'

Elsie rinsed the mugs and slotted them into the dishwasher. She'd been completely honest when she'd told Anthony she was past even thinking about bumping into her soulmate and being swept off her feet to fall hopelessly in love. So why did it feel as if her heart was beating a little faster than normal right now?

Or that being told he'd invented a reason to have a chat with her was giving her an odd curl of pleasure?

That the thought of spending time with him again made that rather pleasant sensation even more noticeable?

And that the fact that he was single had suddenly become far more significant than it had any right to be?

A Fontan procedure was the third major surgery in the series for children who had been born with only one ventricle instead of two, which meant that the way the blood circulated had to be drastically altered if the baby was going to survive. The initial, and most risky, operation could take six to eight hours and usually happened in the first week of life. A second surgery happened at around six months of age and was an intermediary stage before the third, Fontan procedure, that created a way for deoxygenated blood to bypass the heart completely and go straight to the lungs, which decreased the workload in a single ventricle and could dramatically improve the quality of life for the child.

Anthony Morgan was a very well-respected, experienced cardiac surgeon across the entire spectrum of congenital, paediatric and adult cardiac surgery and the Fontan procedure was one of his favourites. He'd been part of the lives of these children since they were born and had a vital role in supporting their families. It was a long and complex enough surgery to shrink the world down to purely what was happening within the four walls of an operating theatre and that had always been the place Anthony felt most at home in. His happy place, where anything personal was irrelevant and he could focus purely on the job at hand—a job he knew he was good at which made him confident and calm, despite any emotional involvement with his patients and how invested he was in getting a successful result.

Oh, things could get tense, of course. There were often complications to manage during and after the surgery where a major blood vessel got disconnected from the heart and joined to the pulmonary artery, with a connection created that would control the flow of blood to the lungs until the body adjusted to the new anatomy. Occasionally a battle was lost, along with a young life, and that was deeply upsetting.

Anthony had never had a post-op disruption quite like the one he got today, however, when he finally turned his phone back on after seeing Penny transferred from Recovery to the PICU, to find a voicemail waiting for him.

One that had been left a few hours ago now.

Hearing his son's voice on the recording was enough to make him catch his breath. Hearing a siren in the background, along with Jonno's words, made it impossible to let it go.

'Hi, Dad. It's Jonno. The operator put me through to your phone when she found out you were in Theatre. I'm on my way to St Nick's with Felix. He's had a seizure. He's still having one, actually. We've got him intubated to protect his airway.' There was a long moment's silence and Anthony could almost feel the struggle his son was having to find the words to say something else. And perhaps he gave up.

'… I just thought you should know…'

Sitting beside her precious grandson, who had a ventilator breathing for him as he lay in the intensive care unit waiting for decisions to be made in the next stage of his treatment, made Elsie Henderson feel like this had been one of the longest ever days in her life and it wasn't even lunchtime yet.

That dreadful call from Brie to tell her they were on the way in to the hospital had been hours ago now but it felt a lot longer. Being in here alone while Brie and Jonno were talking to Felix's neurosurgeon had made the minutes drag past even more slowly, especially when it seemed that Brie had been gone for too long. Her daughter's face was so pale when she returned that Elsie felt as if her heart was breaking. She was holding Felix's hand with one of hers and she stretched the other towards her daughter to draw her closer.

'We've signed the consent forms,' Brie told her. 'They'll be getting Felix ready any time now to go up to Theatre. They have to take the shunt that drains the cerebral spinal fluid out so they can treat the infection that's causing all the problems.'

Elsie nodded. And swallowed hard. 'Where's Jonno?'

'In the relatives' room. He's talking to his father and I knew how important it was so I left them alone. Oh...' Brie turned her head. 'Here they come now...'

The concern in Anthony's eyes as he came into the room was almost like a physical touch for Elsie.

A hug?

'I thought you might need a bit of a break,' he said as Elsie stepped back to let both Jonno and Brie get closer to their son. 'A coffee down in the cafeteria, perhaps? My afternoon outpatient clinic doesn't start for a while yet.'

Felix's neurosurgeon came into the room at that moment, with a nurse carrying a kidney dish with drug ampoules and syringes in it. Elsie knew they would be in the way as things got busier so she touched Brie's shoulder.

'We won't be far away,' she said. 'Just send a text if you need us.'

Us...

Even walking away from her daughter, Elsie wasn't alone in dealing with this crisis, was she? It was a very new feeling, knowing that there were now other people who would be in Felix's life. Caring about him. Caring about *her*, even?

It felt as if their family was magically becoming bigger. Stronger.

This new circle of caring went both ways too. Anthony was looking pale, Elsie thought. Shocked, even, and she had room in her heart to be concerned for how he might be feeling right now. He was seeing his son for the first time in many years. He had a grandson he'd only just discovered, but there was a possibility he could lose both of them in the blink of an eye.

He needed support as much as any of them so Elsie found a soft smile for Anthony as she followed him out of the unit. She even touched his arm to give them a physical connection for a moment—because the emotional connection they had right now was verging on being overwhelming.

'Do you think they'll have any sausage rolls in our cafeteria?' she asked.

St Nick's cafeteria did have sausage rolls, along with little mince pies and tiny quiches in the glass-fronted cabinets for hot food.

'No squeezy plastic tomatoes for the sauce.' Anthony handed Elsie a small plastic sachet. 'I don't think Felix would approve.'

He'd put cups of coffee on the tray as well as a hot snack for himself but it turned out that they weren't remotely hungry after all. Elsie found herself blinking back tears as she remembered going to the café with Anthony and Felix and how special it had been until her world had quite literally started crashing into chaos around her.

'I thought everything was coming right too,' she told

Anthony. 'Last night, Brie and I were talking properly for the first time in so long. She told me that Jonno had gone to that music and movement class with Felix and then they went and had hamburgers together afterwards and she said there was a rumour that he might be applying for a permanent job in Bristol and...' she had to swallow hard '... I started thinking that it was the right time to tell him that he has a daddy. And a grandpa...'

'It will be,' Anthony said quietly. 'Soon.'

'But he's so sick... I had no idea. He was a bit off-colour yesterday and we thought he was coming down with something. Brie thought she should stay home with him when he didn't seem any better this morning but I still thought it was just a cold, which was why I agreed to fill a gap in the roster here instead of staying home with them both.' She dragged in a shaky breath. 'I'm so worried about him...'

'I know. But Jonno tells me his team are confident they're going to get on top of this. They'll take the shunt out and treat the infection with antibiotics. When he's recovered enough, they're looking at a procedure which could mean he won't need another shunt. He's in exactly the right place to get the treatment he needs, Elsie. He's got both his parents with him.' Anthony seemed to be blinking as if he needed to clear moisture from his eyes. 'And both his grandparents. I'm his grandfather...' he added slowly, his tone almost surprised.

'Of course you are,' Elsie said.

'No... I really *am* his grandfather, I think. Jonno told me that he never actually did a DNA test—he just said he did because he was so angry with me back then. Brie was there in the relatives' room at the time and she said she'd always thought Felix looked like Jonno and now she can see the Morgan genes even better. She said we were like peas in a pod with us all having the same eyes.'

'You do,' Elsie said softly. 'And they're lovely eyes. Such a warm, dark brown.' She looked away quickly then, suddenly realising she'd been holding Anthony's gaze far longer than was polite. And what on earth had prompted her to say something as personal as that?

Anthony didn't seem as if he'd noticed, but maybe that was why he glanced at his watch and made an excuse to leave. 'I should probably go and get on with my clinic,' he said. 'If you'll be okay?'

Elsie nodded. 'I need to ring my neighbour so she can let Dennis out for a bit. And then I should stay close to Brie. I know she's got Jonno's support but we've been here before, waiting for Felix to get out of Theatre and... it's not easy.'

'I know.' This time it was Anthony who made a physical connection by touching Elsie's arm. 'I'll pop in later, when I can.'

Anthony could see how exhausted Elsie was when he made a final visit late that evening.

'You really should go home and get a decent sleep,' he told her. 'Felix is stable now. His temperature's coming down. He's probably going to wake up tomorrow morning and surprise us all with how well he's doing.'

'I'm okay. When Brie gets back from having some dinner I'll go and have a lie down on the couch in the relatives' room.'

But Brie didn't think much of that idea when she came back into the room with Jonno.

'Go home, Mum,' she said. 'I'll call you if anything changes, I promise.'

Jonno could obviously also see how tired Elsie was. 'Are you okay to drive?' he asked. 'I could call you a taxi.'

'There's no need for that,' Anthony said. 'I'm heading home myself and I can drop you off, Elsie.'

The neat little end-of-terrace house with its pretty garden looked like just the kind of family home he would have wished for his grandson to be living in. And how lucky was Felix to not only have a devoted mother but a grandmother who was such an important part of his life.

'Thank you so much.' Elsie undid her seat belt as she spoke but her movement wasn't enough distraction to hide the wobble in her voice and there was enough light from the streetlamp down the road for Anthony to see that her cheeks were wet. Was that why she'd been so quiet on the drive home? Had she been crying the whole way?

When she shook her head it seemed like a response to his unspoken question.

'It's just the thought of going inside to an empty house,' she said. 'But I'll be fine. Dennis is there and... sometimes a dog can be the company you need most of all.'

'Would you like me to come in with you?' Anthony unclipped his own seat belt.

Elsie seemed to have gone very still as she met his gaze. 'That's very sweet of you, but honestly, I'll be fine.'

Anthony held her gaze, trying to gauge whether or not he should insist on making sure she really was going to be fine. He'd hate the thought of her going inside to cry alone with only the company of a small dog who couldn't possibly understand. Seeing the glimmer of those tears on her face was reminding him of when he'd found her in the park. When she'd touched a part of his heart he'd almost forgotten existed. Before he'd even learned of the connection they had. And now, thanks to Elsie, his son was talking to him again and he could see a future in which he wasn't entirely alone and that was making that part of his heart expand so much it almost felt as if it could break.

Perhaps that was why he felt compelled to reach out and use the pad of his thumb to brush some of those tears away from Elsie's eyes. To smile at her to try and convey how much she'd changed his life—in a good way—in such a short period of time.

She still hadn't broken their eye contact. She did move, just a little, by leaning her face into his hand so that he found himself cupping her cheek. He brushed away another streak of moisture, following the silvery track down to the corner of her mouth.

Maybe it was the way her lips parted slightly at his touch. Or the way her gaze was still holding his own. Perhaps it was just because it was the end of an astonishingly emotional, exhausting day and being even closer to another human being was irresistible.

Whatever the reason, the pull seemed to be mutual as Anthony leaned towards Elsie. And she leaned towards him? His fingers were still touching her face, cradling her chin as he got even closer.

Close enough to brush her lips with his own.

To close his eyes for a brief but oh, so delicious moment as he let time stop and the brush of contact became a real kiss.

CHAPTER FIVE

THERE WERE SOME lines in life that were an invisible boundary that couldn't be *un*crossed once you stepped over them.

You could pretend that nothing significant had happened—the way both Elsie and Anthony did in the wake of that late-night kiss in the car. It hadn't been long enough or passionate enough to qualify as being significant, had it? It had simply been a moment of comfort in the wake of a very intensely emotional day for both of them. Elsie had even managed to summon an embarrassed laugh as she offered a reason for that unexpected line-crossing.

'I think I need to stop crying all over you...'

'We're family now. Kind of...friends, at least?'

And there it was. A new line that felt safe.

'Definitely friends. And yes...if we share a grandchild, that does make us family, doesn't it?'

'It does indeed. So you can cry on my shoulder any time, Elsie.'

'Nope. Not going to happen again.'

'Okay...'

The echo of that awkward conversation was at the

back of Elsie's mind as she opened a cupboard to find her best—and largest—oven dish to put together one of her most familiar recipes because this was more than the usual family-sized lasagne. There were visitors coming to her house tonight.

New friends. Except, despite what Anthony had said that night, it was a lot more than friendship, really. Complicated bonds were being renewed, or formed, on all sorts of levels and Elsie was thinking about them as she layered her savoury meat sauce with sheets of pasta, grated cheese and béchamel sauce.

The line that the kiss between Elsie and Anthony had crossed wasn't the only one in the roller coaster that had started for both the Hendersons and the Morgans when Felix got sick enough to be rushed into hospital. Felix was blissfully unaware of some of the significant changes happening around him as Jonno began reconnecting with a father he hadn't ever been able to get really close to, at the same time as recognising how deeply in love he was with Brie. As far as six-year-old Felix was concerned, he'd wished upon a star and got the daddy he already loved and that was enough to make him the happiest small boy in the world. He not only had a daddy, he now had a grandpa as well.

He bounced his way back to being well enough to have a procedure that meant he didn't need to have another shunt inserted to drain excess cerebral spinal fluid and he was back home within a couple of weeks as everybody tried to get used to the new normal of those adjusted lines.

Jonno had started his new job with a helicopter rescue service by the time Felix had recovered enough to go back to school and he and Brie began coordinating their rosters so that they could spend as much time as possible with their son, to cover child care, medical appointments and therapy sessions or to be together to enjoy this special time of bonding as a new family.

Anthony had already decided it was time for him to downsize and, as he and Jonno got a little more comfortable with each other, an offer he'd made to let Jonno, Brie and Felix take over ownership of the old family home in a lovely, leafy suburb of Bristol was reconsidered and finally accepted.

To outward appearances, Elsie seemed to be the least affected. She wasn't changing her job or adjusting to new, important relationships like gaining a parent or a committed partner and she didn't need to deal with the disturbance of moving to a new home. If anything, life was being made easier for her because Jonno's involvement meant less responsibilities in Felix's life. She was being given more freedom to do whatever she wanted to do with her own life. She could work more hours at St Nick's or take on some volunteer work with children or, perhaps for the first time in her life, focus on herself and not working nearly so hard.

With a final grating of Parmesan cheese and some slices of tomato for decoration, Elsie slid the heavy dish into the oven to bake. She had a green salad to toss now and some garlic bread to make but she found herself pausing for a moment with a long baguette in one hand and a bread knife in the other.

It was a bit daunting to know that she would be living alone in a matter of only weeks. Even Dennis was leaving. Not only because both the little dog and Felix would pine without each other but he would be living with a wonderful big garden to play in and close to the forest park with endless exciting walks. Elsie needed to swallow the lump in her throat and get on with slicing the bread and spreading garlic butter. She wasn't losing the people she loved the most, was she? She was gaining more family, with a son-in-law she was coming to be very fond of and a…a co-grandparent. A friend who was also a colleague.

A doctor that Elsie had enormous respect for. A person she liked very much. The man who'd kissed her…

Not that there had been the slightest hint that Anthony had even given that friendly kiss another thought but, despite the visible drama of life changing so much for the people around her, Elsie was very aware that, while it might be completely invisible to others, something fundamental had changed for her as well.

They might have both been relieved to dismiss that kiss as simply a moment of comfort between friends but Elsie knew, for her, it was more than that. Because she couldn't forget about it. Sometimes, she even found herself touching her lips against her forefinger—a gentle touch that was no more than a brush but the ability that it had to retrieve the memory of Anthony's kiss didn't seem to fade. Worse, Elsie could also remember the way she'd felt just before he'd kissed her. When he'd been brushing those tears from her face and looking at her like that…

When she'd realised how much she'd *wanted* him to kiss her…

It had been years since Elsie had been kissed on her lips but it had been a very much longer time since it had had this kind of effect on her. Not since she'd been younger than Brie, in fact. Before tragedy and the busyness of life apparently stifled the ability to feel…

…attraction?

No. It felt like more than that. It was an awareness that wasn't going away. If anything, although Elsie was more than capable of keeping it completely hidden, it was getting stronger. Things were getting back to normal, with Felix back at school and Elsie back at work, but how she felt whenever she saw Anthony on the ward was anything *but* normal.

She noticed so many things about him now, like the colour of the shirt and tie he'd chosen to wear that day and the way he'd combed his hair to tame the waves. She could gauge the warmth of his smile so easily when he greeted her and that tiny beat of time that he held eye contact with her was definitely longer than you would with a colleague. Or even a friend?

She was also very aware that even thinking about that eye contact could make her aware of her heartbeat and that tingle of sensation that seemed ridiculous for a woman her age to be feeling.

Yeah…it was more than attraction. Elsie had to admit that she fancied Anthony Morgan. For the first time in… good grief, it felt like for ever—she had wanted to be kissed. She *still* wanted to be kissed.

Okay…a whole lot more than kissed.

How unfortunate was it that the man who'd sparked this level of desire was the one man she couldn't possibly consider going to bed with, even if he found her attractive. He was Jonno's father—a man who was now her daughter's chosen life partner, which made him pretty much her son-in-law.

Judging by the bottle of expensive French champagne Jonno was carrying when he arrived with Brie, bringing Felix back from his riding lesson that they all loved attending, the 'pretty much' part of that designation was about to change.

They all looked happy enough to burst.

And Brie had a sparkling new ring on *that* finger.

'We've got news,' Jonno confirmed, heading towards the fridge with the bottle. 'But we'd better put this on ice until Dad gets here.'

They were engaged.

To be married.

The son who'd told Anthony so many years ago that he wasn't going to follow in his father's footsteps and risk living the kind of lie his parents' marriage had been was grinning from ear to ear as he told the story of how Felix had helped him propose to Brie during his riding lesson that afternoon.

'We'd made a plan, Felix and me,' Jonno told them. 'Because we decided that if I'm his daddy and Brie's his mummy and we're all going to be living together in our new house very soon, then it would be a good idea if we got married before then.'

Anthony caught Elsie's gaze and he could see a reflection of his own surprise at how fast things were moving. Jonno and Brie were planning to move into the old Morgan homestead as soon as he moved out, which was only a matter of a few weeks away. Neither of them wanted to interrupt the storytelling by pointing that ticking clock out, however.

'So Felix had the ring hidden inside his boot,' Jonno continued. 'He told his mum that he might have a stone in his shoe which was making it hard to ride so she took it off while he was sitting on Bonnie and…'

'And she said, "How on earth did this get in here?"' Felix was trying to mimic the surprise in Brie's voice but it made him laugh.

'I realised what it was,' Brie said softly. 'And then I couldn't say anything at all.'

'I wasn't going to get down on one knee. Because… you know, what horses do all over the place.'

His wide eyes made Felix giggle again but then he straightened his face and his back as he shared his important role. 'But I told her that if my daddy and my mummy are taking me and Dennis to live in the big house then we were going to be a real family like my friend Georgia, and *her* mummy and daddy are *married.*'

'And I said I thought that was a very good idea if that was really what Jonno wanted,' Brie continued.

'And I said I've never wanted anything as much as this,' Jonno finished quietly. 'Except, perhaps, for Felix to get better when he was sick.'

He caught Anthony's gaze then, as if he was thinking of adding something else to that list. Like wanting to build on this new relationship he was finding with his own father? One that encompassed an adult understanding of how complicated things had been and a forgiveness that could allow them both to build something new. Better, even? Anthony had a lump in his throat that was making it a little difficult to swallow. He wanted that himself. Very much.

He had Elsie Henderson to thank for it even being possible to happen and her daughter to thank for making his son look happier than he'd ever seen him look. Ever…

Anthony had to clear his throat to try and get rid of that lump. He needed to distract himself from an emotional overload as well.

'I *am* better,' Felix said helpfully. 'And we're going to be a *real* family. You can come and live there too, can't you, Nana?'

Anthony took another sip of his champagne as Elsie responded carefully, getting up to check on whatever was in the oven and was filling the kitchen with a very delicious aroma.

'We've talked about this, darling, remember? I'll come and visit but you're going to be living in your special house with Mummy and Daddy and Dennis. I'm going to stay in my wee house here.'

'So Grandpa's coming to live here with you?'

Everybody laughed but Anthony could hear the embarrassment in Elsie's voice as she spoke hurriedly.

'No…your grandpa's found a lovely new apartment he's going to move into soon.'

Anthony was quite certain she was deliberately avoiding looking at him and that made him wonder if she wanted to avoid eye contact because she was thinking about what he was thinking about.

That kiss…

He still wasn't quite sure how it had happened. And

he had no idea why it was so difficult to dismiss as nothing more significant than, say…a hug between friends.

No, that wasn't true, was it?

He knew perfectly well why he'd remembered it every time he'd seen Elsie since then. And quite a few times when she wasn't anywhere near him.

He was attracted to her, that was why.

And it had only taken a brush of their lips to let him know that there was something very different about her. Something very desirable but also totally inappropriate, given that their children were about to marry each other. But they could be friends and he would make sure that she felt safe with him. It would be nice if they could both forget about that moment in the car that night as well. A distraction might help?

'It's not that much time to plan a wedding. Let me know if there's anything I can do to help.'

'It's not going to be a big wedding,' Brie said. 'It's just for us. We're going to find a celebrant and have a very simple ceremony—maybe at the beach or a nice garden. Felix will be there, of course, and we're really hoping you will both be able to come. We just need to look at rosters and find the first date that suits everybody.'

Anthony cleared his throat again. 'Are you going to get away for a honeymoon?'

'Not for a while.' Jonno shook his head. 'We think we'll get through the messy business of moving first and then we'll get settled into being a family and then we can all go on honeymoon together in a few months.'

'What a lovely idea.' Elsie was bustling about. She put a huge bowl of fresh green salad on the table and opened a long foil package and fragrant steam came from the hot garlic bread. Then she put on mitts and turned back to the oven. 'Maybe you just have a day or two to yourselves to celebrate your engagement, then. A night in Paris soon, perhaps? I'd be more than happy to look after Felix.'

Anthony saw the way Jonno and Brie looked at each other. He could actually feel the wave of love that flowed between them and how much they both loved that idea.

'We do both have this weekend off,' Jonno murmured.

'Let me sort tickets and a nice hotel for you,' Anthony offered. 'As an engagement gift. I'll help Elsie too. Between us, we'll be able to keep Felix—and Dennis—entertained for a weekend, I'm sure.'

'Can't I go somewhere too?' Felix begged. But nobody responded.

Elsie put a huge baking dish onto a trivet in the centre of the table. 'Dinner's ready,' she announced. 'Come and sit down, everybody. Felix, let's get your chair into your spot. Dennis, get out of the way—dogs are not allowed lasagne. Or garlic bread.'

'I hope I am,' Jonno said fervently. 'This smells *so* good.'

There was a happy, family sort of bustle as they settled themselves around the table in the Hendersons' kitchen and helped themselves to the food. There was still some champagne to finish as they continued celebrating the happy news of the engagement and imminent marriage and maybe that had something to do with the impetuous offer that Anthony found himself making to Elsie.

'Why don't you and Felix come and stay at my place on Saturday night?' he suggested. 'That way, Felix gets to go somewhere too. You haven't even seen the place yet and it would give Felix a chance to get familiar with it all before the move.'

'What…?' Elsie's fork had paused in mid-air. 'You mean staying at your house?'

He nodded. 'You could both choose your own bedrooms. My housekeeper would be delighted to get everything ready. It's a bit untidy with the packing I've already started but I'm sure we can work around that.'

'But…' Elsie looked taken aback. 'Brie and Jonno haven't even decided if they're going yet.'

Brie and Jonno shared a glance that made them both smile.

'Oh, I think we have,' Jonno murmured.

'We'd love to go,' Brie confirmed. 'Just a night or two would be amazing. We could fly out on Friday evening and be back by dinnertime on Sunday. If that's okay with you, Felix? Do you want to stay with Nana and Grandpa?'

Felix's eyes were wide. '*Yes*… At my new house?'

'We can visit.' Elsie's tone was cautious. 'On Saturday afternoon, perhaps? It would be lovely for me to see where you're going to live.' She smiled at Anthony. He smiled back.

'But I want to stay,' Felix insisted. 'So does Dennis.'

Elsie laughed. 'We'll see,' she conceded.

But Felix knew he was winning. He was beaming.

'We're going to have a *sleepover*,' he crowed. 'At my new house.'

Anthony and Elsie shared another glance. They were still both smiling but, again, he had the feeling that Elsie was thinking about exactly what *he* was suddenly thinking about yet again.

That kiss…

Nothing was going to happen, of course.

Because it couldn't be allowed to happen.

Not even in the unlikely event that Anthony was also feeling any of this level of…what *was* it, exactly?

Attraction? Anticipation? Desire?

An urge to jump someone's bones that was powerful enough to feel a little bit dangerous but, at the same time, more than a little bit pleasurable because Elsie had forgotten long ago how exciting it was to feel like this. But didn't that make it unbelievably inappropriate for a woman as mature as Elsie Henderson? Good grief, the way she found herself glancing towards the door to her patient's room, hoping to catch a glimpse of Anthony Morgan walking past, was the kind of way a teenager with a hopeless crush on the new boy at school might behave.

She needed to focus on the task at hand, which was washing the face of four-year-old Oscar when all he wanted to do was to go back to sleep.

'Being sick is quite a common side-effect of the sedative they gave Oscar for his MRI,' she reassured his anxious mother, who was perched on the edge of an armchair beside the bed. 'I expect he'll doze off again soon and feel much better when he wakes up.'

She wrung out the facecloth she had dipped in warm water and touched it to the small boy's chin but Oscar pulled away and shook his head.

'Would you like Mummy to wash your face, darling?' she asked.

Oscar shook his head again. He pushed at the bowl of water Elsie was holding, tipping it over before she had time to step back.

'Oops...' Elsie put the bowl down and then scooped Oscar away from the wet patch. 'Never mind, we needed to change these sheets anyway. How 'bout you sit on Mummy's knee for a minute while I get everything sorted?'

Wrapped in a blanket and snuggled into his mother's arms, Oscar instantly fell asleep again. Elsie quickly stripped the bed and headed for the door with her arms full of damp, dirty linen to find that Anthony Morgan was not walking past this room, he was coming into it.

There was no shirt colour to notice today or a tie she hadn't seen before. Anthony must have come straight from Recovery or the ICU after a stint in Theatre because he was still wearing scrubs. He even had the disposable paper booties over his footwear and his hair was flattened from having been squashed by a close-fitting hat for a prolonged period.

And Elsie's heart did that skippy thing where it sped up and then dropped a beat to reset, because he looked far sexier in these baggy, pale green scrubs than he did in those beautifully tailored suits and shirts.

'Sorry,' she said, not quite sure what she was apologising for. The dirty sheets in her arms, probably, or was it in case he'd noticed her noticing *him*? 'I was just heading for the linen hamper.'

'Of course.' Anthony was smiling as he stepped back to let her pass. 'I've got the right room for Oscar Smythe, yes?'

'Yes…' Elsie hastily dumped the laundry and was back in the room by the time Anthony had introduced himself to Oscar's mother.

'I know there's a meeting tomorrow with the whole team,' she heard Anthony say, 'but rooms full of strangers can be a bit intimidating, so I wanted to come and meet you—and Oscar—before then.'

Elsie knew that smile would be reassuring the mother that Anthony understood just how scary it was to put your child's welfare, if not his life, in the hands of strangers but, if she was Oscar's mother, she would already instinctively know just how trustworthy he was.

'You're the heart surgeon the cardiologist told me about, aren't you? You're going to do the operation to take out the…' the frightened young mother closed her eyes and her voice dropped to a whisper '…the cancer?'

'The tumour,' Anthony corrected gently. 'We think it's unlikely to be malignant but we can't be completely sure until we can examine the tissue after the operation. It's most likely to be something called an inflammatory myofibroblastic tumour, which is very rare and usually benign. I'll print off some information about it and drop it in later for you and your husband to read.

That way you can write down any questions you want to ask any of us.'

Elsie was busy smoothing a clean sheet over the bed and tucking it under the mattress but she caught the surprised glance from Oscar's mother. She smiled back, giving a silent response that yes, this doctor would actually find the time to do something like that. Because he was not only an excellent surgeon, he was a genuinely admirable person.

'They said something about the operation I didn't understand. About swapping valves?'

'The initial tests have shown that the tumour is growing in Oscar's heart. We know that it's not affecting the conduction system, which is good because it means his heart rhythm is normal, but we also know that it's affected the aortic valve, which is the one that lets the oxygenated blood back to the rest of the body. That's why Oscar's lips have been going a bit blue and he's been having the fainting episodes when he's exercising—he's not getting enough oxygen.'

Elsie pulled up the fluffy blanket with a blue teddy bear print and folded the top sheet over the edge. A couple of clean pillowcases and she would be finished in here, but she was slowing the task down because she wanted to hear what Anthony was saying. Not just because she liked the way he was making it easy for Oscar's mother to understand but in case it was all rather overwhelming and she might need Elsie to remind her of some of the things that had been said.

'We need to replace the aortic valve when we take out the tumour,' Anthony was saying now. 'And we've found the best way to do it is to swap it with the pulmonary valve, which normally takes blood from the heart to the lungs.'

'Why?'

'The heart has to pump blood pretty forcefully through the aortic valve to make sure it gets to the entire body, which means that a mechanical or donor or bio-prosthetic valve wouldn't last as long. The pulmonary valve is under much less pressure so it will last much longer—maybe twenty years or so and then it can be replaced again. It's called the Ross procedure. I've got some really good information on that too, with lots of pictures. I'm sure Elsie would be able to go over it with you later if she can find the time?'

Anthony turned to Elsie, an eyebrow raised, a smile tilting one corner of his mouth and…was it her wishful thinking or was he holding her gaze with what felt like almost a physical touch?

'Of course.' Elsie hastily broke the eye contact and fluffed the pillow on the bed with a little more vigour than strictly necessary. Again, she wanted to make sure that Anthony couldn't read what was going through her head.

That ridiculous teenage kind of thinking that it would be impossible to say no to anything this man asked of her.

Even if she knew it was something that could never be allowed to happen?

Something…intimate?

Yes, even that was a thought she could allow herself to play with. Perhaps *especially* that thought. Because she couldn't imagine Anthony Morgan doing anything inappropriate himself, let alone asking someone else to.

So it was perfectly safe.

And surprisingly delicious.

CHAPTER SIX

'So, did Oscar's surgery go ahead yesterday?'

'It did. Took most of the day, in fact, from seeing him pre-operatively to getting him out of Recovery and settled into the unit. His parents looked beyond exhausted by then, as I'm sure you would understand. But they were very relieved.'

Anthony was feeling quite relieved himself with the familiar comfort of slipping into work talk. It wasn't until Elsie had knocked on the door this afternoon that he'd realised he hadn't invited a woman, other than his housekeeper, into his home for…well…decades. It wasn't that he'd never had any female companionship over the years, he just hadn't welcomed them into his home. He had learned long ago how important it was to guard his private life.

This was different, of course. Because Elsie wasn't alone and if anyone was going to be welcomed into Anthony's private life now it was his grandson. Felix's excitement over exploring what was about to become his own house and garden was making this visit a joy already but he had to admit there was more than a slight awkwardness between himself and Elsie. Especially now that Felix had disappeared from the lawn into the wooded area at the bottom of the garden and they were suddenly alone together.

Because Anthony had to be very careful not to step over any boundaries here. How horrified would Elsie be if she knew how attracted to her he was? To be honest, he'd been worried that his impulsive offer to help entertain Felix while Jonno and Brie were in Paris this weekend might have been a mistake, but Elsie was making this easy too, by letting him talk about something that put them both into a very safe space.

'It went very well,' he added. 'I love a complex case like that. The time it took to tease that tumour out of the interventricular septum and up into the left ventricular outflow tract and aortic valve only made it all the more satisfying. The icing on the cake, though, was the confirmation that the tumour was benign.'

'Oh…' Elsie's smile lit up her face. 'That's *such* good news.'

She was genuinely happy for her small patient and his family. The warmth of this woman was impossible not to respond to and Anthony was smiling back at her, basking in the glow.

Grinning, even…

'Grandpa… Grandpa…come and see what we found…' Felix appeared from behind the trunk of an enormous old oak tree, with Dennis at his heels, shouting with glee. He was walking fast enough to risk tripping over with his uneven gait but he wasn't about to slow down. 'It's a *boat*…'

'Do you know, I'd forgotten this was even here.' A

minute or so later, Anthony was pulling ivy from the overturned rowing boat.

'Can I play in it?'

'It would need to be turned over and we can't do that until all these weeds are cleared away. I'm not sure that it would be much fun for Nana.'

'You might be surprised,' Elsie said. 'I love being outside in a garden.'

Felix was almost bouncing with excitement. 'Does it float?'

'I doubt it. It's been rotting out here for a very long time.' Anthony helped Felix with the strand of ivy he was struggling to pull off the boat. 'There are probably holes in it under all this ivy and the pond is deep enough to be dangerous for small people. You remembered not to go too close by yourself, didn't you?'

Felix nodded. 'But I wanted to. Will you show me?'

There was a plea in that small face that squeezed Anthony's heart so hard it hurt.

'Let's have a look in the shed and see if we can find some gumboots that might fit you. Maybe some for Nana too?'

'Nana's got boots.'

'Yes, but they're her good boots. She doesn't want to get them wet and muddy if we stay out in the garden for a while.' Anthony led the way to an old potting shed, deliberately not turning to look at what Elsie was wearing on her feet. He didn't need to because he'd noticed everything about what she was wearing the moment he'd opened his door today.

They were the same long black boots she'd been wearing in the park that day when he'd stopped to talk to her. With jeans tucked into them again and this time a casual oversized knitted jumper in a shade of chocolate brown that was pretty much identical to the colour of her eyes. Anthony was wearing jeans himself and a very old black cable-knit jumper, which made it the most casual he'd been in Elsie's company but that awkwardness was still there. Even more so now, thanks to thinking about what Elsie was wearing. And about the colour of her eyes...

'Here we go.' The potting shed door creaked as he pulled it open. 'There's a whole pile of gumboots in here.'

'What's this?' Felix headed past the boots. 'Is it for fishing?'

'I don't think there are any fish in the pond. Lots of frogs, mind you. There might even be tadpoles at this time of year.'

'*Oh*...' Felix had gone very still, holding the small net on a stick in his hand and looking up at his grandfather as if he were a magician who'd just pulled something astonishing from a hat. 'I *love* frogs...'

'So do I,' Elsie said. 'My frog scrubs are my absolute favourites at work.'

She had a look of admiration in her eyes that was not that different from the way Felix was looking at him, but the real magic was that suddenly the awkwardness between himself and Elsie was gone. Not only that, there was a new bond between the three of them. Two grandparents and a small, happy boy. They were all grinning at each other—like a gang of small children planning to do something a little bit naughty but a whole lot of fun.

'There are some big old jars here. Let's put some boots on and go and see if we can catch some tadpoles, shall we? Maybe we can have a go at turning the boat over too.'

They all got muddy and damp and cold over the next couple of hours, but Anthony hadn't enjoyed himself this much in what felt like for ever. With a concerted effort they cleared the tangle of growth around the old rowing boat and turned it over to let Felix pretend to be a pirate until the lure of frog hunting took over. When they finally carried Felix back into the house because his legs were too tired, with Elsie carrying the jars containing tadpoles in various stages of turning into frogs, he found old towels to dry Dennis, lit the fire in a smaller room near the kitchen that had once been a library but he'd always used it as a living room and personal space to relax in, and then found more towels that he handed to Elsie.

'There's more than one bathroom upstairs but I think Felix might like the big clawfoot bath in the bathroom near the bedroom he chose and it's going to be the quickest way to warm him up, I think. It might help those tired legs too.'

'I'm not cold,' Felix said, but his teeth were chattering. Then his eyes widened. 'Can the tadpoles come in the bath with me?'

'No…' Anthony laughed. 'They only like cold pond water. I'll look after them down here while Nana gives you a bath.' He caught Elsie's gaze. 'Have you got some dry clothes for Felix to change into?'

'I've got my jammies,' Felix told him. 'Nana said I didn't need to bring them but I put them in my bag when she wasn't looking because *you* said we could have a sleepover.'

Elsie's cheeks had gone very pink but, oddly, that awkwardness hadn't snuck back and Anthony knew something was changing between them. Something rather nice…

'I did say that,' he told Felix. 'But we'll let Nana decide later, shall we? After dinner? Are you getting hungry yet?'

Felix nodded.

'What's your favourite thing to eat? We could get pizzas delivered. Or fish and chips. Or…anything, really. Because this is the first time you've been here and that makes it extra special, doesn't it? Have a think about it while you have your bath and then you can let me know.'

It was Felix who had the pink cheeks when they came back down the stairs he insisted on managing by himself by sitting down and sliding, step by step. His pyjamas had dinosaurs printed on them and he had fluffy green slippers with claws on the toes, but even the distraction of the fish and chip dinner wasn't enough to dim his fascination with the tadpoles. He had one of the big jars right beside his plate with tadpoles swimming around in the murky water and Elsie had to remind him more than once not to speak with his mouth full.

'How long does it take for the bumps to grow into legs?' he wanted to know. 'And where does the tail go when it disappears?'

Anthony shared an amused glance with Elsie. 'Can you remember what that app was that was all about frogs? The one that little boy who'd had the bypass surgery for the aneurysm due to Kawasaki disease was so taken with? Didn't that have a really detailed timeline of the development stages?'

Elsie nodded. 'That's a brilliant idea,' she said. Her smile suggested that she was remembering more than the patient. The conversation they'd had that day, perhaps? When they'd both agreed how good it was to be single? When they'd connected as both parents and grandparents, which had led to a very special afternoon that Anthony wasn't ever going to forget.

Felix fell asleep in front of the fire, with Anthony's laptop still open, inches away from his face, still showing the animated transformation of the tiniest tadpoles into fully formed frogs.

'He's going to be dreaming about frogs all night,' Elsie murmured. She found herself having to blink away a sudden mistiness. 'And it's going to be a memory of something that he did with his grandpa that he'll have for the rest of his life.' She was holding Anthony's gaze. 'Thank you for that,' she finished in a whisper.

He didn't respond immediately. Instead, he picked up his wine glass from the coffee table in front of them and took a long sip. Elsie's glass had barely been tasted. Because she would need to be driving very soon.

'Do you know,' Anthony said slowly, 'I once collected tadpoles for Jonno from that same pond and it was just as much fun as we had with Felix today. And then his mother came home. The nanny got fired shortly after that, presumably for having allowed Jonno to get so wet and muddy. The tadpoles disappeared the next day and she disappeared the day after that—with Jonno.

I think they went to some child-friendly resort in Florida. Or maybe it was Spain. They were away for a month that time.' Anthony let his breath out in a long sigh. 'I think we both knew it wasn't worth ever looking for tadpoles again.'

Elsie could hear an echo of something Anthony had said to her about his wife that day they'd taken Felix to the park.

'...if she thought he was getting too attached to me when we did get time together, she'd whisk him away on holiday. Somewhere tropical usually, with her latest lover in tow...'

So he'd been punished for spending time with his son. For loving him.

'Do you know,' she said quietly, 'I bet Jonno still remembers catching tadpoles with you that day.'

For a long, long moment, Anthony held her gaze with a silent message of gratitude. And then he smiled.

'You're a very nice person, Elsie Henderson,' he said softly. 'I like you. A lot.'

Maybe it was the warmth in his tone. Or that his words were a verbal caress. More likely, it was that look in those dark eyes. A look that made her think that what had seemed so very unlikely was actually a definite possibility.

That Anthony Morgan fancied her as much as she fancied him?

Elsie could feel her cheeks getting very warm. Flustered, she pushed a stray curl back from her face to tuck behind her ear. She wanted to tell Anthony that she liked him as well. Definitely a lot. But she couldn't quite find the courage.

'I should get Felix home to bed,' she said instead.

'Or I could carry him upstairs and tuck him into bed here,' Anthony said. 'You could bring one of the jars of tadpoles and put it on the bedside table and then, if he wakes up in the night, he'll remember what we did today and where he is and he won't be frightened.'

'But…' Elsie's words died in her throat. Had she really been about to tell Anthony that she couldn't stay the night because she hadn't brought any pyjamas of her own?

But what if he gave her one of *those* looks again? The kind of look that suggested pyjamas might be the last thing she was going to need?

Oh, my…

Elsie picked up her own wine glass and took a gulp rather than a sip of a rather delicious Merlot. And then she took another because it seemed quite likely that she wasn't going to be driving anywhere too soon.

Or maybe she wanted to make sure she had a very good reason not to.

'…love you, Nana…'

'Love you too, sweetheart. Sweet dreams.'

Anthony watched Felix snuggle under the duvet of the bed his own son had slept in so long ago. He was smiling as he watched Elsie come to the door, with the soft glow of the night light behind her. He thought Felix was already sound asleep so it was a surprise to hear that little half-asleep voice again.

'…love you, Grandpa…'

His smile vanished. His own voice wobbled. 'Love you too, buddy.'

He didn't say a thing as they went back downstairs. He couldn't. What he could do, however, was to stoke up the fire and then find some more wine because by the time he'd refilled Elsie's glass the bottle was empty. When he had finally settled on the couch again he thought he could trust himself to speak without emotion overwhelming him.

'He's amazing, isn't he?' he asked softly. 'There's something about Felix that just creates joy for anyone who's lucky enough to be part of his life. I can't tell you how long it is since someone told me they loved me.'

Oh, help…maybe he'd been wrong about trusting his voice. He tried to wash the lump in his throat away with a mouthful of wine. He could feel Elsie watching him but he definitely wasn't ready to catch her gaze.

'Felix is lucky to have a grandpa in *his* life now,' she told him. 'And the more people we have around us who can tell us we're loved, the better.'

Anthony managed a nod. He felt safe enough to confess something, even.

'I know I wasn't a great father,' he said quietly. 'It was so much easier to keep a safe distance and focus on my work and providing for my family than getting caught up in feeling… I don't know…unloved, I guess. Not up to scratch or really wanted—as a proper husband or father, anyway.' For the first time since he'd started this conversation, he let his gaze catch Elsie's. 'This feels like a second chance. Perhaps I can be a much better grandfather than I was a father.'

There was something very like the kind of energy Felix was so capable of sharing in the way Elsie's eyes crinkled at the corners and the gentle curve of her smile.

'I'm so sorry,' she said softly. 'That you ever felt unloved. Or that you had to hide how you felt about your son. I can promise you'll get back any love you give Felix—in spades. And I can also tell you that you deserve it. I think you're one of the nicest people I've ever had the privilege of meeting.'

That did it. That warmth in her voice. That look in her eyes. And, most of all, the way she reached out to touch his arm, as if she wanted to underline the sincerity of her words with a physical touch. To his horror, Anthony felt a tear escape and slowly trickle down the side of his nose. He knew Elsie had seen it too, because she lifted her hand from his arm and caught that tear on her fingertip.

And suddenly they were back in that moment in his car, when he'd taken Elsie home that night and she was crying in the wake of what had been an exhausting, emotional day for both of them.

He'd known then that Elsie had already touched a part of his heart that was almost forgotten. A part that had been blown even further open only a matter of minutes ago when a small boy had said, '...*love you, Grandpa*...'

What was even more astonishing, however, was that he knew he didn't have to hide. Or be ashamed that someone had seen him shed a tear. That possibly for the first time in his adult life—at the grand old age of sixty-two—Anthony Morgan felt safe to let someone see who he really was. And how he really felt.

It was inevitable that they ended up in each other's arms, wasn't it? Just holding each other close. Sharing a moment that acknowledged they were both part of something life-changing. Potentially scary because personal relationships were not an area of life that Anthony had any great confidence in but…oh…this was a risk worth taking. He couldn't *not* take it, with that little boy asleep upstairs.

His grandson…

Maybe it was also inevitable that when they drew apart far enough to make eye contact it was another part of being in the car that night that was surfacing with all the subtlety of a runaway train coming towards something stuck on the railway track.

This kiss was very different, though. It didn't seem to be taking either of them by surprise. It felt as if it had been waiting to happen. Anthony knew, the moment his lips touched Elsie's, that he'd been very wrong in assuming she'd be horrified if she knew how attracted to her he was.

It *felt* as if she'd been thinking about this just as much as he had.

That she wanted it as much as he did. The tiny sound Elsie made as he deepened the kiss and his tongue invited hers to dance only confirmed what he was thinking. But as much as he wanted to pull her even closer and let his hand move just far enough to touch her breast, he had to stop. To pull away again.

For a long, long moment they simply stared at each other, and it seemed that an entire conversation could happen without a single word being spoken aloud.

We really shouldn't be doing this.

But any fear in Elsie's eyes looked as if it wasn't going to win over a level of desire that mirrored his own.

I'd forgotten how much it's possible to be attracted to someone.

Our kids would be appalled.

But the way Elsie caught her bottom lip between her teeth suggested that disapproval could potentially go the same way as any nervousness.

Is it any of their business?

I haven't taken my clothes off in front of anyone for so long. I'd be so embarrassed...

Anthony could almost feel her beginning to cringe. Preparing to run away?

Don't be... Please... You're gorgeous, just the way you are.

And then he spoke aloud.

'You're safe. I promise...'

CHAPTER SEVEN

MAYBE IT WAS true that you could only find the true magic in life by taking a risk.

By daring to step out of your comfort zone and taking a big risk.

By making yourself vulnerable.

And okay…that first time had had its moments of awkwardness. Acute embarrassment even, when Elsie knew there was no way to hide the changes in her body that inevitably happened as you got older, like the saggy bits and the wrinkly bits.

But in the end it didn't actually matter at all. It didn't matter that they were both more than a bit out of practice either, because any fumbling was excused by laughter and, when it really mattered, the need for this kind of intimacy and the astonishing reminder of the physical pleasure it could provide made any imperfections totally irrelevant.

It wasn't just the sex either, although that had been surprisingly good the first time and even better every time since. It had been decades since Elsie had shared her bed with anyone other than a wriggly grandson arriving for an early morning cuddle and she'd totally forgotten what it was like to fall asleep aware of another human's breathing and the warmth of their skin. How safe it could make you feel knowing that you weren't alone.

By tacit agreement, knowing how inappropriate this level of connection might seem to others—in particular, their own children—they had kept it a secret right from that first night.

Elsie had got up very early the next morning because she didn't want Felix discovering she hadn't slept in her own room and asking any awkward questions, or—worse—reporting the shenanigans that had gone on in his new house to his parents when they got back from Paris later that day. So she'd been in the kitchen, making breakfast when Anthony came downstairs. Felix was sitting at the table with his nose only an inch away from the glass jar as he watched his tadpoles swimming so he didn't notice the way his grandparents were looking at each other, trying to hide smiles that were both delighted but a little shy.

'How was your first night in your new house?' Anthony had asked Felix. 'Was it special?'

Felix nodded. 'I woke up but Dennis was on my bed and the tadpoles were there too, so I didn't need Mummy. Or Nana.'

'That's good,' Anthony murmured. His lips twitched and he seemed to be actively avoiding Elsie's glance as he cleared his throat. 'And you know what?'

'What, Grandpa?'

'I know I said that some things are extra special because it's the first time, but sometimes things get even better when you do them again.'

This time it was Elsie's turn to avoid catching his gaze but she was smiling as she turned to catch the toast popping up beside her.

Felix simply nodded. 'I like my new room,' he said. 'So does Dennis. And the tadpoles.'

The tadpoles were growing legs and their tails were shrinking fast and Elsie had to not only agree with Anthony that some things got a whole lot better on repetition but she was also realising that she wasn't too old to enjoy being a bit of a rebel.

There was an element of guilt, of course, in keeping a secret because she knew that what she was doing might not be acceptable, but Anthony had been right all along, hadn't he? What they chose to do in private, as independent single adults, was their own business. They'd both agreed right from the start that if or when either of them wanted it to stop, or things just faded by themselves, they would navigate that space harmoniously and not let any change in their relationship interfere with their involvement in the lives of their children and grandchild. They were clearly old enough and wise enough to be thankful for some unexpected joy in their lives but to also be able to let it go without the kind of angst it might have caused a decade or two ago.

And it was remarkably easy to keep it secret because it wasn't something that couldn't be controlled and, while it was impossible not to think about it a lot of the time, physically indulging in this astonishing new pleasure and satisfaction certainly didn't need to happen every day and it was no big deal when other things got in the way. And there were quite a few things lining up to do just that with so much going on in everybody's lives after Jonno and Brie returned from their romantic mini break. Moving house was always a big deal and nobody thought anything of the way Elsie stepped in to help Anthony not only search for but to move into the sleek modern apartment he found in the central city.

Both Brie and Jonno were clearly delighted that their parents seemed to like each other and they were grateful for the time they spent with Felix to help out with their own house move that had to happen around their work commitments. On top of all the disruption of moving, there was a wedding to plan and that took any focus away from just how much Anthony and Elsie might actually like each other.

Brie certainly hadn't noticed anything unusual. If anything, she was worried that her mother might be feeling lonely after she and Felix and Dennis had moved out.

'Are you sure you're not too lonely being on your own?' she asked a couple of weeks after she and Felix had moved out and she was back to collect a few final items. 'It must seem awfully quiet.'

'Mmm…' Elsie's response was accompanied by a smile. 'But I'm fine really… I know you're not far away and it's not as lonely as I might have expected.'

Not when Anthony had turned up on her doorstep last night, with a bag full of delicious take-out Thai food. When they'd spent the evening using the internet to share clips of bands from their youth playing favourite songs and discovered they'd actually been to more than one concert for the same band, quite possibly at the same time.

It was fortunate that Elsie was busy packing a shelf of Felix's favourite books into a box so that Brie couldn't read anything in her face. Like the memory of just how thoroughly Anthony had ended up kissing her last night. How they'd run upstairs to Elsie's bedroom like a pair of teenagers who couldn't wait to rip each other's clothes off.

How the touch of his hands and lips—and tongue, even—on her skin was becoming increasingly familiar but not even a little bit less thrilling. Quite the opposite, in fact.

Brie scooped up some forgotten plastic dinosaurs that were lurking in a corner of the room.

'That's enough for today,' she announced. 'We've got a couple of hours before Felix needs picking up from school and I need your opinion on something.'

'Oh? What's that?'

But Brie hesitated for a beat before responding. She was staring at her mother. 'Are you okay? Your cheeks are very pink.'

Elsie made a dismissive gesture with her hand, hoping it would make any memories of those hours with Anthony last night evaporate before her cheeks got any pinker.

'We've been working hard. But we're almost done.' Elsie pushed her wayward curls back from her face. 'You'll want to leave a few things here for when Felix comes for a sleepover so it still feels like his room. Why don't we put those dinosaurs on the windowsill?' She reached out to take them from Brie. 'What did you want my opinion about?'

'You'll have to see it,' Brie said. 'I've found a dress

that I think might be the one for the wedding but I want to see what you think because it's not exactly traditional.'

Elsie laughed. 'Your relationship hasn't been exactly traditional either, so I suspect your dress is perfect.'

Brie didn't take her mother to anything like a bridal boutique.

'I didn't want anything frilly or white,' she said. 'I want something I can wear again and again that will remind us both of the day we chose to let the whole world know how much we love each other.'

One of the biggest department stores in Bristol had a section specifically for cocktail dresses and it was a real pleasure to be amongst the beautiful array of gorgeous designs and fabrics like silks and velvets and shimmering sequins draped on mannequins and hanging on racks.

Brie had the same mid-brown eyes as her mother but the streaks of lighter colour in her curly auburn-brown hair were gold rather than silver. She suited any earthy tones but her favourite colour had always been green and the dress she had found was a forest-green that couldn't have been more perfect. It was a simple A-line design but with a chiffon layer to the ballerina-length skirt and exquisite beadwork on the bodice that made it very special.

'Let me buy it for you.' Elsie smiled. 'As my gift.'

Brie hugged her mother tightly. 'Only if you let me buy *you* a dress to wear to the wedding.'

'I don't need a new dress,' Elsie protested. 'It's not as if I need to impress anybody, is it?'

Oh, really...?

That little voice at the back of Elsie's mind took her by surprise.

Wouldn't you like to impress Anthony? He might say you're gorgeous just the way you are but he's never seen you really dressed up, has he? What if he saw you and looked at you as if he really did think you were something really, really special? And even if there wasn't anybody you wanted to impress, how good would it feel just to do that for yourself...?

Elsie did her best to silence that voice by speaking aloud. 'Why don't we find a cute bowtie for Felix to wear? Maybe a bright red one to match the frames of his glasses?'

'Next time,' Brie said firmly. 'This is about you enjoying my wedding as much as I intend to. It's the only one I'm going to have, after all. Like you...' She threw a soft smile over her shoulder before she turned to start flicking through another rack of dresses. 'I never really understood why you never got married again, but I do now. I could never feel the same way about anyone else as I do about Jonno. You must have loved my dad *so* much.'

'Mmm...'

Elsie turned to another rack but she wasn't really looking at the dresses at all. She was trying to untangle a knot of emotion that was suddenly confusing enough to make her feel...guilty?

Not because she was keeping a rather big secret from her daughter, but because it felt as though she'd turned her back on Brie's father. For a moment, it was actually difficult to pull up a clear picture of his face in her head, let alone how it had felt to be with him. Were her memories being overwritten by what was happening with Anthony?

But, if they were, was that so terrible? It was more than thirty years since she'd lost the man she'd loved so deeply and right now it felt as if she were seeing the cover of a familiar book on someone else's shelf. She knew she'd loved it so much she'd never gone looking to replace it, but the storyline wasn't that clear any longer so she was tempted to read it again, just to remind herself of how it had made her feel to have her heart captured like that.

No…

Those confusing emotional strands were being smoothed out in her head, and her heart, enough to reveal a truth Elsie hadn't seen coming.

She didn't need to revive old memories to feel the intensity of what it had been like to fall head over heels in love because Anthony was capturing her heart more and more. Maybe it had started happening that very first time she'd spoken to him, when she'd sensed how deeply hurt he'd been by the breakdown of his relationship with his son. It had, without doubt, grown immeasurably stronger with the genuine care he had shown her when Felix had been so sick, but what had drawn her inexorably into the pages of a completely new love story had been their lovemaking.

Or was it a combination of everything? Of getting to know—and trust—a man who made her feel so cared for?

So…safe…

But *was* she safe? She knew that Anthony had no interest in a permanent or significant relationship. What would happen if she ended up having her heart broken? Would she have the strength and courage to do what she'd promised she would do and make sure it didn't have a ripple effect on the other members of their newly blended family?

'Look at this, Mum…' Brie's voice cut through, and fortunately short-circuited, that sudden fear. 'This would be the perfect colour for you.'

Elsie actually laughed. 'You want people to think *I'm* the bride?'

Brie shrugged. 'Who cares what anyone else thinks? And it's not white, it's pale grey.'

'Silver.'

'Okay…' Brie grinned. 'Pale grey that's a little bit sparkly. But it's amazing. Like something from the nineteen-twenties with that dropped waistline, but so elegant. And I love the long jacket that goes with it. Try it on, Mum. Please…?'

Elsie bit her lip. It *was* a beautiful dress and out of all the thoughts that had just been rushing through her head, one in particular had resurfaced—that desire to look her absolute best.

To impress the man she had fallen in love with…?

Or just to celebrate the woman she had become? Someone she could—and probably *should*—feel very proud of?

Whatever. The colour would be the perfect foil for Brie's dress, it had been a very long time since she'd had a new outfit and it would be for a very special day.

Smiling, she reached out her hand to take the hanger from Brie.

* * *

Wow…

Anthony Morgan knew his attention should be firmly on the bride in her beautiful green dress and his son, standing beside her, in his dark, elegantly cut suit. It would have been quite understandable that he couldn't stop looking at his adorable grandson in his dark trousers that matched his father's, a white shirt and the bowtie—the same shade of bright red as the frames of his glasses, that his father was also wearing today, but no…

Anthony couldn't take his eyes off the mother of the bride.

Elsie simply sparkled, and it wasn't just the effect of that silver dress in the sunshine on a day that was perfect for a beach wedding. She was glowing with a level of happiness that was making her have to catch more than an occasional tear. And…was that his handkerchief she was using? The one he'd given her in the park that day?

He was tearing up himself, to be honest, and not just because he could remember the way his heart had been caught by Elsie's grief over the loss of a small patient. Or that he was listening to the vows that Jonno and Brie were exchanging in front of the celebrant, with Felix sitting in his wheelchair between them and Dennis the dog lying beside the chair, a red bow tied onto his collar.

All those things were part of what made it necessary to blink hard to stop any tears falling, but they added up to a change in his life in a matter of only a few short months that was so huge it was a bit overwhelming.

He was part of a family. A *real* family that was not only making a formal commitment to each other on the beach today but he knew it was glued together with genuine love for each other—something he'd thought he would never have in his life. He had a relationship with Jonno that was getting closer than it had ever been before. He had the absolute joy of having Felix in his life too, but the totally unexpected icing on the cake was the connection he'd found with Elsie Henderson—the mother of his new daughter-in-law. The grandmother of his precious grandson.

A woman he was coming to care about on a level that went far beyond the enjoyment of her company or the deep physical attraction that was something else he'd never expected to find again.

Brie told Jonno that she had fallen in love with him even before she'd met him because she heard his voice so often over the radio and knew what a hero he was in his job. She told him that he had never known, but he'd been missed every day of her life since they *had* met, by both herself and then their son, because he knew that his father was a hero and he'd loved him even before he'd met him too.

'And when he did meet you, he started wishing on a star that you could be his daddy before he knew that you always had been. His wish has come true, and today my wish is coming true as well. I love you, Jonno. I always have and I always will…'

Yeah… Anthony was pretty sure that it *was* his hanky that Elsie was using to press under her eyes to catch those tears and he liked that. He would have liked to be holding that hanky himself, mind you. Or catching a tear with his thumb, the way he had in the car on the night he'd first kissed her. No…maybe what he really wanted was to be standing beside her and holding her hand, but that would have given their secret away and that might spell the end of the magic Elsie was letting him share.

It was Jonno's turn to say his vows.

'My life has been filled with adventures,' he began. 'But this…becoming a family and moving into our future together…this will be the best adventure I could have ever dreamed of. I love you too, Brie. I couldn't be happier that I'm becoming your husband today.'

'And Felix?' Jonno crouched down in front of the wheelchair. 'I've always been your daddy and I couldn't be happier about that either. I love you too. So much, it kind of makes my heart hurt—in a good way…'

Anthony's heart was hurting in a good way too. Full of love. For his son and his grandson. For his daughter-in-law and…

And for Elsie…

Yeah…this was more than enjoyment of her company, or the astonishing satisfaction that being intimate with her could bring.

He was in love with her.

He hadn't seen it coming. Perhaps because he'd never felt this way before in his life, he hadn't seen any warning signs. He might have ignored them anyway, because he knew that Elsie didn't want that kind of relationship. She'd already met, and then tragically lost, the love of her life and she'd never tried to replace the man who had been Brie's father.

It was one of the things that had made them feel so safe with each other because Anthony had never considered finding another wife. Why would he when he'd always have doubts that any relationship could ever be totally trusted? So he wasn't considering it now either—he just wished he could have felt like this about the woman he had married so long ago.

Or would it have only made things worse to be in love with someone who hadn't felt the same way? He could feel the edges of angst trying to muscle in on the happiness of this moment and he pushed back. How stupid would it be to let anything ruin this wonderful day? How right had he and Elsie been to agree how good it was to be past all the nonsense of romantic relationships and the heartache they could create.

'Congratulations,' the celebrant was saying. 'You are now husband and wife.' She smiled down at Felix. 'And still Mummy and Daddy. You are a family and I wish you all the greatest happiness that life can bring for you all.' She looked up, past the trio and the little dog right in front of her. 'For you too, Nana and Grandpa. You're an important part of this family and their future.'

There were more photographs to be taken now, before the celebrant and photographer left them alone to enjoy the picnic they'd brought with them to this simple family wedding. Gorgeous shots were taken of a barefoot Jonno and Brie both holding Felix's hands as they lifted him over the gently breaking waves, with a happy small dog frolicking nearby. The young photographer suggested more dignified shots of the older generation, however, with Elsie and Anthony sitting on a large old driftwood log.

Close enough to touch, but that was okay because nobody could guess how much closer they had already become. Smiling at each other because that was perfectly acceptable in public, given that their family already knew they liked each other's company.

'You look stunning today,' he told Elsie quietly. 'I love that dress.'

He loved it even more now, because the soft folds of the coat she was wearing over the sparkly dress hid the fact that his hand was close enough for him to let his fingers tangle with hers as they smiled for the photographer. And for each other as they shared another glance.

'You know what?' Elsie whispered.

'What?'

'I'd rather be taking my shoes off and playing in the waves. Do you think that the photographer thinks we're too old to do something that fun?'

Anthony held her gaze for a heartbeat and he could feel himself falling into the softness of those brown eyes of hers. That warmth…

Oh, man…his heart was hurting again. Still in a good way, but there was a warning there that it could tip into something less good. If Elsie knew how he felt about her it would change everything, wouldn't it? She'd probably back off as fast as she could. Nicely, of course, but it would be different. And Anthony didn't want anything to be different. He wanted things to stay just as they were, for as long as possible.

But most especially for today. Today was a celebration. Of family.

Of love.

'I think we should show him that fun doesn't have an age limit.' His smile stretched into a grin. 'But we are definitely old enough to make our own choices.' He reached down to pull off his shoes and socks. 'I can't remember the last time I got sand between my toes. How sad is that?'

'There's no time to lose then.' Elsie had already slipped off her shoes. She dropped her coat beside them and caught the swirl of her dress into one hand. 'Let's go…'

CHAPTER EIGHT

It was a rare occurrence for a cardiothoracic surgeon to be called into the emergency department of a paediatric hospital, especially when it was a trauma case being brought in by helicopter.

It was a first for St Nick's, on two counts. One was that it was a penetrating chest injury and the other was to have a father and son involved in the same case, at the same time. It was Jonathon Morgan who brought in the ten-year-old boy with a length of a metal reinforcing rod protruding from his upper chest and it was Anthony Morgan who had rushed down to join the trauma team, having been alerted to an incoming lung impalement injury with possible cardiac involvement.

It wouldn't have been surprising if the child had not survived the transfer to hospital but Jonno was calmly giving the handover as Anthony arrived.

'Jack was playing with his friends after school on a construction site they'd broken into. He fell approximately two metres onto concrete blocks that had reinforcing rods poking out. Ambulance and fire service were on scene within fifteen minutes and pain relief and sedation were provided before the rod was cut. Air rescue was called in for rapid transport when both a pneumothorax and potential cardiac injury were suspected. He has a right-sided pneumothorax, current respiration rate of thirty-two and his oxygen saturation is ninety-eight percent on a rebreather. He's in normal sinus rhythm but he's tachycardic and getting frequent ectopic beats. I'm querying cardiac tamponade but didn't consider a pericardiocentesis. We've got bilateral IV access but restricted fluid resuscitation for permissive hypotension.'

Jonno caught his father's gaze for a moment, his hand still on the donut dressing around the base of the rod to help prevent any movement that could increase the level of injury. Anthony could see the concern that their patient's condition could deteriorate at any moment, along with the hope that the treatment they could provide here would be enough to save this boy's life. And maybe he also wanted reassurance that his emergency management had been the best it could have been?

Anthony nodded his approval. 'If there is a tamponade, it could be what's controlling any major bleeding from cardiac vessels.' He looked up from his first impression of the patient's condition and level of respiratory distress to the monitors above the bed, taking in the latest measurements of blood pressure and oxygen levels, the heart rhythm and respiration rate.

'Let's get a supine antero-posterior chest X-ray stat. If he remains stable I'd like a CT scan but we'll get a theatre on standby immediately. Jonno, are you okay to keep stabilising that rod?'

Jonno nodded. 'My shift's about to finish. I don't have to be anywhere else.'

Anthony stepped closer, to drape one of the heavy lead aprons over his son's shoulders so that he could stay where he was while the X-rays were taken. 'In that case, you're welcome to come into Theatre with us if you want to follow up on your patient. You could even scrub in and keep looking after that rod until it's safe to remove it, if you like.'

Through the doors of the resuscitation area they were in, Anthony could see an ambulance crew had arrived in the department and it was Brie who was talking to the triage nurse.

Jonno had seen them too.

'Brie was first on scene,' he told Anthony. 'She's brought in one of Jack's mates who also fell into the basement of the building, but he's been lucky enough to get away with only an ankle fracture. Could you let her know that I'll be late home? I'd really like to stay and go up to Theatre with you.'

Anthony passed on the message but when the images from the X-rays were coming up on screen as Brie went past, having handed over her patient, he called her back.

'Want to see?' Anthony invited. 'This is your patient as well. Jonno told me your crew were first on scene.'

Brie nodded. 'And it's not the first time I've been very relieved to have Jonno turn up,' she admitted. 'He'll be thrilled to be able to follow up with watching the surgery. Will it be the first time he's seen you working in Theatre?' Her smile was a little shy. 'That's kind of special.'

It was time Anthony headed back into Resus to co-ordinate the next steps in managing his patient but for a split second her words distracted him because he felt surrounded by something he'd never had at work before.

The feeling of family?

He'd said something to Felix about the first time being special when he'd stayed with his grandfather—the same night that he and Elsie had made love for the first time. And now he was with his daughter-in-law—at work—and about to have his son watching him do his job for the first time ever.

Brie was peering closely at the screen. 'Oh, my goodness. That rod is right inside the heart, isn't it?'

'It's penetrated the right shoulder and lung and it looks like it's sitting in the right atrium. Could be through the septum as well and I'm concerned about the pulmonary artery. Hopefully we can get a CT and a better view of what's going on before we open him up. We'll have to put him on bypass. Your man might be rather late home.'

Her man.

His son.

Brie was the mother of his grandson and she had become his daughter through marriage and would be part of his life from now on. That squeeze on his heart, from the idea of family, was because it was growing. Changing to accommodate both the giving and the receiving of love.

'No problem.' She smiled up at Anthony. 'Mum's got Felix today and I'm due to finish before too long.' Brie turned away as her pager sounded. 'Good luck…'

Yeah… With the mention of Elsie and Felix, the last pieces of the family puzzle had just slotted in to create the full picture. Anthony allowed himself just another heartbeat of time to be aware of how precious that image—and everything it represented—was and how much it had changed his life.

And then it was gone. This case might be another thread that would bind his family together even more closely, but it was ten-year-old Jack who was going to have Anthony Morgan's totally undivided attention now, for as long as it took.

A few days later and the shared case became the topic of conversation amongst the group of adults sitting on the terrace of the old Morgan homestead. Felix was playing hide and seek with Dennis amongst the large shrubs in the garden. Jonno was getting the barbecue ready to cook steak for their dinner and Brie was placing a bowl of salad beside a basket of fresh bread. Elsie had just finished setting out cutlery and napkins and she sat down on the other side of the outdoor table from Anthony. She caught his glance for a moment and they had one of those rapid, silent conversations they were getting rather skilled at.

See? There was nothing suspicious in Jonno suggesting I picked you up on my way here this evening.

It does seem as if our secret is still safe.

Even if they guess they might not be that bothered, you know.

I wouldn't bet on it.

The best part is that I get to take you home again. You might want to invite me in…?

Oh, yeah… I think I might…

Elsie couldn't hide her smile so she made it about

something else. 'Guess who I got as a patient on my ward today?'

'Who? Oh…' Brie's face lit up. 'Is it Jack? Is he out of intensive care already?'

'He's doing amazingly well.' Elsie confirmed the guess with a nod. 'He had a television crew in to interview him and his parents today. They showed me that picture of the metal rod spearing his chest that went viral on social media.'

'I had no idea his mates were taking photos.' Brie shook her head. 'I would have stopped them.'

'You were kind of busy keeping Jack alive.' Jonno smiled at his wife as she passed him a lager with a wedge of lime stuffed into the neck of the bottle, but then his gaze slid past her to rest on his father and the smile faded into an expression of respect. 'I wish you could have seen the way Dad handled that surgery. It was incredible.'

Anthony's shrug was modest but Elsie could see how much the praise meant to him. She loved that he and Jonno were getting closer with every passing week. The fact that she and Anthony were both here for dinner this evening so that they could hear all about the plans being finalised for the family 'honeymoon' holiday was a celebration of this new extended family that would probably make her tear up if she didn't distract herself.

'It's no wonder nobody can believe he survived the accident,' she said aloud. 'Or that everybody wants to know all the details.'

'I hope it will be used as a warning for kids not to break into construction areas and use them as playgrounds,' Anthony said. 'There's a reason they're fenced off.' He shook his head. 'He's one lucky boy, that's for sure. We went into that surgery not knowing what was going to happen. One wrong move could have been catastrophic.'

'Jonno told me all about it.' Brie was smiling. 'He's only just stopped talking about it.'

'Just getting him onto bypass and clearing the haemothorax was dicey,' Jonno said. 'But then the heart had to be opened and the rod removed. There was still the potential for a massive bleed at any moment. It was... tense...'

'I've never moved anything quite so slowly and carefully as pulling that rod out,' Anthony agreed. 'We had to repair the damage in the atrium and then, when we pulled it a bit further, that was when we found the pulmonary artery had been torn as well. If that rod had moved at all during transport we'd never have got him anywhere near Theatre.' He smiled at his son and then at Brie. 'You guys did an awesome job.'

'And now Mum's looking after him on the ward,' Brie said. 'How wild is that? I love that our whole family has been part of the same patient's story.' She stood up to walk to the edge of the flagged terrace. 'That's probably enough running around for now, Felix. Don't you think Dennis might need a rest?'

'We're being wolfs, Mumma,' Felix called back. 'We're good at running.'

'He'll tire himself out soon enough,' Elsie said. 'Or get sore. He's a wolf with a limp already.'

'Wolves...' Jonno was putting the meat on the barbecue '...are the new obsession in this household.'

'That's what we want to talk to you about.' Brie nodded. 'We've decided on the south of France for our holiday. As soon as Felix heard there was a wolf park we could visit to see them in the wild, he got super excited.'

'It's up in the mountains, near the Italian border,' Jonno added. 'But if we based ourselves near the coast, somewhere like Villefranche-sur-Mer, we'd have gorgeous beaches and all the medieval villages to explore nearby, with their restaurants and markets and all the history. I've already looked into renting a van or a big enough car, like an SUV that'll make it easy to take the wheelchair and everything with us.'

'We'll need a car,' Brie said. 'Because there's so much for kids in the area as long as we've got our own transport. Aside from the wolf park, there are some gorgeous parks and playgrounds, an aquarium in Antibes and the Gorges du Verdon, where you can hire kayaks. We thought we could rent a big villa—maybe with a pool—so that there's room for all of us.'

'Sounds gorgeous,' Elsie said. 'But it doesn't need to be that big, does it?'

'That's the other thing we'd like to talk to you about.' Brie shared a glance with Jonno before continuing. 'We want you both to come with us. It would make it a real family holiday.'

'A familymoon.' Jonno was grinning. 'Instead of a honeymoon. And we're not inviting you just so Brie and I can sneak out for a romantic dinner somewhere one evening.' He and Brie exchanged another private glance. 'Although that would be really nice.' His grin faded to make him look almost serious. 'We thought it would be great for us all, especially Felix. What do you guys think? Are you in?'

Elsie breath caught in her chest as she met Anthony's gaze. She could tell he was at risk of tearing up now. She was too. Because this couldn't be better, could it? A time where they could all be together. Having fun and adventures. Being close enough for long enough to really cement new bonds and lay solid foundations as they moved into their new future for their extended family.

'It sounds perfect,' she said with a wobble in her voice. 'I can't wait.'

'We'll get on with making the bookings after dinner, then,' Jonno said. 'These steaks are about done and I don't know about the rest of you but I'm starving…'

The familymoon was all they talked about over dinner, as they agreed on dates, how long they could be away for and who would look after Dennis. Felix was still talking about it when Elsie and Anthony went up to say goodnight to him after his bath.

'Did you know that wolfs have forty-two teeth? That's way more than grown-up humans have.'

'I did not know that,' Elsie said.

'And did you know, Grandpa, that wolfs live in families, just like people do?'

'I think I did know that.' But Anthony was distracted, looking up at the ceiling as Felix snuggled down under his duvet. 'Where did all those stars come from?' he asked. 'I don't remember them being here before.'

'Mumma stuck them up there,' Felix said.

'They were in his old bedroom at my house,' Elsie told him. 'There's a bit of a family tradition of making a wish before you go to sleep.'

'Star light, star bright, first stars I see tonight,' Felix

was happy to demonstrate. *'I wish I may, I wish I might, have the wish I wish tonight.'*

'I bet I know what your wish is tonight,' Elsie said as she kissed him. 'Does it have something to do with going to see the wolves in France?'

Surprisingly, Felix shook his head. 'It's about my baby sister,' he said.

Elsie's jaw dropped as she shared a startled glance with Anthony. Was there something they hadn't been told tonight?

'Mumma says it's not something I should wish for too much,' Felix added sadly. 'Even if my friend Georgia's mummy *is* going to have another baby soon and she's going to get a baby sister or brother.' He sighed heavily. 'Maybe I'll make another wish. About the wolfs.'

'That's a good idea.' Anthony ruffled Felix's dark curls gently. 'Sweet dreams, buddy.'

Perhaps the idea of Jonno and Brie adding to their family was giving Anthony and Elsie so much to think about as they went back downstairs that they couldn't find anything to say aloud. And maybe that was why it was so easy for them to hear the voices of their children, despite the rattle of dishes being loaded into the dishwasher when they were just outside the kitchen door.

'We'll have to find a place with at least four bedrooms. One for us, one for Felix and one each for my mum and your dad.'

'Do you think they're really okay with the idea of going on holiday together?'

'They seem to be getting on remarkably well. That

photograph of them running into the waves at our wedding was quite something, wasn't it?'

By tacit consent, both Anthony and Elsie had stopped in their tracks. Wide-eyed, they stared at each other. Was Elsie wrong in thinking that their secret was still safe? It seemed as if Brie might be about to enlighten Jonno that there might be something going on between their parents, but the conversation appeared to have fizzled out as the clink of cutlery being dealt with suddenly turned into silence. Then, just as Elsie was about to start moving and lead the way into the kitchen, they heard a sound that could have been described as a groan from Jonno.

'They wouldn't,' he said slowly. 'Would they?'

'Surely not.' Had Jonno and Brie been sharing a long and horrified glance perhaps, as the very idea of their parents hooking up occurred to them? 'They're too old to be doing stuff like that. Old enough to know better, anyway.'

'I hope you're right.' Jonno sounded grim. 'Can you imagine trying to explain that to Felix?'

'I don't even want to *think* about it,' Brie said with a huff of laughter. 'It's so gross, it might put me off the idea of going on holiday at all.'

'And imagine how awkward it would be if something was going on and then it didn't end well?'

'I know, right? We might have to toss a coin to see which grandparent got to come to dinner. And birthdays and Christmas would be a bit of a nightmare, wouldn't they?'

Elsie didn't want to hear any more. She was instinctively backing away from the door. She didn't really want to make eye contact with Anthony but the pull was too strong. She needed one of those silent conversations that could happen in the blink of an eye.

Not that she expected any kind of reassurance, mind you.

It was going to be an acknowledgement that they were in trouble here.

A cry for help, even?

Dealing with an unexpected complication was something Anthony Morgan was well used to during surgeries and overhearing that damning conversation was kind of like a sudden bleed that could be fatal if it wasn't controlled very quickly, wasn't it? It needed to be clamped. Deciding how to fix it could come later, but doing *something* was urgent.

So Anthony caught Elsie's gaze to let her know he had this in hand. He cleared his throat loudly to advertise his arrival and then walked into the kitchen ahead of Elsie as if nothing was amiss. He even found a broad smile.

'I timed that perfectly, didn't I?' He ignored the guilty glance that flashed between Jonno and Brie. 'Look at that, you've done the dishes already.'

Elsie came in a few seconds after him. 'Sorry... I meant to help with that.'

'It was far more important that Felix got a goodnight kiss from his nana and grandpa,' Brie said a little too brightly. 'Are you ready for a cup of tea? We can go online and see what we can find in the way of a villa to rent in France.'

'I should head home.' Anthony could hear the forced

casual tone in Elsie's voice. 'I've got a day shift tomorrow so it's an early start.' Her gaze met Anthony's for no more than a split second. 'It's no trouble to get a taxi if you want to stay for a cup of tea and some internet surfing.'

'No... I'm not going to let you take a taxi.' Creating some distance suddenly seemed like a very good next step in dealing with this complication. Or was it that he needed to be alone with the only other person who was being directly affected by what they'd overheard? 'I've got an early start myself and...' his smile was wry '... we're not getting any younger, are we?'

It was kind of mortifying that their children apparently thought they were old enough to know better.

But it was almost understandable that they would be very surprised that people their age could possibly be having the best sex of their lives. Even more so that it would be horrific that they were having it with each other...

'Are you happy for us to book something, then?' Brie seemed to be giving the bench a very thorough wipe-down with a dishcloth. 'We were thinking of a villa that's big enough for us all to have our own space.'

Elsie was already turning away to collect her coat and bag so her voice was slightly muffled.

'Sounds perfect.' Her words were an echo of what she'd said earlier this evening but there was no emotion in her voice this time. 'I can't wait.'

So the unexpected bleed of the complication was clamped but Anthony found himself at a bit of a loss, as he drove Elsie back home, to decide on the best next step to try and fix things. If he was honest, he didn't want to think of how to start a conversation he didn't really want to have. Not when he knew the right thing to do would be to offer Elsie a way out. To give her the opportunity to not have to worry about how appalled her daughter would be if she found out her mother was sleeping with her father-in-law and the inevitable rift in his new family that would ensue.

The only way to guarantee safety, of course, was to make sure it wasn't happening any longer so they could stop keeping secrets and potentially telling lies. It had probably only taken that photograph at the beach wedding for the idea that something 'gross' might be going on to lodge itself somewhere in Brie's brain. Living in the same villa for a week, with the romantic backdrop of medieval French villages and gorgeous restaurants thrown in, it would be impossible to guard every glance or avoid being too close and, if that overheard conversation was anything to go by, the 'familymoon' would be totally ruined by the truth coming out.

He'd told Elsie it was nobody's business but their own but that wasn't true, was it? There were three other people involved, and one of them a small boy who wouldn't understand but could still be hurt by any fallout.

Anthony parked his car outside Elsie's house and killed the engine. He was thinking about the first time he'd done this and how, when he'd looked at Elsie, she was crying. He could remember exactly how he'd felt— as she'd found that space in his heart to nestle into. The space that had been far too protected to let anybody in for so long. And it had been a big part of the major changes that had made his life so much better.

It was all too obvious how much he was going to miss those secret, private times with Elsie.

Too much…?

If she'd been crying now, he wouldn't have hesitated to gather her into his arms and reassure her that they could find a way to make it work. But Elsie wasn't crying. And he knew better than anyone that you couldn't blindly trust that a relationship was going to work out long-term. He might have fallen in love with Elsie but he'd never told her that because he knew it would be an unwelcome pressure for someone who wasn't looking for a relationship.

For someone who'd found and then had to cope with losing the love of her life. She might even be relieved at being offered a way out, especially one where they could remain friends.

Where they could both be invited for birthday celebrations and Christmas dinner with their children and grandchild.

Grand*children*, if Felix's wish came true one day.

And there it was. A whole future that could be damaged and that would hurt Elsie as much as anyone else involved.

Anthony wasn't about to let that happen.

How hard was it to try and make this easy for both of them?

Elsie didn't know quite what to say. She needed to let Anthony know that she understood how important it was that he had reconnected with his son. That he had family around him for the first time in decades.

The first time in for ever, really.

He already knew how much importance she placed on his presence in his grandson's life because she'd been the one to tell him about Felix's existence. She'd offered him the chance to meet Felix and that had, in effect, brought the two of them together.

And, yeah…she was in love with Anthony, but she knew he might never trust someone enough to commit himself to a real relationship and, while their lovemaking had been unexpectedly wonderful, it wasn't enough to make it worth threatening these new and precious relationships he had in his life with Jonno and Felix. And Brie as his daughter-in-law, for that matter.

Elsie had had a taste of falling out with her own child in the wake of having secretly arranged for Anthony to meet Felix and she couldn't let that happen again. Brie needed her support as she settled into her new life with the man *she* loved and Elsie had been programmed to put her daughter's needs before her own for almost as long as she could remember. It had been a lifesaver to do so, in fact, when she was facing the trauma of having become a pregnant widow.

Anthony was such a gentleman, he was probably wondering how to redefine their relationship without causing any embarrassment or awkwardness. He certainly wouldn't want to lose his son again for the sake of the sexual benefits they'd added into a friendship. How relieved would he be if it was Elsie who made the suggestion that it would be better to go back to being simply friends?

What she really wanted to do was to invite him into her house—and her bed—for the rest of tonight.

She loved him enough to do the opposite.

'I don't want us to have to take turns having Christmas dinner with the people we love,' she said quietly.

'It was a bit of a wake-up call.' Anthony nodded slowly. 'We're lucky they were just guessing. That they don't really know the truth.'

'They *can't* know the truth.' Elsie's voice was a whisper. She didn't want to say it aloud, but Jonno had spent many years hating his father and the connection between them was new. Fragile. If it got broken again, it was quite likely it would never be repaired.

'I think the solution might be to create a truth that we don't need to hide,' Anthony said. 'That we're parents and grandparents and…friends. Just friends.'

Elsie swallowed hard. This was what Anthony wanted, wasn't it?

What he needed.

So she nodded.

'Just friends…' she echoed. 'We can do that.' She tried to smile but couldn't quite manage it. It was hard, but she caught his gaze. 'It has been…lovely, though, being…more than friends.'

'It has.'

Elsie could see the muscles in Anthony's neck moving, as if he was also finding it hard to swallow. She could see the way he was looking past her, to her house, as if he was thinking of suggesting one last night together?

Oh…how much harder would that be, knowing that every touch, every kiss, every shared glance with a silent message was never going to happen again? Elsie could feel the tears gathering and knew it was imperative that she got herself inside before she began to cry.

Otherwise, it would only make this more difficult for Anthony and she wasn't going to let that happen.

She leaned towards him and gave him a swift kiss on his cheek. The kind a good friend could bestow without crossing any boundaries.

'Thank you for bringing me home,' she said. 'I'm going to go and see what interesting facts I can find out about wolves for the next time I see Felix.'

She didn't give Anthony time to respond, pushing her door open and scrambling out of the car.

If she moved fast enough—if she could get inside so that Anthony would never know how hard this was for her—then, in the longer term, this would be so much easier for both of them.

CHAPTER NINE

IT WAS AS though nothing had ever happened, really.

Here she was, in the secure room for drug and medical supplies within the paediatric surgical ward, helping the most senior nurse on duty tidy up after an exceptionally busy day that had created an unacceptable level of chaos in an area that needed to be precisely organised. A perfectly normal task in a working day and she would go home for a perfectly normal evening. Alone.

There were no secret assignations to anticipate which would give her a thrill whenever she thought of them. Nobody to cook something special for or stimulating company to look forward to and oh, yeah…no sex that was better than any Elsie Henderson had ever had in her life—perhaps because she was finally old enough to know that it didn't actually matter if your body wasn't perfect and that it didn't have to be any kind of performance that you could potentially fail—it was simply a physical conversation to be cherished and, if you were lucky enough to find the right person—you might discover joy and a satisfaction that you hadn't even realised was possible.

But there was none of that in her life any longer and

it was proving rather difficult to get used to its absence, which was a bit silly, really, after nearly a couple of weeks to adjust. Had she really thought that things like secret assignations and mind-blowing sex could be anything other than a fantasy for someone her age? Surely even falling in love should have been something she'd lost interest in long ago?

'Can you come and double-check the records with me, please, Elsie?' Laura was going through a set of keys in her hand, looking for the one to unlock the controlled drug cupboard. 'I want to make sure the numbers tally and get a requisition form off to the pharmacy to restock anything we're getting low on.'

'Of course.' Elsie picked up the clipboard where staff had to record details and sign for any drugs taken. 'Wow…we've had a few procedures needing sedation and analgesia today, haven't we? I helped with that central venous line and I heard about the spinal tap that was ordered. What else was there?'

'A naso-gastric tube insertion and a urinary catheter on two different but equally terrified toddlers.' Laura shook her head as she unlocked the door to the cupboard. 'Plus there was that severe asthma attack, and two seizures that weren't easy to control. That reminds me…' She glanced sideways at Elsie. 'How's your grandson doing? He was sick enough to be in intensive care not that long ago, wasn't he?'

Elsie nodded. 'He's absolutely fine now. He's getting very excited about a family holiday that's coming up. In the south of France.'

'Ooh, nice…' Laura was lifting cardboard boxes full

of ampoules down from a shelf. 'I could do with one of those.'

'It's a honeymoon, really. My daughter, Brie, got married recently.'

'Mmm… I heard…' Laura's glance was curious this time. 'I'm not one to engage in gossip, but I couldn't help hearing something about your daughter marrying Anthony Morgan's son.'

Elsie's smile was wry. 'And they thought they were keeping it all so quiet. You can't beat a hospital grapevine for spreading the news, though, can you?' She bent her head, knowing that she needed to focus so that no mistakes were made in the important task of a drugs tally but she was also letting her breath out in a small sigh of relief. Thank goodness she and Anthony had been so discreet. If anyone had noticed that she and the esteemed paediatric surgeon seemed to be noticeably friendly, they probably just assumed that it was because their children had married each other. They were part of the same family now so it was…well…unthinkable that they would hook up with each other, wasn't it?

Gross, even…?

It hadn't felt gross at the time. It had felt more like something rather miraculous…

'It's a bit of a true love story, isn't it?' Laura asked a moment later. 'It's no wonder everyone's been talking about it. It's like one of those "true life" magazine articles.'

'Sorry, what?' Elsie's head jerked up, her heart sinking like a stone. She could only imagine how appalled Anthony was going to be if he found himself the subject of gossip in his workplace for a second time in his career. A fierce need to protect him followed the fear and the need to see him and talk to him felt like a physical pain.

'The romantic reunion.' Laura's outward breath was a satisfied sigh. 'Creating an instant family with the child that is actually their own.'

'Mmm...' Elsie let her own breath out in a sigh as well. This wasn't about *her*. Or Anthony. It was easy to find a genuine smile. 'It *is* a very happy ending. It was a gorgeous wedding too. Just a quiet one, on Sugar Loaf Beach.'

She turned a page on the clipboard, looking for the page for the controlled drugs like morphine and fentanyl and midazolam that had to be behind two separate locks, but she'd been distracted into thinking about something very different that she'd been sorting through just yesterday evening. Having found a very pretty silver heart-shaped frame when she'd been out shopping in the afternoon, she had wanted to choose a photograph of that special day on Sugar Loaf Beach to put into it.

Unexpectedly, it had turned out to be a far from easy choice. Did she want the stunning picture of Brie and Jonno looking into each other's eyes as they exchanged their vows, with Felix between them and gazing up at both of his parents adoringly? Or the one where they were swinging Felix above the foam of a breaking wave and clearly all laughing with the joy of both the setting and the occasion?

Maybe the one she really wanted to go on her bedside table was the one of herself sitting with Anthony on that driftwood log and they were smiling at each other. Elsie would never forget that his fingers were tangled with her own in that moment, hidden beneath the folds of that beautiful silver dress. Even now when he was nowhere near her, she could feel exactly how she'd felt with that touch—both physical from his hand and oh, so emotionally from losing herself in the way he was looking at her.

As if he was as much in love with her as she had been with him?

No…she couldn't think of that in the past tense. You couldn't feel like that about someone and have it just evaporate like magic because it wasn't convenient.

'Must be a bit weird for you, though. With Anthony?'

Elsie made a noncommittal sound that could have been amusement, but it actually was a bit weird now. Because it was when she saw him on the ward or passed him in a hospital corridor that it really felt as if nothing so deeply intimate had ever happened between them. As if they were merely colleagues. Friends. And…he looked perfectly happy. As though calling it quits on their secret relationship wasn't bothering him at all.

That he might, as she'd suspected, be relieved that they could dial things back to something that couldn't go wrong and threaten his new relationship with his son and grandson?

The columns that held the time of day, drug name, dosage and signature of the person removing it blurred in front of Elsie's eyes and, for a horrible moment, she thought she might burst into tears. This was a roller coaster she really, really wanted to get off.

But Laura was smiling. 'I mean, he's a wonderful doctor and his patients' families think he's marvellous, but Anthony Morgan's a bit…um…aloof, isn't he?'

Aloof...?

Elsie shook her head by way of a response this time.

'Not really,' was all she said. It was time they got stuck into the job at hand. 'I've got a total of six ampoules of morphine listed as used today. That means there should still be twelve in the box.'

The glass ampoules rattled as Laura counted them and Elsie waited for the tally with that word still echoing in the back of her head.

Aloof meant distant, didn't it? Unfriendly. Uncaring, even?

She was taken back to the very first time she'd spoken to him, in the early hours of that morning when she'd been so surprised to find him in the staffroom. Yes...she would never have described him as being particularly social. He did his job and he did it extremely well, but you could see his personal boundaries a mile off. She could remember the way he'd shut her out as soon as she'd asked a question about one of his patients that she might not have been entitled to ask. She could remember how emotional he'd seemed when he'd seen that photograph of Jonno in the newspaper. He was a private person, certainly, but then he'd had good reason to learn to be like that, hadn't he? She could even remember thinking that he was the kind of man who could keep a secret for ever if he needed to.

But aloof...?

In another lightning-fast thought process, Elsie could remember the way he'd looked at her in the car that night. The concern in his eyes because she was crying. The way he'd touched her so much more deeply than simply on her lips when he'd given her that gentle kiss. The way he'd kissed her that night in front of the fire and, later, the way he'd made it so easy—joyous, even—to rediscover a kind of intimacy she'd thought only happened to other people. Much younger people…

No. Anthony Morgan wasn't aloof. He was an intelligent, gentle, caring man who'd been so badly hurt in his private life that he was afraid to trust that it wasn't about to happen again and…

She loved him, for all those reasons and more.

…and she was missing him so much that it hurt.

The morphine ampoules tallied. So did the fentanyl, midazolam and ketamine. They quickly checked the antibiotics and steroids and a dozen other drugs and then they both signed the charts to record their findings. Then Laura looked at her watch.

'It's nearly time for shift change. I'll go and get the requisition form done for the pharmacy if you want to go and check your patients before handover. Someone on night shift can do a stocktake of the IV supplies and dressings.'

'Thanks. I don't want to be late home today. Brie's dropping Felix around because both she and Jonno are working night shifts. I've been looking forward to it all week.'

'You must be missing him terribly,' Laura sympathised.

'I am.' Elsie's response was heartfelt. And she wasn't just talking about her grandson.

'Nana… Nana…we're *here*…'

'I think Nana knows that, Felix.' It felt like too long since Brie had stepped through the front door of her childhood home. 'Dennis, be quiet! You won't be welcome here if you keep making a noise like that.'

But her mother didn't seem to be minding when Brie got to the kitchen to find Elsie crouched down getting one of Felix's fiercest hugs, with Dennis trying to push in to get his share of the love.

'It's a sleepover,' Felix was telling his grandmother.

'It is. Did you remember to bring your PJs? And your favourite stories?'

Felix nodded. 'Mumma said I couldn't take the stars off the ceiling, though.'

'That's okay. Remember we left one behind, right above your pillow, just for special nights like this, so you can still make a wish?'

She was smiling as she looked up to see Brie come into the kitchen, but her smile faded so fast Brie knew she wasn't doing the best job in hiding her thoughts. She found herself blinking fast too, in the hope of making sure no tears were forming.

Felix hadn't noticed anything amiss. He was grinning from ear to ear as he finally stopped trying to strangle his grandmother. 'There's a surprise, Nana.' He was clutching his favourite soft toy horse that was the star of the series of Nobby the pony books he loved so dearly. 'Nobby isn't a cowboy pony any more.'

'Isn't he?' Elsie managed to sound excited about stories they all knew by heart, having had to read them aloud to Felix on a nightly basis. 'Did he go back to the circus?'

'No.' It was Brie who answered. 'You're not going to believe this. Nobby's—'

'Don't tell her,' Felix ordered. 'I'm going to hide it under my pillow so it's a proper surprise.'

Brie handed him his backpack so he could find the precious book and then he was gone. They could hear his slow but determined progress up the stairs a few seconds later, his backpack thumping on each step behind him.

'Got time for a cuppa?' Elsie asked. 'I just made a pot of tea.'

'I guess.' Brie couldn't sound as cheerful as she was trying to. She couldn't help the sigh that escaped as she sat down at the kitchen table either.

'What is it, love?'

'Nothing. I'm just a bit tired. It's not helping that I seem to have picked up a bit of that tummy bug Felix had last week.' Brie knew she wasn't fooling her mother, but she could at least try and distract her. 'There's a position on a new shift coming available. A daytime one which would fit much better with school hours and I wouldn't have to do any night shifts. I've applied for it, so keep your fingers crossed for me, Mum.'

'I will.' Elsie put a mug of tea in front of Brie. 'Do you want me to check on Felix and watch him coming down the stairs?'

She shook her head. 'We've got stairs too, remember? He's got a new technique of sliding down on his bottom instead of coming down backwards, which he thinks is great fun.'

Elsie sat down and picked up her own mug but she was looking up at the ceiling. 'He's taking a long time putting that book under his pillow.'

'He's probably reading it for the millionth time. I

shouldn't spoil the surprise, but Nobby's having a holiday at a riding school and there's a little disabled boy who's always been too scared to ride. I won't tell you the ending but Felix thinks the whole story is about him.'

'Aww…' Elsie's smile was misty. 'I can't wait.'

'I should warn you about the wish too. Just so you know what to say.'

'He's not still wishing for a little brother or sister, is he? Like Georgia's getting?'

Brie's jaw dropped. 'How did you know that?'

'He told me. And Anthony. That night we were both there for the barbecue?'

'You didn't say anything.'

'No…'

The odd look on her mother's face made Brie wonder if there was something going on that she'd missed. 'You and Anthony haven't even been around at the same time since then, come to think of it.'

'Haven't we?' Was it her imagination or was Elsie avoiding meeting her gaze? 'We'll make up for it with our time in France when we're all together. That's only a few weeks away now.'

'I know.' Brie nodded. And then, to her horror, she felt a tear escape.

'Oh, love…' Elsie reached to pull a few tissues from a box at the end of the table. 'I knew there was something more than just being tired. What is it?'

'I don't think it's just Felix who wants a little brother or sister. I'm pretty sure Jonno wants another baby too.'

'Oh…' This time, it was a sound of trepidation.

'I can't do it, Mum. I couldn't face going through another pregnancy.'

She could see that Elsie understood exactly why. Of course she did. She'd been through every moment with her, from the shock of learning of the accidental pregnancy to the terrifying experience of having her baby operated on before he was even born. Good grief, Elsie had even mortgaged her house to pay for the in utero surgery that they'd had to travel overseas to access.

'Jonno thinks he understands how difficult it was,' Brie added quietly. 'And I know he was there when Felix got the infection and had those awful seizures and needed the surgery but…'

'But he can't really know how terrifying it would be to take that risk again,' Elsie finished for her.

'He did say the risk of having a second child with a neural tube defect is very small—only about four percent.' Brie had to catch another tear. 'But that sounds like a huge risk to me. And what if it *can* be detected a lot earlier than it was for Felix? I wouldn't want to be faced with being offered a termination again. Do you remember how heartbreaking that was?'

Elsie was nodding. There were tears in *her* eyes too. 'I'm so sorry, love,' she said softly. 'This should be such a happy time for you all. I hate that you're having to think about this.'

'It *is* a happy time.' Brie blew her nose. She could hear the thump of Felix beginning to slide down the staircase. 'And Jonno hasn't actually said anything other than that he heard Felix making a wish that isn't even unreasonable.' She sniffed and blinked away the last of any tears. 'I got the feeling that Jonno thinks it would complete our family, and it *would*. And it's not that I don't want another baby. I just don't think I could do it, and that makes me feel like I'm letting him down...'

'You're not.' Elsie reached to put her hand over Brie's. 'He's got a whole new, amazing life thanks to you. You both adore each other. He's got the most amazing son he could ever wish for. He's got his own dad back in his life and he's living in the home he grew up in again. These are all huge changes. Wonderful changes. When he's had a bit of time to get used to them all, he'll realise it's more than enough. I'm sure he would never expect you to do something that would be so traumatic.'

'He wouldn't. But...oh, Mum...you should have seen the look in his eyes when he told me what Felix was wishing for... I just know how much he wants it too and I love him so much that a big part of me wants to give him exactly what he wants.'

'Are you talking about me?' Felix appeared at the kitchen door, with Dennis at his heels. 'What *do* I want?'

'A biscuit?' Elsie suggested brightly, hurriedly getting to her feet. 'I think there's just enough time before dinner for you to have one. I made chocolate chip biscuits last night.'

'A chippy bickie.' Felix licked his lips. 'Can Dennis have one too?'

'No.' Brie also got to her feet. 'Come and give me a kiss, darling. I've got to go to work. I'll be back in the morning in time to take you to school.'

A tetralogy of Fallot was a complex cardiac condition in that it involved four different but related defects that interfered with how much oxygenated blood could be pumped around the body.

Anthony Morgan had first met Jemma when she was only a couple of months old and her parents noticed how blue she was becoming when she cried for a prolonged period of time. Having been born slightly prematurely, she had been too small for a complete repair but a less invasive procedure had been done to improve her blood flow.

Now, more than a year later, Anthony had spent several hours in Theatre already, with confidence that his work today would let this little girl live a full life with a very good long-term outlook. He had patched the hole between the ventricles and removed the obstruction to the flow of blood to the lungs by enlarging both the pulmonary valve and the associated arteries. They were now ready for the crucial step in the surgery of taking Jemma off the cardiac bypass machine that had allowed the heart to be disconnected from the body's circulation while the delicate work to repair the defects had been done.

The rewarming of Jemma's body had begun, the aortic cross clamp was removed to allow the heart to re-join the circuit of blood flow and air was removed from the chambers of the heart. Using internal paddles with a small electrical charge to restart the heart and reinflating the lungs were part of a stepped algorithm that was automatic to follow, but difficulty in weaning a patient off bypass successfully was not that unusual and Anthony had to be prepared to deal with any complications.

It wasn't until he had closed the chest and Jemma

was safely in Recovery with all monitored parameters within acceptable limits that Anthony could feel both his focus and that tension finally drop to a level that was low enough to allow anything else some space in his head. It was in that moment, as he turned to walk out through the swing doors of the recovery area, that the first thought of Elsie Henderson snuck into his mind.

Well, no…that wasn't entirely true. It was always one of the first thoughts he had every single day, when he woke up in that huge bed. Alone. It had become automatic to think of her again when he walked into the pristine kitchen area of his new apartment to make a coffee before heading to work, because he couldn't help comparing this sleek and impersonal modern design with the cosy warmth of the little kitchen in Elsie's old, terraced house. Anthony was increasingly hating his new home but, in a way, that was a good thing. It was close to the hospital and work had always been his escape from the disturbing emotional aspects of a life that was less than ideal in other areas.

He wasn't about to let himself get too hung up on where he lived either, because he had so much in his life to be very thankful for. He and Jonno were getting closer with every passing week and he was a firm part of his delightful grandson's life now. He dropped in at least once a week to spend time with Felix, often out in the garden where Jonno would sometimes help with what needed to be done. Felix had another jarful of tadpoles on the go and Brie was always welcoming. His daughter-in-law had a soul as warm as her mother's, Anthony had decided, and she was genuinely happy that he and Jonno had not only reconnected, they were building a better relationship than they'd ever had in the past.

What was wrong with him, he wondered as he pressed the lift button that would take him down to the ward for a quick round of his inpatients? With so many amazing things in his life that he'd never dreamt of having, why wasn't he the happiest man on the planet? Why was it such a relief when he had a day that included complex surgery that precluded any kind of personal reflection for many hours on end?

Because it felt as if something was missing?

Because he was missing Elsie so very much?

It wasn't as if the feeling was mutual. He'd probably hit the nail on the head when he'd thought that Elsie needed to be offered a way out of the intimate relationship they'd somehow fallen into so unexpectedly in order to protect what was most important to her—her daughter and her grandson. She certainly looked happy enough every time he saw her at work these days and he couldn't help thinking that it might be a deliberate move on her part not to turn up to their children's home at the same time.

Finding her in Jack's room when he went in a few minutes later was bittersweet. Just being this close to her was filling a tiny part of that huge space her absence had left in his life, but it was like stepping back into his past. He needed to pull defensive walls around him and put on a performance that was capable of making how he felt undetectable.

'Look, Jack, it's Dr Morgan. I told you he'd be here as soon as he could.' Elsie's smile filled another part of that space in his heart. 'Jack's hanging out to get the final okay that he can go home today.'

'I know.' Anthony managed to return the smile with warmth that was equally genuine, but he cut the eye contact before it became even a heartbeat too long to be normal for a space between colleagues and friends. 'Sorry, Jack. I had a bit of a long operation to do. That's why I'm still wearing my scrubs.'

'How come your scrubs don't have frogs on them, like Elsie's?' ten-year-old Jack wanted to know.

Anthony shrugged. 'Maybe I'm a bit too boring for frogs.'

'That's not true.' Elsie winked at Jack. 'I happen to know that Dr Morgan has *real* frogs in his garden. Sometimes, he even has tadpoles in a jar in his kitchen.'

Jack's jaw dropped. 'How do you know that?'

'We're kind of friends.' Anthony had seen a flash of something like panic in Elsie's eyes. Did she think she might have overstepped a boundary? Or that Jack's mother might say something to someone else on the ward that would start the rumour mill churning? He wanted to reassure her that it wasn't a problem but avoided looking in her direction as he spoke, however. Perhaps he didn't want to see any relief or the nod that might back up his bland description of any connection between them?

Jack's mother was more than ready to back him up. 'People that work together are often friends, Jack. And you could follow Dr Morgan's example. Doing something like going out looking for tadpoles with your mates would be a much better idea than breaking into building sites.'

Jack was scowling now. 'They'd think I was just a stupid kid. Or a scaredy cat.'

'I don't think so,' Elsie said. 'I bet they've all seen you on TV or the internet. You'll be a bit of legend. Maybe you can be someone whose example they can follow.'

'You could have died, Jack,' his mother said quietly. 'Dr Morgan saved your life. Friends that let that kind of thing happen aren't the kind of friends you need, if you ask me.'

Anthony tilted his head to catch Jack's gaze. 'You'll figure it out,' he told the boy. 'Right now I'd like to see how well your wound is healing. Could you unbutton your pyjama top for me?'

Jack complied. 'They took some stitches out today.'

'I know. That was the hole that was there for the chest drain. You don't need to get any stitches out from the main incision. They just melt away under the skin.' Anthony was looking at the wound on the centre of Jack's chest, gently pressing on the skin. 'This is healing nicely.' He looked up at Jack's mother. 'Keep an eye out for any redness or ooze or if Jack starts running even a bit of a temperature. Anything over thirty-seven point five and you should go and see your family doctor or come into the emergency department here at St Nick's.'

'Thanks, Dr Morgan. They said he can go back to school in a week or two, is that right?'

'Yes, but you'll need to be careful with the weight of the schoolbag he's carrying and make sure it's not over two kilograms. Has the physiotherapist been in to give you some exercises to do at home?'

She nodded. 'She said it's really important to do them

to stop any stiffness in his neck or shoulders. And the breathing exercises to keep his lungs clear.'

Elsie had the discharge papers ready to be signed. 'Have you seen the pre-discharge results from the chest X-ray and ECG and the echo that got done this morning?'

'I have.' Anthony's smile was for Elsie this time but he turned swiftly to Jack's mother. 'And they're all looking reassuringly normal. We've set up an appointment with the cardiology department for Jack in a month's time, just to keep an eye on him, but do remember you can come in any time you're worried, like if he seems unusually tired or short of breath or something.'

'So I can go home now?' Jack asked.

'You can. But you still need to be a bit careful. You've got wires holding the bone in the front of your chest together. The sternum.' He touched Jack's chest again. 'If you put your fingers here you can feel the little bumps where they're healing.'

It was no surprise that it felt irresistible to lift his gaze to catch Elsie's right then. Anthony was never going to forget the drama of that day they'd first worked together, opening Vicky's little chest to try and save her life. With merely a split second of eye contact, he knew that Elsie was thinking about that same tragic scenario and he knew that it was still enough to distress her.

He also knew in that same fraction of time that they hadn't lost the ability to have a lightning-fast telepathic conversation.

We did the best we possibly could.
I know.
I'll never forget it either.

I know...

Of course she did. And it was only one of the threads of connection that had bound them together so easily.

And so intimately.

It felt as if they both looked away at exactly the same time.

'It needs twelve weeks for the sternum to heal properly,' Anthony told Jack. 'You need to avoid any jarring movements like jumping, and any twisting like you might get if you play football or use a skateboard. Don't use just one arm to pull or push anything either.' He turned to Jack's mother. 'It might still be uncomfortable for a while but paracetamol should be enough to deal with it.' He took a pen from the pocket of his scrub tunic and scribbled his signature on the discharge form.

'Take care of yourself,' he said to Jack. 'I don't ever want to see you coming into my hospital with anything else poking out of your chest, okay?'

'Okay.'

Jack was laughing and Anthony was smiling as he said goodbye to his mother, acknowledged her effusive thanks with a modest nod and then left the room.

He didn't look back at Elsie.

CHAPTER TEN

ANTHONY HADN'T EVEN looked at her when he left Jack's room and it had made Elsie feel almost like a piece of the furniture.

And he'd been *smiling*.

Happy. As if being 'kind of friends' was perfectly okay.

And it was for her too. But only because it had to be. Elsie's heart felt as heavy as a piece of furniture for the rest of her shift. She helped Jack and his mother pack all his belongings and then his dad arrived to take them home and other staff gathered to wave them off and celebrate what really had been a miraculous survival and recovery story. They'd be talking about his case for a long time and it was already tucked into Elsie's memory banks, along with the fact that it had been Anthony who'd done the daunting and delicate surgery needed to save the boy who'd speared his heart with a metal rod.

It was another connection between them. Another addition to the weight of what was missing from her life now.

What could have been if they'd just happened to

meet, perhaps, and neither of them had any baggage from their past lives?

Elsie's breath came out in a huff, as if she was laughing at herself, when she was changing out of her scrubs and into her civvies when her shift ended. As if anybody their age didn't have an entire trailer-load of baggage that had to be dragged along behind them. It was a bit over the top that she and Anthony shared a grandchild, but if they didn't Elsie knew they would never have connected in the first place. Not on the kind of level they had, anyway, because Anthony's baggage meant that he would never have trusted anyone to that extent.

And that trust would still be there, even if they were only friends, wouldn't it? If she could just get over missing him so much on a deeper level, they could end up being the best of friends, rather than just 'kind of friends' and they could be there for each other for support as well as sharing family times.

Coincidentally, it was Elsie's closest family member whose name came up on the screen of her phone as she walked into the section of St Nick's car park where her little, bright blue hatchback was waiting.

'Hey…' She tried to sound much brighter than she was actually feeling. 'Everything okay, love?' She opened her car door and threw her bag onto the passenger seat before getting in. 'How did the riding lesson go for Felix today?'

'It's still going. He's learning how to groom Bonnie so we'll be here for ages. And then we're meeting Jonno for hamburgers. I… I just needed a moment away from him so I could call you.'

Elsie's breath caught in her chest as she heard the

undercurrent of emotion in her daughter's words. Something was seriously wrong. With Felix? With her relationship with Jonno?

'Tell me what's wrong,' she said gently. 'I'm sure, whatever it is, it's not as bad as you're thinking.'

'But it is.' Brie's indrawn breath was a strangled sob. 'I'm pregnant, Mum...'

Elsie was still sitting in her car, with her head bent and her eyes closed, almost an hour later.

The knock on her window wasn't loud but it was certainly enough to make her nearly jump out of her skin. Her heart was racing as her eyes snapped open to find that it was Anthony knocking on her window.

His face was a picture of apology.

'Sorry,' he said loudly enough for her to hear through the window. 'I didn't want to give you a fright but...' He shook his head and walked around her car to open the passenger door. 'Can I get in for a minute?' he asked. 'I've...um...just been talking to Jonno.'

Elsie pulled her shoulder bag from the seat by way of giving permission for Anthony to get in, but it felt as if the new hurdle in the lives of the people she loved the most had just become even more real and urgent because Anthony obviously knew about the pregnancy as well.

'He'd been at his gym,' Anthony said as he sat down. 'He said he'd needed a session on the toughest run of the climbing wall to try and clear his head, but it hadn't worked and he needed to talk to someone before he went to meet Brie and Felix. I'm guessing you've heard the news too?'

Elsie nodded. Brie had told her everything that had happened since she'd done the pregnancy test and told Jonno the result. That she'd walked out on him after telling him that an unplanned pregnancy was the last thing she'd wanted to happen. That she couldn't even think about it yet, let alone talk about it. It had been a relief that she'd had the excuse of needing to collect Felix from school and take him for his lesson at Riding for the Disabled and she'd hoped talking to her mother would help her get her head around the news.

And Jonno had been to talk to his father, which was another step in the trust they were building as they strengthened their relationship, and that was something Elsie knew she should be celebrating, but right now that seemed irrelevant. And on top of the emotional overload she was already dealing with, having Anthony so close to her in a confined space after keeping their distance so carefully for the last couple of weeks was almost overwhelming. She could even catch a whiff of that familiar, delicious scent of his skin and hair. She had to force herself to focus.

'How does *he* feel about the pregnancy?' she asked. 'I don't think Brie's given him a chance to say anything yet.'

'He's over the moon. He said he'd never thought he'd want a family at all, but he fell in love with Felix pretty much the moment he met him and he couldn't love Brie any more than he does, so having another baby with her is like a gift. And this time he'll be there for the whole journey. The pregnancy. The birth. Watching the baby grow and celebrating every milestone. All those things he missed out on last time.'

Elsie swallowed hard. She could understand that. She could sense that Anthony was just as thrilled at the idea of sharing all the important moments of the life of a new grandchild from this moment on but...

Anthony said it for her. 'But Jonno thinks it's the last thing that Brie wanted to happen. You're right, she wouldn't even talk to him about it and he's...well... I think he's scared that she might not be able to cope. He's really worried about her but he doesn't know how to fix it.'

'*Fix* it?' Elsie shook her head. 'This isn't something that can be fixed. Brie's terrified. She knew Jonno wanted another child and she felt like she was letting him down but she couldn't face it. Not again.' Her heart was breaking for what she knew her daughter was going through at the moment. 'And she shouldn't have to.'

'So how did it happen?' Anthony sounded puzzled. 'I can understand the one accidental pregnancy that happened with Felix, but *two*?'

Elsie felt herself bristling. 'Brie was on the pill the night she met Jonno. She'd been on the pill for months to regulate her periods because they were so irregular it was a real problem. She got sick which made the contraception fail so it was hardly her fault.'

'I wasn't saying it was.'

Elsie ignored him. 'She went off the pill while she was pregnant, of course, and never went back on, even though her cycle was still irregular when it finally came back. She wasn't keen to be taking something on a permanent basis if she didn't really have to. I don't know how it happened this time. Or when but, you know, there are two people involved here. The responsibility—or blame—isn't just on Brie.'

'Blame?' Anthony was staring at her. 'You're making this sound like it's a catastrophe. This might be an unplanned pregnancy but it's not an unwanted one, by any means. Not by the father, anyway.'

'It's too much for Brie,' Elsie snapped. 'She's got more than enough on her plate at the moment. She's just got married. She's settling into a new career and a new house. She's already got a disabled child to care for.'

'Now you're making it sound like it's a given that she's going to have another disabled child.' Anthony gave his head a single shake as he corrected himself. 'That *they're* going to have another disabled child.'

'That's what she's scared of.'

'But the odds of that happening are very small. Four percent, Jonno said, and it can be picked up in a scan as early as about eleven weeks. How far along is she?'

'She doesn't know. Looking back, she said she's felt a bit off and tired for weeks but she put it down to the stress of moving and getting settled. They're making an appointment as soon as possible with the obstetrician who delivered Felix.' Elsie pulled in a deep breath. 'Do you really think it's that easy? That if you find out something is wrong with your baby you can just pull the plug and get rid of the problem?'

'I'm not suggesting any of it is easy. I'm just saying—'

But Elsie hadn't finished what *she* wanted to say. 'We didn't find out until Brie was twenty weeks along with Felix. She'd already been feeling her baby moving for a couple of weeks. But it wouldn't have made any difference if we'd found out even a couple of months earlier. We loved him from the moment we knew he existed, after we'd got over the surprise of it all. And you can't possibly know how much of a shock it was for her to be offered a termination. Or how hard it was for me to be the only person Brie had for support and to wonder whether I was doing the right thing in helping her in what felt like a fight to do the best thing for her baby. My grandbaby.'

'Mine too,' Anthony said quietly.

'You weren't there.' Elsie knew her words were cutting but she couldn't swallow them. 'You have no idea.' She put her hand over her eyes. 'It wasn't just the pregnancy. Or the surgery he had months before he was born and the waiting to see if the pregnancy would even last. There's been all the surgeries since. All the hospital visits and specialist appointments and knowing that any pain he's going through won't be the last. The fear that something worse could happen and that might mean we could lose him. Or he won't get the kind of future he deserves to have—it's there like a cloud on the horizon. Even if we manage to not think about it, we know it's there, every minute of every day…'

Elsie's voice trailed into silence. It wasn't just Brie who was terrified of the thought of going through it all again. For a long moment there was silence in the car and then Anthony spoke quietly.

'I'm here now. So is Jonno. And we would have been there for Felix if we'd known. We *were* there, both of us, when he was sick enough to be in danger last time. We will be here from now on. Both of us. For every minute of every day if that's what's needed.'

'I know.' Elsie bit her lip. She could hear echoes of the impassioned words she'd just thrown at Anthony and she knew it wasn't fair. She could almost feel the distance between them increasing, despite how close they were sitting in this small vehicle. It felt as if some of those threads of connection between herself and Anthony were fraying and breaking.

Or being deliberately cut?

'I'm sorry,' she said. 'This is a bit of a shock. Right now, all I can think about is trying to support my daughter. I know how scared she is and we're programmed to protect our children, aren't we?'

'Indeed,' Anthony agreed. 'And my son is just as much a part of this as your daughter.'

She met his gaze then and that feeling of distance went up another notch but it wasn't enough to kill that ability to communicate silently.

Are we taking sides here?

Are we going to stand by our own offspring on any battleground if it turns out that unbearable decisions have to be made?

What about Felix? Will he be in the middle of some ghastly tug-of-war?

It couldn't be allowed to happen.

'I think I've said enough.' Elsie turned to look through the windscreen. 'Too much, probably. I need to go home.'

'Of course.' Anthony reached for the door handle. 'I agree that there's probably nothing else that needs to be said at the moment. Not until we know more.' He opened the door but then hesitated before climbing out. 'I want to do everything I can to support Brie as well as

Jonno,' he said. 'And you too, Elsie,' he added quietly. 'I want you to know that.'

She nodded. But she didn't turn her head to look at him as he got out of the car and the door clicked shut behind him.

Had she really thought such a short time ago that they could end up being the best of friends and able to be there to support each other as well as sharing family times?

Right now that felt like as much of a fantasy as being in an intimate relationship with the man she'd fallen in love with.

Elsie put her bag back onto the passenger seat, trying to ignore the heat she could feel from the fabric that had been supporting Anthony's body. She fastened her seat belt and started the car, focusing on her driving enough for everything else swirling in her head to get pushed behind a safety barrier.

At some point on the route home, however, she felt something new merging with the weight of sadness that had been all about missing Anthony. It was almost a touch of relief, in a way. An acknowledgement that if choosing sides in supporting their children was breaking that very personal connection between them, it would make it a lot easier being in each other's company going forward.

Especially for something like going on a shared holiday.

Or would the rapidly approaching 'familymoon' get cancelled as this new development, with all its dangerous undercurrents, meant that being together could become an emotional whirlpool they would all prefer to avoid?

* * *

This was why the relationship between them had had to end.

Marriages and families were complicated enough without adding a dimension that could fuel the flames and increase the intensity of any crisis. It was automatic that they would both try and see any situation from their own child's point of view. They might be coming from opposite ends of the spectrum—Elsie had been over-protective of Brie since before her daughter had even been born and they couldn't be closer, whereas Anthony was only beginning to forge the kind of relationship he had been denied for decades—but the end result was the same. It was creating a gulf between them.

How much worse would it be now if they had still been in that close, secret relationship? Being forced apart on a personal level by how they were reacting to Brie's unexpected pregnancy but also being held together because they both needed to support their families.

Family.

Ironically, they had got to know each other and become so close because they were part of the same family, but it was *because* they were part of the same family that the relationship couldn't have been allowed to continue.

And that was why Anthony shouldn't be where he was, right now—on the doorstep of his old family home. Not when he was perfectly well aware that Elsie was going to be here babysitting Felix while his parents went to the appointment with the ultrasound technician who specialised in advanced techniques for diagnosing foetal abnormalities.

But it was well past the time he'd expected to hear some news. Maybe Jonno had simply forgotten to turn his phone back on after the appointment this afternoon, but if that wasn't the case and they still weren't home he knew that Elsie would be on tenterhooks just as much as he was.

More so, perhaps. Because, as she'd pointed out so clearly, he hadn't been there the first time so he couldn't actually have any idea how awful it had been for both Brie and Elsie.

He *had* been there, however, when Felix had been unwell enough for them all to be worried sick. When he knew his support had been something Elsie had appreciated. When those first connections had been made. Connections that had steadily deepened and strengthened until he'd thought he'd found someone he could trust enough to… Well, he hadn't been brave enough to get as far as imagining the shape that a future with Elsie Henderson might have. He'd given up on the idea of marriage, so long ago that it wasn't a consideration, but he'd known he was in love with her and, given how much he'd missed her in recent weeks, being simply friends was definitely not what he'd begun dreaming of.

So he'd come here instead of tackling that overdue paperwork in his office or going home to pace the polished floors of his apartment. And when it was Elsie that answered his knock on the door he could see instantly that he'd been right in thinking she would be unbearably anxious.

'Oh, no…' she said as she opened the door. 'Have

you heard something? Are they…? Is it…?' She couldn't find the words for what she needed to know.

'I haven't heard anything,' Anthony told her quickly. 'I thought I'd drop by just in case they were home already.'

Elsie shook her head. For a moment she seemed to be clinging to Anthony's gaze, as if she needed something that she knew he could provide.

Strength perhaps?

Yes. He would always be able to do that for Elsie. 'We'll hear soon,' he said. 'And it's going to be okay.'

Oh, man… As a doctor he knew better than to offer reassurance that could not be guaranteed. Except that he meant this.

'Whatever the result,' he added softly. 'We'll take it one step at a time and we'll manage. It *will* be okay.'

He saw the way Elsie took a gulp of air as she nodded. He could also see the way those anxious lines around her eyes softened just a little and he felt his heart squeeze as he realised she was accepting his support.

That she needed him, even?

'Would you like to come in and wait?' she asked, stepping back. Then she shook her head. 'How weird is this? Me inviting you into the house that's been your home for most of your life?'

Anthony smiled. 'Everything's a bit weird at the moment, isn't it?'

Elsie's cheeks were pink and she wasn't meeting his gaze. 'I'm sorry about the other day. I shouldn't have said a lot of what I said.'

'You were upset.' Anthony took his coat off and, without thinking, hooked it over the large decorative wooden acorn on top the newel post at the bottom of the staircase, just like he always had. 'I do understand.'

'Would you like a cup of tea? Or something stronger?' Elsie glanced at her watch. 'I reckon the sun's over the yardarm.' There was a hint of a smile curving her lips. 'And even if it isn't I don't think it matters right now.'

'Sounds like a great idea to me.' Anthony nodded. 'What's Felix up to?'

'He's watching his new favourite movie. You know the one about the zebra who grows up to become a racehorse?'

'No.'

'I'm sure you'll get to know it very soon. You can go and catch the end of it now, if you want to?'

Anthony shook his head. 'I'd rather have a glass of wine with you.' He raised an eyebrow. 'If that's okay…?'

'Of course.'

Anthony couldn't interpret the tone in Elsie's words as she led the way into the kitchen but it seemed almost businesslike. And then it brightened. 'Let's see if the kids have got anything nice that's already cold.' She threw a glance over her shoulder as she opened the fridge. 'I expected Jonno and Brie home ages ago. Why do you think it's taking so long?'

'It could be that they were running late to start with, but it's a very detailed assessment so it was always going to be a long appointment.'

'Can't they see instantly if there's an abnormality in the spine?' Elsie pulled out a half empty bottle of wine. 'Is a Pinot Gris okay? Or there'll be a bottle of red wine somewhere, I'm sure.'

'White's fine. And I'm sure Jonno won't mind if we finish that off.' Anthony took his glass and went to sit on an old couch that was positioned against the wall close to one set of French windows to provide a view of the lovely garden stretching beyond the flagged terrace.

'It's more complicated than simply checking the baby's back,' he told Elsie. 'Especially at this early stage of development. It's more to do with precise measurements of intracranial anatomy like the posterior fossa. The translucency is important as well. Even the shape of the head at this stage can be an indicator for a neural tube defect like spina bifida.'

Elsie had come to sit beside him. 'You sound like you know a lot about it.'

Anthony let his breath out in a sigh. 'I confess I've been reading all the latest information I could find ever since we spoke the other day.'

'So you're worried too.' Elsie took a mouthful of her drink. 'Even though the blood test showed that Brie's level of Alpha-fetoprotein is only slightly raised?'

Anthony caught Elsie's gaze and held it just that bit longer than he knew he should. Maybe because it kind of felt like he was holding her hand?

'Worrying is part of the job description of any parent, isn't it?'

Elsie seemed as reluctant as he was to break the eye contact. 'And grandparent,' she added. 'But I do wish they'd call.'

'Jonno said they're hoping that their doctor will be available to go over the results with them straight away. Maybe that's what's keeping them so long.' Anthony took a swallow of his wine. 'It's kind of lucky that Brie's cycle has always been so irregular, in a way. We might have had to wait a lot longer if she hadn't already been so far along by the time she did the test. And we're even luckier that the technology's so advanced now. 3D and transvaginal scanning make early detection a lot more accurate.'

He leaned back on the soft cushions of the couch as they both sat in silence for a while.

'I've always loved this room,' he said then. 'Which is funny because I was hardly ever in it. I love it even more now, though. Maybe it takes a happy family to make a kitchen really come alive.'

'That's true. It's where you make the food to nurture the people you love. Where you come together to share it. I guess you used the dining room here more than the kitchen?'

'We rarely ate together,' Anthony admitted. 'Unless it was a formal dinner party. I think Jonno always had his meals in here. With his nanny.' It had been another area of that unhappy marriage that he'd been taught not to interfere with.

'It's different now.' Elsie smiled. 'And we get to share it sometimes.'

Like the last time they'd been here together? At the barbecue that had ended with the realisation that their relationship couldn't continue. Anthony tried to distract himself by letting his gaze roam around the room. There were pictures held onto the front of the fridge by magnets and one of them looked like a portrait of a wolf that Felix had created with felt pens. The animal had bright yellow eyes and an extraordinary number of teeth.

'I can't believe how different it feels,' he agreed. 'Or

how lucky I am to share it.' He cleared his throat. 'Can I confess something else?'

Elsie looked startled. Wary? Did she think he was going to say something about missing what they'd discovered they could give each other?

At least he could reassure her that he wasn't about to step on forbidden ground.

'I hate where I'm living,' he told her. 'Even if it was never like it is now, this old house always felt far more like a home than that apartment ever will.'

Elsie opened her mouth to say something, but in the same instant they heard the sound of the front door opening.

Anthony could sense that they were both holding their breath as they listened to the footsteps on the tiled hallway floor getting closer. He took Elsie's glass and put it by his own on the table as they both stood up to face the internal door of the kitchen. Brie came in first and she looked tired. And pale. Jonno was right behind her and he put his arm around his wife's shoulders as soon as she stopped.

For a long, long moment, nobody said anything. And then Jonno cleared his throat.

'It's fine,' he told them. 'Everything's perfectly normal.' His voice caught and Brie looked up at him so they were looking at each other as he finished speaking. 'It's a girl,' he said softly. 'We're going to have a baby girl and she's going to be fine...'

There were hugs that needed to be had. A celebration of the kind that could bind families together tightly enough to last for ever, but for just a moment longer neither Anthony nor Elsie moved an inch. They too were sharing a glance and Anthony could see how enormous the relief was that Elsie was feeling. The love for her family, including the new baby girl on the way, was almost blinding but Anthony thought he could see something else there as well.

That a part of that limitless love was his. And his alone.

That Elsie was just as much in love with him as he was with her.

It should have been heartbreaking, but nothing could dampen the joy of this moment. Especially when Felix came into the kitchen to see what all the noise was about and he was finally told that he was going to get a baby sister in the not too distant future.

His face lit up. 'I knew I would,' he exclaimed. 'I didn't change my wish into something about the wolfs even when I said I was going to.' He was almost dancing in his excitement. 'Did you see the picture I did, Grandpa? It's on the fridge.'

'I did. I love your wolf's teeth.'

'We're going to see them. It's…how many sleeps now, Mumma?'

'Nine,' Brie told him. 'Single figures already.'

'So we're still going to go?' Elsie had crouched down to hug Felix.

'Why not? I'm pregnant, Mum, not sick.' Brie was looking at Jonno again and the love between them was such a solid thing that Anthony could swear it was visible. 'And what better way to celebrate this than by having a familymoon?'

'We'll keep Mumma safe from the wolves, won't we, Felix?' Jonno scooped his son up into his arms.

The solemn nod from the little boy as he wrapped his arms around his father's neck brought a lump to Anthony's throat. So did the way Brie caught her mother's gaze and they exchanged misty smiles.

He was part of this. This was *his* family.

And it was everything he could have ever dreamed of. Until Elsie's gaze brushed his own and he felt a part of his heart that wasn't open enough to absorb that joy.

But it was almost everything he could have ever dreamed of. And it was more than he'd ever had before so it was enough.

It had to be enough.

CHAPTER ELEVEN

THIS WAS AS good as it got.

The sun was still shining late in the afternoon when the Morgan/Henderson family set out to explore the small French town that would be their home for the next few days. The flight had been smooth and swift and the spectacular views as they'd landed, with mountains towering on one side and the deep blue of the Mediterranean sea sparkling on the other, had already set the bar high for the best holiday ever.

Jonno drove the rental car the short distance to Villefranche-sur-Mer and they stayed in their luxurious accommodation just long enough to unpack what they needed and admire the huge terrace and sea views before setting off on foot to explore a place that their guidebook promised would be unforgettable.

They had known they would need to navigate steep hills and many steps as they wandered towards the sea, admiring picture-perfect pastel-coloured houses and cobbled streets with hanging baskets of bright flowers, but Felix and Jonno had already made a plan.

'Dadda's going to be a real-life Nobby,' Felix told

them. 'I can ride on his back when it's too bumpy in my chair.'

With his toy horse Nobby tucked firmly under his arm, that was exactly the perfect way to go sightseeing. His small wheelchair was light enough to be easily pushed when it was empty and Anthony took responsibility for it when Jonno was giving his son a piggyback. They naturally fell into a pattern where Brie walked beside Jonno and Anthony walked behind the younger couple with Elsie beside him, happily taking far too many photographs.

They explored the sixteenth century citadel and then headed for the old town along the harbour road to find a restaurant for dinner so that they could get Felix to bed at a reasonable hour.

'Oh, look…' Elsie exclaimed. 'What a gorgeous chapel.'

The tiny building was on the sea side of the road, painted in soft earthy colours and richly decorated with various patterns.

'It's got *eyes*.' Felix lifted one of his hands from his father's head to point.

'It's the chapel of Saint Pierre,' Anthony told them, scrolling through the information he'd found almost instantly on his phone. 'He's the patron saint of fishermen and the eyes are there to watch over the fishermen and keep them safe when they're out at sea. And look, Felix. Can you see what the cross on the steeple is made of?'

Elsie took a photograph of the three generations of Morgans peering up at the steeple. How could Anthony have ever believed he wasn't Jonno's biological father? The family resemblance was unmistakable. Even the way they were all squinting in the fading sunlight, their heads tilted to the same side, was identical. Brie had obviously seen it too because she was laughing. She also had one hand resting gently on her belly and the reminder that a precious new baby was on its way to join this family made Elsie feel as if her heart was so full of joy it was in danger of bursting.

'Can you see, darling?' she asked Felix. 'It's four fish that are joined together to make the cross. Isn't that cool?'

But Felix had had enough of sightseeing for now. 'I'm hungry,' he announced.

They found a restaurant on the flat waterfront with outdoor seating beneath an awning, an enchanting view of the harbour dotted with small boats and plenty of room for a wheelchair. There were fairy lights that trailed from the awning into the branches of trees filling big terracotta pots and a child-friendly menu that included pizza and lasagne.

'We are almost on the Italian border,' Jonno said. 'But I don't reckon the lasagne will be as good as yours, Elsie.'

'I'm going to eat something French,' Brie said.

'Like snails?' Jonno laughed.

'Don't be silly, Dadda,' Felix chided. 'Nobody eats *snails*.'

For a split second, as Elsie caught Anthony's gaze in the burst of laughter, she completely forgot that she needed to keep her distance. Or that that distance had increased all too easily when they'd both stepped into their own corners to protect their own children. They'd both felt the same overwhelming relief at the reassuring news about their unborn grandchild's development and they were both determined to make this family holiday a celebration of their new—and growing—family.

But how romantic was this? A setting sun and a harbour view. Fairy lights and cobbled streets. The sound of the most beautiful language in the world around them, classic French music coming from a sound system nearby and a tall flute of the champagne Anthony had ordered already in her hand.

So…just for that moment, Elsie let herself hold Anthony's gaze for longer than she knew she should and he didn't look away. He held up his glass to touch hers instead, and they shared a smile that shut the rest of the world away for a heartbeat and then another—because Anthony seemed to want this contact that was like no other. Physical but without touching. Intimate but perfectly acceptable in public. Something that could only happen with two people who cared for each other far more than any kind of 'friend'. The thought that Anthony might, in fact, be missing her as much as she was missing him filled Elsie's heart even further and it was aching by the time she took a sip of her champagne and opened her menu as though food was uppermost in her mind.

It was only then that she noticed an odd note in the silence at the table and she glanced sideways just in time to catch Brie looking down at her menu—as if she didn't want to make eye contact with her mother.

As if she'd noticed something more than a friendly toast to a shared holiday that she had just exchanged with Anthony?

Oh, help…

Elsie felt a tiny shiver slither down her spine. This was a wake-up call, that was what it was. She couldn't afford to let her guard down for even a moment. Not even if they were in the most romantic country ever.

Not even if it seemed that Anthony would be just as happy to close that distance.

'Haven't you noticed anything? Anything at all?'

'Can't say I have.' Jonno was watching Felix, who had his nose pressed against a glass panel on the raised deck which was one of the many viewing platforms in the wolf park.

'What about last night, at dinner? The way Mum was looking at your dad at the table.' Brie shook her head. 'It reminded me of when I was just little and she got the photograph albums out and told me stories about *my* dad and how wonderful he was and she'd get all misty and cry sometimes.'

'Guess I was too busy choosing my dinner,' Jonno said. 'How good was that steak and the mashed potatoes with truffles?' He grinned at Brie. 'I'm glad I didn't go for the snails just to horrify Felix. And then we all went to bed early, didn't we? We knew we'd need a bit of stamina for today's adventures.'

But Brie wasn't going to be distracted. She'd been thinking about this during the spectacular drive up through pretty villages and forests and gorges carved into cliffs above the river to get this close to the Italian border in the Alps. She'd hardly taken in any of the information in the introductory session in the old stone stable either, although she was aware that there were three wolf packs in the park and Felix was currently waiting for the feeding session to begin with the Canadian wolf pack.

After that they had a busy few hours planned at the park. They were going to a falconry show to see owls and eagles and vultures perform with their handlers, give Felix time to explore the attractive children's playground, have lunch in the café or a picnic in a designated area of the forest and then catch another feeding session with a different wolf pack later this afternoon. No doubt Felix would be sound asleep in the car by the time they headed back to the coast, especially since he'd been up since the crack of dawn with the excitement of this long-awaited trip to the wolf park becoming a reality at last.

Brie saw Anthony pointing at something in the trees and caught a glimpse of something pale moving behind the tree trunks. She saw Felix shake his head sadly, however, letting Anthony know he hadn't seen it, so his grandfather scooped him up to hold him higher. Now it was Elsie who was pointing and a few seconds later Felix was clapping his hands with excitement. But Brie wasn't scanning the forest again or watching for the park rangers who would be coming out with chunks of meat in a bucket to feed the wolves. No…

She was watching her mother. And the way Elsie was watching Anthony as he held his grandson safely in his arms.

'I think she likes him,' she muttered. 'In fact, I'm sure of it.'

'What's not to like?' Jonno draped his arm around her shoulders. 'Like father, like son. Or should I say like son, like father? I'll bet he likes her too. Like daughter, like mother.'

He pulled Brie a little closer but she nudged him gently with her elbow. 'We talked about this. How weird it would be if our parents liked each other. As in, you know...*liked* each other.'

'Like we do, you mean?' Jonno's gaze was soft as he held hers. Then he bent his head and kissed her. And Brie kissed him back. How could she not? She'd never been this happy in her life.

And she wanted the people she loved to be just as happy.

'What if they heard us that night? When we were joking about it while we did the dishes? When we said we might have to toss a coin to see which grandparent got to come to a birthday party or Christmas dinner?'

'Well...it could be a bit awkward if they ended up not wanting to talk to each other.'

'But what if we stopped something happening that might make them as happy as *we* are?'

'You've got a point. It's not as if Dad had anything like a good marriage the first time round and I didn't exactly make life any happier for him for a long time, did I?' Jonno raised an eyebrow. 'Do you think we should encourage it? Send *them* out for a romantic dinner tonight while *we* babysit Felix, instead of the other way round?'

'That might be a bit obvious.' Brie had a more subtle idea. 'Why don't I sit in front with you on the drive home, instead of being in the back with Mum and Felix?' She bit her lip. 'No one else can drive because the rental car is under your licence and being in the front seat might help me not to feel car sick on all those bendy bits in the gorges. You know…the way pregnant women can get?'

Jonno's face softened even more. And then he kissed her again. 'I love you,' he murmured. 'Even if you are a devious matchmaker.'

Felix had turned in his grandfather's arms to search for his parents. 'They're coming, Mumma. The man with the wolfs' lunch. Come and see, Dadda… *Quick*…'

Jonno was already moving closer to the window but his smile advertised that he'd caught Brie's mouthed words.

'Love you too…'

Felix was almost asleep by the time the straps of his car seat were clicked into place, so it wasn't surprising that Brie suggested she sat in the front beside Jonno. Not that Elsie had noticed her daughter feeling queasy on the tight curves and tunnels in the road through the gorges on the way up to the mountains but it was a perfectly reasonable swap and she certainly wasn't going to complain about seeing more than the back of Anthony's head on the journey.

It had been a perfect day and it turned out that the timing had also been perfect because there were some rather dramatic dark clouds gathering above the mountain peaks and it looked as if they might be in for a storm.

'Maybe we should go straight home and not stop in any more of the villages,' Jonno suggested. 'I've heard that the storms in this part of France can be quite violent.'

Anthony was nodding. 'They hit the news quite often. With floods and hailstones the size of golf balls.'

'Oh, stop…' Elsie said. 'I'm sure we'll get home well before it arrives.'

Brie laughed. 'And I reckon Felix will sleep through any size of hailstones. He's *so* tired…'

'And *so* happy.' Jonno smiled as he glanced sideways at Brie. 'Could be that everything else on this trip is going to be an anti-climax after the "wolfs".'

Or maybe not.

The enormous clouds, with inky black centres and eerily bright edges as they did their best to block the sun, were filling the sky by the time they reached one of the narrowest parts of the road, with a stone wall on the cliff side and the river, with its churning white rapids, only metres away down the bank on the other. A few heavy drops of rain hit the windscreen and Jonno reached to turn on the wipers. The first crack of thunder was terrifyingly loud, so close the flash of lightning came simultaneously and the combined effect of both the sound and light was enough for them to feel it vibrating in their bones.

And it all happened in a blink of time, too fast for Jonno to be able to do anything to prevent it. A truck coming around the curve ahead of them was suddenly on the wrong side of the road and there was simply nowhere for him to go to try and avoid a head-on collision. Into the cliff on the right or towards the riverbank on the left? With his ability to analyse and respond to emergencies, Jonno must have realised in that nanosecond of time that they stood more chance heading towards the open side than becoming a sandwich between a much heavier vehicle and a wall of stone. He pulled on the steering wheel and started to brake at almost the same time but a second bolt of lightning, followed instantly by the crack of thunder, split the weird darkness outside and covered the scream of...who was it?

Brie?

Felix?

Elsie twisted within her seat belt as she turned to put her arms around Felix to protect him, only to find that Anthony's arms were already there. The car tipped and bounced and cracked against what felt like rocks. Elsie could feel Anthony holding *her* as well as providing an extra layer of protection for Felix but she kept her eyes squeezed shut so tightly she could only see stars, convinced that these were her last moments on earth. It took only seconds but it felt like for ever and then numerous airbags went off with sounds even more frightening than the thunder.

'*Mumma...*' Felix was screaming beneath his grandparents' tight hold. '*Dadda...*'

'It's okay, buddy. I'm coming to get you.'

Jonno's voice was astonishingly calm and Elsie's eyes snapped open. The car was still rocking but it was staying in one place.

And they were still alive.

'Brie?' There was an urgency in Jonno's voice now. 'Does anything hurt? Take a deep breath for me, hon.'

'I'm...okay...' But there was panic in Brie's voice. 'There's water around my feet. Jonno...we're *in* the river. We've got to get out. We've got to get Felix out.'

But Jonno took another second to assess their predicament.

'Dad? Elsie? Are you okay? Felix?'

'*Dadda...*' Felix was sobbing. 'I want to get *out*. I don't like this car...'

'Elsie?' It was Anthony asking this time. He was reaching to touch her face. 'You're not hurt, are you?'

'I don't think so.' But then Elsie tried to move and cried out in pain. 'My foot...' she said. 'I can't move it. I think it's caught under the front seat.'

'I can't get this door open.' Jonno had taken off his seat belt. He was holding the door catch open and trying to thump the frame with his shoulder. 'And the window control isn't working.'

'I'll try mine.' Brie reached for her door but Jonno stopped her.

'Don't. We have to get out this side. The rapids are too close.'

Elsie was undoing the clips of Felix's safety belts so that she could gather him into her arms and cuddle him to try and stop the heartbreaking sobbing.

'It's okay, darling,' she told him, over and over. 'We'll get out really soon.'

There were people climbing down the bank beside them now and she could hear them shouting. On the road above, traffic had come to a standstill and the vehicles' headlights were shining into the sheets of rain now falling.

Anthony was pushing the button beside the headrest on the driver's seat and pulling it upwards. 'Use the spikes on the bottom,' he told Jonno as he passed the headrest through the gap between the front seats. 'Break the window.'

Was it the effort Jonno was putting into smashing the glass that made the back of the car grind and slip on the boulders that had caught them in the shallow edge of this fast-moving river? Elsie saw the flash of fear in Anthony's eyes as he looked past her to the foaming rapids that were far too close and she knew that, while they had survived the crash, they would not survive the car being caught and swept away by the river's current. She cuddled Felix even closer so that he couldn't see that she was crying with fear herself.

The car window broke and shattered, tiny pieces of the safety glass showering Jonno, but he kept going as fast as he could, to get more of the pieces still clinging to the frame. A man outside was helping. They were talking to Jonno but it quickly became obvious that he didn't understand. Another man came closer.

'Help is coming,' he said in English. 'We must get you out.'

Jonno twisted. 'Pass me Felix,' he ordered.

'*No...*' Felix clung to Elsie, even as Jonno reached back to get hold of his son.

It was one of the hardest things Elsie had ever done to prise Felix's arms from around her neck and push him towards Jonno. He dragged him through the gap between the seats and then through the window into the arms of the people outside, who were standing almost knee-deep in water, amongst slippery rocks, in a chain leading back to the firm ground of a narrow shoreline at the base of the bank.

'You're next, Brie.'

'But I can't... There's no room... You'll have to get out first.' And then Brie turned to the back of the car, her face scrunched into lines of terror. '*Mum...* Have you got your foot free?'

'Yes.' It was a lie, but the only thing Elsie was concerned with right now was that her daughter got safely out of this car. 'It's okay, love. You get out. I'll be right behind you.'

Jonno had squeezed himself out of the window and was reaching back to catch and help Brie. She could hear Brie's groan as she squeezed herself through the narrow gap of the window frame but she couldn't afford to add any fear about the baby Brie was carrying to her state of mind just yet. There was too much else to be frightened about.

Jonno was halfway back through the window as soon as others had taken over supporting Brie to safety. 'I can reach the lever on the seat,' he told Anthony. 'If you come into the front, we can push the back of the seat flat and it'll make it easier for us to get to Elsie.'

Elsie tried again to pull her foot free but it was stuck fast. It felt as if sharp edges of metal were biting into her skin as she pulled even harder. She had to give up and in that moment she felt the front of the car, now much lighter, swing sideways and the whole vehicle rocked as the waves of the rapids tried to snare it.

Elsie could hear the sound of a helicopter hovering overhead already and there were even some flashing lights of emergency vehicles on the road above them now, but were any rescuers going to be too late?

'You have to get out,' she told Anthony. 'Quick... I think the car's going to be washed away.'

'Come out, Dad.' Jonno's voice was a command. 'I'll get in and see how I can get that foot free. There's someone with a crowbar and a police car is here. They're saying a fire truck is not far away.'

But Anthony didn't move. He was holding Elsie's hand very tightly. 'I'm not going anywhere,' he told her. 'Not until I know you're safe.'

Amazingly, amongst all that terror, there was something wonderful to be found. That look in Anthony's eyes.

The fear.

The *love*…

But then he let go of her hand. 'I'm going to see what I can feel under the seat,' he told her.

Elsie could feel his hand on her ankle and then on her foot. 'There's a spike of metal,' he called above an increasing sound of rushing water and shouting outside the vehicle. 'It's right through your shoe. I can't tell if it's in your foot because everything's twisted.'

'I'll come in,' Jonno said. 'Maybe I can use the crowbar to lift the seat.'

'I've got one end of the shoelace,' Anthony called back. 'I'm going to see if I can untie it and loosen the shoe but…it's all under water…'

So far under that Anthony's face was almost touching the water as he reached beneath the seat. The level was rising and the car felt less and less stable but there was nothing Elsie could do except focus all her energy on the man right beside her.

'Please…' she whispered. 'Please get out, Anthony… Save yourself…'

He either didn't hear her or was simply ignoring her. 'I've loosened the lace,' he shouted. 'And I'm going to hold your ankle and help you pull. Try again, Elsie…'

She pulled and felt her foot slip a little. She pulled again with Anthony's fingers a tight band adding extra weight. There was a flash of pain but her foot slipped further.

And then it was free. Anthony was upright in a heartbeat. He was pulling and then pushing her towards the window only seconds later and Elsie held out her arms. It was Jonno who caught them first and then there were others as she felt her body squeeze through the gap and into even more of the icy river water. But she didn't feel safe yet. Not even when she knew they were on solid ground. She pushed at her rescuers and told them to wait. To put her down.

She wasn't going to feel really safe until she knew that Anthony was. She could see that his head was out of the car window. That he was holding onto Jonno's arms and that his son had a firm grip on his father's upper arms, but she could also see that the car was moving. Swinging further into the rapids. And then, in the space of time it took for Elsie to realise she'd been holding her breath for far too long, it happened. The car twisted and then rolled, turning upside down and then sinking as it got claimed by the vicious current of the rapids, and in that final dramatic moment Anthony was pulled free. By his son.

She heard the cheer going up from what was now quite a crowd of onlookers. There were the flashing lights of more emergency vehicles and she could see Brie and Felix looking down on the scene, wrapped in blankets and coats and the arms of total strangers. But then Jonno was beside her, his arm around his father's waist as he helped him out of the river, and suddenly there was only one place that Elsie needed to be.

In the arms of the man she loved.

And, judging by the way he was holding her, he was feeling exactly the same way...

CHAPTER TWELVE

THE STEADY BLIP-BLIP-BLIP was the best sound they had ever heard.

The sound of an unborn baby's heartbeat as part of an ultrasound that told them this tiny girl had been well protected in her mother's womb and by the technology of a modern car.

The only physical injury was to Elsie's foot, which was badly bruised after being half crushed and twisted in the seat mechanism. There were no broken bones but it was heavily bandaged and she had been sitting in a wheelchair ever since they had all been transferred to the hospital in Nice to be checked.

'Just like me,' Felix had told her approvingly. 'When my legs are tired.'

When their rescuers discovered that both Jonno and Brie worked for emergency services in England, that Anthony and Elsie were a doctor and nurse and that the little boy had the challenge of living with spina bifida they had all been treated like royalty. When they came out from the ultrasound exam there were still members of the French rescue team waiting to hear the results.

'The baby is fine,' Jonno told them. 'But we're going

to cut our holiday short and go home so that we're close to our own doctors, just to be on the safe side.'

Jonno might be being overprotective of his wife and baby but nobody was going to argue with him. Elsie wanted to be in her own home, safe and sound, herself. The shock of coming so close to losing her life today was going to take a while to wear off.

'But you'll come back, yes?'

'Absolutely. As soon as we can.'

A smiling fireman stepped forward from the back of the group with something wrapped in a towel.

'This was found by the river after you went in the helicopter,' he told them. 'We thought it might be special.'

Felix's face lit up when the towel was unwrapped to reveal a still rather soggy toy.

He was still cuddling Nobby, sitting on Elsie's knee, as their well-wishers finally left, more than happy with the part they had played in a highly successful mission. 'I was going to wish for you when I went to bed,' Felix told the toy horse. 'Except I knew we didn't have any stars here.'

'There are always stars,' Anthony told him, crouching beside the wheelchair. 'Sometimes you can just feel them rather than see them but that doesn't mean you can't make a wish.'

Felix's eyes were wide. 'Do you wish on stars too, Grandpa?'

'I do.'

Felix tilted his head to look up at Elsie. 'Do *you* wish on stars too, Nana?'

'Sometimes,' she admitted. She didn't need to look

up because Anthony was at eye level, having crouched down to talk to Felix.

'What do you wish for?'

Jonno and Brie exchanged a glance and Brie held out a hand to Felix. 'Let's go and find a taxi to take us home, shall we?'

But Felix shook his head. 'But I want to know.'

Elsie caught her lip between her teeth, but everybody seemed to be smiling and suddenly it felt as if it was about more than the sheer relief of a whole family having survived a potentially catastrophic accident.

It really did feel as if there were imaginary stars in the air around them. And that wishes could come true.

'We know,' Jonno said quietly to his father. 'You would have stayed in that car if we hadn't been able to get Elsie out, wouldn't you?'

'Yes.' The single word was raw.

Felix's eyes were very wide. 'Because you didn't want Nana to be lonely?'

'Because I love Nana,' Anthony said. 'Very, very much.'

Oh… Elsie could see the truth of that in Anthony's eyes and she could feel the truth of it. She just hoped he could see a reflection of that same kind of love in *her* eyes. For *him*. Because she wasn't going to find any words right at this moment.

Felix was nodding. 'I love Nana too,' he said.

'So do we,' Brie said. 'Which is why we need to leave her alone with Grandpa for a minute. Come on…'

Felix obediently slid off Elsie's lap but he was scowling. 'I still want to know,' he muttered, 'what Nana's wish is.'

'I wish...' Elsie had to clear the lump from her throat. 'I wish that I could kiss Grandpa.'

Felix looked unimpressed. 'Why can't you?'

Brie and Jonno exchanged another meaningful glance. 'No reason at all,' Jonno said.

'We think it's a great idea, in fact,' Brie added. 'You're perfect for each other—just like your kids are.' She caught Felix's hand. 'Now, come *on*, bubba. We need to get Nobby home and dry before he catches a cold. And then we've got a plane to catch to really go home.'

It was just the two of them, then. Temporarily, anyway, because they'd need to follow their family soon and share the taxi to get back in time to gather their belongings and get to the airport again, but neither of them was in a hurry to move just yet.

Anthony laid his palm gently on Elsie's cheek without breaking the eye contact between them.

'I think it's a great idea too,' he said softly. 'I do love you, Elsie. So much. It's thanks to you that my life is as perfect as it's ever been but...but is it wrong to want more? To want to have you in my life as a lot more than just a friend?'

'If it's wrong, then I'm just as guilty.' Elsie was smiling. 'I love you too, Anthony, and I've been missing you *so* much. I think I fell in love with you the moment I saw how lost you were. When I knew you'd never been loved the way you deserve to be. The way I will always love you.'

Anthony was smiling but his eyes looked suspiciously bright. 'You know what?'

'What?'

'I'm about to make your wish come true.'

And he did. Although Elsie knew perfectly well that he was kissing her as much as she was kissing him. A soft kiss that was perfectly within any limits for a public place, but…oh…there was passion simmering beneath that softness. A desire that might need to be contained but they had plenty of time, didn't they? The rest of their lives might just be long enough…

She also knew that Brie had been right. She and Anthony *were* perfect for each other and they were lucky enough to be finding something as precious as this kind of love at a stage in their lives when it felt like no small miracle.

They broke the kiss to find a breath and to smile into each other's eyes. Maybe it was even better to find it now because they were old enough and wise enough to know they needed to make the most of every minute of every day they could spend with each other.

Starting right now.

With another kiss…

EPILOGUE

One year later...

IT WAS THE last day of the second 'familymoon' for the Morgans.

A holiday that had been jam-packed with adventures, including a whole day at the wolf park for seven-year-old Felix.

Five-month-old Bella had spent most of her time in the front pack that was her daddy's favourite new fashion accessory but, judging by the frequency of the baby's gurgling laughter and beaming smiles, she seemed to think her first family holiday was the best thing ever.

The bride and groom from the recent wedding were just as happy. The ceremony to celebrate Anthony and Elsie's commitment to each other had been held in the garden of the big old family homestead—the one with the pond that was so full of frogs. Elsie had worn the same silver dress she'd worn for her daughter's beach wedding and Brie, as her bridesmaid, had worn the same pretty green dress she'd got married in. It was

Felix who'd begged to have the red bowties again and this time Anthony wore one too.

So did Bella, as a tiny velvet bow on a headband, nestled amongst her wispy dark curls. Everybody agreed she looked exactly like Felix at that age and, as a big brother, he couldn't have been prouder. He loved his little sister so much that he read her a bedtime story every day. The same story. And there was already a soft toy Nobby hidden in a cupboard to be ready for her first birthday.

There had been anxious times as well as so many happy ones, of course. Everybody had watched Brie like a hawk until she was well past the timeframe that could have revealed any problems the accident might have caused. Elsie had been off work for some time while her foot had healed, but Anthony had assured Felix that he wasn't letting Nana get lonely.

He would have been happy to move into Elsie's little terraced house, in fact, and couldn't wait to leave the apartment he hated, but she'd wanted them to start their life together somewhere that would be chosen by them both but completely new to them both as well. Somewhere they could be together for the rest of their lives with no ghosts from the past lurking anywhere.

They didn't want to be too far away from their family, because that was a huge part of their present and future, but they didn't want to live in each other's pockets either, so they'd bought a small cottage in a village on the outskirts of Bristol. Close enough to make it easy to keep working for as long as they wanted to, but far enough to be their very own space.

Just for them.

Because they were as much in love with each other as it was possible for a couple of any age to be and all lovers needed that kind of space.

To be alone.

Together…

*****

COMING SOON!

We really hope you enjoyed reading this book.
If you're looking for more romance, be sure to
head to the shops when new books are
available on

Thursday 30th March

To see which titles are coming soon, please visit

millsandboon.co.uk/nextmonth

MILLS & BOON

MILLS & BOON®

Coming next month

TEMPTED BY THE REBEL SURGEON
JC Harroway

'Mason!' The name flew from her lips before she could stop it, before she had a chance to dampen her shocked reaction at seeing her ex standing there in all his jaw-dropping glory.

He was dressed like any other surgeon: green surgical scrubs, a theatre hat covering his dark unruly hair, a stethoscope slung around his neck, but as well as the last man she thought she'd see standing in her department, he was surely the sexiest doctor to have ever existed.

'Dr Harvey,' Mason replied with a twitch of his lips and a smile in his piercing grey-blue eyes. The look, which could have lasted a split second or a hundred years, somehow conveyed everything that they'd once been to each other, every intimate moment and whispered promise. But Lauren must surely have imagined those things, because on second glance she only saw polite recognition, as if they were total strangers, which of course they were now. It had been six years, after all.

Lauren swallowed, relieved to find that her mouth wasn't hanging open. What was he doing standing in her ER without explanation, resembling a surf bum not a doctor, all tanned and relaxed as if he'd just strolled in from the beach?

'What are you doing here?' she asked automatically, her feelings bruised and her mind abuzz with questions. But now wasn't the time or the place for an in-depth reunion. Despite what they'd once been to each other, he was just the registrar she would need to put in his place for keeping her and the patient waiting.

Relaxed, in control and in no way surprised to see her, Mason moved to the patient's bedside. 'You called me,' he said in an obvious and reasonable answer while mirth danced in his eyes. 'I'm the locum on-call surgical registrar.'

Fresh annoyance bubbled in her veins. He must have known that she still worked at Gulf Harbour. He would have been prepared for their paths to cross when he took the locum position. Why hadn't he called, warned her that he was back? Had she meant so little to him that he hadn't given her a single thought?

Continue reading
TEMPTED BY THE REBEL SURGEON
JC Harroway

Available next month
www.millsandboon.co.uk

Copyright © 2023 JC Harroway

MILLS & BOON

THE HEART OF ROMANCE

A ROMANCE FOR EVERY READER

MODERN — Prepare to be swept off your feet by sophisticated, sexy and seductive heroes, in some of the world's most glamourous and romantic locations, where power and passion collide.

HISTORICAL — Escape with historical heroes from time gone by. Whether your passion is for wicked Regency Rakes, muscled Vikings or rugged Highlanders, awaken the romance of the past.

MEDICAL — Set your pulse racing with dedicated, delectable doctors in the high-pressure world of medicine, where emotions run high and passion, comfort and love are the best medicine.

True Love — Celebrate true love with tender stories of heartfelt romance, from the rush of falling in love to the joy a new baby can bring, and a focus on the emotional heart of a relationship.

Desire — Indulge in secrets and scandal, intense drama and plenty of sizzling hot action with powerful and passionate heroes who have it all: wealth, status, good looks…everything but the right woman.

HEROES — Experience all the excitement of a gripping thriller, with an intense romance at its heart. Resourceful, true-to-life women and strong, fearless men face danger and desire - a killer combination!

To see which titles are coming soon, please visit

millsandboon.co.uk/nextmonth

OUT NOW!

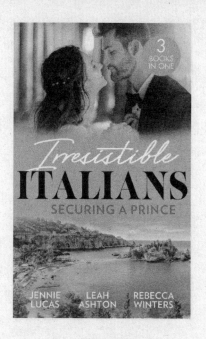

Available at
millsandboon.co.uk

MILLS & BOON

OUT NOW!

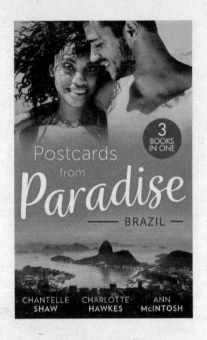

Postcards from Paradise — BRAZIL

3 BOOKS IN ONE

CHANTELLE SHAW   CHARLOTTE HAWKES   ANN McINTOSH

Available at
millsandboon.co.uk

MILLS & BOON

MILLS & BOON
A ROMANCE FOR EVERY READER

- **FREE** delivery direct to your door

- **EXCLUSIVE** offers every month

- **SAVE** up to 25% on pre-paid subscriptions

SUBSCRIBE AND SAVE

millsandboon.co.uk/Subscribe

JOIN US ON SOCIAL MEDIA!

Stay up to date with our latest releases, author news and gossip, special offers and discounts, and all the behind-the-scenes action from Mills & Boon...

 @millsandboon

 @millsandboonuk

 facebook.com/millsandboon

 @millsandboonuk

It might just be true love...

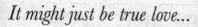